D0035860

FIRE AND ICE

"I hardly recognize you, Miss Alden. You clean up rather well."

Sierra started violently, shocked to find Ram standing beside her. How had he approached her without her knowing it?

"You are no gentleman to mention my—unfortunate accident," she said with asperity.

"I'm glad you noticed. I'd hate to be mistaken for something I'm not." The chuckle started deep in his chest and rumbled from his throat in a low, sexy growl.

"You aren't fit for polite society, Mr. Hunter. I'm surprised Father invited you tonight."

"Perhaps your father is a better judge of character than you are," Ram returned with a taunting smile.

"Perhaps he doesn't really know you," Sierra said shortly.

"And you do—a girl barely out of the schoolroom?"

Ram watched her eyes narrow into shards of pure silver, captivated by the fire smoldering in their bright depths. Idly he wondered if she'd show the same kind of spirit in bed.

Other *Leisure Books* by Connie Mason:
WIND RIDER
TEARS LIKE RAIN
TREASURES OF THE HEART
A PROMISE OF THUNDER
ICE & RAPTURE
BRAVE LAND, BRAVE LOVE
WILD LAND, WILD LOVE
BOLD LAND, BOLD LOVE
TEMPT THE DEVIL
FOR HONOR'S SAKE
BEYOND THE HORIZON
TENDER FURY
CARESS AND CONQUER
PROMISED SPLENDOR
MY LADY VIXEN
DESERT ECSTASY
WILD IS MY HEART

SIERRA
Connie Mason

LEISURE BOOKS **NEW YORK CITY**

*To my brother and sister-in-law, Salvatore and
Louise Roti.*

A LEISURE BOOK®

July 1995

Published by

Dorchester Publishing Co., Inc.
276 Fifth Avenue
New York, NY 10001

Printed in the United States of America.

PROLOGUE

Colorado Territory, Summer 1850

The little girl toddled aimlessly between the bodies of her mother and father, unable to understand why they didn't move or answer her. They lay sprawled on the ground beside their overturned wagon, and for a time she sat beside them, sucking her thumb and crying. She was hungry and thirsty and her head hurt. She wondered why she couldn't find her brother or sister. Huge tears gathered in her silver-gray eyes and flowed down her chubby cheeks. At the tender age of three, she did not recognize the cold reality of death. Having been hastily hidden in a trunk by her mother during the Indian attack, she had not witnessed firsthand the brutal slaying of her parents.

The huge lump on her head pained her, and she touched it gingerly, unaware that she had sustained the injury when Crow raiders overturned the wagon and the trunk in which she had been hidden spilled out. When she finally awakened and tumbled out of the trunk, her three-year-old mentality could not grasp the gory scene of death and destruction.

Unable to rouse her parents, little Sierra Larson wandered off to look for her siblings. She knew Ryder and Abby would know what to do. Unfortunately, her brother and sister had been carried off by a Cheyenne hunting party who had crossed paths with the Crow raiders and taken the children. The Cheyenne had not seen the little girl inside the trunk and had left her to the mercy of wild animals and the elements.

Chapter One

San Francisco, August 1868

Ramsey Hunter pushed through the swinging doors of the Lucky Lady Saloon, pausing briefly on the raised wooden sidewalk constructed to keep pedestrians out of the mud. He dug impatiently in his pocket for a match, struck it against a scarred pillar badly in need of paint, and held it to the long, tapered cigar clamped between his teeth. A brisk, salt-laden breeze blew the life from the fragile flame and nearly took his expensive Stetson with it. Pulling the brim down firmly over eyes as blue as a cloudless sky, he fished in his pocket for another match, struck it, and shielded the resulting flame with a cupped hand. The flame faltered and died as another gust of wind blew in from San Francisco Bay.

Muttering an oath, he flung the match into the muddy street and stuffed the cigar into his vest pocket. Ram Hunter wasn't the type to pursue lost causes. Had he been, he would have remained in Texas and meekly accepted what fate had dealt him instead of spending the last eight years trying to settle old scores. Lady Luck had rewarded him in ways he hadn't expected, and he had named his saloon in honor of that capricious damsel.

Ram gazed at the sea of mud that served as a street and grimaced. The recent rains had turned the thoroughfare into a quagmire. If not for the board meeting at the bank across the street, Ram would not attempt the crossing at all this morning. As one of the town's wealthiest citizens, he had invested in several business institutions and real estate ventures, all of which were paying handsome dividends.

Ram's sensual lips curved upward in a wry smile when he thought of the changes these last ten years had wrought in him. He had gone from naive boy to a man who had learned the hard way to trust no one but himself. Now look at him. Property owner, investor, board member, and businessman. He had all the wealth he could ever want, including a saloon with a lively clientele of gamblers, guzzlers, and men in search of female companionship. He provided all three diversions, but only quality stuff for the Lucky Lady. He didn't cater to rowdies. He employed high-class whores, and his whiskey was the best in town. No diseased doxies or rotgut for the Lucky Lady.

"Nice morning, Ram."

Ram smiled at the passerby, recognizing him as one of his regular customers and owner of the mercantile next door. "If not for this infernal wind, it would be perfect, Stan," Ram returned. "And a curse on the muddy road, which I'll have to cross whether I like it or not."

Stan Walton's gaze took in the muscular length of Ram's long legs encased in meticulously creased trousers and expensive boots and nodded in commiseration. "I've got to cross to the bank myself later this morning. Maybe one day the streets of San Francisco will be paved."

"If they can build a railroad into the city, they sure as hell can pave the streets," Ram grumbled.

"Won't that be something, though?" Walton said, amazed. "They say it will be at least another two years before service starts. I can't wait for them to drive in the last spike. California will really boom then. Well, I'd better get going. I see Mrs. Healy is already waiting for the store to open. See you tonight, Ram. Maybe my luck will change at the tables."

Another gust of wind caught Ram's coattails, sending a chilling draft skidding up his spine. Catching the flapping ends neatly, he buttoned his jacket, pulling the elegantly tailored garment taut against his broad back and wide shoulders. Then he sent a look of distaste over the sea of mud that stretched the length of the street and, finding no alternative, prepared to step down from the sidewalk.

Meanwhile, on the opposite side of the street, Sierra Alden contemplated the same muddy quagmire Ram had been deploring only moments before. She had come to town early this morning to do some shopping and was now faced with crossing the street to the mercantile. She hated the thought of ruining her dress and boots, which were the latest up-to-date style, part of the extensive and expensive wardrobe she had brought with her from New York, where she had attended a fancy finishing school. She had arrived home by ship after a two-year absence just two weeks ago and this was her first trip to town.

Ram spied Sierra the moment she stepped out of the bank onto the sidewalk. He paused for a moment in pure enjoyment at the sight of her slim, supple figure. She looked like a fashion plate right out of a magazine, all ruffles and fluff, and the most ridiculous hat he'd ever seen perched atop her lustrous dark hair. A smile sketched his lips as he watched her fight the wind as it snatched at her skirt and petticoats. She wasn't completely successful in holding her skirt down, for he caught a tantalizing glimpse of a neatly turned ankle and a brief flash of shapely calf.

Holding her skirts as high as she dared, Sierra stepped daintily into the street, sinking almost immediately in mud to the top of her ankle-length boots. Her lips thinned in annoyance as she pulled her foot free and took another halting step. For modesty's sake, she dared not lift her skirts another inch higher, so her hem dragged in the mud, making progress difficult. This would never happen in New York, Sierra thought, recalling the elegant shops lining the sidewalks of New York. Not that she wasn't happy to be home again with Holly and Lester Alden.

Sierra had become so accustomed to the luxuries of New York life that it had been difficult to return to a raw town like San Francisco. She thanked God that their modern house on the hill was as fine as any New York had to offer, and she rarely encountered the unpleasantness found in those parts of New York where rowdies gathered. Stepping daintily through the sucking mud, Sierra tried to concentrate on the items she hoped to purchase for the party her parents were giving in her honor Saturday night.

Sierra shuddered as a violent gust of wind whistled down the street, wrapping her muddy skirts around her trim ankles. Faced with muddy skirts and ruined boots, she found herself wishing she had remained home and entrusted the errands to one of the servants. Suddenly she felt the feather-and-lace confection she wore on her head lift and blow away. In moments it was airborne, flitting hither and yon, finally landing in the mud only a few feet from where Ram stood. Since it was her favorite hat, Sierra grit her teeth, set her stubborn little chin and waded through the mud after it.

Thoroughly amused by the little drama, Ram chuckled aloud. It had been a long time since he'd been so well entertained. He watched with rapt attention as the young woman bent to retrieve her hat. What happened next could only be appreciated by someone with Ram's wry sense of humor. When Sierra bent over, a vicious breeze caught the hem of her skirt, flipping both it and her petticoats up and over her back, exposing a generous portion of deliciously rounded derrière clad in lace-trimmed pantalettes. Then, adding insult to injury, a dray lumbered past, blessing Sierra with a muddy benediction. Startled by the sudden turn of events, Sierra became entangled in her flapping skirts and sat down hard in the mud.

Unable to control himself a moment longer, Ram burst out laughing. He laughed until his sides hurt, laughed while Sierra screeched in rage, laughed until tears came to his eyes. Finally remembering his manners, he dried his eyes and reached out a hand to help her.

Sierra glowered in unrestrained fury at the obnoxious man who dared to find humor in her lamentable situation. The sight of his immaculate, finely tailored clothing added fuel to the fire of her temper. No one, absolutely *no one*, had ever laughed at her. She swiped a hand across her face to flick away a glob of mud and succeeded only in smearing the mess across her smooth white cheek.

To her utter humiliation, the man's grin widened, his white teeth flashing attractively in his tanned face. Unbidden, her eyes slid downward over thickly muscled chest, narrow waist, and slim hips. But she didn't stop there. Her naughty gaze traveled along his long sturdy legs, then upward again, where she paused a moment, thinking that in all her twenty-one years she'd never seen such a blatantly sexual man.

Nor one so infuriating.

How dare he laugh at her! Just who did he think he was? When he finally stopped laughing and reached a helping hand out to her, she looked at it as if it were a snake.

"Take my hand, miss. I'll help you up," Ram urged, reaching out to her.

She glared up at him through sooty lashes and Ram was utterly enthralled by the startling silver flash of her eyes. Their sheer brilliance rivaled the shiniest metal he'd ever brought up from his silver mine. Unfortunately, they were filled with more anger than he'd ever seen any woman exhibit.

Sierra had taken just about all she could take of the rude stranger who dared to laugh at her. She assumed he was a stranger in town since she couldn't recall seeing him before she went off to school. Just because he didn't know she was the daughter of a prominent and wealthy banker didn't excuse his offensive behavior.

Devilment turned Sierra's eyes to pure silver as she reached out to grasp Ram's outstretched hand with both of hers, as if accepting his help.

When he bent toward her, she pulled with all her might. His face a mask of disbelief, he tottered at the edge of the sidewalk, then tumbled headlong into the mud. He came up cursing, his blue eyes dark with shock and fury.

"You little witch!"

He tried to rise, skidded, then fell back down with a thud, his big body displacing its weight in gooey mud. Sierra's complacent smile turned from a discreet giggle to outright laughter when she saw Ram floundering in the mud as he attempted to gain his feet. His expensive Stetson had flown off his head and lay in the mud beside him. The sun reflected brilliantly off the top of his thick, dark blond hair. He was glaring at her with such ferocity that she thought it prudent to leave before he did her serious harm.

"Wait until I get my hands on you," he sputtered menacingly.

"It's no more than you deserve," Sierra retorted haughtily as she lifted herself from the quagmire with regal grace and dragged through the slime to the sidewalk. "That will teach you to laugh at a lady."

Never had Ram seen such a bedraggled sight as she flounced down the sidewalk, looking as if she had wallowed in a pigsty in all her dazzling finery. He knew it was ungentlemanly of him, but he couldn't help shouting with laughter, earning a malevolent look tossed over one elegant shoulder from the enraged miss.

While Ram was bathing and changing his clothes in his room at the Lucky Lady, Sierra paraded angrily before her elderly father, complaining bitterly about the man who had the gall to laugh at her misfortune. She looked nothing like the fashionably dressed young lady who had come to town with him this morning. Not only was she missing the feathered fancy she called a hat, but her lovely green dress had been transformed into a muddy brown creation. She was covered in slime from head to toe and her boots were completely ruined.

"The man is a foul beast, Papa!" Sierra raged. "I've never seen him before, but I can tell you he is no gentleman."

Frail, gray-haired Lester Alden listened indulgently to his only daughter. "From what you tell me, sweetheart, your retaliation was anything but ladylike. You pulled him down in the mud with you, you say?"

A feline smile curved Sierra's lush lips. "He deserved it," she said sweetly.

"And you have no idea who the man was?" She shook her head, spraying droplets of mud over the fine turkey carpet. "He's probably a stranger in town. Forget the incident. If you're lucky you'll never see him again. Meanwhile—"

"Mr. Alden." A young man stuck his head inside the door. "Excuse me, but Mr. Hunter has arrived and the other board members are waiting in the boardroom. Mr. Lynch has already joined them."

"Thank you, Figby, I'll be there directly." The clerk withdrew, trying not to stare at his boss's elegant daughter and failing miserably. She looked as if she'd been dragged through the mud.

"Clean up as best you can, then go buy yourself something new, sweetheart," Lester urged. "There's water in the pitcher and a clean cloth nearby. You'll have the office to yourself while I'm in the board meeting. Try to forget what happened. I'm sure you'll never see that obnoxious man again. After you finish your shopping, I'll take you home."

Somewhat mollified but still angry, Sierra nodded absently. Then she gasped in surprise and tried to hide behind the furniture when the door opened and a man entered.

"Lester, I'm sorry I'm late, but you'll never believe what happened. Some scatterbrained brunette—"

Coming to an abrupt halt, the breath caught in Ram's throat when he saw an incredibly filthy Sierra trying to disappear behind a chair. His shock was nearly as great as hers.

"No problem, Ram," Lester said, oblivious to the shimmering tension vibrating between Sierra and Ram. "We can go to the meeting together. But first I'd like you to meet my daughter. Ramsey Hunter, my daughter, Sierra. Sierra has been away at school, but she's home for good now."

"Miss Alden," Ram said, removing his hat and executing a sweeping bow that would do credit to a duke. "Pleased to meet you." A mocking smile hovered over his lips as his eyes roamed freely over her mud-splattered clothing.

"You'll have to excuse Sierra, Ram. She had an unfortunate accident this morning."

Sierra's lips thinned as her gaze slid over Ram's impressive figure. He was elegantly turned out in dove-gray suit, dark gray vest, pristine white shirt, and blue neckcloth. His boots were polished to a high sheen and his Stetson looked new. She glanced down at her own disreputable appearance, grimacing at her muddy dress and ruined boots.

When Sierra refused to return his greeting, Ram cleared his throat and said, "See to your daughter, Lester. I'll go on ahead. Join us when you're able." He turned abruptly and strode away.

Sierra stared at his departing back, her expression mutinous. How could someone who looked like Ramsey Hunter be so thoroughly disagreeable? Under normal circumstances she would be intrigued by his raw appeal. Though still an innocent, she had done her share of flirting at school and even kissed a man or two at those tedious dances and social events she had attended. Gordon Lynch couldn't hold a candle to Ramsey Hunter, but at least Gordie was a gentleman. If she and Gordie did marry, and she supposed they would, she would have the love and respect due her. The longer she thought of how Ramsey Hunter had laughed at her, the angrier she became.

"You *know* that man, Father?" Sierra asked, rounding on her hapless parent. "That's the despicable beast I was telling you about."

"Are you sure? I always considered Ramsey Hunter a gentleman. He's one of the richest men in town. Owns the Lucky Lady and has an interest in several other businesses. Since he came to town two years ago, I've not heard one bad word about him."

"He's a saloon owner, isn't he? I would assume that his occupation would place him on the fringe of polite society. I don't care how rich he is, I want nothing personally to do with him."

"Listen, Sierra, I don't have time now to discuss the merits of Ramsey Hunter. I'm sorry about what happened today, and after Saturday you can ignore him all you want."

Sierra went still. "Saturday? Are you speaking about my party? Oh, Father, surely you didn't invite that—that odious saloonkeeper to my party, did you?" She stamped her small foot. "I won't have it! I simply won't have it."

"Be reasonable, Sierra," Lester cajoled, "Ram is a board member. How would it look if I invited the others and not him? He's invested heavily in the bank and in San Francisco real estate."

"Where does he come from? What do you know about him?"

"What does it matter? A man's past is his own affair. Now I really have to go, Sierra. I'll meet you here later this afternoon." He turned and strode out the door.

Seething in impotent fury, Sierra watched her father leave. Until she'd learned that Ram Hunter was going to attend her party, she had looked forward to it. Now she wasn't sure how she felt. He had seen her at her absolute worst and she had acted like a shrew in his presence. Not that he didn't deserve it. With Ramsey Hunter there, her party could turn out to be a resounding disaster.

Ram couldn't recall when he'd been so distracted during a meeting. The image of the bedraggled little witch who had pulled him into the mud kept floating before his vision, making concentration impossible. The meeting was blessedly short, and Ram made a hasty exit before Lester could corner him. The banker was looking at him strangely, and he wondered if Sierra had told him about their encounter earlier. He was in no mood to face an irate father. Funny, he thought distractedly. He knew Lester had a daughter, but it never occurred to him that she'd be as young and beautiful as Sierra. Lester was at an age when one would expect him to have grown grandchildren, not children barely out of the schoolroom.

Grateful that the sun had dried some of the mud, Ram carefully avoided the puddles as he crossed the street and headed back to the saloon. Before he pushed through the swinging doors of the Lucky Lady, he saw Jody Carlson from the telegraph office hurrying toward him.

Carlson was hailing him and waving a piece of paper in the air.

"Mr. Hunter! Telegram just came for you. Thought I'd deliver it personally."

"Mighty good of you, Carlson," Ram said, smiling his most personable smile.

"Well, it's the least I could do, seeing as how you're always so nice about allowing me credit at your saloon."

He handed the sheet of paper to Ram, tipped his hat, and walked back in the direction from which he had just come. Ram read the message quickly, spat out a curse, and read it a second time. Then he wadded it up and stuffed it into his pocket. On his way through the saloon, he barked out a crisp order to the bartender. "Send Lola up to the office, Slim—now!"

"Yessir, boss, right away." When Ram spoke in that tone of voice, Slim knew he meant business.

Brassy-haired, green-eyed Lola Snodgrass sauntered into Ram's office a few minutes later. All of thirty years old but still desirable, still voluptuous in a blatantly sexual way, Lola had been Ram's right hand since he'd purchased the saloon from its previous owner. He'd inherited her with the establishment and hadn't regretted keeping her on. She managed the girls with an iron fist and made damn certain none of the dealers cheated the house. From the moment of Ram's arrival on the scene, she had reserved her time exclusively for him, eschewing all other men for the privilege of sharing his bed.

"You wanted me, honey?" Soft and seductive, her voice held a note of promise. If Ram wanted her for anything other than business, she was more than willing to oblige him. She draped herself across the desk, giving him an unrestricted view of two plump breasts pushing over the indecently low neckline of her scarlet dress.

Ram glanced at her, hardly noticing the sexual innuendo in her words or the brazen display of flesh. He'd seen and heard it all, too many times to count. If he no longer valued Lola as a lover, he certainly valued her as a friend and astute businesswoman.

Not wasting words, Ram said, "I have to go away, Lola."

"Go away?" She leaped to her feet, no longer the seductress. "What the hell does that mean? Where are you going? How long will you be gone? You're not pulling a disappearing act, are you? What about your business?"

"That's what I want to talk to you about, Lola. I want you to take over here while I'm gone. Unfortunately, I can't predict how long I will be gone. Weeks at least, months maybe. I'm not sure. I wouldn't leave if it wasn't necessary."

"Dammit, Ram, I can't run this business without you."

"I think you can. You've proven your worth to me many times over. Will you do it? I'm going to ask Lester Alden to keep an eye on my investments during my absence. I'm sure he'll give you a hand here too if you need it. What do you say, Lola, will you do it?"

Lola stared at Ram through narrowed lids that slanted upward at the corners, giving her face an almost feline appearance. Her lush red lips drew together in a pout. "I'm gonna miss you, honey. No one can make love like you."

Ram laughed, pulling her into his arms and giving her a quick kiss. "I'm sure there are others equally adept in bed, but I appreciate the compliment. Seriously, honey, I need you here to look after things for me."

"Sure, Ram. Since you put it that way, I don't see how I can refuse."

"You won't be sorry. When I return I'll see that you get a fair share of the take during my absence."

"For you I'd do it just for the sake of our friendship," Lola said, giving him a speaking look. "You've been damn decent to me since taking over the Lucky Lady. I'll be waiting for your return, honey. Waiting and eager," she added, giving him a lingering kiss.

"Go along with you now," he teased, swatting her rump playfully. "There's much to be done before I can leave."

Ram watched her sashay from the room, exuding sex from every fleshy pore. In the past two years he'd enjoyed her voluptuous body more times than he cared to count, but he had never felt more than a passing affection for her. In his experience, women were users and he knew that Lola would use him too, given half a chance. He intended to stay one step ahead of all deceitful females.

Take that little hellion this morning, he reflected idly. She had no call to yank him into the mud as she'd done. He had laughed at her, true, but she had looked so comical when her ridiculous little hat flew off and the wind flipped up her skirts, exposing her delicious rump, that he couldn't help himself. Unlike Lola, her trim figure bore no signs of plumpness, yet she still managed to look damn enticing.

He shifted uncomfortably in his chair to ease his loins as he imagined the luscious brunette spread beneath him, her supple legs twined around his hips. He wondered if she was still a virgin. Not that it mattered, he told himself. She happened to be the daughter of the town banker, whom he liked and respected. He hoped the feeling was mutual. Ram didn't have many friends and that's the way he wanted it. But since his arrival in San Francisco, he'd found he could trust Lester Alden, though no man would ever have his complete trust again.

Ram found it difficult to believe that the young beauty was the same daughter that the elderly Alden had spoken of with such fondness. The Aldens were such a mild-mannered couple that he wondered from whom Sierra had inherited her headstrong, impulsive nature. That she was spoiled outrageously was apparent. He'd like to turn the little beauty over his knee and give her the paddling she so richly deserved.

Ram smiled to himself, wondering if she knew he had been invited to her party on Saturday night. He gleefully anticipated her shock when he showed up. Since it would take him a few days to finalize his plans, Saturday would be the earliest he could inform Lester of his departure and ask him to look after his interests during his absence. He trusted Lola as far as he trusted any woman, but it wouldn't hurt to have the astute businessman check his accounts from time to time.

Ram nearly burst out laughing when he recalled how adorably disheveled the spoiled Miss Alden had looked with her clothing and skin covered in mud, her face mottled with anger, and her sable hair straggling down her back in a sodden mass. Then he remembered how she had repaid his well-meaning offer of help by yanking him into the mud, ruining his new suit and favorite Stetson. Damn, he'd like to get his hands on her and . . . He shook his head to clear it of thoughts that were far too disturbing, not to mention arousing. He could think of more pleasant things his hands could be doing to Miss Sierra Alden than administering punishment.

Fortunately the entrancing little witch was safe from him. He wanted nothing to do with innocent virgins. To his detriment, he'd learned that virgins were no more trustworthy than whores. Dora had taught him to put women in their proper place in his life.

Dora and Jason . . . If there was a God, this time he'd find them.

Chapter Two

Sierra glanced into the upstairs hall mirror one last time before descending the stairs to greet her guests. Early arrivals were already mingling in the parlor, and she wanted to be on hand when Gordie walked through the door, eager to give him the full benefit of her dazzling appearance tonight. She'd taken great pains choosing just the right dress and jewelry and knew she looked her best in a gold tissue silk that hugged her slim curves and displayed her smooth white shoulders and upper breasts most becomingly.

She hoped Gordie appreciated her efforts. She had even piled her hair atop her head in a bouffant style in an effort to appear more mature. In addition to being a homecoming party, tonight was a celebration of her twenty-first birthday. Since Sierra had no knowledge of her birthdate, she had chosen August as her birth month. All she had recalled when the Aldens found her wandering on the prairie was her first name and age, quite an accomplishment for a three-year-old.

Sierra descended the stairs slowly, aware that she was the center of attention. A dazzling smile sketched her lips, then faltered slightly when she saw that Gordie had already arrived and was waiting for her at the bottom of the steps. She'd known Gordie all her life, and everyone assumed they would marry one day. She'd always thought she wanted Gordie until . . . until she'd encountered that obnoxious saloon-keeper. How could poor Gordie possibly compete with a man as outrageously attractive as Ramsey Hunter? Dear God, how could she even think of Ram Hunter in the same breath as Gordie Lynch? They were nothing alike.

True, they both had blue eyes. But Gordie's were a rather pale imitation of Ram's. They both had blond hair, but Gordie's was thin, wispy, and lifeless while Ram's was thick, wavy, and lustrous. Gordie was only an inch or two taller than her own five-feet-five, while Ramsey Hunter towered over her. Why did Gordie's features look so pale and pinched? she wondered distractedly. And why hadn't she noticed it before?

When Sierra reached the bottom of the staircase, Gordie took her hand, drawing it into the crook of his arm in an annoyingly possessive manner. He gave her appearance a quick perusal, pursed his lips in vague disapproval, and said, "You look lovely, my dear, but isn't that dress rather revealing? I'd prefer you save your charms for the privacy of our bedroom once we're married."

"Gordie, really," Sierra snapped, annoyed more than she cared to admit. "This dress is quite respectable. If you think it's revealing, you should see what the women in New York are wearing."

Gordie scowled, his displeasure apparent. "Sending you to school in New York was a mistake. Your parents are far too indulgent. Once we're married, I'll expect you to act like a banker's wife. One day I'll take over at the bank for your father and become one of the town's leading citizens. Lester is getting too old to manage so large an enterprise."

Sierra bristled indignantly. Her father might be elderly, but he still managed his businesses with great finesse. He was sharper than any man she knew.

"How is a banker's wife supposed to act, Gordie?" she asked sweetly.

"With decorum, dear, with decorum," Gordie said, oblivious to Sierra's irritation. "We really ought to set the date, dear," he continued blithely. "You're not getting any younger, and we should get started on our family. If you had seen fit to return from New York sooner, we'd already be married with a child or two in the nursery."

"I'm in no hurry to get married, Gordie. I

want to enjoy myself before settling down and raising a family." What did he think she was, a brood mare?

"As I said before," Gordie persisted, "you've had sufficient enjoyment out of life. Your parents indulge you shamelessly."

"Ah, there you are, children," Lester beamed, forestalling Sierra's scathing reply as he and his wife strolled up to join them.

Sierra welcomed their arrival with a warm smile. For some reason, everything Gordie said tonight set her teeth on edge.

"You look beautiful, dear," Holly Alden gushed, proud of her only child.

"You look lovely, too, Mama." Sierra smiled, thinking her mother looked somewhat paler than usual tonight.

A pretty, frail woman, Holly Alden looked every one of her sixty-five years. Unable to have children, she had given up hope of ever raising a child of her own when they found Sierra, looking so lost and pitiful that she and Lester had taken her to their hearts immediately. They later discovered the bodies of Sierra's parents, who had been slaughtered by Indians. When no relatives could be found, the Aldens happily adopted Sierra and took her with them to California.

"Are you certain you don't want to make this affair tonight even more joyous by announcing your engagement to Gordon?" Lester asked, earning a scowl from Sierra. Lester was looking forward to turning his business acumen in another direction, but until Sierra married a man capable of running the bank, he felt obligated to remain. Not that he wanted to rush Sierra, but Gordon Lynch was a skilled businessman fully capable of taking over at the bank. He was also extremely eager to marry Sierra.

"I suggested the same thing just moments ago," Gordon contended, "but Sierra says she isn't ready yet to marry."

Attuned to her daughter's innermost feelings, Holly said, "Sierra just returned from school, Gordon. She's been away from home a long time. She needs time with her family before settling down with a husband and raising a family of her own."

Sierra sent Holly a grateful smile. She could always depend on Holly to understand her needs. Sierra was fond of Gordie, but marriage was forever. She needed time to learn if she could truly love Gordie instead of thinking of him as a friend.

"I don't care what Sierra says," Gordie retorted. "I will consider us engaged despite the lack of a formal announcement. Now, shall we dance?" He pulled her toward the open patio doors where a band played beneath the stars and several other couples were already dancing to the music.

Sierra did not see Ramsey Hunter greet her parents at the front door. Nor did she know that they had urged him to join the younger group outside on the patio. He paused in the doorway a moment, surveying the crowded area illuminated by hundreds of Chinese lanterns, his gaze sweeping the couples twirling on the dance floor. He spotted Sierra almost at the same moment she saw him. The breath caught in his throat. He thought she looked like a regal princess placed on earth for the visual pleasure of lowly mortals.

Ram recognized her partner as the vice president of the bank and a man who frequented his establishment often to purchase the services of Lola's girls. Absently he wondered why it upset him to think of Sierra with a man who couldn't match her in fire and spirit. In his estimation, Gordon Lynch was a rather colorless imitation of a man. Even the whores spoke disparagingly about his lack of finesse in bed.

"If you're looking at Lester's daughter, forget it."

Ram smiled at Donald Simpson, who had just come up to join him. Don was a business acquaintance and about as close to him as he allowed any man to get. "She's a fetching little thing," Ram allowed.

"She's all but engaged to Gordon Lynch. I hear the old man is grooming him to take over at the bank after Gordon marries his daughter."

"Is that so?" Ram said, feigning disinterest. "She sure doesn't look like the kind of daughter old Lester and Holly would produce, but I suppose stranger things have happened."

Don sent him a searching glance, saw that he was serious, and said, "I forget you're relatively new to San Francisco. Sierra is adopted. Don't know the whole story, but rumor has it her family was slaughtered by Indians."

"That explains a lot," Ram murmured, unable to take his eyes off Sierra as she swayed gracefully in Gordon Lynch's arms.

"Well, have a good time, Ram," Don said as he spied his wife across the patio. "I'm going to claim my wife for a dance."

Sierra smarted beneath Ram's intense gaze. She'd been torn between wishing he'd not attend her party and praying he would. Their meeting a few days ago had been a disaster. The man was possessed of incredible gall. He should feel guilty for making fun of her misfortune.

Sierra was still thinking of Ram when the dance ended and Gordie led her from the dance floor. "Would you like something to drink?" Gordie asked, unaware of her preoccupation with Ramsey Hunter.

"Yes, thank you," Sierra said with alacrity. She waited until Gordon disappeared inside the house, then moved into the shadows to watch the other dancers. When she looked to where she had last seen Ram, he was gone. A sigh left her lips. Vaguely she wondered if it was one of relief or disappointment.

"I hardly recognize you, Miss Alden. You clean up rather well."

Sierra started violently, shocked to find Ram standing beside her. How had he approached without her knowing it?

"You are no gentleman to mention my—unfortunate accident," she said with asperity.

"I'm glad you noticed. I'd hate to be mistaken for something I'm not." The chuckle started deep in his chest and rumbled from his throat in a low, sexy growl.

"You aren't fit for polite society, Mr. Hunter. I'm surprised Father invited you tonight."

"Perhaps your father is a better judge of character than you are." Ram turned with a taunting smile.

"Perhaps he doesn't really know you," Sierra returned shortly.

"And you do—a girl barely out of the school-room?"

Ram watched her eyes narrow into shards of pure silver, captivated by the fire smoldering in their bright depths. Idly he wondered if she'd show the same kind of spirit in bed. He'd bet his last dollar she'd be a passionate bed partner, but regrettably he wouldn't be the man to unleash those passions. He'd leave that to Gordon Lynch. That thought produced a burst of laughter. Lynch was as passionless a man as he'd ever encountered.

"I'm glad I amuse you," Sierra snapped when she heard Ram's snort of laughter. "Think what you like, but I assure you I'm no child."

His gaze roamed freely over her lush figure. "No, you're no child, Miss Alden. Any fool can see that."

"Here you are, Sierra. I've been looking all over for you." Gordon appeared beside Sierra, bearing a cup in each hand. "I've brought you some punch." He sent Ram a dark look and nodded brusquely. "Hello, Hunter, I'm surprised to find you at such tame entertainment. You'll find no stimulating diversions here."

Sierra took the cup from Gordie's hand, somewhat surprised by his unfriendly manner toward Ram. At least everyone wasn't as enamored of Ram Hunter as her father was, she thought smugly.

Ram sent Gordon a mocking smile. "I find the company and atmosphere highly stimulating, just as you do the entertainment in my establishment. There's no accounting for men's tastes."

Judging from the fierce scowl on Gordie's face, Sierra sensed that a challenge had passed between the two men, but she had no idea what it was all about. It was unsettling to think that Gordie had visited a notorious gambling saloon, but she supposed men needed diversion occasionally. It never occurred to her that Gordie might buy the services of a whore. Gentlemen didn't do such things, did they?

Gordon's face turned beet red. He had never liked Ramsey Hunter and liked him even less now. He sensed a rift developing in his relationship with Sierra and laid the blame at Ram's feet. How dare the scurrilous bastard hint in front of Sierra that he visited the Lucky Lady. Grasping her elbow, he propelled her away.

"You mustn't neglect your guests, Sierra," he said, aiming her in the direction of a group of people standing nearby. "Have a good time, Hunter," he threw over his shoulder, "though it's hardly the type of entertainment you're accustomed to."

Sierra glanced back once, not surprised to see Ram's lips spread in a wide grin. Was he always so easily amused?

"Was Hunter bothering you?" Gordon asked once he and Sierra were out of earshot. "I'm surprised your father invited him tonight. He may be rich, but no one seems to know much about him. He just appeared in town one day and started buying up property. I'd swear there's something unsavory in his past, something he prefers to keep hidden."

"He wasn't bothering me, Gordie. Forget Ramsey Hunter. I already have."

Sierra sincerely wished she meant those words. In truth, she had never been more aware of a man than she was of Ram. He looked elegant in his exquisitely tailored black suit. His chest and shoulders were as beautifully muscled as a Greek statue, but vibrant with life, more intoxicating than stone could ever be. His face wasn't classically handsome, but exceptional in a rugged, masculine sense. His thick blond hair brushed the collar of his white shirt, and his intense blue eyes had the ability to look into one's soul. She could tell he was accustomed to laughing a lot by the tiny network of lines spreading outward at the corners of his eyes and generous lips.

"I saw you talking to Ram Hunter." Sierra sat in the powder room adjusting her stockings when one of her girlfriends entered and sat down beside her. "My, but he's handsome. Too bad he's so enamored of that Lola woman who works for him down at the Lucky Lady. Decent women don't seem to interest him."

"I think he's an obnoxious lout," Sierra sniffed disdainfully. "He's rude and certainly no gentleman. Lola, whoever she is, is welcome to him."

"My goodness," Sally Dreyfus exclaimed, her eyes wide with curiosity. "What did he do to get you so riled?"

Sierra flushed and looked away. She certainly didn't want to get into it with Sally, an incurable gossip. "Nothing. I just don't like the man, that's all."

"I don't think Gordon likes him either," Sally observed. "He couldn't wait to get you away from Mr. Hunter. My father says he is an astute businessman as well as a rich one."

A few minutes later, Sierra returned to her guests, Sally's words still ringing in her ears. Her friend's revelation about Ram and that saloon woman served only to reinforce Sierra's observation about Ram's character.

Ram watched Sierra glide gracefully about the room, speaking with her guests. She was a good hostess, he'd give her that much. But for some unexplained reason he was extremely resentful of the way Gordon Lynch clung to her. Ram noted that Lynch was deeply engrossed in conversation with Lester Alden, and without conscious knowledge he moved unerringly toward Sierra, yearning to engage in another round of stimulating conversation with the little vixen. Halfway across the room he realized what he was doing and stopped abruptly. His coldly analytical mind told him that Sierra Alden would create havoc in his life at a time when he least needed it. The pampered young beauty could easily make him forget the one constant in his life.

Revenge.

Turning away from the entrancing sway of Sierra's hips as she moved from group to group, he waited to catch Lester alone. His travel plans were in place now, and there was no time like the present to ask Lester to keep an eye on his investments during his absence, since he had no idea when he would return from Denver.

Sierra wandered over to a group of her father's business associates, listening politely to their conversation. One of the men mentioned that he had just returned from Denver, and her attention sharpened.

"I tell you, gentlemen, it's a strange story, indeed. For years tales circulated about a white Indian who rode with Red Cloud. Turns out the rumor was true. The man was raised by the Cheyenne people after his parents were killed in a raid. Real savage, he was. According to stories making the rounds in Denver, both he and his sister had been integrated into the tribe."

"Astounding," one of the men exclaimed. "What became of the man and his sister? Are they still with Indians?"

Sierra held her breath. Could it be? Could it possibly be? After all these years to finally hear substantial proof that her brother and sister might still be alive filled her heart with hope. Her father—her adoptive father—insisted that neither of her siblings could possibly be alive after all this time. Sierra thought the story too much of a coincidence to let it drop without further investigation.

"The white savage was called Wind Rider," the speaker continued. "Don't recall his white name. The army had him in jail for a time, but the governor intervened. Don't know why, or what became of him. But I do know his sister left the tribe and married a prominent Denver businessman. Can't recall her name, either."

"Is her name Abby?" Sierra asked breathlessly. Dear God, let it be so, she silently prayed.

The man gave Sierra a startled look. "Could be. Have you heard the story before, Miss Alden?"

"No, no, nothing like that, it's just . . ."

"I've heard talk about white savages but always assumed it was foolish nonsense." Gordon had joined the group in time to hear part of the conversation and didn't like where it was leading. "If you'll excuse us, gentlemen, I wish to dance with my fiancée." Sierra was so reluctant to leave that Gordon had to literally drag her away.

"I wanted to hear the rest of the conversation, Gordon," she hissed angrily. "If my brother and sister are still alive, I want to know."

Gordon gave a snort of exasperation. "I thought Lester disabused you of that notion years ago. It's time you stopped dreaming and accepted that your brother and sister are dead. I don't want to hear anymore talk about it." Brooking no argument, he pulled her through the open doors and onto the dance floor.

Sierra's mind worked furiously. If there was even a remote possibility that her brother and sister were the white savages the guest had referred to, she owed it to herself to find out. She had to go to Denver, she just had to. She didn't want her need to find her siblings to hurt her adoptive parents, but for as long as she could remember she'd dreamed of finding them. Though they were vaguely defined in her mind, she'd known from the moment Lester and Holly had found her wandering on the prairie that she had a brother and sister. For a long time she had missed them dreadfully, until they slowly faded from her memory. But she had never completely forgotten them. And lately she'd been haunted by thoughts of her siblings, who had been taken from her before she'd really gotten to know them.

Fearing they would lose their beloved daughter, both Lester and Holly had brushed aside all inquiries Sierra made concerning her family. Sierra was aware that her parents were dead, but in her heart she'd always felt that Ryder and Abby lived. And if she had her way about it, she would soon find out. Nothing, absolutely nothing, would prevent her from going to Denver and finding her lost siblings.

The moment the dance ended, Sierra excused herself to go to the powder room. But it was just an excuse to rid herself of Gordie. She really wanted to speak with her father. She fumed impatiently when she saw Lester and Ram Hunter enter the study and shut the door behind them. Leaning against the panel, she settled herself to wait until Ram left so she might speak with her father privately. Curiosity got the best of her when she heard voices, and she leaned her ear to the door.

"What is this about, Ramsey?" Lester asked as he settled into a chair and offered Ram a cigar. "Can't it wait until next week?"

"Sorry, Lester, but I wouldn't ask for a private word with you if it wasn't important. I plan on leaving early next week and need to ask a favor of you. If you refuse, I'll understand."

"Well, you've certainly got my attention. What can I do for you, Ram?"

"I'm leaving for Denver on the next stage. Don't know how long I'll be gone, but I'm counting on you to keep an eye on my investments for me during my absence."

"I won't ask why you're going away. I'm smart enough not to invade a man's privacy, but isn't this trip rather hasty? What about the Lucky Lady? I hope you're leaving it in good hands."

"I left Lola in charge of the Lucky Lady. She knows the business, and I trust her not to cheat me. If it's convenient, I'd like you to check the books every week or so until I return."

"Of course, if that's what you want." Lester gave Ram a searching look. "Do you want to tell me about it?"

"It's personal," Ram replied succinctly. "Perhaps I'll tell you when I return."

"Very well, Ram, you have my promise to keep you solvent. Any other requests?"

Sierra moved away from the door when she heard the scrape of a chair and footsteps. She didn't want her father and Ram to think she'd been eavesdropping, though in truth that's exactly what she'd been doing.

When the door opened, Sierra ducked into a nearby room, waiting until Ram strode out of the study and down the hall before entering the study and closing the door behind her. Lester looked up in surprise, a smile curving his lips when he saw Sierra.

"Well, sweetheart, to what do I owe this pleasure? Are you having a good time?"

"It's a wonderful party, Papa, thank you. You don't know how grateful I am." If not for her party, she'd have never heard about the white savages who quite possibly were her missing brother and sister.

Lester raised a shaggy white eyebrow. "Am I missing something here? You sound almost too grateful."

"I heard something tonight, Papa—something that could very well change my life."

"Sounds ominous. Do you want to tell me about it?"

Sierra paced the room, much too excited to

sit down. "I heard a rumor tonight that confirms my belief that both Ryder and Abby are alive. One of the guests told an extraordinary story about a white savage and his sister who were raised by Indians. The man, Wind Rider, rode with Red Cloud. I think Wind Rider is my brother Ryder. Evidently he and his sister, who I believe is Abby, left the tribe and are now living in or near Denver."

Lester felt an ache begin deep in his chest and spread outward throughout his body. He'd dreaded this moment ever since Sierra was old enough to ask questions and wonder about the fate of her siblings. He had sent her East to school in hopes that she'd forget them, but obviously she'd never quite given up the dream of finding her brother and sister. He and Holly couldn't bear the thought of losing their beloved child and had routinely denied the possibility of Sierra's finding her siblings. As far as Lester was concerned, he and Holly were Sierra's only family. He knew it was selfish of him, but that was the way it had to be.

"There's been talk of white savages for years, sweetheart, but that doesn't mean they exist. We both know how remote the possibility is that your brother and sister are still alive."

"But this time it's different, Papa!" Her voice trembled with emotion. "This is the first concrete evidence we've had that white savages actually exist. Denver isn't all that far away. It would take so little to learn the truth once and for all. Take me to Denver, Papa, please. Can't you understand? This is something I have to do for my own peace of mind."

Lester's lined face looked even more haggard as he regarded his determined daughter. Surely she knew that he and Holly were much too old to undertake so arduous a trip, didn't she? "Be reasonable, Sierra," he cajoled. "It isn't realistic to assume that your siblings are alive after all this time. You can't believe everything you hear. If I thought they were alive, I'd do all in my power to reunite you with them. But if you recall, I hired a detective years ago and he turned up no trace of them. I don't want to see you hurt, sweetheart. It's best for all concerned if you forget this foolishness."

Sierra's chin rose fractionally. She'd heard these same arguments time and again, but this time she wouldn't be so easily dissuaded. This time there was solid evidence that a brother and sister raised by Indians existed. Lester had told her that the bodies of her siblings were never found, but she strongly believed they had been taken by Indians and integrated into the tribe. She *had* to believe it.

"I want to go to Denver, Papa."

"Look at me, Sierra. Take a good look. I'm not young anymore, and your mother is far too frail to venture across mountains and prairies. If the railroad was in operation, it would be different, but we're still two years away from coast-to-coast travel. Can't we compromise? I promise to purchase the first rail tickets and take you to Denver the moment they are available."

"But that's two years in the future, Father!" Sierra wailed. "Two years of not knowing, of waiting, of hoping. I don't think I can stand it."

"It's the best I can offer, sweetheart, since I absolutely refuse to allow you to go alone."

"I can hire someone to act as chaperon."

"You've led a sheltered life. You have no conception of the hazards you might encounter. A young, beautiful woman is vulnerable to every disreputable character in the West, despite a suitable chaperon. No, Sierra, you'll not travel to Denver without proper escort. Besides, even by stage the journey would be much too arduous for a pampered young lady like yourself."

Sierra could see that her father was distraught, so rather than upset him further, she pretended to accept his argument as the final word on the subject. But her mind was already made up. "We'll talk later, Papa," she said gently. "I suspect Mama and our guests are wondering where we disappeared to."

A look of immense relief lightened Lester's wrinkled features. Thank God Sierra had listened to reason. It was true that he didn't think himself capable of undertaking an overland journey through rough country, but more importantly, he couldn't bear the thought of losing his daughter to a family she couldn't even recall.

"Run along, sweetheart. I'll join you directly," Lester urged, feeling in need of a moment alone to compose his ragged nerves.

Sierra's mood was pensive when she left her father's study. She hated causing him undue anguish, but she was determined to go to Denver. Unfortunately, there was the small problem of finding a way to leave without the Aldens' knowledge or help. Money was no hindrance, for she had a bank account with a healthy balance, thanks to her father's generosity and the fact that he never questioned how she spent her allowance.

The rest of the evening passed in a blur. She supposed she danced and made small talk, but she remembered little of it. It wasn't until the guests began leaving and she saw Ram speaking with her father that she recalled their conversation in the study earlier. The information she had heard could very well prove useful to her. Ramsey Hunter was going to Denver. Very soon. She made a point of being on hand to bid him good-bye.

Ram saw Sierra standing near the door and felt something shift inside him, creating a moment of vulnerability he hadn't experienced in a long time. Some sixth sense warned him to be very careful where Miss Sierra Alden was concerned or repent the rest of his life.

"Miss Alden, I had a delightful time," Ram said politely as he paused beside her. "Meeting you has been an . . . experience I won't soon forget."

Sierra grit her teeth and smiled. "Indeed, Mr. Hunter, a most unusual meeting. I hear you're leaving town soon."

One sandy brow rose in lazy question. "Now where did you hear something like that? You weren't eavesdropping, were you?"

Sierra brushed aside his insinuation. "I hope you aren't too upset with me over our unfortunate—er, confrontation the other day."

A nerve jerked in Ram's jaw. Unfortunate confrontation wasn't exactly how he'd describe their meeting. Explosive better expressed their reaction to one another. "What exactly are you getting at, Miss Alden?" She was smiling so sweetly that he assumed she was up to something.

"Oh, nothing, I just wanted to wish you bon voyage to Denver." He felt the effects of her devastating smile clear down to his toes.

"Few people know I'm going to Denver."

"I know a lot of things about you."

"Did you like anything you heard?"

He stepped closer, until her sweet breath fanned his cheek. The way she looked at him made him want to reach out and pull her softness against the hard length of his body, to kiss her until she grew breathless, to lay his body atop hers and make her his in the most basic way.

She gave him a coquettish grin. "Not much, but I'm willing to change my mind."

Warning bells went off in Ram's head. Coyness didn't work with him. If she wanted something, he preferred that she just come right out and ask. "Good night, Miss Alden. We can finish this conversation when I return from Denver."

Sierra watched him walk away, a smug smile curving her lips. "We'll finish this conversation a lot sooner than that, Mr. Ramsey Hunter," she said beneath her breath.

Chapter Three

Sierra paused outside the Lucky Lady, gathering the courage to push through the swinging doors. It was still very early, and the popular saloon was likely to be deserted, but it was definitely off limits to a lady no matter what the time of day. But few women were as determined as she. Few women had so much at stake.

She had spent long, futile hours trying to convince Lester to either hire someone to escort her to Denver or take her himself. When Holly grew panicky at her continued insistence that she find her siblings, Sierra had finally given up, no less determined but with a new plan forming in her mind. A plan that involved Ramsey Hunter. Though she couldn't stand the infuriating man, she reluctantly admitted that he was her last

51

hope of reaching Denver before snow closed the passes.

Since faltering courage was not Sierra's style, she squared her shoulders and stepped through the swinging doors. She had a mission to accomplish and nothing was going to deter her. Come hell or high water, she was going to convince Ramsey Hunter to escort her to Denver.

At first, Slim Hankins failed to notice her; he was busily replacing empty bottles of liquor with fresh ones in anticipation of the evening crowd. Sierra had to clear her throat rather loudly before he acknowledged her. The moment the bartender saw Sierra standing in the dim saloon looking oddly out of place, he gave her his full attention.

"Can I help you, miss? If you're looking for a job, you'll have to wait until Lola wakes up for an interview." Slim didn't think Sierra was a whore, but one never could tell in this day and age. He looked her over carefully, thinking she was beautiful enough to challenge any of Lola's stable of girls and would be a real attention grabber at the Lucky Lady.

A slow flush crept up Sierra's neck. Did she look like a woman who . . . who . . . She couldn't even think it, let alone say it. "My business is with Mr. Hunter. Where might I find him?"

Slim's eyebrows rose fractionally. She wasn't the type of woman the boss usually consorted with. Women like Lola were more Ram's style. Not that Ram couldn't get any female he wanted. "Is the boss expecting you?"

"Are you saying I need an appointment?"

"Er . . . no ma'am, I don't reckon you do. Ram hasn't come downstairs yet. He's in his room. Up the stairs, third door on the right."

Ram hadn't seen the need to rent or buy more suitable lodgings and seemed perfectly content with the large two-room suite above the saloon that served both as office and sleeping quarters. He liked being on hand around the clock to settle disputes and supervise his business. Since his days usually ended in the wee hours, he normally arose late in the morning and worked in his office during the afternoon and early evening.

"Thank you," Sierra said coolly. Her back rigid, her jaw firmly set, she started up the stairs.

Watching from below, Slim couldn't recall when he'd seen a more determined woman. Just looking at her made him thankful he wasn't Ramsey Hunter.

Shirt sleeves rolled up and neckline gaping open to reveal a generous expanse of muscular chest, Ram finished his third cup of coffee and sat back in his chair to admire the view from the window. With no tall buildings blocking his view, he enjoyed an unobstructed panorama of San Francisco Bay. The sight never failed to stir him. Having been born and raised in a small Texas town miles from any large body of water, he had fallen in love with San Francisco upon his arrival two years ago. His thoughts were miles away when a tentative knock on the door brought him abruptly from his reverie.

"Come in," he called absently, still immersed in the mesmerizing sight of the sun's reflection on the sparkling water. Assuming his visitor was Lola, he didn't bother turning his head as he greeted her. "Kind of early for you, isn't it, Lola? Have you had your coffee yet, honey? Help yourself, there's plenty left in the pot."

Sierra's face flamed at the mention of Ram's . . . mistress. Mistress was the only word she could think of to describe the relationship between Ram and the soiled dove.

"It's not Lola," she said tersely.

Ram's head jerked around and his body tensed. He had recognized her voice instantly but was nonetheless shocked to see Sierra in his room at the Lucky Lady. He rose gracefully to his feet and executed a mocking bow. "Miss Alden, what brings you to my humble abode? Does your father know you're here? Your business must be urgent for you to breach the lion in his den."

Sierra raised her chin fractionally, gaining courage when she remembered the importance of her visit. "I wanted to speak with you in private, Mr. Hunter. My business is indeed urgent, else I wouldn't be here."

Ram sent her a wry smile. "What could be more important than your reputation? I know it's still early, but you could have been seen entering the Lucky Lady."

"I have a proposition for you, Mr. Hunter.

One that demands prompt attention before you left town."

Ram's blue eyes narrowed speculatively. "What kind of proposition?" Knowing Sierra as he did, he was confident he wasn't going to like anything she had to offer.

"I need your escort to Denver and I'm willing to pay handsomely."

To his credit, Ram kept a straight face. "Let me get this straight, Miss Alden. You wish to go to Denver and you're willing to pay for my escort?"

Sierra smiled sweetly. "That's right, Mr. Hunter. How much?"

"Now wait a damned minute, Miss High-and-mighty Alden. I'm not for sale."

Sierra bristled indignantly. "I'm buying nothing but your escort to Denver. It's urgent that I reach Denver with all haste, and it isn't proper for a young lady to travel alone. I'd prefer to travel with an escort, if possible."

"Excuse me, but isn't that your father's responsibility? Shouldn't he be the one providing escort?"

Sierra flushed and glanced at her feet. "Father is . . . you know he can't . . ."

"The truth, Sierra. May I call you Sierra?" Sierra nodded absently. "I need to know everything before I commit myself to this scatterbrained scheme of yours."

Sierra raised her head and looked directly into his eyes. Her silver gaze nearly blinded him. "Father refused to take me. He said we'd visit Denver when the railroad was completed, but I can't wait that long. He refuses to listen to reason."

"I'm sorry, Sierra, but I agree with your father. Denver by stagecoach is a grueling journey. You'd never be able to withstand the ordeal. Stay home where your parents can pamper you. After one day of eating dust and bone-breaking jostling over rutted roads in an uncomfortable coach, you'll be ready to turn back."

Sierra sent him a scathing glance. "You have a very low opinion of me. I can survive the ordeal if you can. Besides, it's imperative I reach Denver."

"What is so urgent to make you beg for my help when you don't even like me?"

"It's a long story, but suffice it to say this isn't some reckless adventure I'm embarking on. How much will it take to change your mind? I'll agree to anything you say."

"Anything?" Ram's eyes took on a devilish gleam.

"Anything within reason."

A wide smile sketched Ram's lips as he closed the distance between them. When they were standing toe to toe, he tilted her head and brushed her lips with his. The kiss was so fleeting, so softly given, that Sierra thought she'd imagined it.

"What if I want something other than money,

Sierra?" He stroked her velvety cheek with the back of his hand.

Sierra sent him a wary glance. "Not want money? I don't understand."

"I think you do. You're a beautiful, desirable woman. There are some things a man wants from a beautiful woman that have nothing to do with money. I have enough money of my own."

Sierra's silver eyes grew wide as saucers when his meaning became clear. His bold words gave her pause for thought. Just how badly did she want to reach Denver and how far was she prepared to go to obtain what she wanted? Evidently Ramsey Hunter aimed to find out.

The finger that lifted her chin for his kiss followed the line of her throat down to her collarbone, where it paused for the space of a heartbeat. Sierra gasped in dismay when that finger continued down to the first button on the front of her blouse. Nimbly he released the button, lingering with dramatic effect before moving down to release the second, smiling wolfishly at her all the while. Catching her lower lip between her teeth, Sierra held herself stiffly when he continued on to the third button. Ram's eyes gleamed with wicked delight when he glimpsed a generous portion of plump white flesh through the opening he'd created in her blouse.

"Shall I continue, Sierra?"

Sierra could only stare at him. If she said no, she might as well forget about getting to Denver anytime soon. If she said yes, she'd be placing herself on the same level as Lola and her kind. She chose to remain mute, hoping Ram would remember that she was a lady and act the gentleman for once in his life.

Another button slipped through the buttonhole, baring more of Sierra's upper breasts. She closed her eyes, refusing to watch as Ram continued his subtle seduction. Two more downward strokes and Sierra's blouse hung open to the waist. When she felt him tug at the strings of her chemise, her eyes flew open and she grasped his hands.

"Wait! Is—is this necessary?"

"It's your call, Sierra. You want to go to Denver, don't you? How eager are you? How far are you willing to go? Perhaps you're not as innocent as I thought. Maybe you did more in New York than go to school. Has Gordon Lynch already sampled your sweet charms?"

Ram knew he was deliberately goading her, but she needed to be taught a lesson. Dimly he wondered how far he'd have to push her before she'd come to her senses. Not even the promise of her sweet body could tempt him to take this spoiled child on an overland journey fraught with danger. He hoped the little charade he was playing with her would convince her that she was ill-prepared to match wits with him and how recklessly she had behaved by coming to the Lucky Lady alone. Unfortunately, he hadn't counted on his body's response to the dark-haired beauty. But he was confident of retaining full control of the situation.

The predatory look in Ram's eyes made Sierra realize how irresponsibly she had acted by coming to the Lucky Lady and entering a man's room, especially this man's room. As Ram's words sunk in, she came out of her stupor into raging anger. No one had ever said such vile things to her. Jerking back her arm, she swung at him, putting all her weight behind it. Ram saw the blow coming and ducked. Retaliation was swift and startling.

Grasping Sierra's arms, he pinned them behind her back, bringing her hard against him. Then his mouth slammed down on hers. The moment his lips touched hers, she stiffened and tried to back away, but he tightened his grip, pressing her resisting body more intimately against his lean, hard length. He didn't force her into responding; it just happened as his tongue thrust coaxingly against her closed lips until her mouth opened of its own accord and she was assailed with a weakness so overwhelming that her legs buckled beneath her.

She gasped into the warmth of his mouth as he released her hands and placed his own hands on the lush swell of her bottom. Contrasting emotions skittered through Sierra as she felt the sizzling warmth of his hands sear through the layers of her clothing. She tried to protest but couldn't think past the sensations Ram was producing inside her.

Relentlessly he renewed his assault on her lips, tantalizing her with his hot kisses. Sierra's senses whirled as raw pleasure such as she'd never experienced before shot through her, sending tingling heat through her veins. A true innocent, she had no conception of the danger she courted if Ram was really bent on seduction. With a will of their own, her arms crept around his neck.

With enormous satisfaction, Ram felt Sierra's surrender in the softening of her body and realized that he could take her now and she would offer little resistance. To test his theory, one hand left her bottom, slowly moving upward to cover her breast. Sierra whimpered, feeling the heat of his hand through the boned corset she wore. He groaned when he felt her melting against him. The will he took so much pride in nearly deserted him when Sierra moved against him in a most disturbing manner.

Abruptly Sierra tore her mouth away from his, her eyes wild with sudden alarm when she realized that she was behaving as wantonly as Lola. Ram came to his senses at the same time and shoved her away from him with a brutal thrust. He was breathing hard; the temptation to take what the little witch offered was proving stronger than he would have expected. She was seducing him to her will almost as effectively as he was seducing her to his. He hadn't fallen so low, he thought wryly, that Sierra or any other woman could buy his services with her tempting little body.

"Go home, Sierra," he rasped. "Your tactics won't work with me. I wouldn't escort you to

Denver for all the money in the mint. I respect your father too much to agree to your reckless proposal."

Her blood still singing with her first taste of real passion, Sierra's silver eyes glowed darkly as she glared at Ram. He seemed to enjoy her struggle to gain her composure. "But you said— you wanted—what made you stop?"

Ram snorted in disgust. "My good sense. You're trouble, Sierra, the kind of trouble I don't need right now. No woman is worth it. You're a spoiled little princess who wouldn't last a day on the road. Go on," he shouted, angry at his startling loss of control, "get out of here before I change my mind and give you what you want. I hate to disappoint you, Miss Alden, but I'm certain Gordon Lynch will satisfy you if you ask him nicely."

Sierra's temper hung by a slim thread. Unfortunately, Ram Hunter offered her the best chance of reaching Denver. Too stubborn to give up, she resorted to tears. It wasn't necessary to force the emotional outburst, it came quite naturally as large tears gathered in the corners of her eyes and rolled down her pale cheeks. Ram appeared unmoved as Sierra's narrow shoulders shook with the force of her unrestrained sobs.

"You don't understand, Ram," she sniffed, using his less formal nickname. "Perhaps you'll change your mind if I explain."

"I doubt it," he remarked dryly. He rather liked the sound of his name on her lips.

She explained anyway.

"I was adopted by the Aldens. My own parents were killed by Indians eighteen years ago. I was just three. My brother and sister disappeared and no trace of them was ever found. We speculated on their fate, but it was all conjecture until I listened in on a conversation at my party. A recent visitor to Denver spoke of a white savage who had been raised by Indians."

"White savage?" Ram asked skeptically. "There have always been rumors about white savages, but no one has ever proven that white men rode with Indians."

"This time it's different. A white brother and sister, both rumored to have been raised by Indians, are supposed to be living somewhere around Denver. Don't you see?" she pleaded, "I have to find them. Instinct tells me those white savages are my brother and sister."

Ram stared at her, refusing to be influenced by her story, no matter how heartrending. He had a story of his own, one equally heartrending. "Does Lester know why you want to go to Denver?"

Sierra nodded, feeling her confidence return. "He knows. He claims he's too old and Holly too frail to make the journey by overland coach. He adamantly insists that my brother and sister couldn't possibly be alive after all these years. I get the impression that he doesn't really want me to find Abby and Ryder."

"I think Lester is right. Listen to him. You have no idea what you might find when you get to Denver. If your siblings were indeed raised by Indians, they might not feel about you the same way you feel about them. They couldn't possibly survive the experience without being changed in some way."

Sierra felt something snap inside her. "What kind of man are you, Ramsey Hunter? Have you no heart? No compassion?"

A muscle twitched in Ram's jaw. At one time he'd had a soft heart and a multitude of compassion, but no longer. He'd learned from experts to guard his heart and trust no one. As for compassion, experience taught him to dispense with that useless emotion.

"As you've probably discovered, Sierra, I have no heart. What I lack in sympathy I make up in passion. I am quite relentless in the way I hate and the way I make love. I do both with equal zeal."

"You're an insensitive dolt, Mr. Hunter. I don't know why I ever thought you might help me."

"Because you're a naive child, Miss Alden. Don't you realize how easily I could have seduced you? I could have taken you on the floor, in my bed, or any place else in this room if I'd really wanted to. Fortunately I had the good sense to resist the temptation."

"You could have fooled me," Sierra snapped irritably. "You were the one who suggested I pay with my body."

Ram's blue eyes sparkled with amusement. "If I'm not mistaken, you didn't consider the price too high. After one kiss, you were quite eager to meet my demands."

"I—I was desperate," Sierra said shakily, "and you knew it. Only a cad would take advantage of a woman's desperation."

"Ah, but I didn't take advantage of you, did I, sweet Sierra? Like a gentleman, which I'm definitely not, I'm sending you on your way barely touched. Had I really wanted to take advantage of you, you'd be beneath me in my bed, taking the full measure of my thrusts between your sweet thighs."

Sierra's face drained of all color. His crude words made her realize she was no match for Ram Hunter. Obviously he was trying to shock and embarrass her, making her regret asking for his help. He almost succeeded until Sierra recognized his intent and decided she wasn't going to be frightened or bullied by him.

"Has nothing I've said gotten through to you?" she asked, searching his face for a hint of understanding.

"Nothing at all. One last time, Sierra—go home before someone discovers you in my room. Gossip travels fast in a town like San Francisco. Think what Gordon would say if he heard nasty rumors about you and me. And since I'm leaving town on tomorrow's stage, I won't be around to squelch the rumors and save your reputation."

Sierra smiled ruefully. At least she had gained something from this ill-advised confrontation. Ram had just divulged a useful piece of information she hadn't had before.

"Very well, Mr. Hunter," she said with a sweetness that immediately placed Ram on his guard. "I'll leave, but you haven't—"

Sierra halted in mid-sentence when someone rapped lightly on the door and entered without being invited. She gaped in surprise when Lola, dressed in a nearly transparent negligee, sashayed into the room. Lola seemed as shocked to see Sierra as Sierra was to see her.

"What in the hell is going on here?" She pinned Sierra to the wall with her catlike green eyes. "Who in the hell are you and what are you doing in Ram's room?"

Ram groaned aloud. Why did Lola pick now of all times to barge into his room? He felt confident the two women weren't acquainted, but he was taking no chances.

"The lady and I are conducting business, Lola," he said evasively.

"Yeah, monkey business," Lola returned shortly. "She doesn't look your type, honey."

"She isn't my type," Ram concurred, "And she was just leaving."

"Good," Lola replied. She sidled up to Ram and leaned against him, giving him an eye-popping view of her partially exposed breasts. "You and me got some business of our own, don't we, honey?" She radiated raw sex, leaving little doubt in Sierra's mind about the kind of business Lola referred to.

Sierra gave Lola an assessing glance, thinking she looked every bit as notorious as her reputation. She thought Lola's red hair ugly and her attire quite indecent for mixed company. But she supposed Ram had seen the woman in less clothing than she wore now. That notion flooded her cheeks with color and gave her an uncomfortable feeling in the pit of her stomach. Not that she cared how many women Ramsey Hunter bedded, she tried to tell herself. The only thing she found interesting about Ram Hunter was the fact that he was going to Denver, and that's exactly where she wanted to go.

Aware that Ram was eager to be rid of her, Sierra turned to leave. She was halfway through the door when Lola said, "Shut the door behind you, honey. Me and Ram want to be alone." Sierra slammed the door so hard the walls rattled.

Despite her setback, determination burned hotly within her. She still had one other option, which she fully intended to explore. There was still Gordon. Girding herself with resolve, she directed her steps toward the bank.

"Sierra, what are you doing here?" Gordon asked when he looked up and saw Sierra enter his small office.

"Do you love me, Gordie?"

"What! Why would you ask me that now? We're going to be married, aren't we?"

"But do you love me?" she persisted.

"Well, of course. I'm really busy, dear. Can't we discuss this at a later time?"

It was the most unromantic declaration Sierra had ever heard. "No. I'm going to ask something of you, and I needed to know if you loved me first."

"Ask if you must, Sierra, so I can get back to work."

"We'll get married whenever you wish if you escort me to Denver."

He looked annoyed. "Denver? Whatever for?"

"I want to look for my brother and sister. I have good reason to believe they're alive."

"I refuse to feed your fantasies, Sierra. Lester believes they perished long ago and I agree with him. You're going to have to accept that reality and stop badgering us with your ridiculous demands. As for our marriage, I knew you'd come around," he said smugly. "I'll set things in motion, and we can be married next month." He returned to the papers spread before him, Sierra already forgotten.

Gordon paused but did not reply when Sierra said with quiet emphasis, "I *am* going to Denver, Gordie." Whirling on her heel, she left in a flurry of lacy petticoats swirling about her shapely legs.

"You seem distracted, honey," Lola said as she perched on Ram's lap. "Who was that woman anyway, and what did she want?"

"No one of importance, Lola; forget about her."

Ram wished he could follow his own advice, but somehow the vision of a thoroughly disgruntled Miss Sierra Alden, her silver eyes snapping with fury and her adorable little chin tilted in the air, remained firmly entrenched in his memory. He recalled with relish the tantalizing view he'd had of firm white breasts that appeared the perfect size to fit his hands.

God, she was magnificent. Why did she choose him to torment? He could have taken her so easily had he wanted to. And God knew he wanted to. It had both annoyed and amused him when she'd pretended to consider the price he demanded for escorting her to Denver. To his regret, he'd never know if she actually would have offered her body in lieu of money. Hell, he didn't want her money, and he definitely didn't need her body. He had Lola, didn't he? And dozens of others like her.

"You're leaving tomorrow, Ram," Lola purred seductively. "Let's not waste a moment of the time you have left." She rose from his lap, took his hand, and pulled him toward the bed. "Last night you said you were too busy. You've got no excuse now."

True, Ram thought, somewhat repelled by the sight of her large breasts straining in unrestricted freedom against the thin material of her negligee. With sudden insight, he realized that he no longer preferred breasts the size of small melons, or liked flesh liberally scented with strong perfume. He much preferred the subtle scent of violets and firm breasts that fit his hands perfectly.

Using all the diplomacy he could muster, Ram gently disengaged himself from Lola's grasp. "Look, honey, I've got a lot on my mind right now. I wouldn't do you justice."

"Ram Hunter unable to do a woman justice? Ha!" Lola snorted in disbelief. "That will be the day. Does this have something to do with that little bit of fluff who came calling on you this morning? Maybe she is your type after all."

"Let's not argue, honey. Your friendship is too important to me," Ram said earnestly. "I'm trusting you to run my club, aren't I? I made you no promises about our relationship. We're both free to do as we please."

Lola's face fell but she quickly recovered. It had been good while it lasted, but she'd always known Ram would dump her one day. He wasn't the kind to hang around with one woman for any length of time. Hell, she couldn't blame him. A realist, Lola knew she had Ram's trust, and in the long run that might be more important than having him as a lover.

"You're right, honey, you made me no promises, nor me you. Hell, it was fun while it lasted. You're damn good in bed, Ram Hunter. But if friendship is what you want, I can live with that. And don't worry about the Lucky Lady. Nothing will happen to it while I'm here to see that things run smoothly. You've been good to me, honey, and I always pay my debts. But if you change your mind, I'm here for you in any way you want me."

Alone in his room, Ram cursed himself for a fool. Had he lost his mind? He'd be weeks on the road without a woman, and he had just turned down his last chance in a good long time to bed an obliging one. What in the hell had Sierra done to him? he wondered dismally. He had barely touched her, and suddenly no other woman appealed to him. He could hardly wait to board the stage tomorrow and get as far away from Sierra Alden as he could.

* * *

For the first time since learning about her siblings, Sierra's determination faltered. Denver might as well be on the opposite side of the world for all the good it did her. She was astute enough to know that it wouldn't be safe to travel alone, and desperation had forced her to reexamine her options and consider things she might not attempt under normal circumstances.

Men, she thought disparagingly. In her opinion, most men were overbearing, inconsiderate beasts who considered themselves superior to women. Why must women be subjected to the will of men? Just wait, she'd show them she wasn't just any woman. She needed to get to Denver, and it suddenly occurred to her exactly how she was going to get there.

Chapter Four

Sierra suffered a moment of intense anxiety and another of remorse as she carefully placed the note she had written the night before on her pillow. If her father had been more receptive to her plea to take her to Denver, she wouldn't be sneaking out of the house like a thief in the night.

Since neither she or her mother normally left their rooms before noon, Sierra felt certain no one would bother checking on her before then. Her father habitually arose at eight, consumed his breakfast alone, and left for the bank promptly at nine. Since he had no reason to suspect anything out of the ordinary this morning, Sierra assumed he would follow his usual routine and leave without knowledge of her hasty departure. By the time he reached the bank, the stage would already have left, carrying her away from San Francisco and toward her long-lost siblings.

Sierra had gone over all the aspects of her plan carefully before drawing most of her money out of the bank the day before and purchasing a ticket at the Wells Fargo office that would take her through to Denver by stagecoach. She'd even had the foresight to wear a hat with a veil to hide her identity to prevent anyone recognizing her and reporting her purchase to her father. The ticket clerk hadn't been the least bit curious.

Sierra tiptoed down the staircase, carefully avoiding the squeaky stair halfway down. Hampered by her heavy valise, she finally reached the landing, where she paused to catch her breath. She heard nothing but the ticking of the hall clock as she let herself out the front door.

It was still very early. A mauve-tinged dawn was just a vague promise in the gray sky, and Sierra knew the help wouldn't begin arriving for at least an hour. Without a backward glance, she walked down the street at a brisk pace, hindered only by her heavy valise and long skirts. She had estimated the distance to the Wells Fargo depot at about a mile, but since the stage didn't leave until six, she knew she had plenty of time to reach it.

Last minute preparations for his journey had left Ram exhausted as he climbed aboard the stage and took a seat beside an itinerate preacher carrying a dog-eared Bible. A salesman sat across from him, holding a worn leather case across his knees. A man who appeared to be a prosperous businessman was hoisting his considerable bulk aboard the sturdy Concord coach.

Ram shifted his weight on the leather seat, wedging his big frame into his allotted fifteen inches of space. His head came into brief contact with the rolled-up leather curtain, which could be let down to keep out inclement weather, and he shifted positions again, finally finding one that allowed him a modicum of comfort. He glanced impatiently at his watch, noting that departure time was a scant five minutes away.

Leaning his head against the basswood panel, he closed his eyes and surrendered to exhaustion. He'd had precious little sleep last night and had the pampered Miss Sierra Alden to thank for his sleeplessness. Not only did his body remember the arousing softness of her supple curves, but he could still taste the sweetness of her mouth. It was probably a good thing he was leaving town for a while, he thought, annoyed at the direction of his thoughts. By the time he returned from Denver, the little witch would be safely married to Gordon Lynch and he would have worked her out of his system.

Pulling his hat low over his eyes, Ram sank deeper into the seat and promptly fell asleep, his dreams fraught with the image of a dark-haired beauty who had skidded into his life on a sea of mud. Her timing couldn't have been worse. He had neither the time nor the inclination to tame an impudent child who demanded more of him than he was willing to give. Ram had learned about women's wiles early in life and had suffered the consequences. Never again would he trust a woman.

Sleep claimed Ram so abruptly that he did not hear the coach driver holler, "All aboard! Awaaay!"

Sierra careened around the corner moments before the coach door slammed shut, out of breath and perspiring from her long walk. She had failed to take into account the numerous hills she had to traverse or realized how much the heavy valise would slow her progress. She was just rounding the corner of the depot when she heard the last call for passengers to board. Fortunately, the driver spotted her and waited, albeit impatiently, for her to clamber aboard. He stripped her valise from her hand, tossed it into the boot, and slammed the door behind her. Out of breath, she sank into a vacant seat next to a nattily dressed, overweight man in his middle forties.

She saw Ram immediately. He was seated directly opposite her, his hat pulled down over his eyes and a soft snoring sound escaping from between his full lips. His long legs were bent at the knees, nearly brushing hers as she settled her green-and-white voile skirts around her and straightened the fruit-topped confection she wore on her head.

A few moments later, the coach rattled off at runaway speed, the team of half-broken Western mustangs lurching forward beneath the driver's expert handling. He held three pairs of reins in the fingers of his left hand, his right wielding the whip with amazing dexterity, "talking" to the six horses through the ribbons.

When the coach jerked forward, Ram grunted but did not stir. Having traveled by stagecoach before, he knew exactly what to expect during the lengthy trip. They would be allowed two stops during each twenty-four hours at a home station, and for a few hours they would be able to stretch their cramped legs, quench their hunger and thirst, and fall into a fitful sleep in beds provided by the company. Since conversing with passengers did not interest him, Ram dozed off again, determined to sleep as much as possible before the harrowing trip through mountain passes made rest impossible.

Sierra took advantage of Ram's inattention by covertly observing him, thinking him the finest specimen of manhood she'd ever seen. If only he wasn't so confounded infuriating, she thought sourly. She ducked her head and flushed when she recalled the heat of his big body, the intoxicating masculine scent of him, and the warmth of his mouth as it moved with maddening purpose over hers.

The conceited oaf knew exactly the effect he had on women and reveled in the seductive power of his magnetic personality. The raw intensity of his kiss and the mysterious need it roused in her had given her a kind of pleasure she'd never experienced before, and he had taken advantage of her inexperience. She had no idea what Ram would do when he awoke and discovered her on the same stagecoach, but she mentally prepared herself for his anger.

Ram slept for hours. The coach had left the cool coastal breezes of San Francisco and entered the desert heat of the Sacramento Valley before he finally stirred. He flexed his arms and stretched his legs, then tilted his Stetson back from his forehead and opened his eyes.

"Oh, no!" He groaned in dismay, convinced his imagination was playing tricks on him again. Wasn't it bad enough that Sierra haunted his dreams? Why must he contend with her image during his waking hours?

If he didn't know better, he'd swear she was sitting across from him, more beautiful and tempting than in his dream, wearing clothing so impractical for stagecoach travel that he nearly laughed aloud. Logic told him that not even a spoiled little princess like Sierra would travel across country in a fancy dress that already exhibited signs of wilting and wearing a silly little hat topped with several varieties of fruit.

Maybe if he blinked she would go away, he thought hopefully as he closed and opened his eyes several times in rapid succession. God, no, he thought, thoroughly annoyed, she was still there, sitting beside the businessman, her skirts tucked primly around her long legs. When she smiled at him—more like a gloat, actually—Ram knew he wasn't dreaming.

"What in the hell are you doing here?" His demanding voice awakened both the preacher and the salesman and startled the businessman.

"I'm traveling to Denver, what does it look like?" she answered sweetly.

"I ought to wring your pretty little neck," Ram bit out from between clenched teeth. "Don't you ever take no for an answer?"

"Now see here, mister, you can't talk to the little lady that way," the businessman said, coming to Sierra's defense.

"If you know what's good for you, you'll keep your opinions to yourself," Ram retorted, fixing the hapless man with a steely glare. Pegging Ram for a man who didn't give threats lightly, the businessman gave Sierra an apologetic smile, then abruptly turned his head toward the window to study the passing scenery.

"I paid my fare, Ram Hunter; you can't do

a thing about it," Sierra said complacently. She knew better than to expect help from her fellow passengers, who understandably were intimidated by Ram.

"You think not?" Ram replied. "I can wire your father from Sacramento and make damn certain you don't get on the stage when we leave. Your father must be out of his mind with worry. I swear you don't have the brains you were born with."

Sierra's silver eyes flared angrily as she fought for control. Was there no end to the man's audacity? "If you're worried about my parents, don't trouble yourself. I left a note explaining everything."

What she didn't tell Ram was that her note was worded in such a way as to suggest that she was traveling under Ramsey Hunter's protection. That he had generously agreed to escort her to Denver since he was going there himself. Of course she had fabricated the whole story, but she already felt enough guilt for the way she had sneaked out of town without causing her parents more grief.

Ram sent her an icy glare. "Nevertheless, I'm sending your father a telegram. Sacramento isn't all that far from San Francisco, and he can be there to meet you within hours. I owe him that much."

"If you do, Ramsey Hunter," she threatened, "I swear I'll leave town before Father arrives. I'll take off across country on my own if I have to." The stubborn tilt to her pointed little chin warned Ram that she was prepared to do exactly as she said. He also realized that if she did as she threatened, she'd be in worse circumstances than if she stayed with the stagecoach.

"Now, miss, that's not a good idea," the preacher cautioned. As a man of God, he felt duty-bound to interfere at this point. "You appear to know this gentleman. Perhaps he has your best interests at heart."

Sierra glared at him. "Ramsey Hunter doesn't know what my best interests are. I am twenty-one, and he has no say over what I do or don't do. Reaching Denver is more important to me than any imagined danger I might face in getting there."

"I don't know what the world is coming to," the preacher opined piously, "when young unmarried women traipse across the country without proper escort and lacking permission from their guardians. God made women to be submissive to men, to bear their offspring without complaint, and to abide by their wishes." Having given his final word on the subject, he opened his Bible and promptly lost interest in his fellow travelers.

Ram nearly laughed aloud at Sierra's fierce expression. Evidently the preacher's words were not to her liking, although the belief he had just expressed was held by most men. Personally, he liked women with spirit. What he didn't care for were women like Sierra Alden, who were deliberately willful and self-destructive.

Nor did he like selfish, grasping, or deceitful women like Dora. He had lost two entire years of his life because of that mercenary bitch. Now that he finally had Dora within his sights, he wasn't about to let anything or anyone interfere.

"You win, Sierra, but I still aim to telegraph your father and let him know you're all right. What you do after that is your business. I wash my hands of you. Travel at your own risk, Sierra, but don't look to me for help."

Ram's words brought a wicked gleam to the salesman's eyes. An opportunist by nature, the suave man recognized a stroke of luck when he saw one. "Miss, I couldn't help overhearing the conversation, and while I don't condone women traveling alone, I admire your courage and fortitude. My name is Thurman Baker, and I'm traveling to Virginia City," he continued with sly innuendo. "I'd be most happy to offer my protection for that part of the journey during which we will be traveling companions."

"How kind of you, Mr. Baker, but I don't . . ."

"If you were going to say you don't need protection, I beg to differ with you. We have several overnight stops before reaching Virginia City, and danger abounds for a beautiful young lady like yourself."

Ram suppressed a groan, only too aware of Baker's predatory nature. Danger did indeed exist for Sierra, and Baker was a part of that danger. Ram felt it as surely as he felt his own rage at the thought of Sierra and the handsome Baker together.

"Miss Alden doesn't need your protection," Ram bit out, sending Baker a scalding glance.

Sierra was on the verge of declining Baker's offer when Ram rudely interrupted. A small smile hovered over her lips when she saw how he reacted. And since Ram had publicly renounced all responsibility for her, she saw a way to repay him for his unforgivable rudeness.

"I am perfectly capable of replying for myself, Mr. Hunter," she said coolly, while treating Thurman Baker to a devastating smile. "It's rare to find a true gentleman. I think Mr. Baker's offer is extremely kind, which is more than I can say for another gentleman of my acquaintance, although in his case I use the word 'gentleman' loosely."

Baker sent her a brilliant smile. "I accept the responsibility quite willingly, Miss Alden."

"I'll bet," Ram muttered darkly.

Later, while Ram gazed absently out the window and Sierra appeared to be dozing, the businessman leaned over, winked at Baker, and hissed beneath his breath, "Lucky dog. I'd trade places with you in a minute. If you find the lady too hot to handle, feel free to call on me."

Fuming inwardly, Ram heard every word. They hadn't been on the road a full day, and already Sierra was inviting trouble. Did the spoiled little minx have no clue to the problems she was creating for herself? Clenching his fists, he managed to remain calm, determined to let Sierra Alden handle her own affairs. He'd washed his hands of her, and he was a man of his word. Or he had been until he'd met the infuriating, willful, reckless Miss Sierra Alden. She had been so coddled by her doting parents that she was impossibly ignorant of the dangers and hardships she'd encounter on this perilous journey.

Ramsey Hunter did not aspire to the title of reluctant guardian. He had his own problems to resolve.

Sierra awoke from her doze with a queasy stomach. The jolting coach had upset her entire constitution, but she wouldn't give Ram the satisfaction of knowing how desperately close she was to losing the meager contents of her stomach. Swallowing hard, she became aware of a raw throat and burning eyes, irritated by thick alkali dust that had quickly coated her clothing and hair.

"Doesn't this coach carry water for the passengers?" Sierra asked, licking her dry lips.

"I assumed you knew," Ram said blandly. "Each passenger is allowed to bring along a canteen and two blankets in addition to twenty-five pounds of luggage."

Sierra sent him a startled look. "You mean I was supposed to bring my own water?"

"Don't worry, Miss Alden," Baker said smugly. "You can share my canteen. I'll refill it when we reach Sacramento." He handed the container to Sierra and she drank greedily.

Shortly afterward they had their first rest stop of the day. The passengers wandered off into the woods in different directions, and Sierra followed their lead. When she reappeared, Ram was waiting for her. It appeared that he had been standing guard, but she knew better than to think he cared enough about her safety to put himself out for her. Before she realized his intent, he grasped her arm and pulled her behind a tree.

"Ramsey Hunter, what *are* you doing?"

"We need to talk, Sierra."

"We've nothing left to say to each other. You've made your position clear. We are merely traveling companions, forced to share the same coach for the next fifteen days or so."

"I'm warning you, Sierra, don't push your luck. Do you have any idea of the position in which you placed yourself when you accepted Baker's protection? The man is expecting payment for his trouble, and I think you know what I'm talking about."

Sierra gave him a startled look. "I presume you're judging all men by your own standards. Mr. Baker was merely being gentlemanly."

"Gentlemanly! Bah. I've seen his kind too often not to recognize what he's after."

Sierra went still. "Is that all you have to say, Ram? If so, it's time to board."

"No, there's more. The clothing you are wearing is unsuited for cross-country coach travel. It's neither necessary nor desirable to look like a fashion plate. Do you have nothing practical to wear?"

Sierra fumed in impotent rage. How dare he tell her what to wear!

"Ah, there you are, Miss Alden." Baker gave Ram a searching look. "Is this gentleman bothering you?"

Ram nearly laughed in the dandy's face.

"No, we were merely talking, Mr. Baker," Sierra said, giving him a dazzling smile. "Shall we board the coach? I see the driver motioning the passengers back inside."

She accepted Baker's arm, blatantly ignoring Ram's glowering expression. "Don't say I didn't warn you," Ram called after her. Sierra heard but did not give him the satisfaction of a reply.

"Damn-fool woman," Ram muttered to himself as he boarded the coach. He didn't know why he even bothered.

Sierra smoothed a hand over her rumpled dress, sadly aware of its pitiful condition. No amount of washing would ever restore the beautiful material to its original brightness. What in the world had ever possessed her to wear anything as unsuitable for long-distance travel as a voile day dress? She hadn't really given her appearance much thought when she'd packed, haphazardly choosing a few of her favorite outfits and hats, and she hated to admit that Ram had every right to criticize her clothing. She saw now that a serviceable gray or brown serge traveling dress and unadorned bonnet would have been much more appropriate. Tomorrow she'd choose a plain, dark outfit from her valise. At least she'd had the good sense to wear her sturdiest boots.

The sun was diving behind the horizon when the stagecoach pulled up in front of the Wells Fargo office in Sacramento. Stiff from constant jolting, every bone in Sierra's body ached. She took comfort in the fact that they were to stay at a real hotel tonight and relished the thought of a bath, decent meal, and soft bed. Truth to tell, she thought she'd gotten through the first day remarkably well. For the most part, the scenery had been rather dull and unexceptional. She felt confident that the rest of the trip would prove equally uneventful. Not that she would call having to endure Ramsey Hunter's company uneventful.

"The hotel is just a few steps down the street, Miss Alden," Baker said obsequiously. "I'll see that you receive the best room available. And if you're not too tired, I'd be honored to have you join me for dinner."

Sierra was about to refuse when she saw Ram glaring at her. "I'd be delighted, Mr. Baker. Shall we say seven? That will give me time to bathe and change."

She tried to maintain her smile when she saw Ram stride purposely toward the telegraph office. Not that it mattered. The stage would be long gone before her father could send anyone after her. Let Ram Hunter do his worst.

Thurman Baker had high hopes for the night. He felt confident that Sierra Alden was experienced enough to know what he expected from her. Proper young women did not travel unchaperoned in this day and age, and from the exchange he'd heard between her and Ramsey Hunter, it appeared they were more than mere acquaintances. Evidently something had caused a rift between them, and he intended to take advantage of it until he disembarked in Virginia City, where a wife and three children awaited him. But Sierra Alden didn't need to know that, he told himself smugly. During his years of traveling around the country, he'd seduced more young women than he could count, and he would probably continue to do so for as long as there were gullible young women to take advantage of.

Fatigued beyond belief, Sierra set her fork down on her empty plate and sat back, replete. "Thank you for the company, Mr. Baker. I felt much safer sitting in the dining room with an escort. Now, if you'll excuse me, I'd like to retire. The driver said we are to leave at six in the morning."

Baker scraped back his chair. "I'll see you to your door."

Seated across the room, Ram's blue eyes narrowed thoughtfully when he saw Sierra and Baker leave the dining room. Spitting out a curse, he rose abruptly to his feet. Then, thinking better of it, he sat back down, forcing himself to finish his coffee. He tried to convince himself that Sierra knew what she was doing, but instinct told him she was too naive to recognize her danger. Dimly he wondered if she was really the innocent he thought her. Or had she learned more at that fancy school in New York than he gave her credit for? The hell with Sierra Alden, he thought sourly as he took another sip of tepid coffee. He was more than a little surprised to note that his hands were shaking.

"Good night, Mr. Baker," Sierra said, offering her hand to the handsome traveling salesman.

Baker scowled. This certainly wasn't the way he intended the night to end. He took Sierra's hand, released it after a quick squeeze, then hovered over her while she unlocked the door and stepped inside. A pool of light greeted her, and she was instantly grateful to the thoughtful maid who had lit a lamp for her. But before Sierra could turn and lock the door behind her, Baker pushed inside and leaned against the panel, leering hugely.

Confused, Sierra took a step backward. "Mr. Baker, what do you think you're doing?"

"It's all right, Sierra, no one saw me. We'll not be bothered the rest of the night." He pushed himself away from the door and slowly walked toward her. "Take off your clothes, pretty lady. I want you naked beneath me."

Sierra blanched. "Please leave before I scream." She spoke calmly, willing her voice not to betray her rising panic.

"Don't worry, honey, I won't let on tomorrow that we spent the night together."

"Go away!" Sierra said through clenched teeth. "I'm sorry if I gave you the idea that I wanted . . . this."

"Your message was loud and clear, honey. I know you're no innocent. If you were, you'd not be traveling alone. I got the impression that you and Ramsey Hunter were friends—real good friends," he said with a knowing grin. "I'd like a little of the same kind of friendship."

"I'm going to give you one last opportunity to leave," Sierra said tightly, not wishing to cause a ruckus but prepared to do so if it meant ridding herself of Baker's obnoxious presence. "If you persist with this silliness, I swear I'll scream the house down."

Suddenly Baker leaped at her, bearing her down to the floor and covering her mouth with his hand. "You little tease. Do you enjoy leading men on? This time you've met your match." He began tearing at her bodice while she kicked and scratched and fought to dislodge his hand from her mouth.

How could she have been so stupid? she silently lamented. Ram had warned that she was asking for trouble, but she had chosen to ignore him. This incident with Baker clearly demonstrated just how naive she had been to travel alone. Damn Ram Hunter! She hated to admit that he had been right. Then all thought ceased as Baker ripped her bodice apart, baring her breasts and pawing them with his free hand. Sierra's whimpers grew frantic when she felt his teeth clamp down on a tender nipple.

Ram tried to ignore his gnawing anxiety but failed miserably. Sierra was so damn stubborn, he thought distractedly, that she wouldn't admit he was right if her life depended on it. He couldn't understand his concern for Sierra, and it alternately confused and troubled him. He had already washed his hands of the little witch. If he was smart, he'd let her fend for herself. It infuriated him that a pampered princess with a stubborn streak a mile wide tugged at his emotions when he had more important things on his mind.

Unfortunately, no amount of reasoning had changed his mind. Rising abruptly, he threw down his napkin and walked briskly through the lobby, taking the stairs two at a time. All the stagecoach passengers had been given rooms on the same floor, and he had taken special note of the fact that Sierra's room was just a few doors beyond his. With grim determination, he strode past his own room and stopped before Sierra's door. He pressed his ear to the panel, cursing himself for a fool when he heard nothing. No doubt Sierra was sleeping soundly by now, and he had worried needlessly. He turned to leave, then went still, suddenly aware of a sound he hadn't heard before.

The raspy noises, sounding suspiciously like frightened whimpers, made Ram's hair stand up on end. Was Sierra crying? Had something happened to her in the short time since she'd left the dining room in the company of that bounder, Baker? Without a thought for propriety, Ram tried the knob. He frowned in consternation when he found the door unlocked, more certain than ever that something was amiss. Moments before he pushed open the door, he heard a muffled cry from within. He reacted instinctively, fearing he wouldn't be in time.

Sierra felt Thurman's free hand slide along her inner leg, inching her skirts upward as his hand moved higher. Distracted by the satiny texture of Sierra's inner thigh, Baker's hand slipped from Sierra's mouth long enough for her to let loose a muffled cry.

"Do you like that, honey?" Baker asked, mistaking her cry of distress for one of passion. "This is only a taste of what I can do for you." His hand had reached the place where her thighs met and Sierra lurched upward, trying to dislodge him, but his body was firmly wedged atop hers.

Ram burst through the door, took one look at the struggling couple on the floor, and roared in outrage. Before Baker realized they weren't alone, Ram charged, picking him up bodily and flinging him across the room.

"You vile bastard! What in the hell do you think you're doing?"

Dazed, Baker stared at Ram until he finally found his voice. "I wasn't doing anything the lady didn't want. She invited me inside her room. Hell, she's been coming on to me all day."

Sierra gasped in outrage as Ram swiveled his head to glare at her. He thought she looked like a bewildered child, sprawled on the floor and holding the gaping edges of her dress together. She wasn't entirely successful in covering herself, for Ram caught a tempting glimpse of round white breasts. Tearing his gaze away, he returned his attention to Baker.

"Get the hell out of here, Baker. If you ever approach Miss Alden again, you won't live long enough to tell about the experience. And," he added ominously, "I strongly urge you to take another stage out of town."

Lifting himself up from the floor, Baker dusted his rumpled suit with shaking hands and glared belligerently at Ram. "Who made you Miss Alden's keeper? I heard enough to know she wants nothing to do with you."

The threatening growl that came from Ram's throat convinced Baker that Ram meant business, and he was too cowardly to test the mettle of the dangerous-looking man. When Ram took a step in his direction, he hightailed it through the door. Ram slammed and locked the door behind him. Then he rounded on Sierra, who had risen unsteadily to her feet, still clutching the gaping edges of her dress.

"Well, did you?" He grasped her shoulders in a bruising grip, his face a mask of fury. "Did you invite that bastard in your room tonight?"

Utterly astounded, Sierra blinked up at him. Then she pressed her hands against his chest and pushed him away. "Go away, Ram Hunter! Leave me alone."

Chapter Five

Sierra turned her back on Ram, retreating across the room. Ram stalked her aggressively. "Answer my question, Sierra."

"Your question is an insult to me personally and a slur upon my reputation," she retorted angrily spinning around to face him.

Ram studied her through narrowed lids. Her silver eyes blazed with anger and her chin trembled despite her best efforts to remain calm. Ram thought she looked like a little girl, vulnerable, hurt, lost. A melting sensation began deep inside him, and he reached for her. Still upset over Thurman's abominable behavior and stunned at Ram's unfair accusation, Sierra whimpered in protest but offered scant resistance when he drew her into his embrace. She desperately craved comfort, and Ram's muscular arms provided the kind of comfort she couldn't resist.

The harsh lines of his face softened as he asked, "Do you want to tell me about it?" She felt so damn good in his arms that he could barely think past the pleasure. At that moment, hard-bitten, distrustful, sardonic Ramsey Hunter experienced a gut-wrenching desire such as he had never known or imagined before.

The feeling was so savage, so unexpected, that it sent him searching for reasons for his surprising response.

He inhaled the sweet scent of her skin and hair, faintly reminiscent of violets. The narrow curve of her waist felt small and supple beneath his hands, her bones as fragile as a bird's. Just the thought of what he wanted to do to her sent a stab of fire through his loins. Why didn't she resist him? he wondered as his hands clasped her hips and brought her hard against the rigid thrust of his manhood. He knew instinctively that she would be passionate and wild in bed, and that unbidden thought made him even harder.

Suddenly realizing where his thoughts were taking him, Ram thrust her away, holding her at arm's length while he searched her face, trying to decide if she really was a witch or just a very clever woman who knew how to beguile a man until he lost his mind.

Sierra felt the loss of his arms immediately. Where moments ago she had been encompassed by warmth, now she felt cold, bereft even. Was Ram still angry with her? Did he still believe she had invited Thurman Baker into her room?

"Regardless of your belief, I didn't invite that despicable man inside my room." There was a raw edge of desperation to her voice.

She reached out to him in silent supplication, forgetting about her torn bodice until she saw Ram staring at her breasts. The smooth white globes were marred by ugly bruises, the result of Baker's crude mauling. A small cry escaped her lips, and she tried to pull the gaping edges together, but Ram pushed her hands aside, grasping her wrists in one fist and holding them captive in front of her. With his other hand he pushed aside the torn edges of her bodice, his eyes narrowed on the vivid purple bruises. His face was grim, his lips taut with fury. He brought the tip of his forefinger to the injury, startling Sierra with the gentleness of his touch.

"Did Baker do this?"

Sierra nodded, unable to speak around the lump in her throat.

"What else did he do?" His body thrummed with barely suppressed rage. If the bastard raped her, he'd kill him with his bare hands.

Sierra swallowed hard and said in a shaky whisper, "Nothing. Thank you for arriving in time."

"My pleasure," Ram said tightly. "Dammit, Sierra, I warned you what would happen! Are you always so blasted reckless?" Now that he knew Sierra hadn't been badly hurt, his anger returned in full force. "Have you no sense at all? You'd be smart to wire your father and remain here until he sends someone after you."

Sierra tugged her hands free and brought them up to shield her breasts. "No! I'm wiser now. I won't let this happen again. I told you before that nothing will stop me from reaching Denver, and I meant it." Deliberately she turned her back on him.

Ram cursed, low and long and shockingly graphic as he swung her around to face him. "If you weren't so damn spoiled, you'd listen to reason. You have no business traveling alone."

"I'm not alone," Sierra said, raising her chin fractionally. "There are several passengers aboard the coach."

Ram stared at her lush lips and felt a sudden, inexplicable urge to kiss her. He felt it as keenly as he felt the need to breathe. Sierra's silver eyes widened as Ram's head started a downward path that ended when his lips found hers. She opened her mouth to protest, leaving her vulnerable to the satin slide of his tongue. The breath left her throat on a soft sigh as his arms gathered her close, closer still, until her warmth penetrated the layers of his clothing.

"Oh God, you're so soft and warm," Ram whispered against her lips.

His breath mingled with hers. Every inch of Sierra's skin trembled with anticipation. Her blood thickened and a sweet, drugging tension flowed through her veins. His fingers laced through the dark silkiness of her hair, releasing

96

it from its prim bun. Transfixed, he watched as it flowed over her shoulders in glorious disarray. Her scantily clad breasts fitted snugly against his chest, reminding him in a most provocative way of their hardened points.

Her mouth was so sweet that he was loathe to leave it, kissing her again and again, deeply, solidly, first with little teasing nips, then with soul-destroying thoroughness. His tongue found hers, drew upon it, sucked it into his mouth. She felt his hand slide up to cover her breast, the palm caressing her nipple. He explored her boldly with his large palms, traveling downward to cup her hips, her buttocks. With a hoarse cry, his lips lifted from hers and he touched his mouth to her throat, the tip of his tongue bathing the pulse there with wet, hot strokes.

Sierra felt herself slide into oblivion, driven by the wild pulsing of Ram's body against hers and the slick wetness of his tongue. She felt him thicken and lengthen against her, felt him press his hardness into the soft valley between her legs, and felt powerless against his almost magical allure. Her entire body was practically vibrating with need, her nerve endings stretched taut with erotic tension. It was galling to think that an infuriating scoundrel like Ramsey Hunter could affect her so profoundly.

Sierra had listened avidly when girls at school described their somewhat innocent experiences with passion. She often wondered what it would feel like to respond with wild abandon to a man, and now she knew. It was disconcerting that a rogue like Ramsey Hunter, who apparently held women in low esteem, would be the man who would teach her about passion. She'd always supposed she'd experience passion with Gordie, but Gordie's tepid kisses had been a great disappointment to her.

"I want you, Sierra." Ram's muffled groan jerked Sierra back to reality. The meaning behind his words pounded against her brain, but reason had already deserted her.

"The bed," he said, sweeping her from her feet. He bore her to the narrow bed pushed against one wall.

God help her, Sierra thought, held in thrall by the magic he wove around her senses. When had this attraction between them grown out of control? Waves of pure, raw want radiated between them, pulling them together like a giant magnet. She wanted Ram; wanted what he would do to her, for her, wanted everything he had to give her.

Ram knew nothing, felt nothing but the churning need in the heated mass of desire that had once been his body. He struggled against the overwhelming impulse to strip her bare and impale her. He knew she wanted him. He could feel it in her racing pulse, in the furious pounding of her heart, and in the hardened nipples pressed against his chest. She was panting, as breathless and needy as he was.

So great was his lust for the black-haired beauty that she was spread out on the bed with him atop her before his craziness left him. With a massive effort, he jumped to his feet, staring down at her as if she were a snake who had just bitten him.

"My God, what am I doing?"

Dazed, Sierra gaped at him, stunned by the unnatural tightness of his jaw, the sudden darkening of his features. He looked different, his lusty exuberance transformed by a raging mixture of disbelief, shock, and denial.

"This shouldn't have happened, Sierra." His voice was cool, remote, holding no trace of the warmth he'd displayed just moments ago. "It *won't* happen again. I don't know what kind of spell you cast over me, but it isn't powerful enough to make me change my mind or forget the vow I made long ago. You're a tempting little morsel, Sierra Alden, but I'm going to pass. Save your charms for Gordon Lynch. Or some other hapless victim."

If Ram intended to anger Sierra, he had succeeded beyond his wildest dreams. He had destroyed her pride and rejected her, all in one breath. Leaping to her feet, she rounded on him viciously. "I did nothing to you, Ram Hunter! If you recall, I asked you to leave me alone. I don't need a watch dog. From now on I'll thank you to mind your own business."

"You tried to seduce me once before and found it didn't work. Nothing, absolutely nothing, will persuade me to act as your chaperon. You don't need a chaperon, you need a keeper."

Ram knew he had gone too far, but only his

anger prevented him from succumbing to his raging need to make love to the exasperating little miss. Once he let his guard down, he had a sneaking suspicion that Sierra could seduce him with very little effort. As Dora had once done. Never again would he become a woman's victim. He was too wary to fall for a pretty face and magnificent pair of breasts.

Sierra glared up at Ram rebelliously. The harsh lines of his face bespoke a cynicism she'd rarely beheld before. And then she found her tongue, flinging insults at him like stones. "Why, you conceited ape, if I wanted to seduce someone, I'd find a man with a more pleasing personality. You've the disposition of a grizzly bear being chased by angry bees. You mistook my intention if you thought I was offering myself to you in an effort to win you to my cause."

"You could have fooled me," Ram muttered, fighting a losing battle with his resolve.

Sierra looked so damned beautiful that his overpowering need to make love to her made him dizzy. Her face was flushed, her lips swollen from his kisses. Her nearly nude breasts rose and fell in splendid fury beneath the gaping edges of her bodice. She was magnificent. And if he didn't leave this minute, he'd never be able to walk away from the room with his heart intact. He had no right to touch Sierra Alden, no right at all. He had enough problems without taking a pampered brat under his wing.

Ram knew he had to get out of Sierra's room fast, or he wouldn't be responsible for his actions. His heart pounded like a wildly beating drum in the explosive silence, and he knew a moment of panic. Spinning on his heel, he strode toward the door.

"Coward," Sierra challenged softly. Ram paused but did not stop.

"Lock the door behind me," he threw over his shoulder, ignoring Sierra's challenge. The soft click of the latch left a hollow feeling deep in the pit of her stomach. Bandying words with Ram was headier than the strongest wine.

Still shaking from the encounter, Sierra wasn't too naive to recognize a man's arousal. She knew instinctively that Ram Hunter wasn't as immune to her as he'd like her to believe. She wondered about the demons driving him. Instinctively she knew that whatever was taking him to Denver was so dark, so compelling, that it made his life a living hell. She respected his privacy, understood his need to resolve his problems, for she felt the same demanding urgency to find her siblings. What she didn't understand was his hostility. Didn't he know how easily she saw through his pretense?

The morning stage to Denver, via Placerville, Carson City, Virginia City, and Salt Lake City, left promptly at six the following morning. Thurman Baker was conspicuously absent. Joining the preacher and the businessman were the Sysons, newlyweds traveling to Salt Lake City to visit the husband's parents, and a woman whose flamboyant appearance was a blatant reminder of her profession.

After all the passengers had boarded and their luggage was stowed away, Sierra found herself wedged in between Ram and the preacher. More crowded than previously, Sierra was grateful for her fifteen inches of allotted space and felt a pang of pity for Ram, whose much larger frame was literally squashed into the same narrow section. At the crack of the driver's whip, the coach jolted forward with bone-jarring speed.

Most of the day Ram sat with his hat slanted over his eyes, doing his damnedest to ignore Sierra. Meeting her had come at a time when he least needed the kind of distraction she provided. If he wasn't already . . . His thoughts fractured. No sense thinking about it now, for he wasn't free to pursue the bewitching beauty even if he wanted to, and if he failed to catch up with Dora he might never be free.

Sierra struck up a conversation with Willie Mae Syson, which provided welcome relief from the distracting friction of her hip resting firmly against Ram's. It was worse when the coach rounded a curve, throwing her body fully against his. Once, when she sprawled awkwardly across his lap and had to brace herself against his chest, he raised his hat from his face long enough to send her a wicked grin.

Ram was profoundly aware of every soft curve of Sierra's body where it came into electrifying contact with his. How in hell could he be expected to concentrate on his mission with

Sierra sitting next to him, touching him, driving him crazy? No woman had ever touched him the way Sierra did, not even Dora.

At noon they made their first stop of the day. Most of the passengers rested beneath trees, eating the box lunch provided by the hotel for a price. When the Sysons moved away for a few moments of privacy, Sierra sat down beside the preacher and the businessman. When she dared a glance at Ram, she was far from pleased to note that he was wandering off toward the trees with the colorful woman Sierra suspected was a soiled dove.

Ram had no interest in the rather obvious Clara Phillpot, but he let himself be coaxed into strolling with her since he needed to stretch his legs anyway. When she made a rather startling suggestion as to how they might while away a few minutes, Ram declined politely, stating that there was hardly enough time to do them both justice. When they returned to the coach, the passengers were already boarding.

Their final stop of the day was the home station, where they would change horses and put up for the night.

Ram was the first to step down when the coach stopped that night to discharge passengers. Exhausted and bruised from constant jouncing, Sierra followed him out the door. But when she touched the ground, her legs buckled beneath her. From the corner of his eye, Ram noted her distress. Spitting out an oath, he whirled on his heel and caught her before she reached the ground.

"So you think you're strong enough to travel overland by stagecoach, do you?" he taunted as he carried her toward the station. "This is just the first leg of your journey. You'd be doing yourself a favor by returning home on the next westbound stage."

"Put me down, Ram Hunter." Sierra heaved an exasperated sigh. Why did she have to appear weak before the overbearing brute? "I'm perfectly capable of walking."

"You could have fooled me." Ram stood her on her feet, and when she seemed steady enough, he reluctantly dropped his hands from her waist. He was debating with himself whether he should leave her to her own devices when Clara sidled up beside him and took his arm.

"I declare, that ride made me absolutely dizzy. Do you mind if I hang on to you for support?" Her dark, inviting eyes promised delights Ram didn't even want to think about.

These past few days, Sierra had driven him so wild with desire that he was tempted to take what Clara so generously offered. His problem lay in the fact that Clara Phillpot's blond, over-blown beauty and fleshy charms held little appeal for him. At the moment his tastes ran to ebony hair, entrancing silver eyes, and willowy curves.

Not at all amused by Clara's overt flirtation, Sierra flounced off toward the station, where supper and bed awaited her. Had Sierra known she'd be required to share a lumpy, flea-ridden bed with Clara, she might have chosen to bed down in the barn with the men. But the following morning, Sierra did not dare complain about her sleepless night for fear that Ram would harangue her again about returning to San Francisco.

The stage stopped briefly in Carson City and then Virginia City, where both the businessman and the preacher debarked. The remaining passengers were joined by a dandified gambler, an elderly woman going to visit her son, a young soldier returning to duty at Fort Bridger after home leave, and three cowboys who climbed atop the stage, carrying their saddles aboard with them.

Tree-studded hills and flat-topped buttes sped by the coach so fast that at times Sierra feared for her life. In places the roads were so narrow that she was certain the wheels would fall off into space. Once the passengers were asked to disembark while the driver and his relief led the skittish horses around a narrow blind curve. When they returned to the coach, Ram managed to sit beside Sierra.

"Don't be frightened," he said, trying to ease her fears. The jehu is experienced. But don't say I didn't warn you. Unfortunately, it gets worse. The Rocky Mountains will present the biggest challenge."

"I'm not frightened," Sierra denied. Her pale face made a mockery of her words. She was experiencing hardships she'd never even imagined, situations that scared her nearly out of her wits.

She dreamed endlessly of a hot bath, good food, and soft bed with satin sheets. The reality was a throat clogged with dust, skin itching from sand gnats, sleepless nights, burning eyes, and filthy clothes. Not only could she smell her own stench but that of every passenger crowded inside the coach. And her journey had just begun.

That night she was stubbornly determined to avoid sleeping with Clara Phillpot at a home station. She'd had all she could take of the woman's snoring and cloying perfume. She'd noticed a stream running behind the station, and on the spur of the moment decided to sneak out when everyone was sleeping to bathe. Since the night was warm, perhaps she'd sleep in the soft grass growing along the bank.

Clutching a small bundle of soap, a blanket, and a change of underwear, Sierra quietly tiptoed out the door and moved noiselessly through the yard to the stream that flowed lazily behind the station. The horses snorted in welcome when she passed the corral, but she paid them little heed.

The night was shimmering and golden beneath a full moon. Sierra paused on the bank of the stream, admiring the play of light on the water, like millions of tiny diamonds dancing on the surface. Never had she been so utterly captivated by the beauty of nature. Strange, she thought as she stripped off her clothing, she'd never given much thought before to the natural wonders of the land and sea and the animals that inhabited them. She'd always been too concerned with creature comforts to take nature seriously. But this trip had shown her that the most rewarding beauty was the product of nature.

Sighing rapturously, Sierra stripped away her corset and stays. True, the garment was necessary in order to enhance a woman's figure, but during the past few days she'd cursed the uncomfortable corset more times than she could count. It would be wonderful, she thought blissfully, if she wasn't obliged to conform to the dictates of fashion.

Nude but for her thin chemise, Sierra thrust a toe into the water. It was cool but bearable. In fact, it was so inviting that she plunged into the stream, not stopping until the water lapped at the undersides of her breasts. She washed leisurely, ducking beneath the water several times to rinse the soap out of her hair.

Ram stood in the shadows, captivated by the cavorting water nymph. He couldn't blame Sierra for wanting a bath; he'd had one himself before retiring to the barn. Unable to sleep, he'd heard the horses snorting and decided to investigate. He'd seen Sierra slip past the corral and followed. Fire sped through his veins when he saw her strip to her chemise and enter the water. He knew he should leave, that she wouldn't welcome his intrusion upon her privacy, but his legs refused to obey his brain's command to walk away.

Sierra waded through the water to the dark shore, wringing out her wet chemise. Her long legs glistened wetly in the moon-drenched night, and the fire within Ram blazed out of control. She reached for the blanket, found it missing and cried out in dismay.

"Are you looking for this?" Ram appeared from the shadows as if by magic, holding the blanket between his outstretched arms.

Alarm quickly turned to anger as Sierra glared at Ram. "What are you doing here?"

"I couldn't sleep. I see you had the same idea as I did. I bathed earlier." He stepped forward and wrapped the blanket around her. "Take off that wet shift. It's a warm night, it will dry by morning if you spread it out on a bush."

Being naked but for a blanket didn't appeal to Sierra. She didn't trust Ram and trusted herself even less. "Go away. I'm going to sleep outside tonight, and I don't need protection."

"Are you sure that's what you want? Are you aware that prowling animals often come to the stream at night to drink?"

"Animals? No. You're trying to frighten me."

"Just giving you a friendly warning." A rare smile lit his face. He could tell that Sierra knew nothing about nature or the dangers she might encounter. Not that he expected any wild animals to pounce on her this close to the station.

"Thank you. Now please leave. I'd like to get

dressed, and I don't trust you to behave like a gentleman."

Ram nodded in acquiescence. Sierra was right. He couldn't trust *himself* to behave like a gentleman around the bewitching brunette. Sierra was too great a distraction—a distraction he couldn't afford right now. Circumstances demanded that he forget the fire of her response, that he ignore her irrepressible spirit and beauty. "Good night, sleep well." He turned to leave.

Sierra breathed a sigh of relief. If she ever did marry Gordie, his brand of tepid passion would be a welcome relief after Ram's effortless power and volatile masculinity. This explosion of wills and dark forces swirling between her and Ram was so overwhelming that it left her feeling weak and confused.

Without warning, a screech owl perched in a nearby tree set up a nerve-shattering racket, frightening the wits out of Sierra. She cried out Ram's name, groping for him in the darkness. He turned immediately and opened his arms, deftly catching her against him as she ran into his embrace. She had been so unnerved, she wasn't even aware that she had allowed the blanket to slip to the ground, or that Ram's hands could feel every curve and indentation of her lush body beneath the wet chemise. All she could think of were those terrifying night sounds and how comforting Ram's arms felt.

When Ram realized what had frightened Sierra, a low rumble of laughter rattled his chest.

"Silly little goose. It's only a screech owl. He won't hurt you." He tried to set her aside, more aroused than he had a right to be. She felt too damn good pressed tightly against him; her thinly clad body was doing incredible, provocative things to him. But to his astonishment, Sierra clung to him with almost desperate urgency, her fright very real. Her arms twined around his neck, and she pressed up against the daunting length of his hard body. Ram did the only thing a man in this position could do. He lowered his mouth and kissed her.

Ram moaned softly. She tasted so good and felt even better, all fluid friction and soft white flesh. If he followed the dictates of his body, he'd pull her down into the cool grass and take her measure with his thick length, thrusting into her again and again as she writhed beneath him and cried out in sweet, lilting passion.

When her lips parted and their tongues met in silent battle, he nearly succumbed to his driving need. But his conscience told him he had no right to take Sierra Alden. He might be a bastard, but he hadn't lost all sense of propriety. Summoning all the will at his command, he broke off the kiss and stepped away from her.

"I'm sorry, Sierra."

Sierra stared at him uncomprehendingly. Ram was giving her a glimpse of real passion, and she didn't want it to end. But obviously Ram Hunter didn't feel the same kind of passion that burned within her. Once again he had reacted negatively to her display of passion, brushing her aside like unwanted baggage.

Ram recognized her confusion and cursed the wretched luck that delighted in throwing them together like this, driving him to the very edge of sanity and sorely testing what little remained of his tattered control. Didn't she realize he was protecting her virtue?

Never had Sierra felt so abandoned, so humiliated. How long would it take for her to realize Ram wasn't attracted to her? How many times must she hear him say he wanted nothing to do with her? It wasn't exactly that she *wanted* to throw herself at him, she just couldn't help herself where Ram was concerned. She was quickly learning that she had no pride when it came to Ramsey Hunter. But tonight he had made it abundantly clear that he didn't want her.

"Go back to the station, Sierra, and get some sleep. The road to Salt Lake City is a difficult one at best. It's still not too late to return to San Francisco. Think about it."

Please think about it, Ram pleaded in silent supplication. *I don't know how much longer I can keep my hands off you. If I took you like I wanted, I could never face your father. I'm not free. I may never be free.*

Sierra shuddered, stepped back, and picked up the blanket, pulling it tightly around her shoulders. "I'm not going back, Ramsey Hunter. I'm going to sleep out here, just as I planned. You needn't worry. I'll be fine."

She retained her haughty posture until she heard Ram's retreating footsteps. Only then did she allow her shoulders to sag beneath her wilting pride.

Chapter Six

The following days and nights were more difficult than Sierra had ever imagined they would be, despite the breathtaking and ever-changing vistas. The stark beauty of the passing landscape captivated her, from the vast prairie-dog towns and herds of shaggy buffalo to stupendous waterfalls and strange rock formations.

They had traveled through violent storms twice, suffering unbearably in the suffocating closeness of the coach when the leather shades were lowered to keep out the driving rain. And afterward they all had to leave the coach while the men helped push through knee-deep mud. Too many times for Sierra's peace of mind, the brakes smoked as the coach careened down a ledgelike road above a chasm. Sierra couldn't recall ever experiencing so harrowing a ride.

She felt sorry for the men riding atop the coach.

On the other hand, when the road was flat and wide, the ride was almost enjoyable, if one ignored the throat-clogging dust. On the good days, the gambler would produce a dog-eared deck of cards and the men would play poker for small stakes. Bad food, lumpy beds, often infested with fleas, and lack of privacy all combined to make Sierra wish she'd not been so impetuous in undertaking this trip—until she recalled her reason for such an arduous journey, making it all worthwhile.

As the third day progressed, Sierra eagerly looked forward to their next stop and roundly cursed the winding, rutted road that delayed their arrival. They were climbing a steep incline up a magnificent mountain peak when her body swayed against Ram's, unable to maintain her balance in the jostling coach. After their rest stop earlier in the day, she had found herself sitting beside Ram, something she usually tried to avoid. Ram managed to snag himself the seat by the door, as far away as he could get in such close confines from the persistent Clara Phillpot.

From the corner of her eye, Sierra noted that Ram was staring fixedly out the right window. She stretched her neck to see what had captured his attention so thoroughly. A small explosion of breath left her lips when she saw that the road at the right of the coach dropped away sharply into a deep ravine.

"What is it?" Sierra hissed in a voice pitched

deliberately low to avoid frightening the other passengers. By now she knew Ram well enough to recognize when something worried him. If he was worried about something, she wanted to know what it was and prepare herself.

"I'm sure it's nothing," Ram said evenly. But when she saw his muscles bunch and his body tense, she knew he was lying.

Suddenly she felt the coach shudder and tilt sharply to the right. If she hadn't been so attuned to Ram's instincts, she would not have been alarmed. When a crunching noise followed, Ram's distress grew more pronounced. Truly concerned now, Sierra looked to Ram for an explanation. His intense expression sent a thrill of apprehension racing down her spine. When the coach started sliding to the right, Ram's superbly fit body reacted with a swiftness that stunned her.

Sierra gaped in dismay when Ram kicked open the door. Trees whizzed past at an alarming speed, and she had only an inkling of what he intended when he grasped her around the waist and hollered, "Brace yourself!"

"Ram!"

Then she was hurtling out the door, rolling over and over as the coach wheels missed her by scant inches, and coming to rest at the foot of a tall spruce tree. Protected from serious injury by Ram's big body, Sierra lay dazed and panting, finding no sane reason for Ram's odd behavior. Then she heard a horrible crash, heard the gut-wrenching screams of terrified horses and passengers, and saw the coach careen over the lip of the ravine and slide out of sight down the sloped incline.

"No—oh no!" Thoroughly shaken, she buried her face in the curve of Ram's neck and trembled against him. They had come too close to death for comfort. How had he known?

He anticipated her question. "I felt the right wheels leave the roadbed and realized the ledge had fallen away. For a few seconds the coach's momentum carried us forward, literally on thin air. When the coach tilted to the right, I knew it would be only a matter of time before we slid into the ravine. The jehu saw it too, but there was nothing he could do but continue forward and pray for solid ground. Stopping would have been just as disastrous as continuing forward. Are you hurt?"

Sierra shook her head. "I don't think so. You saved my life. Do you suppose any of the others made it?"

"I don't know, but I aim to find out. Will you be all right if I leave you here?"

"What are you going to do?" Her voice rose on a note of panic.

"I'm going to climb down there and see if anyone survived the fall."

She clutched his sleeve. "Be careful, Ram. I couldn't bear it if . . . please be careful."

He stared at her, his expression stripped bare of cynicism and more vulnerable than she had ever seen it. Without warning, he cupped her face in his hands and kissed her hard. "Rest," he said as he turned away. "I'll be back as soon as I can."

She wanted to beg him not to climb down that ravine and endanger his life, but she had no right. She wasn't the only one who needed him. Her heart thumped wildly against her ribcage as Ram disappeared over the edge of the ravine.

She waited for what seemed like an eternity. Her head pounded and her body thrummed with fear. When the rapid discharge of gunfire blasted up from the depths of the ravine, Sierra's breath caught in her throat. She struggled to her feet. A sharp, stabbing pain in her ankle brought a ragged cry from her throat. She felt as if every bone in her body had been jarred out of alignment. Unable to walk on her injured ankle, she dropped down on elbows and knees and dragged herself across the road to peer over the ledge.

She saw the coach lying on its side at the foot of the ravine. She shuddered in relief when she saw that Ram had reached the bottom and that he and the soldier, who appeared unhurt, stood over the horses, their guns drawn and smoking. Her eyes dimmed with regret when she realized that Ram had used his guns to put the poor animals out of their misery. Her gaze made a sweeping search of the area, looking for other survivors.

The driver was sitting with his back resting against the overturned coach, one leg stretched out before him at an awkward angle. Clara

Phillpot was sitting beside him, looking dazed and disoriented. The Sysons were a short distance from the coach; Willie Mae was bending over her husband, who appeared to have suffered some kind of injury. The grandmother was sitting beside a wheel, which was still spinning crazily, holding her arm and moaning. A few feet away, the gambler was sprawled on the ground, holding his head and groaning. Blood seeped from a head wound into his eyes.

Casting about for the other passengers, Sierra counted four bodies sprawled on the ground where they had been thrown. Obviously the top riders and the second driver hadn't fared as well as those passengers inside the coach. She watched as Ram spoke to each passenger, dispensing blankets and canteens he'd retrieved from the boot. When she recalled how close she had come to becoming one of the victims, she thanked God for Ram's trigger reflexes.

Exhausted, she crawled back to the tree, shaking from pain and shock. She lay back and closed her eyes, grateful to Ram for saving her life. She must have dozed, for when she awoke Ram and the soldier were pulling themselves up over the rim of the ravine, each dragging a bundle up with them.

"I brought your valise so you could retrieve your valuables," Ram said as he set the bag before Sierra. "Corporal Trotter has blankets and canteens."

"Thank you. Most of my money is in my valise. What about the others?"

"We made them as comfortable as possible, but none are in good enough shape to make the climb up the ravine. Except maybe for Mrs. Syson. And she refuses to leave her husband. Corporal Trotter was the only person who sustained no injuries."

"What can we do?"

"The driver says there's a way station not too far away," Trotter told her. "It's the last stop before entering the Great Salt Lake Desert, no more than a day's walk, ma'am. Mr. Hunter and I can make it easy, and we have plenty of water. We'll summon help as quickly as we can."

"It's nearly dark—what if you get lost?" The thought of being left alone in the wilderness terrified her.

"We won't get lost, Sierra, trust me. I've brought you a blanket and canteen. I'm sorry I couldn't find anything to eat."

"No! You can't leave me here alone!"

"There are people down in the ravine, Sierra. You won't be alone."

"You want me to climb down there and join them?"

Ram tunneled a hand through his thick hair, sending Sierra a thoroughly disgusted look. "I don't want you to go down there at all. You're to stay right here until I return."

"I'm going with you."

"We should start right away, sir." Corporal Trotter looked from Ram to Sierra, aware of the volatile clash of wills. "If the lady can keep up with us, I don't mind taking her."

119

"I mind," Ram retorted, his patience growing thin. "She's staying here. Let's go, Corporal."

"I'll follow," Sierra threatened. If Ram thought he was going anywhere without her, he was sadly mistaken. "And if I get lost and eaten by wild animals, it will be your fault. You're the one who will have to explain to my father."

Ram sent his eyes heavenward. What had he done to earn this kind of torment? Didn't she realize she'd be safer waiting for help to arrive than she would be traipsing over rough country? To Ram's regret, she looked so frightened that he couldn't find it in his heart to refuse her.

"Very well, Sierra, you win. But if you can't keep up, I swear I'll leave you wherever you fall." His voice was gruff, giving her the impression that he meant every word. "The lives of the people in the ravine depend upon us reaching the way station as quickly as possible."

Sierra swallowed hard. Would he really abandon her if she lagged on the trail? "I understand."

Ram eyed her skeptically. Then he and Trotter turned stiffly and walked away. "Very well. Take what you need from your valise, we're leaving whether you're ready or not."

Rummaging in her valise, Sierra removed a drawstring bag containing her money and stuffed it into her pocket. Since none of her clothing was suitable for a hike through the mountains, she left it behind, taking only a silver-backed comb and brush, a treasured gift from her adoptive parents. Ram and the corporal were already disappearing around a hairpin turn in the road ahead when Sierra staggered to her feet.

Pain. Sharp. Excruciating.

She tested her right ankle again and groaned aloud, grateful that she lagged too far behind to be heard. She knew that if Ram realized she'd injured her ankle, he'd make her stay behind. She held her breath and took a tentative step, gratified to find that the pain had settled down to a dull throbbing. At least it wasn't broken, she thought with ragged relief. She hobbled forward a few steps, discovering that by limping and placing most of her weight on her left ankle she could walk. Clenching her teeth against the pain, she set off after Ram.

Ram heard Sierra scrambling after him but did not look back. Since she couldn't be dissuaded from tagging along with him and Trotter, she had to take responsibility for her own decisions. He refused to pamper her despite the strong urge within him to sweep her into his arms and carry her all the way to Salt Lake City. As long as he knew she was trailing behind him, he kept his protective instincts firmly in hand.

Tears rolled down Sierra's cheeks as she fought the pain, the heat, and the rough terrain over which she traveled. Her complexion was chalky; her stays were digging so fiercely into her narrow waist that each breath was sheer agony. With each faltering step she had to fight four petticoats, each one clinging tenaciously to her legs, and her bruised body felt as if it was

121

being consumed by fire. Pure stubbornness kept her on her feet. She'd drop from exhaustion before she'd beg Ram to slow down or tell him she'd been injured. The loss of the sun, which had slipped behind a wooded mountain crest, brought another kind of torment.

Cold.

That morning she'd donned a gray skirt and silk blouse, throwing a short cape over her shoulders to complete the fashionable outfit. The sleeves of the blouse had been shredded during the fall and the cape offered scant protection against the cool evening breeze.

They were climbing upward now, nearly at the peak of a pass whose downward descent led to the Great Salt Desert. Sierra estimated that they had been walking for nearly two hours, and the only things that kept her on her feet were pure grit and determination. She began to fear she'd never make it to the way station. When she stopped once to catch her breath, she had checked her throbbing ankle and saw that it was grotesquely swollen above her boot. But she'd had no time to loosen the laces, for Ram was already out of sight.

Ram slowed his steps fractionally, dimly aware that Sierra lagged far behind. For the past two hours she'd followed doggedly, and he felt grudging respect for her fortitude. Few women of his acquaintance would attempt so dangerous a journey.

Abruptly his face turned to stone when he recalled all the daring things Dora had attempted and gotten away with. Women were capable of just about anything, he decided, be it daring feats or deception. He'd put nothing past them.

Sierra grit her teeth against the shimmering pain tugging at the edges of her brain. Her ankle throbbed so badly now that each step became pure agony. The road wavered before her eyes, and darkness seemed to close in all around her. Her distress increased when she stepped on loose stones, and her bad ankle twisted beneath her. She cried out, clutched at air, and began a slow spiral to the ground. Then she knew no more.

Ram knew a moment of panic when he heard Sierra cry out. Whirling on his heel, he saw her sag to the ground. She lay so still that fear shuddered through Ram. Had she suffered an injury and been too stubborn to tell him? He dropped to his knees beside her, alarm and anger warring within him. He was alarmed by her pallor and angry because she'd failed to confide in him.

The tension ebbed out of him when he saw the shallow rise and fall of her chest. His fingers moved swiftly to loosen the top buttons of her blouse and ease her breathing. She was pale and sweating and seemed to struggle to achieve each intake of breath. He cursed long and loud when he noticed her tightly cinched waist. Trotter, who waited a short distance away, heard and sprinted back to join him.

"What's wrong with her?" he asked anxiously.

"I'm not sure, but the tight stays she's wearing

can't be doing her any good." With grim determination, he unfastened the remaining buttons on her blouse.

Embarrassed, Trotter looked away. "Perhaps I should go it alone from here and you stay with the lady. She doesn't look in any shape to continue."

Ram spat out another oath. "I warned her to remain behind. I hadn't planned on playing nursemaid."

Trotter blushed. "I'd offer to stay with her, sir, but you seem to know the lady. I'm sure she'd prefer you to remain with her. I'll send someone back for you and the others when I reach the home station. Will you be all right?"

Ram sighed in resignation. He couldn't in all conscience leave Sierra behind, nor did he feel comfortable leaving her with a stranger who appeared too embarrassed to do what was needed to make her more comfortable.

Running his fingers through thick, rumpled hair, he nodded distractedly. "Leave a blanket and canteen. We'll be fine here until help arrives."

Trotter sent Ram a look of profound relief. Then he turned abruptly and walked briskly away. Ram watched him disappear through the gloomy dusk, then turned his attention back to Sierra. She was still pale, and he didn't like the way she was struggling for breath. Picking her up with utmost care, he carried her through the woods to where he thought he'd heard the unmistakable sound of water rushing over rocks.

Sure enough, he found a mountain stream about one hundred yards from the road and laid Sierra down carefully on the grassy bank. She moaned but did not awaken.

Concentrating on easing Sierra's discomfort, Ram ripped the gaping edges of her blouse apart and loosened the waistband of her skirt. It didn't take a wizard to realize that her tightly laced stays were restricting her breathing, and his stark features hardened with resolve. Using his pocket knife, he slit the strings and pulled the garment free. Sierra shuddered and drew in a ragged breath.

"Little fool," he muttered darkly. "I'd like to strangle the idiots who dictate fashion to gullible females. These instruments of torture should be outlawed." With a great deal of satisfaction, he flung the offending garment into the stream and watched it disappear beneath the surface.

"Now these petticoats," Ram continued conversationally, though Sierra was beyond hearing. He was momentarily distracted by an incredibly narrow waist, breasts that seemed a perfect fit for his hands, and hips that flared gently down to shapely legs. He imagined how wonderful it would feel to strip off his clothes and press his naked body against hers. The thought sent a surge of hot blood to his loins.

Disgusted by the direction of his lusty thoughts, Ram shook his head to clear it and turned his efforts toward making Sierra comfortable. Lifting her skirt, he released the tapes holding her four petticoats in place, then tugged them down her hips and legs. After he removed the petticoats, he stared in stunned silence at her grotesquely swollen right ankle.

"Oh, my God!" He sat back on his heels, gently palpitating the swollen flesh above her boot.

Sierra stirred restlessly but did not awaken. It was just as well, Ram thought as he carefully removed her boot and stripped off her stocking. How could she have hiked so far on an ankle that must have given her intolerable pain? Any other woman would be crying and begging him to stop, but not proud, foolish Sierra. No, rather than ask for quarter, she'd stoically borne the agony in silence. If she hadn't fainted, he probably would never have known about her injury.

At least Sierra's petticoats were good for something, Ram thought as he tore one of them into strips and wet them in the icy stream. With exquisite tenderness, he bathed her pale face and neck, then her ankle, using pads of folded cloth as cold compresses. When that didn't seem to bring down the swelling to any appreciable degree, he moved her closer to the stream, positioning her so that the injured ankle dangled in the icy water. When she began to shiver, he thought of the blanket and realized he'd left it back on the road. The next best thing, he decided, was to share his own warmth with her. Dropping down beside her, he cradled the upper part of her body in his arms and simply held her.

And he was warm—oh yes, very warm. Sierra's blouse was gaping open and her skirt pushed up around her thighs, revealing more of her flesh than he had a right to see. He stared at the alluring roundness of her full breasts rising impudently against her thin chemise, the nipples drawn into tight little buds, and the outline of her long legs, which were spread apart to accommodate her injured ankle. Not only was he extremely warm, but his constricting chest made breathing difficult. Taking advantage of a helpless woman was not Ram's style, so he gritted his teeth and turned his thoughts to unpleasant matters.

Dora.

At one time Dora had been everything to him. He had been so damn young and trusting then. But Dora and a man he'd trusted and admired had taught him a lesson not easily forgotten—or forgiven.

Jason Jordan.

His memory traveled backward in time. He had just turned twenty-one. Ten years later, his dreams were still haunted by the metallic sound of steel doors closing behind him. He'd never forget the crushing loneliness, the oppressive silence, the hellish years of bad food, back-breaking labor and beatings—especially the beatings—and the sure knowledge that Dora and Jason were on the outside, laughing. What a gullible fool he had been.

Never again. Afterward he'd sworn never to allow a woman to get too close to him, and he had renewed the vow countless times during the years that followed. Two years had been carved out of his life. Miserable years that could never be returned to him or replaced; years in which he'd lost his innocence and learned through cruel experience to trust no one. That young, impressionable boy no longer existed. From the ashes emerged a man—a stronger, harder man, one immune to a woman's wiles, a man unable to trust.

Sierra moaned and shifted in his arms, jerking Ram from his painful memories. "It's all right, little love," he murmured softly into her ear. "You're going to be just fine." His arms tightened around her, forgetting the jeering ghost of his memories and the vow he had made. He'd had plenty of women since Dora and expected he'd have many more in the years to come, but he doubted any would affect him in quite the same way that Sierra Alden did. Unfortunately, he couldn't afford the luxury of falling in love.

That jarring thought didn't prevent him from wanting to hold Sierra in his arms, from imagining how it would feel to make love to her, from wanting to hear her call his name in ecstasy.

He wanted to be her first lover.

And her last.

My God, she was more dangerous to him than he had thought!

Sierra awoke to the feeling of warmth and comfort. Her eyes opened slowly, adjusting to the first dim rays of daylight. She saw trees swaying gently above her and frowned, trying to recall where she was and why. She moved abruptly and her body screamed in protest, reminding her precisely how close she had come to death. She moaned and tried to rise, startled to find herself reclining in the warm nest of Ram's arms. She gazed up into his eyes and saw that he was watching her. His expression revealed more than he intended, giving her an unguarded glimpse of his innermost feelings. He was angry, very angry, but beneath the anger lay something deeper. She saw concern, and another more complex emotion she didn't attempt to interpret.

"How do you feel?" His words had a jolting effect.

She moved experimentally. "Not too bad, considering. Did I sleep long?"

"All night."

She flushed and looked away. "I'm sorry, Ram. I tried not to complain, but the pain just got too bad." Truth to tell, she was more than a little grateful that Ram hadn't left her behind as he'd promised. Did that mean he cared just a little about her? "What happened?"

"You fainted on the trail. Had I known you were injured, I would have insisted that you remain behind. You're so damn stubborn and reckless you don't use the sense God gave you. Corporal Trotter continued on alone."

Sierra held up her injured ankle and saw that it had been bound tightly with strips of white material. Her petticoat? Then she noticed that her legs were sprawled in decidedly unladylike abandon, with her skirt bunched up around her hips, revealing the lacy edges of her drawers. Dimly she wondered why she felt so light and unfettered. She hadn't been able to take this deep a breath since she was a carefree child running about in ankle-length skirts. Abruptly her hands flew to her unbound breasts and the shocking truth dawned on her. With shaking fingers she pulled the gaping edges of her blouse together and glared at Ram.

"My God, what have you done to me?"

Ram laid her gently on the ground and rose to his feet, stretching the kinks out of his muscles. "I merely made you comfortable."

"Where are my—my—" She blushed. One simply did not mention unmentionables in mixed company.

"Your stays?" He seemed amused. "I dispensed with them. I suspect they're several miles downstream by now. It's beyond me why women torture themselves with stays. This trip is torture enough without making it worse by restricting your breathing."

"All proper ladies wear stays," Sierra said defensively.

"Why? You're slim as a rail. I can make no sense out of women's fashions. Needless to say, you won't be wearing them anytime soon." He eyed her narrowly and offered his hand. "Can you stand? We should walk back to the road to meet our rescuers when they arrive."

Sierra flipped down her skirt and grasped his hand. She felt positively wanton without her stays and petticoats. Once on her feet, she tested her ankle, surprised to find that it held her weight. Whatever Ram had done last night had certainly helped. "Where is my boot and stocking?"

"Right here." He held the boot in his free hand. Her stocking and garter were stuffed inside. "Let me help you."

He dropped to his knees, gently lifted her foot, and slipped on her stocking and boot while she balanced herself against his broad shoulder. The boot wouldn't lace but it lent support to her weak ankle. When he would have adjusted the garter on her leg, her face flamed and she snatched it from his hand. Turning her back, she slipped it in place herself.

"How does your ankle feel?"

"Bearable," Sierra said stoically. Her bald lie didn't fool Ram one damn bit.

"Sure it is." Before she realized what he intended, he swept her off her feet and carried her toward the road.

"Wait!" He paused, one sandy brow raised. "I want to button my blouse first. I'd be embarrassed if someone saw me like this."

Ram slanted her a wicked grin. "I'm thoroughly enjoying the sight myself. But you're right—I sure as hell wouldn't want to share it." His words shocked him and he sobered immediately.

The tantalizing sight of her unfettered breasts

bobbing beneath her thin chemise made him acutely aware of how dangerous she was to him. He imagined how their milky roundness would feel cradled in the palms of his hands, speculated on their taste, their scent, knowing she would taste delicious everywhere his lips roamed. With an effort born of desperation, he directed his gaze away from her tempting flesh.

"All right, I'm as decent now as I'll ever be," Sierra announced, giving him a shaky smile.

Blissfully unaware of Ram's distraction, Sierra snuggled deeper in the cradle of his arms. She loved being held by him. He felt wonderful and smelled even better, faintly reminiscent of spicy cologne and tobacco. She wished she could stay in his arms forever. With startling insight, she realized that she could never be happy with Gordon Lynch. Not after knowing a man like Ramsey Hunter.

"I'll settle you at a hotel in Salt Lake City," Ram said conversationally. "By the time the next stage comes through, your ankle should be healed. You'll have to take a feeder line to Denver."

Sierra frowned in consternation. Ram's words indicated that they would be parting soon.

"Won't you be on the same stage?"

Ram shook his head, unable to look her in the eye. During the long night he'd decided that Sierra was too great a distraction, and dangerous besides. She was becoming too important to him, and he couldn't allow that. "I have other plans."

"What kind of plans?" Her voice rose in panic.

"I've decided to buy a horse in Salt Lake City and travel to Denver on horseback. Alone. And no," he said anticipating her request, "I won't take you with me. Don't even think about it. This is one time, Sierra Alden, when your little games won't work."

Chapter Seven

Sierra paced the short length of the hotel room, treading the same worn floorboards she'd followed for the last several hours. She and Ram had arrived in Salt Lake City yesterday. Corporal Trotter had reached the home station and returned with a rescue team, a wagon for the injured, and a pair of horses for her and Ram. After spending the night at the station, a guide had taken them across the Great Salt Lake Desert to Salt Lake City, skirting the huge lake bearing the same name as the city. Trotter had remained behind to help the rescue party bring the injured passengers to safety.

When they reached Salt Lake City, Sierra wasn't surprised that their unfortunate accident had caused them to miss their feeder line stage to Denver, but she was upset when she found out another wasn't due for a week. She was further angered when Ram announced his intention to rent a horse and continue alone to Denver. No matter how desperately Sierra pleaded to be taken along, Ram remained adamant in his refusal. The thought of parting left her with an empty feeling in the pit of her stomach.

Sierra flexed her ankle, pleased with her speedy recovery. Strolling to the window, she gazed absently down at the thoroughfare below. Her attention sharpened when she noticed Ram entering the livery at the end of the block. She muttered an unladylike oath when she realized that he was probably on his way to purchase a horse and leave her behind as he'd threatened. How could she allow him to walk out of her life without a backward glance? She'd do almost anything to convince him to take her along with him. Where Ram was concerned, she had no pride.

From the ashes of her despair, a daring plan took form in her mind and her lips curved upward into a sly smile. Limping only slightly, she left the hotel and hurried down the street toward the livery. If luck was with her, she'd be in time to intercept Ram before he left town.

Ram examined the superb bay gelding with a critical eye. Running his hands down the animal's flanks, he was impressed with the bay's bone structure and sleek muscles. He was a good animal, all right, Ram thought, satisfied with his choice. He'd picked the bay over the sturdy dun mare even though both were fine animals, and the price mentioned by the hostler was surprisingly reasonable.

"Well, mister, what do ya say? Do we have a bargain?" the hostler asked hopefully. "Ye won't find a better animal fer miles in any direction. Save maybe fer the mare over yonder."

"The bay will do," Ram said, restraining his enthusiasm lest the hostler raise the price. He counted out the money and placed it in the man's hands. "Where can I buy a good saddle and trail supplies?"

"Ya going far?" the hostler asked curiously.

"Denver." His terse reply did little to satisfy the hostler's curiosity.

"That's a far piece," he observed, scratching his thatch of shaggy gray hair. "Hear tell the injuns are still plenty riled over their losses at the Wagon Box battle. The area around Denver just ain't safe with Red Cloud and his warriors still on the warpath."

"I heard that Red Cloud and some of the chiefs just signed a new treaty at Fort Laramie," Ram contended. "In return, the peace commission agreed to give up its forts and roads in the Powder River Country."

"That's the truth of it, mister," the hostler said, spitting a brown stream into the soiled straw at his feet, "but there are still hostile injuns in the area, just waiting fer unsuspecting travelers."

"Thanks for the warning, friend," Ram said. "I'll be careful."

Ram led the bay from the livery into the sun-drenched street. "Buy yer saddle and supplies at the general store," the hostler called after him. "Ya won't be cheated. You'll find it at the north end of the street."

Ram waved, indicating that he'd heard the hostler's recommendation, and turned in the direction of the store. He saw Sierra marching resolutely toward him and groaned in dismay. He'd hoped to slip out of town without another confrontation with the tempting little vixen. He'd decided that leaving Sierra behind in Salt Lake City was the only sure way of protecting himself from the devastating attraction that had grown between them. It was for her own good, he told himself. Allowing the relationship to develop further would not be fair to Sierra, since marriage was out of the question.

It took little imagination for Ram to guess what Sierra would do to his emotional tranquility if he allowed her to accompany him. Sierra disrupted his life and kept him in a constant state of turmoil. It was a small miracle that he'd been able to control his lust for her this long. She was too naive to realize the danger of pursuing a man like him, a man who could never be what she needed.

Her face set in implacable lines, Sierra marched up to Ram until they stood toe to toe. "I can't believe you really intend to leave me behind."

Ram sighed inwardly. "Did you doubt it?"

"You're a—a pig-headed ass, Ramsey Hunter," she fumed, blurting out the worst word she could think of. "A gentleman wouldn't abandon a lady."

"You've forgotten one little thing, Miss Alden. I never agreed to act as your nursemaid. Nor did I ever indicate by word or deed that I would be responsible for you on this foolhardy mission of yours. It's ridiculous to believe your siblings are still alive after all this time. This trip was your decision, and it's time you took responsibility for your own actions."

Ram watched without expression as the color drained from Sierra's face. Desperation made him deliberately brutal, but he had to break this invisible bond between them once and for all. If hurting her was the only way to discourage her, then so be it. Sierra frightened him. Frightened the hell out of him. If he let a woman get close to him again, he'd break a vow he'd made long ago. Dora had taught him a lesson about relationships that he'd not forget.

"Perhaps we'll meet again in San Francisco," Ram said coolly. "Then again, maybe we won't. The wife of Gordon Lynch doesn't belong in Ramsey Hunter's world. The way I see it, our paths will probably never cross again. It's been a real pleasure, Sierra," he said dryly. "Once you've had time to reconsider, you'll realize I'm doing you a big favor."

Sierra searched Ram's face, refusing to accept his words. His expression revealed more than his words implied. It told her that he didn't really want to leave her behind. She felt it as surely as she felt her own reluctance to part from him. Did he really think she could go home and marry Gordon after experiencing his kisses? After feeling his arms around her, holding her, protecting her? Ram might lie to himself, but he couldn't lie to her.

Sierra gave him a cunning smile. A daring plan had already formed in her mind. "We *will* meet again, Ram Hunter, depend on it." Sooner than you think, she thought. Ram looked askance at her, but she did not elaborate. He'd find out soon enough, she thought gleefully.

"Good-bye, Sierra," Ram said, "I wish you luck finding your siblings." Grasping the bay's leading reins, he walked away before he was tempted to relent and allow Sierra to have her way.

"So long, Ram," Sierra replied, trying to disguise the excitement in her voice. She had so much to do in so little time.

"The mare's a fine horse, miss," the hostler said as Sierra ran her hands over the magnificent piece of horseflesh. "Almost sold her a few minutes ago, but the gentleman decided on the big bay instead."

The fact that Ram had considered buying the mare for himself was good enough for Sierra. She quickly concluded her purchase and asked directions to the general store.

"I want to buy the same items you sold the man who was in here a short time ago," she told the startled store clerk. In short order she purchased a saddle, saddlebags, canteen, blanket, personal items, trail food, a sturdy pair of boots, and a jacket.

She felt confident she had thought of everything when the clerk said, "I reckon you'll want a rifle. The gentleman bought a Winchester repeater. That all right with you?"

"Er—yes, that will be fine," Sierra said, somewhat flustered. She hadn't even considered a weapon. "Is that all?"

"Well, ma'am," the clerk said, eyeing her attire critically, "you'll need suitable trail clothing. What you're wearing now won't do if you're planing on a long trip."

Sierra looked down on her rumpled skirt and torn blouse and agreed wholeheartedly. "What do you suggest?"

The clerk walked to the back of the store and returned a few minutes later with a soft leather split skirt, long-sleeved blouse, and flat-crowned, broad-brimmed hat. He held up the skirt for her inspection. "This will be more comfortable for riding than what you're wearing. It's practical and all the rage now."

Sierra was intrigued by the functional yet attractive skirt and bought two, adding several blouses in her size. She also included several changes of intimate apparel, but no corset. The clerk pointed out the dressing room and Sierra changed immediately into one of her new outfits. When she came out, the clerk's eyes shone with admiration.

"I'll saddle your horse while you pack your

clothing in the saddlebags," he offered after Sierra settled the bill. "The rifle will fit into the saddle boot and I'll put the foodstuffs in a drawstring sack that can be attached to the saddle horn."

"You're very kind," Sierra said gratefully. The young man blushed as he carried the saddle outside to where her horse was tethered.

A short time later, Sierra was back at the hotel, settling her bill for the night's lodging and collecting the personal items she valued enough to take with her. By the time she mounted and rode away, she had already learned from the clerk in which direction to travel to reach Denver. She knew she couldn't be far behind Ram, for she'd watched him ride out of town not an hour ago. Her plan was to follow a respectable distance behind and keep well out of sight until it was too late to be sent back. Ram Hunter wasn't the only one with brains, she thought smugly, refusing to dwell on his implacable anger when she finally caught up with him.

Ram set a southeasterly course. The climate was more temperate than in the Great Salt Lake Desert they had passed through. Dense woods rose on either side of the trail, interspersed with fertile valleys fed by mountain streams, tributaries of great rivers. Geographically scenic marvels such as deeply incised canyons, natural bridges and arches, and towers and turrets of every description provided a feast for his eyes. Despite the glorious scenery, Ram's thoughts wandered. He looked forward with relish to his long overdue confrontation with Dora and Jason. Dimly he wondered how they would react to seeing him. Did they know they were both wanted by the law? Ram still wasn't certain how he was going to punish Dora, only that she would pay. Was she still heart-stoppingly beautiful? he wondered idly. Did her silky blond hair still brush the elegant curve of her hips? Were her provocative, almond-shaped eyes the same incredible shade of amber that had beguiled him so thoroughly?

Vividly he recalled her long, shapely legs and all the other considerable attributes she had used to entrap him. And how could he forget her plump, milk-white breasts crested with pouting coral nipples? He even remembered the powerful allure of that soft, inviting place between her legs that had seduced him so effortlessly. They had been good in bed, but he had learned volumes about women in the intervening years. He was no longer a green youth captivated by Dora's sexual prowess and insatiable appetites. What a fool he'd been to think she was special.

Dora had never loved him. She loved what he could give her. His wealthy parents had set him up in business when he'd returned from school, and Dora had gone after him like a bitch in heat. He wondered if she and Jason had planned his seduction and downfall from the beginning.

His thoughts turned to Jason Jordan. The man's name tasted bitter on his tongue. An orphan whose parents had been slain by Indians, Jason had been taken in by Ram's generous parents when Jason was ten and he was six. He'd loved Jason like a brother. Like a fool, he'd thought Jason returned the brotherly affection.

Ram made camp that night beside a rushing mountain brook. He bathed in the cold water, built a fire, and cooked a simple meal of beans and bacon. Then he curled up in the blanket and tried to sleep. Lord knew he should have been tired enough to drop off immediately, but instead he lay awake staring at the star-studded sky. Try though he might, he couldn't blame Dora for his restlessness.

It was Sierra who kept him in a constant state of turmoil. He imagined shiny black tresses and eyes the shade of sparkling silver. He dreamed of lithe curves and long slender legs. Sierra had beguiled him as completely as Dora had those long years ago. Fortunately, he had learned his lesson well and was too wise now to fall victim to his lust. He was well pleased with his ability to walk away from Sierra unscathed, and he owed it all to his experience with Dora. And by God, that's the way he *wanted* it, the way it had to be—at least until this business with Dora and Jason was behind him.

His past dealings with women had taught him never to get involved, never to care too deeply for someone, and to guard his heart against beguiling women. At length, Ram drifted into an uneasy sleep, his dreams consumed with Sierra, unaware that she had made her own camp not five hundred yards away.

The dark, shadowy forest frightened Sierra. She couldn't recall ever feeling so lonely. Unidentifiable night sounds assailed her from every direction, a good indication that dangerous animals lurked in the darkness. Building a fire was out of the question since she had no earthly idea how to go about it. She was forced to satisfy her appetite with dry biscuits and that horrible jerky the store clerk insisted she buy. The only way she could swallow the salty dried meat was to soften it in water and nibble at a biscuit to push the stuff down her throat. But at least it was filling.

After her meager supper, Sierra settled down to sleep, wrapping up in a blanket and using her saddle for a headrest. Twice she was awakened by animal noises, and each time she had to forcibly restrain herself from running to Ram's camp and throwing herself into his arms. But she knew it was too soon to reveal herself, and she forced herself to put her fears behind her. If Ram had taken her with him, he could have saved her all this anguish.

Ram rose at dawn, ate two biscuits, and washed them down with several cups of strong, scalding coffee. Then he packed up his gear, saddled his horse, and returned to the trail.

Sierra smelled the fragrant aroma of boiling coffee, and her mouth watered hungrily. She'd even dug the coffeepot out of her gear but quickly replaced it. By the time she figured out how to build a fire, Ram would be so far ahead of her that she might never catch up. She saddled her horse and left, munching on jerky.

It was long past midday when Ram suddenly realized that he was being trailed. He saw nothing, yet the feeling persisted that he was being followed. As the day progressed, he became more and more convinced that someone was keeping enough distance between them so as not to be seen. It was nearly time to make camp for the night, and it took only a split second for Ram to come to a decision. Turning his mount from the trail, he took to the woods, circling around behind his foe. Before the day ended, he intended to learn who in the hell was following him and why.

Sierra watched the sun sink below the horizon and knew Ram would be making camp for the night about now. She reckoned he couldn't be more than half a mile ahead of her and decided to make her own camp. She figured it wouldn't be safe to show herself for at least another day. Selecting a likely place beneath a canopy of trees, Sierra dismounted and removed the saddle from her horse.

"Does that feel good, girl?" she crooned as she rubbed the mare down with the saddle blanket. Then she hobbled her beside a hummock of lush grass and rummaged in her bag for something more palatable to eat than jerky. "Maybe I should build a fire," she said aloud.

She was so hungry for another human voice that she had begun talking to her horse. She hummed to herself as she gathered sticks.

Ram moved quietly through the woods, making surprisingly little noise for a man his size. He had tethered his horse a short distance away and continued on foot. Darkness settled around him, and he moved unerringly toward his prey, guided by the racket made by his mysterious stalker. Only a tenderfoot would make so much noise, he thought with a hint of disgust.

Ram froze when he spied the crude camp through the canopy of trees. Though the figure was little more than a dim shadow, Ram could see him move awkwardly about the camp. Concealed by a large tree, Ram watched intently before concluding that the man was alone.

He dropped into a crouch, body tense, the muscles in his legs bunching reflexively. Uncoiling his body, he launched himself forward, pinning Sierra beneath his hard body before she knew what had hit her.

Sierra felt something slam into her and let out a whoosh of air as the breath was driven from her lungs. Panic-stricken, she feared she'd been attacked by a wild animal and prayed for a quick, painless end. When she felt the thrust of cold steel against her temple, she went limp beneath the crushing weight of a hard, implacable body.

"All right, you bastard, why are you trailing me? Speak or I'll blow your brains out." The metallic click of a cocked gun was more frightening to Sierra than the wild animal she had imagined.

She'd recognized Ram's voice the moment he spoke. He was going to kill her! Raw fear spiraled through her as she tried to speak and failed. The best she could manage was a terrified squeak. But it was enough. That sound, combined with soft, womanly body sprawled beneath him, was all Ram needed to identify his captive, and he let the hammer of his gun fall back into place.

Picking Sierra up by the shoulders, he gave her a rough shake. "You little idiot! Do you know how close you came to being crow bait? What are you doing here? Why are you following me?"

Sierra swallowed. Her mouth moved wordlessly as she fought to control her trembling. After several false starts, the words came tumbling forth. "I didn't want to be left behind. I'd have had to wait a whole week before another stage came through town. Besides," she admitted, peering up at him defensively, "I wanted to be with you."

Ram's fury was awesome. Sierra cringed beneath his barrage of sharp words, threats, and dire predictions. When his initial anger had finally passed, he pulled her roughly against him and hugged her so tightly that she had to fight for breath. It felt wonderful.

"Little fool. Do you realize how close I came to killing you? It makes me shudder to think about it."

Then he caught her mouth with his and kissed her fiercely. At first she feared his kiss was an extension of his anger, until she felt his mouth soften and his hands gentle. With mesmerizing thoroughness, his tongue pushed past her teeth to explore the sweetly scented cavern of her mouth.

Feeling himself losing control, Ram pushed her away abruptly and tunneled his fingers through his thick blond hair. Sierra thought the gesture was wonderfully endearing and rewarded him with a brilliant smile. Her smile nearly defeated him, and he fought for control. She was lovely, utterly and undeniably beautiful.

"Build a fire," he ordered gruffly as he turned away. "I'll get my horse and then we'll talk."

"Can you cook?" Sierra asked hopefully. "I've eaten nothing but jerky and dried biscuits since yesterday morning."

"Don't tell me the pampered little princess can't cook," Ram mocked, slanting her an oblique look.

Sierra shrugged. "There was no reason to learn. But I'm a fast learner, if you're willing to teach me."

A strangled sound came from Ram's throat, and he grit his teeth harshly. There were many things he'd like to teach Sierra, but cooking wasn't one of them. He strode away as fast as his trembling legs could carry him.

While Ram was gone, Sierra gathered an armload of sticks and brush. When he returned he found her crouched before the neat little pile, staring at it as if she expected it to ignite through spontaneous combustion.

"Why haven't you started the fire?"

Sierra impaled him with an innocent, wide-eyed stare. "I don't know how."

"Sweet loving God, can't you do *anything?*"

Sierra thought about that a moment. "I'm sure there is something I excel at. Perhaps you can help me find it." Her words held a wealth of promise. Ram groaned and tried to banish her obvious qualifications from his mind.

She watched him closely as he lit a match to the brush and fed it kindling until it burst into flames. Then he filled the coffeepot from his canteen, measured out coffee, and set it in the fire to boil. While the coffee boiled, he removed a frying pan from his gear, sliced potatoes, and put them in the pan with some bacon to cook. Then he cut two thick slices from a cured ham. When the potatoes were partially cooked, he added the ham to the pan. It smelled wonderful, and Sierra's stomach growled hungrily.

"Where did you learn to cook?" she asked curiously.

"There are a lot of things about me you don't know."

"Like why you don't trust women?"

Ram glared at her. "You're a nosy little baggage." He forced himself into a calmness he didn't feel as he spooned ham and potatoes into a tin plate and handed it to her. "I assume you have your own utensils. Or must we share a fork and knife?"

"I have my own, thank you." Without waiting for an invitation, she dug in. "This is delicious."

Ram merely grunted as he poured coffee into two tin cups. Conversation stopped as they devoured their supper. Ram finished first. He set his plate aside and stared moodily into the darkness beyond the fire. When Sierra placed her plate beside his and sighed contentedly, he stared at her and cleared his throat. "We might as well get this out of the way right now. You're going back to Salt Lake City tomorrow."

"Not on your life," Sierra tossed back, supremely confident that he couldn't make her return if she didn't want to.

"I told you before, I'm not playing nursemaid to a spoiled little princess."

Sierra's chin rose stubbornly. "You can't make me go back, Ram. I'm of age and this is a free country. I can go and do what I please. And it pleases me to follow you to Denver."

"Well it sure as hell doesn't please me to act as your chaperon. If I had wanted the responsibility, I would have agreed to your harebrained scheme back in San Francisco. You're a distraction, Sierra. You limit me, limit my free movement and limit my choices. I can't afford to be distracted right now."

The only word Sierra heard was 'distraction.' "Just how do I distract you, Ram?" Her voice was sweetly seductive.

He stared at her lips, lush and red, at the silky

texture of the luxurious black eyelashes shading her astonishing silver eyes, at her long legs curled beneath her—and nearly laughed aloud. Everything about her was a distraction. And his coldly analytical mind told him she was too damn dangerous to his plans for his peace of mind.

His voice was harsh. "You know damn well what you do to me, Sierra. You're a temptation I don't need. When you're near, I can't keep my hands off you."

"Then why fight it?" Her voice was pitched so low that Ram had to strain to hear her words. When he realized exactly what she was hinting at, he went still. His eyes kindled, all smoke and fire. But just as swiftly they dimmed.

Her question met with cold, tense silence as he rose abruptly and began gathering up the plates. At length he said, "I'm not going to give you what you want, Sierra. I've always tried to steer clear of women like you. Your kind demand too much from a man, like marriage and children. I can offer nothing but a roll in the hay and fleeting pleasure."

"Maybe that's enough," Sierra replied, shocked by her words. How could she throw herself at Ram when obviously he didn't want her? Never in her life had she acted with brazen disregard for her reputation or her pride.

Ram's hands were shaking when he thrust the dirty plates at Sierra. If Sierra continued to behave like a wanton, he wouldn't be responsible for his actions. "There's a stream a few yards to the south." Without further words, he turned and fled in the opposite direction.

"Ram! Where are you going?"

Ram neither paused nor looked back. He acted as if the devil was nipping at his heels as he fled into the darkness. Realizing that she had gone too far, Sierra sighed and went in search of the stream. She found it about one hundred yards away and finished the job quickly. She knew she should return to camp, but the promise of a refreshing bath was too great a lure to resist. Stripping to her chemise, she waded into the shallow stream.

Ram was still shaking when he returned to camp a short time later. His hunger for Sierra was so fierce that it consumed him utterly. Lord knew she provoked him beyond endurance. He had no idea why he was resisting when obviously she was more than willing. Normally he'd have no qualms about taking what Sierra offered, but she was unlike any other woman he'd ever bedded. Instinctively he knew that once he made love to her that first time, he'd lose a part of himself. Furthermore, once would not be enough. He'd want her again and again.

He'd want her forever.

But at this point in his life he could make no commitments, give no assurances. Sierra deserved better than vague promises.

He closed his eyes and tried to imagine what it would be like to make love to Sierra. He had no idea if she was a virgin and didn't care. One quick, driving thrust of his loins and he'd be inside her. She'd be hot and tight and so damn eager that he'd have to exert strict control to keep from exploding immediately.

His fancy ran rampant as he imagined her moans, felt the wet, throbbing heat of her surround his surging sex. In his mind he pictured her beneath him, moaning and undulating, her long legs wrapped around him, taking him all the way inside her.

"Oh, God." Blood filled his loins and he closed his eyes against the forbidden images of his erotic fantasy. He wanted her so desperately that he was nearly beyond redemption. What he needed to douse his ardor was a long dunking in cold water. He wasn't entirely convinced that a soaking would help but considered it worth a try, especially since he was destined to suffer through the night with Sierra sleeping within arm's reach.

Sierra heard a splash and spun around in alarm. She relaxed visibly when she saw arms flashing in the water a few yards downstream and moonlight reflecting off hair the color of ripening wheat. Evidently Ram had the same craving for a bath as she did. She felt certain he hadn't seen her, so she eased toward shore and crouched amidst dense shrubbery growing near the water's edge, hoping Ram hadn't seen her. She exhaled sharply when he stood up in the thigh-deep water a short distance away and walked toward shore, revealing his state of full arousal.

Sierra gasped, shocked at her first sight of a naked man. She and her friends had speculated often about the vast differences between the sexes, but she'd never before had the opportunity to compare those differences. Even in the dim light he was magnificent. *It* was magnificent. It was also frightening.

It fired her erotic fantasies.

Ram was nearing her hiding place now, and she edged closer to the bank. She feared that if he saw her, he might think she'd been spying on him. To her horror, she backed into a deep depression made by fish to deposit their eggs. The water rose up to swallow her.

Ram waded toward shore, his state of arousal still painful despite his dunking in the stream. But at least it had taken his mind off Sierra long enough to allow him to cool off somewhat. A strangled sound directly ahead of him brought him to an abrupt standstill. He nearly laughed aloud when he saw a pair of slim white arms grasping at air and a shiny dark head disappear beneath the surface.

A half-dozen giant steps brought him to Sierra's side. Grasping her arms he yanked her to her feet, sputtering and gasping for breath. Knowing Sierra's penchant for getting into trouble, he wasn't surprised to see her. She had been nowhere in sight when he'd arrived at the stream, and he assumed she'd already started back to their camp. The woods were thick and dark and they could have passed each other and not known it.

Ram couldn't make up his mind whether to be angry or amused. Deciding that anger was safer and wiser, he gave her a shake that was by no means gentle. "Were you spying on me, Sierra?"

Chapter Eight

Sierra was standing so close to Ram that she could feel the rock-hard proof of his desire prodding her stomach. He seemed to walk around in that state a lot lately, she thought. Despite his denial, she knew he was not immune to her, and she definitely wasn't immune to him. Lord knew she'd resisted his appeal as long as she could, but the impossible man seemed to grow on her with each passing day.

Shamelessly, she lay her cheek against his bare chest and breathed in the male scent of him. The blend of masculine odors of tobacco, woodsmoke, and mountain sage filled her with a curiously hot excitement. She felt as if everything in her life, everything that had transpired before she met Ramsey Hunter, had been a prelude to this precise moment. Her body and mind were consumed with the arousing need to touch him, kiss him, and be touched and kissed in return.

Ram's body went taut when he felt the velvety softness of Sierra's cheek against his chest. A roaring filled his ears. His blood ran hot with the pressing desire to make love to her, to taste every inch of her skin, to thrust into her again and again until the fever inside him cooled.

He groaned as if in pain and held her at arm's length, though it nearly cost him his sanity to do so. One of them had to keep his wits about him. "I asked you a question, Sierra. Were you spying on me?"

Sierra swallowed convulsively and shook her head. He searched her face.

"I know what you want," he growled hoarsely, "what we both want."

"I . . . I'm not aware of wanting anything."

His voice was so tight that she could see his vocal cords working. "Trust me, little love, when I say I know. You've been a thorn in my side since the day we first met. When I try to remove it from my flesh, it only embeds itself deeper. I give up," he rasped, pulling her hard against him. "I may be damned for eternity, but I'm through fighting you. I no longer have the strength."

Sierra's insides went liquid. She was so close to Ram that not even a breath separated them. She felt the erotic rasp of his chest hairs through her wet chemise as they brushed against her sensitive breasts, felt the powerful surge of his staff against her stomach, and the need to touch him nearly overwhelmed her. Her arms crept around his neck, her hands tunneling through the wet strands of his thick blond hair. She lifted her head and brought his lips down to meet hers.

Breathing hard, Ram met her lips halfway, kissing her hungrily, filling her mouth with the bold thrust of his tongue, grinding his hips against her to assuage the raw ache of arousal. He couldn't recall when he'd been so excited, so utterly, devastatingly in need. This was passion without nuance, a primitive, desperate need for union that swept away all inhibitions. Constraint was no longer an option.

When he finally broke off the kiss, Sierra stared at him, her eyes as round and shiny as silver dollars. "I don't understand what's happening," she said honestly, "or what it is I want from you. I—I've never acted this way with any other man, and it frightens me."

"It scares the living hell out of me," Ram admitted, panting as if he'd just run a race. "I know what you want, sweetheart, and I'm going to give it to you. I want to show you how wonderful it can be. Lord knows, I've practiced more control with you than a woman has a right to expect. You've got me in such a state, I no longer know my own name. I'll give you one last chance to change your mind. Speak now before it's too late, for once I begin making love to you, there can be no turning back."

Sierra's mouth went dry. How could Ram

know what she wanted when she didn't know herself? Making love. It sounded mysterious. It sounded frightening.

It sounded wonderful.

It was something only allowed in the marriage bed. Would Ram offer marriage if she allowed him to make love to her?

Her hopes along that line were dashed when he said, "I can make you no promises. What we do here, we do for ourselves, for the pure sensual enjoyment it will give us. I can offer you nothing besides pleasure. If you're hoping for something more permanent, then leave now, this instant." His arms dropped away from her.

Walk away? Sierra's face went slack with astonishment. Just like that? She didn't think she had the courage. Her body was thrumming to a primitive tune, and mysterious forces were stealing her will. She needed . . . She wanted . . .

"I . . . can't. I want . . . I want . . ."

"I know exactly what you want, little love."

With ridiculous ease, Ram scooped her from the water and into his arms. With brisk purpose, he carried her back to their campsite. His lack of breath had nothing to do with the fast pace he set for himself and everything to do with the woman in his arms.

"Wait—my clothes," Sierra cried, realizing they had both left their clothing lying on the bank of the stream.

Ram's teeth were clenched so tightly that he could barely speak. "Later."

The fire was nearly out when Ram reached their camp. He set Sierra on her feet and moved away. "Don't move. I want to fill my eyes with you while I build up the fire."

He worked quickly, his steady gaze holding her immoble as he fed sticks to the dying fire. His gaze traveled the length of her body, caressing her, his imagination taking him on an erotic journey as he anticipated the pleasure of their joining. When the fire was burning brightly, he spread out his bedroll and reached out his hand to her. Their fingers touched. Sierra cried out as scorching heat traveled up her arm and spread throughout her body. A rosy flush crawled over her skin, and she knew with agonizing certainty that she blazed hotter than the fire in the firepit.

"This is your last chance, Sierra. You must stop me now if you don't want this." He waited, his blue eyes catching the light of the fire, reflecting the golden, dancing flames.

Sierra knew she should stop him. Knew she should turn and run like hell. She couldn't. She had to believe that Ram hadn't really meant what he'd said about not marrying her. She could change his mind, she knew she could. She'd make him change his mind. She lifted her chin, looked deeply into his eyes, and shook her head.

Holding her gaze, Ram dropped to his knees beside her and stripped off her shift. Their bodies touched, and fire leaped between them. He could feel the coiled tension within her; the quivering excitement pumping through her, and was humbled by it. He wanted to release that excitement and absorb it. He wanted to feel the eager dampness between her thighs bathe his male flesh. He wanted to give her a pleasure she'd remember forever.

"Are you a virgin, little love?"

Sierra swallowed visibly. "I've never been with a man before, not the way we are now."

"Ah, God." He started to rise. He couldn't do it. A virgin expected marriage, and he could not offer marriage. He would be depriving her future husband of the right to take a virgin to the marriage bed. "I can't do this to you."

A small cry of dismay escaped Sierra's lips as her fingers dug into his shoulders. He couldn't leave her now—she wouldn't let him. Her voice held an almost desperate ring. "It doesn't matter, Ram, truly. I want this." She touched her lips to his chest and Ram was lost.

"Witch," he groaned, pulling her into his arms and slamming his mouth down on hers. "You can't say I didn't give you fair warning."

She returned his kiss. When it ended, he said something harsh she didn't understand and pulled her beneath him. She clung to his shoulders, wrapping her arms around his back, afraid he was going to change his mind again. The thought was unbearable.

"Please," she whimpered.

"Oh, yes, little love, oh, yes. Nothing short of death can stop me now. Feel what you do to me?"

He pulled away slightly, grasped her hand and placed it on his swollen member. She gasped and looked down to where her hand clutched him. His staff was thick and ridged with veins, throbbing and glistening wetly. His breath hissed through his teeth in a grating, grunting groan. It took enormous self-control to fight the savage need to release his seed.

Sierra's eyes grew round. "It's so . . . so . . . I never imagined . . ."

"Don't be afraid," he said raggedly. "I'll try not to hurt you."

With marked reluctance he removed her hand, staring deeply into the silver depths of her eyes as his hands memorized the lush contours of her body. Her flesh felt hot and as smooth as silk beneath his touch. He cupped the curve of her buttocks. They were tight and round and lusciously feminine. He was breathing heavily now as his mouth blazed a trail down her throat to her breasts. His lips curved around a pouting nipple, strong and suckling, and utterly without mercy. Pleasure spiraled through her. When he slid his finger deep inside her, her breathing escalated dangerously as wet, drenching heat spread in a growing circle from that secret part of her no man had ever touched. A melting sensation turned her bones to liquid.

Ram felt her warmth, felt the wetness pool around his fingers, and shuddered. A harsh, tearing sound erupted from his throat. If he wasn't inside her soon, he'd disintegrate into ashes. He pushed another finger inside her. She felt pain and stiffened.

"Relax," he whispered soothingly, "You're tight. I'm just preparing you to take me inside you." His fingers stretched her, moving slowly in and out as he suckled her breasts.

Suddenly Sierra was all wondrous feeling, held suspended by the burning sensation of his long, hard fingers and harsh rasp of his breath against her breasts. The flames grew hotter, devouring her, as Ram's fingers opened her, stretched her, making her wet and slippery for his entrance. Something smooth and hard and hot pushed between her legs, probing inside her, stretching her impossibly wide, and she knew a moment's fear. With sudden, excruciating insight, she realized that what she was doing was very wrong. Ram had told her frankly that he had no intention of marrying her, that he felt no responsibility toward her, and was only making love to her because it was something they both wanted.

She looked up at him, struggling for words to tell him she had changed her mind, when he drove into her. She pressed her mouth to his shoulder to smother a cry of agony. He thrust again, embedding himself deeper. The pressure was unbearable, and it hurt like the very devil. But beyond the hurt, beyond the unrelenting pressure, she felt herself gradually gliding from pain into pleasure. She felt the fullness of him; he was thick, hard, and throbbing inside her. He was a part of her now, and nothing had ever felt so right, so good, so utterly perfect.

The pleasure was nearly unbearable. Ram groaned and moved forward, then pulled almost all the way out of her silken sheath. He pushed in again, the rough, sucking thrust and retreat igniting an inferno deep inside her. The pain was gone, but the pressure remained, filling her, thrilling her as she clung to him, straining upward, burning hotter as the pressure grew and intensified.

"God, I can't . . . I have to . . . I don't know if I can wait, little love." His voice was strained; the veins in his neck and forehead popped out prominently as he fought to maintain control of his senses.

His hips pumped furiously, and his breath came in ragged, ripping gasps. He flung his head back, his face contorted, his expression rivetingly sensual. Sierra felt something inside her ignite and leap to life, like tiny little explosions erupting along her nerve endings. She wanted . . . Dear Lord, she didn't know what she wanted, except that Ram had the power to give it to her.

"Please . . . Oh, Ram, please . . ."

"Yes, sweetheart, yes, yes, yes . . ." He gave one mighty thrust, sending Sierra over the edge of pleasure into raw ecstasy. He shuddered violently, surging long and deep inside her as he gave up his seed.

When he had no more to give, he collapsed heavily on top of her. Sierra felt the harsh drag and pull of his breath, the thudding of his heart, and the ripples quivering across his chest. She relished the solid weight of him against her, and her arms tightened convulsively. She held onto him until his breathing quieted. Then he drew out of her and rolled onto his back.

Sierra was astonished at the plethora of emotions swirling around her. Suddenly her senses were keener, sharper, more aware of the sights and sounds around her and of her body's needs. She breathed deeply of the night air, pungent with wood smoke and pine, and sniffed appreciatively the scent of love. The combination was heady beyond belief. She spared a glance at Ram. He sat with an elbow resting on his bent knee, staring into the darkness, his expression guarded.

Words welled up inside her, but she bit them back. There was so much she wanted to tell him but couldn't. Instinctively she knew he would not appreciate knowing just how deeply he had touched her soul and how completely he had captured her emotions.

"I hope you're happy," Ram said with gruff remorse. "This shouldn't have happened. If you recall, I warned you beforehand what your goading would lead to. I meant it, Sierra—I won't marry you."

Sierra swallowed thickly. "I didn't ask you to marry me. It was wonderful, Ram. I've never felt . . ." Her face reddened, and she studied her fingers.

His eyes smoldered darkly. "But you were hoping. Even if I could marry you, I'd make a lousy husband." He turned toward her, pulling her into his arms. "But I'd be a wonderful lover."

"You *are* a wonderful lover," Sierra corrected, sending him a torrid glance that ignited the spark still burning hotly within him.

"How do you know? You were a virgin. You've no one to compare me with."

"I just know. Are you sorry?"

"That you were a virgin?" He laughed harshly. "I should feel guilty, but in truth I feel exhilarated and alive in a way I've never been before. And dammit, I'm proud to be the first. I resisted as long as I could, but—no, I'm not sorry. Are you?"

Her chin came up sharply and she stared at him, her gray eyes glowing like polished silver in the moonlight. "No. No matter what happens between us, I'm not sorry for this night."

"What will you tell Gordon on your wedding night when he learns you're not a virgin?"

"I'll think of something." As if she could ever marry Gordon Lynch—or any other man who wasn't Ramsey Hunter.

"I'm sure you will," Ram commented dryly.

She looked so tempting lying naked in his arms, felt so damn good, that the urge to kiss her burned hotly within him. His lips touched her, and without hesitation Sierra returned the kiss, opening her mouth to the gentle nudging of his tongue. When she felt his manhood growing thick and heavy against her hip, her eyes widened in surprise. Aware of her thoughts,

Ram broke off the kiss and grinned down at her.

"Can you feel how much I want you again?" His breath tasted sweet against her lips.

"Again? Is . . . is it possible?"

He brought her hand to the throbbing length of his staff. "What do you think?"

She touched him lightly with her fingertips, surprised at the burning heat and silky slickness of his skin. She felt him shudder, heard his groan. He filled her hand and she squeezed him gently, wrapping her hand tightly around him. She stroked his thick length to the root and when he made a gasping sound, she released him abruptly.

"Did I hurt you?"

He gave a shaky laugh. "No. You have no idea how good that felt."

Suddenly he swept her beneath him, lowered his head, and licked her breast. His tongue traced its shape, following the fullness from the upper curves to the turgid peak, sucking it into his mouth. Fire exploded inside her, producing a piercing heat low in her womb. His fiery breath bathed her, and his body felt taut and slick beneath her roaming hands. A surprised little scream left her lips when he palmed her mound. With the pad of his fingertip he caressed the lips of her sex, pressing upward, stroking the delicately sensitive spot within her womanly folds. Her breath stopped; her head thrashed from side to side. Arching upward, she undulated her hips, pumping them against his relentlessly stroking finger.

She moaned in pleasure when he eased into her, stretching her, filling her, making her complete again. She pulsated around him, taking him deep, feeling no pain, only delicious waves of fierce splendor, gripping him so tightly that the breath left him on a low, keening moan. He drove into her again and again, lifting her buttocks as he thrust deeply, stroking her clutching tightness until he was plunging with unrestrained vigor.

A powerful climax was building within him; he felt it coming, knew it would be more shattering than any he'd ever experienced before. Like a bursting dam, it started with a tiny trickle of sensation and built until his ears were roaring. Then he burst into so many jagged pieces that he knew he'd never be the same again. Sierra had turned his world upside down; her soft woman's body had utterly destroyed his ability to think coherently. He gave a hoarse shout, a final thrust, and climaxed violently.

Lost in a maze of shooting stars and exploding fireworks, Sierra felt her world disintegrating as ecstasy spiraled through her, in her, around her. She arched, cried out, and reached for the stars.

When Sierra's world stopped spinning and she opened her eyes, she saw Ram braced above her, watching her face as she found pleasure. His expression was oddly tender. "Is it always like this?" she asked breathlessly.

Ram gave her a rare smile and pulled himself out of the slick lips of her sex. Still shuddering, he stretched out beside her.

"I'd be lying if I said it was," he said at length. "What we just experienced is rare."

"Why?"

"Damned if I know. And I'm not sure I want to know."

Sierra remained thoughtful, trying to make sense out of the way she had responded to Ram. She couldn't imagine making love with Gordon, let alone responding in the same exuberant fashion.

"Let's just say we are two sexual animals releasing our passions in a natural and exciting way," Ram commented dryly, attempting to diffuse a potentially emotional situation. It wouldn't do for Sierra to become attached to him when he had no idea what the future held for him. "I wouldn't put too much importance on what we just did. This has been building between us for a long time. For what it's worth, you're damn good for a beginner. I hope Lynch appreciates you."

Sierra went still. If Ram was fishing for a way to hurt her, he had succeeded. Did he fear she'd demand marriage after he'd warned her to expect nothing from him? Her temper flared. "Don't ruin it, Ram. I expected nothing from you and asked for nothing. You made that perfectly clear before—before we . . ."

She flushed and looked away, suddenly embarrassed by her nudity. She pulled the blanket up to her neck, somehow feeling less vulnerable to Ram's potent magnetism.

Ram groaned inwardly. Damn, he was the worst kind of bastard. He wasn't being intentionally cruel, merely truthful about their future, or lack of one.

"I'm sorry, Sierra. I never meant for this to happen. I knew you were trouble the moment I met you."

"I'd say it was the other way around," Sierra said softly. "It's too late now, isn't it, Ram?"

"No, it's not too late. We can start by forgetting this happened. It would probably be best if we didn't see one another again."

Sierra sat up abruptly, forgetting the blanket as it dropped into her lap, baring her breasts. "You're sending me back to Salt Lake City?"

Ram sighed in resignation. "No, I can't do that. It isn't safe for you to return alone, and I can't spare the time to take you. Unfortunately, I'm stuck with you until we reach Denver."

Ram's eyes turned smoky as they focused on the alabaster sheen of her breasts. He swallowed visibly, unable to tear his eyes away. Suddenly aware of the direction of his gaze, Sierra flushed and yanked the blanket up to her chin.

"You won't be sorry, Ram."

"I already am. Get some sleep, Sierra. I want to get an early start tomorrow."

Sierra settled down on the blanket, wondering how she was expected to sleep with Ram lying next to her. She couldn't. "Ram."

"What?"

"Why are you in such an all-fired hurry to get to Denver? You're awfully mysterious."

"You wouldn't be interested." What good would it do to tell Sierra about his problems when it would change nothing?

"I know you think I'm spoiled and frivolous, but I can be a good listener. Why won't you tell me? Is it because you don't trust me?"

"Trust a woman?" Ram laughed harshly. "Not damn likely. I know of no woman and precious few men I'd trust. Go to sleep."

She closed her eyes, mulling over Ram's startling words. She felt intense curiosity about the woman who had earned his distrust and influenced his perception of females in general. She thought he must have loved her a great deal and wondered if he still cared for her.

"Who is the woman and what did she do to you, Ram?"

A string of curses ripped past Ram's lips. "Why can't you leave well enough alone? I have nothing personal against you."

"What about the woman you left in charge of the Lucky Lady? She's your mistress, isn't she? You trust her."

"Lola? Lola is different. She's as honest as the day is long. I'd trust her with my life."

Sierra sniffed. "She's a female. Is it because she's your mis—"

"Dammit, Sierra, leave Lola out of this. Just go to sleep and leave me alone."

"I'm cold."

"Put on your clothes."

"We left them down by the stream."

She heard a rustling sound, then felt a comforting warmth as he scooted close to her and fitted her into the curve of his body.

"Is that better?"

She sighed contentedly. "Much better."

"Now will you go to sleep? And try not to squirm too much." He didn't think he could stand it if she rubbed that delectable little rump against him during the night.

"Good night, Ram. I don't know who the woman was who hurt you, but I can help you forget her if you'd let me."

"Not damn likely," he muttered grumpily.

The bright promise of dawn was just a breath away. The night stars had faded from the sky, and the eastern rim of the earth took on a faint glow. Sierra awoke abruptly, disturbed by Ram's restlessness. He was thrashing wildly and talking in his sleep, his words garbled and disjointed.

"Dora! For God's sake, don't do this to me! Jason, you're my best friend! What have I done to deserve this?"

His thrashing grew more violent, and Sierra flung herself atop him, afraid that he'd hurt himself.

"The bars! God almighty, I can't bear it!"

"Ram! Wake up. You're dreaming."

Ram awoke with a start, confused and feeling the same kind of suffocating fear he had experienced when he'd been shut away from the outside world.

"Sierra, what's wrong?"

"You were having a nightmare. It must have been frightening; you were thrashing around and talking in your sleep." She paused, then blurted out, "Who is Dora?"

Ram went still. "No one important. Forget it."

He felt the points of her breasts digging warmly against the sensitive skin of his chest, felt the curl of heat between his thighs as their groins meshed, and the horror of his dream fell away like ashes before the wind.

"If you're using that as an excuse for me to make love to you again," he said, abruptly changing the subject, "I'll happily oblige." He pushed his hips against hers in a most provocative manner. He was already hard and throbbing.

Sierra arched away from him. "I didn't mean . . ."

"Nor did I." He cocked an eye on the glowing sky. "Besides, we've no time." If he made love to Sierra again, he might never want to stop. She was heaven and hell, and loving her was a luxury he couldn't afford.

Sierra was somewhat subdued when they returned to the trail an hour later. She felt the enormity of what she had done with Ram in every bone in her body and in the dull aching between her thighs. It hurt to think that something so wonderful and fulfilling meant nothing to Ram. How could he have loved her so passionately, then cast her away? He had warned her how it would be, but she hadn't believed him. She knew now that the reason he would not marry her was because there was another woman in his life, and that hurt even worse.

Ram loved a woman named Dora.

Who was Dora and what did she do to Ram? Was she the woman who'd destroyed his faith in all females? If he'd allow it, she'd undo the damage that heartless woman had done. No matter what Ramsey Hunter said, she'd not forget him—oh, no, not damned likely. For a long time she had been confused about her feelings for him, but no longer. Never had anything been so explicitly defined, so abundantly clear.

She loved Ramsey Hunter. She had fallen hard, straight into the arms of paradise.

He was insensitive, impossibly, maddeningly arrogant, and she loved him.

Chapter Nine

Bouncing over the rough trail affected Sierra in ways that were far from pleasant. Unaccustomed to riding for long periods of time, she suffered chafing that left the insides of her legs raw and exquisitely tender. Her back ached, and the throbbing pain between her thighs grew steadily worse by the minute. Riding wasn't the only sport she was unaccustomed to. She hadn't considered the consequences when she and Ram made love twice during the night, and she was suffering for it now. Her shoulders slumped beneath the weight of her exhaustion, and it angered her that Ram appeared insensitive to her discomfort.

If Sierra hadn't been so stubborn, she would have complained long ago, but she couldn't bear being called a pampered princess one more time. Ram had driven them both relentlessly over steep mountain roads, which at times curved so precariously that she feared her horse would fall off the edge. Not for the first time she wondered about Ram's haste to reach Denver. She assumed it was because of that woman whose name he had called out in his sleep. Dora must be someone special, Sierra reflected, to lure Ram halfway across the country.

Ram's thoughts would have stunned Sierra. He relived in his mind every intimate detail of their tumultuous joining the previous night and cursed himself a thousand times over for not stopping it before it got out of hand. The possibility was remote, but the chance existed that his seed had found fertile ground. What if Sierra became pregnant? Since marriage at the present time was not feasible, he hoped the situation would not arise. And the only way to ensure that pregnancy did not occur was to make damn certain he was not tempted to repeat the act.

Ram hardly noticed the spectacular panorama of mountains rising tall and majestic around them, of fertile valleys and wooded slopes. The beauty of nature seemed unimportant compared to his enormous guilt. He had taken advantage of Sierra's innocence and stolen her virginity against his better judgment. But dear Lord, he hadn't been able to help himself. It had been building inside him for so long that making love to Sierra had seemed both natural and desirable. Not to mention one of the most enjoyable experiences of his life.

Now he was plagued by guilt and miserable over what he had done to Sierra. For more years than he cared to count, he had guarded his heart. It had once been ripped from his flesh by a woman, and he had sealed it against human emotions the day those metal doors slammed behind him. Since that time he'd used women for the purpose God intended them, discarding them when they grew tiresome.

But he hadn't always been such a callous bastard. Once he'd been a warm, considerate and loving human being. He'd been contented with life and looked forward to a loving relationship blessed with several children. Then his world had collapsed. For two wretched years he'd suffered anguish, pain, deprivation and back-breaking labor. He'd learned to survive; he had to learn, or perish. Plotting a fitting revenge was all that had kept him sane. When his ordeal ended as suddenly as it had begun, the life he'd once lived no longer appealed to him. He'd matured, hardened, adopted a different set of values, and existed solely for the day he'd have his revenge. He had devoted the following years to that purpose, and at long last his diligence was going to be rewarded.

Dora and Jason had led him a merry chase, flitting from place to place one step ahead of him and the law. By the time he'd learned where they were, they'd taken themselves off to another location, forcing him to start all over again. Fortunately, he'd been successful in one endeavor. During his travels, he'd gone partners with a down-and-out prospector from Virginia City who'd sworn he was within weeks of striking it rich. It wasn't weeks, but eventually they did hit paydirt. After two years of toiling from dawn to dusk, they'd struck silver. The vein was so rich that it had made them both wealthy.

With money to burn, Ram had hired a detective to trace Dora and Jason. The Pinkerton man had finally traced them to San Francisco. Rich enough now to retire for life if he chose, Ram sold out his share of the mine and went to San Francisco. Unfortunately, Dora and Jason had already skipped town. Once again they had eluded him without a clue as to where they had gone.

Ram had liked what he saw in San Francisco. The town was raw but had potential. Since he hadn't a clue where to search next, he bought the Lucky Lady and began investing heavily in real estate. Then he'd received word that the two he sought were now in Denver, and he had dropped everything to give chase. Maybe this time would be different. If luck was with him, he'd arrive before they'd flown the coop.

Cocking an eye on the sun as it dipped behind a wooded peak, Ram reined in beside a mountain stream and waited for Sierra to catch up. It was time to find a campsite, and he decided to take advantage of the stream flowing through a lush valley.

Pain shimmered around Sierra in increasing waves. Pure guts had kept her in the saddle.

Raw determination had kept her conscious. When she saw Ram rein in ahead, relief shuddered through her.

"We'll camp here for the night," Ram said when Sierra reined in beside him. "Gather wood for a fire while I hunt for small game. I've got a hankering for roast rabbit tonight." He dismounted and was unsaddling his horse when he heard a shuffle and thump behind him. He paid it little heed, assuming that Sierra had dismounted clumsily. She was as unsuited to the wilderness as a fish was to living out of water. "Why don't you try your hand again at starting a fire?"

Sierra suppressed a groan, eased her leg from her horse, and slid to the ground. She hit with a thump, and pain exploded inside her. Her eyes rolled back in her head, and the ground came up to meet her.

Unaware of Sierra's distress, Ram started to walk away, then stopped abruptly, alerted by his finely honed instincts. Something was wrong. He whirled on his heel, crying out in dismay when he saw Sierra lying in a heap beside her horse.

"Sierra!"

Sierra was beyond hearing. She had lost her tenuous grip on consciousness the moment her feet touched the ground.

Dropping to his knees beside her, Ram lifted her in his arms and carried her to the stream. Dipping a hand in the cool water, he dribbled droplets into her face. Sierra moaned and opened her eyes.

"What happened?"

"You tell me. I found you lying on the ground. Are you ill?"

Sierra bit her lip and shook her head. How could he not know the source of her pain?

"If you're not sick, what in the hell is wrong with you?"

Sierra's temper exploded. "I hurt, damn you! Have you no clue as to why I'm in pain? I'm not accustomed to riding long hours, and last night . . ." She was too embarrassed to continue.

A glimmer of comprehension brought a frown to his face. "You hurt?" He searched her face, then slid his gaze down her body. "Where? If you had mentioned it earlier, I might have been able to help."

Sierra sent him a quelling look. "How can you help? Obviously you have no idea why or where I hurt."

Ram went still. "Why don't you tell me?"

She flushed and looked away. "You're a big man, Ramsey Hunter, and I . . . I'm not accustomed to . . . to . . ."

Her words confirmed Ram's suspicion, and with it came a generous helping of guilt. "You mean that I . . . That what we did . . . Oh, God, Sierra, I'm sorry. I didn't think. I've only had one other virgin, and the circumstances were different. Since then I've made a point to steer clear of innocent women. Why didn't you say something? We could have stopped earlier."

Dimly Sierra wondered if the virgin Ram referred to was Dora. "I didn't want you stopping on my account. You called me a spoiled child one time too often, and I didn't want to enhance your misconception of me."

"Dammit, Sierra, this is different. You're hurt, and it's my fault. Take off your clothes."

Sierra paled. "What are you going to do?"

"I'm not going to hurt you again, if that's what you're worried about. Just do as I say. I'm trying to help you."

"Are you sure this is necessary?"

His face hardened. "Positive. If you won't undress, I'll do it for you."

Turning away, Sierra slowly removed her blouse and split skirt. Then she looked at Ram hopefully. But her hopes were dashed when he said, "Everything." A tremulous sigh slipped past her lips as she slipped off her shift and drawers. Ram took over then, removing her boots and stockings. When she looked up at him, she was shocked to see that he had removed his own clothing while she was taking off hers.

Before she could protest, he scooped her into his arms and carried her into the cold stream. Sierra shivered, but was pleasantly surprised to find the water soothing against her saddle-bruised flesh.

"Does that feel better?" Ram asked as he knelt and settled her on the shallow bottom. "Lie back and let the cold water soothe your injured flesh." Ram sat behind her, supporting her head as she leaned back against him. A trembling sigh slipped past her lips.

"Little fool," Ram said in a tone so filled with tenderness that it flowed over her like a warm blanket. "You're as stubborn as a mule. I would have understood."

"I knew you were in a hurry to reach Denver and didn't want to slow you. I promised I'd be no trouble and I meant it."

He leaned down and brushed her lips with his. It was no more than a feather-light touch, but Sierra felt the searing heat of his lips clear down to her toes. She lifted her face for more, but Ram quickly turned away. He hadn't meant to kiss her, but he purely couldn't help himself. Furthermore, he knew he had to stop now before it went too far. He'd gladly suffer the fires of hell before he'd hurt her again.

"Sit here in the water as long as you like, Sierra," Ram said as he surged to his feet. "We both need something substantial for supper, and my sitting here with you won't catch us a rabbit. I shouldn't be long."

Sierra watched him walk away, mesmerized by the masculine splendor of his taut body as he plowed through the shallow water. She admired the muscular precision of his tight buttocks and strong legs, the way he moved with easy grace, the utter magnificent length of him. She watched until he'd donned his clothes and disappeared into the woods with his rifle.

When Ram returned a short time later with

two fat rabbits, Sierra was dressed and struggling with the fire. She had managed to ignite a rather sickly blaze and was feeding it sticks when Ram dropped the skinned and cleaned rabbits at her feet.

"I'll see to the fire," he said. "Do you feel better?" Sierra nodded. "Good. Perhaps you can spit the rabbits on sticks while I build up the fire."

"Ram."

"Yeah." His eyes refused to meet hers. Holding her naked body in his arms had been highly arousing. The image of her nude splendor shimmering beneath the water had tantalized him beyond endurance. If he hadn't left when he did, he wouldn't have been able to control his actions.

"Thank you."

Ram cleared his throat. "We'll take it easier tomorrow."

The next day Sierra felt only slight discomfort. She was finally growing accustomed to the bouncing gait of her mount and the rough trail. Ram made things easier by not pushing them so hard. And he was scrupulous about not touching her again. He didn't deliberately ignore her; rather he made sure he found other things to occupy his mind and hands when they stopped to rest during the day and at night when they made camp. Sierra felt certain he regretted making love with her, and it hurt. Since she hadn't pressed for a marriage proposal, she failed to understand his cool regard. She was astute enough to know he wanted her nearly as much as she wanted him.

Each night when they made camp, Ram spread his bedroll on the opposite side of the campfire. After a gruff good night, he usually turned his back on her and promptly fell asleep. Had Sierra known how dearly his pretense cost him, she would have been astounded.

They had been on the trail over a week when they encountered their first fellow travelers—a man and his family traveling by wagon to Salt Lake City to settle among the Mormon population.

"How much farther to Denver?" Ram asked the man, whose name was Jacob Roper.

"Not far," Jacob replied. "Three, four days on horseback. You come from Salt Lake?"

"We left over a week ago," Ram revealed.

"See any Indians?" Jacob asked in a low voice. He didn't want to frighten his family, but Indian activity had been reported in the area and it worried him.

"You're the first humans we've seen," Ram returned.

Jacob, seeing that his wife was deep in conversation with Sierra, leaned close to Ram and said, "The army agreed to abandon the Boseman. Red Cloud rode in triumph through Fort Phil Kearny and burned it to the ground. I heard tell hostile Indians are camped all around Denver, despite the treaty Red Cloud and some of the important chiefs signed at Fort Laramie."

"I don't think you'll encounter any problems from here to Salt Lake," Ram replied confidently. "Nothing I've seen so far indicates the presence of hostile Indians in the area."

"I wish I could give you the same assurance," Jacob said. "A couple of days ago, we saw a war party riding in the distance, but fortunately they didn't see us. Take care, friend. I wouldn't want to be taken by Indians now, not in the mood they're in."

"Much obliged," Ram replied. He didn't relish tangling with hostile Indians, not with Sierra riding with him.

The Ropers continued on, and during the following days Ram remained vigilant. They were one day out of Denver when Ram finally allowed himself to breathe easily again. He felt confident that hostile Indians would not strike this close to the city. They were traveling through a grassy valley between two towering mountains when Ram's theory was shot all to hell.

"Don't panic, Sierra," he rasped harshly as she drew abreast of him, "but there are Indians on the ridge behind us."

Sierra's head swiveled around to peer over her shoulder. Sure enough, a dozen or more painted Indians were spread out over the ridge, watching them. The hair rose on the back of her neck, and her heart pumped wildly. Some of the warriors carried rifles, while others were armed with bows and arrows, but all were heavily armed. Their bodies and faces were slashed with stripes of vivid red, yellow, and black paint. Even their ponies wore war paint. Sierra had heard about the warlike plains Indians but never thought she'd actually see them. The sight sent fear coursing through her.

"What can we do?" Her heart was pounding so loudly that it sounded like thunder in her ears.

"Nothing," Ram said tightly. "We do nothing. Just keep riding as if nothing is wrong."

"Are they going to kill us?" She sounded so frightened that Ram yearned to reach out and reassure her, but he resisted the urge, fearing his gesture would appear cowardly to the Indians.

"Not unless we let them," he said, trying to sound confident and failing utterly. They were in trouble. Deep trouble, and they both knew it. "Try not to look back at them, and maybe they'll let us go."

They heard rather than saw the Indians ride down the slope in hot pursuit. Sierra knew the exact moment they decided to give chase. Bloodcurdling cries echoed through the valley, followed by the thunder of pounding hooves.

"They're coming!" Sierra cried, panic-stricken.

"Ride, Sierra! Ride like hell. Don't look back. No matter what happens, keep riding."

Her heart nearly stopped when she realized that Ram intended to sacrifice himself for her. He couldn't possibly hold off an entire war party by himself, and he knew it. She'd always been stubborn and headstrong and saw no reason to change now. She reined her horse to a skidding halt, turned, and rode back to where Ram waited for the first wave of Indians to arrive.

Ram wondered just how long he could hold off the Indians before they killed him. Long enough to allow Sierra to escape, he hoped fervently. He nearly screamed in frustration when he saw Sierra riding hell-for-leather toward him instead of away as he'd ordered.

"No, dammit, no! Go, Sierra! Get the hell out of here!"

Reining in beside Ram, Sierra squared her pointed little chin and said, "I can't let you sacrifice yourself for me. If we go down, we go down together." Deftly she removed her rifle from the saddle boot. "Show me how to shoot this damn thing."

The air turned blue with Ram's violent curses, his glowering expression effectively conveying his anger, his utter dismay. Did the woman have no sense at all? He'd been willing to sacrifice his life for her so she might escape. For the first time in years, his motives were pure and unselfish. But when she'd returned to fight at his side, his sacrifice was no longer necessary, or even desirable. Now he was faced with a different situation entirely and forced to make a decision that could mean the difference between life and death.

"Throw down your gun!"

Confused, Sierra stared at him. "What?"

189

"You heard me. Throw down your gun."

When she shook her head, refusing to obey, Ram grabbed the rifle from her hands and tossed it to the ground. His followed close behind. Then he grasped the reins from her hands and waited for the Indians. They arrived within minutes, surrounding them, taunting them, waving their weapons in the air and shouting words Sierra did not understand.

"Why did you do it?" Sierra's question hit him like a shot to the gut. He prayed to God he had done the right thing.

"If we fought them, we'd have no chance at all. At least we're still alive."

"But for how long?" Sierra cried as the Indians closed ranks around them.

"Long enough to plan our escape," Ram said. "I couldn't bear to see you slain before my eyes. Why didn't you listen to me? You could have escaped."

Then it was too late for words as one of the Indians struck Ram with the butt of his rifle, sending him crashing to the ground. Obviously amused, the other Indians howled with laughter.

"Ram!" Sliding from her mount, Sierra dropped to her knees beside him.

"I'm all right, Sierra," he said groggily. But Sierra could see he wasn't all right. His eyes were glazed, and blood seeped from a cut on his head.

Sierra tried to assist him to his feet, but one of the warriors grasped her roughly and pulled her away, raising his arm in a threatening manner.

"Don't anger them, Sierra," Ram warned in a voice slurred with pain. "Don't give the bastards an excuse to hurt you."

The Indian who had struck Ram grated out a harsh command and prodded him to his feet. When Sierra reached out to help him, the warrior tossed her on the back of his pony and leaped up behind her. His brown arms closed like steel bands around her. Frantically, she looked back at Ram and saw that his hands were being tied before him and fastened to a long rawhide rope. The Indian held on to the rope as he mounted his pony. When they rode off a few minutes later, Ram was forced to stumble along behind the horse.

Stinging tears made dirty tracks down Sierra's cheeks. She couldn't bear to see Ram being treated like an animal. Blood from the Indian's blow blurred his vision, and he was forced to run to keep from being dragged in the dirt. He wasn't always able to stay on his feet, and the results were terrifying.

"Stop! You're killing him!" Sierra cried, ramming her elbows into her captor's ribs. She earned a clout alongside her head for her efforts. Thirst nagged at her, and she knew Ram must be suffering even more than she. If not for his extraordinary strength, she knew he'd not survive the excruciating pace set for him.

Pain lanced Ram's sides as he fought to stay conscious. He knew without being told that once he faltered, he'd be disposed of without a moment's hesitation. He had to stay alive for Sierra's sake. Together they had a slim chance for survival.

Concentrating on placing one step before the other, Ram managed to keep up the grueling pace. His body became insensitive to pain, his brain immune to everything except the need to survive. He barely noticed when it grew dark and the moon came out. He wasn't even aware that the night approached its darkest hours, or that his ordeal had ended when they arrived at a slumbering Indian village. Several minutes elapsed before Ram's brain registered the fact that they had reached an Indian stronghold hidden deep in the mountains. Only then did his rubbery legs collapse beneath him as he slid effortlessly into oblivion.

Sierra tried to go to Ram's aid, but her captor would not allow it. Panic-stricken, she watched as Ram was dragged over the rough ground and tied to a stake in the center of the encampment. Then it was her turn. Fighting all the way, she was hauled forcibly from the horse and bound securely beside Ram. Then the Indians melted away into various tipis scattered around the clearing. They were alone.

"Ram! Can you hear me? Oh, Ram, please answer me."

Somewhere in the dim recesses of his mind, Ram heard Sierra calling his name. He tried to answer, but his mouth was so dry that his tongue felt like a swollen lump of flesh.

"Ram, please. Are you all right?"

Swallowing thickly, Ram tried to find enough moisture in his mouth to answer Sierra. He succeeded with great difficulty.

"Wh-where are we?"

"They've brought us to their camp. I think they've gone to their beds. It's very late."

He strained to see her face, but in the darkness all he could make out was a pale oval. "Have they . . . Did they hurt you?"

"No. One of the Indians struck me, but not hard. It's you I'm worried about."

"I'd feel a helluva lot better if I had a drink of water. Try to get some sleep, little love. I don't know what's going to happen tomorrow, but we'll face it better if we're alert."

Sierra gave him a sad little smile. "I'll try, Ram." She sighed raggedly. If not for his comforting strength beside her, she'd not be able to face the dawn. But with Ram, anything was possible. Even surviving this wretched situation.

*   *   *

Sierra opened her eyes, and a scream built up inside her. She saw the grinning face of a child leaning so close she could feel his breath fanning her cheek. The child drew back, his face dark with anger. He said something she didn't understand and kicked her in the ribs with a moccasin-clad foot. Suddenly they were surrounded by children, some brandishing sticks, which they wielded against her and Ram with great enthusiasm. Soon they were joined by women, who were even more bloodthirsty than the children. Shielding her head and face, she bore their blows stoically. Ram was shielding her as best he could with his own body, but unfortunately it wasn't good enough. They both suffered numerous bruises over much of their bodies.

After a while the women and children lost interest and wandered away. When the Indian brave who had taken her up on his horse approached, Sierra called out to him. "Water, please. We're thirsty."

"Forget it, Sierra, he doesn't speak English."

"He understood, I know he did," Sierra insisted as she watched him walk away. He returned a few minutes later with a water pouch, which he set carefully in front of her.

Sierra strained toward it. When she realized that he wasn't going to untie her, she let loose a few unladylike curses. Why was he torturing them like this? Intuition told her it was only the beginning of their ordeal.

"It's no use, little love, he's taunting us. It amuses him to see us grovel."

Suddenly a young woman approached, said something harsh to the warrior, and crouched beside Ram. She picked up the pouch and held it to his lips. He drank greedily until he could hold no more. When the woman made to leave, he strained against his bonds and shouted, "Wait! Don't go! Let my woman drink." Ignoring his plea, she walked away.

"Oh, God," Ram sobbed. "I'm sorry, Sierra. I had no idea."

194

"It's all right, Ram," she said, licking her dry lips. "You were thirstier than I was, anyway."

The rest of the day passed in a blur. For the most part they were ignored, but she could tell the Indians were gearing up for some kind of celebration. A celebration in which they were to be the guests. She knew instinctively that she wasn't going to like what followed.

To Sierra's surprise and gratitude, they were untied, given something to eat and drink, taken into the woods to relieve themselves, then promptly retied to the post. From time to time, the warrior who had taken her up on his horse came by to stare at her. His dark, piercing eyes spoke eloquently of his desire, and Sierra dreaded the approaching night. She knew what he intended, and there wasn't a damn thing she could do about it.

The celebration started promptly at dusk. There was feasting and dancing and drinking. The later it got, the wilder the dancing became.

"Sierra."

She turned to stare at Ram. The raw pain in his eyes brought a shimmer of tears to hers. He knew as well as she what was in store for her . . . for them. "Yes."

"Whatever happens tonight, I want you to know that had it been possible, I would have married you. I—I care about you. I never mentioned it before, but there is a slim chance you could already be carrying my child."

Sierra's eyes widened to the size of silver dollars. "I never thought about that. I don't think it really matters anymore, since neither of us is likely to survive this night. Unless . . ." A sudden thought came to her.

"Unless what?"

"Nothing. It was a wild idea, anyway." She resisted telling him what was in her mind. Giving him false hopes would be cruel.

Suddenly the same warrior who had plagued her throughout the day detached himself from the circle of dancers and weaved his way toward them. Sierra could tell he was drunk by the way he staggered. She cried out in alarm when he whipped a knife from the band of his breechclout, brandishing it before her face. When he slid the blade beneath her bonds and cut through the ropes, she knew a terrible fear. Her time had come. When the fierce brave dragged her over the rough ground toward a nearby tipi, she realized that he intended to rape her.

Fear and frustration brought a sob to Ram's lips. He strained against his bonds, desperate to help Sierra. "Damn you! Don't you dare hurt her!" It nearly killed him when he realized what the filthy savage intended to do to Sierra.

Dragging Sierra into the tipi, the warrior threw her down on a bed of soft furs and stood over her, leering. She could smell the stale odor of liquor on his breath, mingled with the fetid stench of his arousal. When the warrior whipped off his breechclout, stark fear raced through her. Common sense told her that if she didn't do something quickly, she'd be brutally raped.

"I know you can understand English," she said, raising her chin in false bravado. "Do you know Wind Rider?" An arrested look came over his features. "I am Wind Rider's sister. If you harm me, he will kill you." Sierra knew it was a long shot, but grasping at straws was all she had now.

His eyes blazed fiercely, and he drew back his hand as if to strike her. She screamed and closed her eyes. When she opened them; he had lowered his fist and was staring at her with a mixture of fear and disbelief.

"Wind Rider." He spat the name harshly. Then he turned and ran from the tipi as if the devil was nipping at his heels.

Chapter Ten

Ram strained against his bonds, cursing violently and calling the heathen savages every vile name he could think of. Never in his entire life had he felt so helpless, so utterly useless, not even when he'd been locked away from society. He'd reacted like a wild man to Sierra's terrified scream, but it had gained him nothing. His futile efforts to rip apart his bindings earned him unbearable anguish and torn flesh.

When Ram saw the Indian burst from the tipi, fastening his breechclout around his narrow hips, he cried out in wretched agony. He would have given his life to spare Sierra this. He watched in trepidation as the warrior charged into a circle of men and began talking and gesturing wildly, pointing toward the tipi where he had left Sierra. A few minutes later, an older warrior whose proud bearing and authoritative demeanor proclaimed him chief, detached himself from the group and strode briskly toward the tipi.

"Oh God, no," Ram moaned, closing his eyes against the pain. Did the savages intend passing her from warrior to warrior? It would have been far better for him to have killed her than to see her suffer this kind of torture.

Sierra knelt weakly on the sleeping mat, trembling as if from fever. She hadn't expected the Indian to run from the tipi when she'd mentioned Wind Rider but thanked God that she'd had the presence of mind to use her brother's name, if indeed Wind Rider was her brother as she suspected. It had been a long shot, but at the time nothing else came to mind. The Indian's surprising reaction gave her fleeting hope that her desperate ploy had worked. What next? she wondered. Desperation had forced her to search for improbable solutions. It was a miracle that this obscure tribe of Indians knew or had heard of Wind Rider.

Suddenly an Indian burst through the tent opening. He looked more fierce even than the first Indian. He stared at Sierra for so long that she felt as if each moment were an eternity. After an interminable length of time, he walked slowly toward her. Abruptly he reached down and hauled her roughly to her feet.

"Who are you?" he asked in halting English. His hawklike features were frightening, his eyes challenging as he glared at her fiercely.

Sierra swallowed thickly. "I—I am Sierra, sister to Wind Rider. Do you know him?"

The Indian grunted noncommittally. "Tears Like Rain is sister to Wind Rider. I, Strong Hand, have looked upon her face when I was in White Feather's camp, and you are not Tears Like Rain."

"N-no, I am their younger sister. I was not raised by Indians as they were. I have come a long way to find Wind Rider and Tears Like Rain."

Strong Hand's eyes narrowed suspiciously. "You are lying."

"No! I swear it. I am Wind Rider's sister. We were separated as children."

Strong Hand merely grunted as he dragged Sierra from the tipi and shoved her toward the campfire. Ram had been nearly out of his mind with fear for Sierra, and when he saw her emerge from the tipi virtually unscathed, he sobbed in relief.

"Sierra!"

"Don't worry," she mouthed before she was swept past. She had no idea if mentioning Wind Rider had helped their cause, but it surely couldn't make their plight any more desperate than it already was.

Strong Hand pushed Sierra toward the huge campfire burning brightly at the center of the camp. Curious yet wary, the other Indians closed ranks around them. Strong Hand said something in his own language, something that must have startled his people, for they stared at

Sierra intently, speculating among themselves about the veracity of Sierra's astounding claim.

Roughly, Strong Hand grasped Sierra's chin, turning her face to capture the glow of the fire. Staring raptly into her eyes, he gave a shout and invited the others to look also. They crowded close, gazing into Sierra's eyes and murmuring together excitedly.

"What is it?" Sierra cried, startled by their reaction.

"Perhaps there is truth in your words," Strong Hand admitted grudgingly. "Your eyes shine like the silver coins so treasured by white men. Wind Rider has eyes such as yours. We will wait for Wind Rider. He will know if you are his sister. If you are not, Firewalker will claim you for his woman."

"How do you know Wind Rider will come?" Sierra asked anxiously.

"He will come," Strong Hand said with such conviction that Sierra was inclined to believe him. "A messenger will leave at dawn. It may take time to find him, but he will come."

"What is going to happen to us?"

"You will not be harmed."

Frowning fiercely, Firewalker gave a shout of protest and stepped forward. He gestured toward Sierra, then pointed at himself, obviously displeased with Strong Hand's decision and arguing loudly in his own behalf. When a woman stepped forward to join in the fray, Sierra stared in confusion. After a few minutes, Firewalker turned and stalked away, but the woman kept haranguing Strong Hand until he made a decision that appeared to please her. With a start, Sierra realized that she had seen the woman before, that she was the same woman who had offered water to Ram while callously refusing to quench Sierra's thirst.

"Go with Prairie Flower," Strong Hand said, giving Sierra a little push. "Firewalker is giving up his lodge for you."

"Wait! What about my—my man?"

Strong Hand glanced over his shoulder to where Ram was straining futilely against his bonds. "I have given Yellow Hair to my sister. Prairie Flower recently lost her man in battle with white eyes and yearns for a child. She thinks your man will make strong sons."

Stunned, Sierra swiveled her head to stare at Prairie Flower, taken aback by the contempt visible in the woman's eyes. Prairie Flower was somewhat older than she but attractive nonetheless, with slanting brown eyes, shiny black hair that hung thick and straight to her waist, and lips that could only be described as lush. Beneath her buckskin tunic, her body was lithe and muscular, with bountiful curves in all the right places.

Prairie Flower returned Sierra's stare, her expression smug as she motioned for Sierra to follow her. Sierra shook her head, turning pleading eyes on Strong Hand. "Ram is my man. You have no right to give him to another."

Strong Hand's face could have been carved in stone. "You talk brave for a woman, sister of

Wind Rider. I will call you Talks Brave." Then he spun on his heel and walked away. Sierra started to follow but was stopped dead in her tracks when Prairie Flower grasped her arm in a surprisingly strong grip.

"Strong Hand has spoken, Talks Brave," Prairie Flower said. "He is chieftain of our tribe, and unless the People dispute his word, it will be as he says. Yellow Hair is mine. Wind Rider might claim you as kin, but he cannot claim your man. It is our right to do with him as we please. If not for me, he would be slain. He is a strong man. He will give me fine sons."

"You speak English."

Prairie Flower sent her a contemptuous look. "The Arapaho have no difficulty with the white man's tongue. Come, it grows late. The feasting is over. I will take you to your lodge."

With marked reluctance, Sierra followed the Indian woman. When they reached Ram, she tried to stop, but Prairie Flower's grip was relentless.

"Do not try to leave the lodge," Prairie Flower warned as she shoved Sierra inside the tipi. "Firewalker wants you. He needs little excuse to take you to his mat. Perhaps Wind Rider will give you to him when he arrives." After that parting shot, she left Sierra to her morbid thoughts.

Ram was completely and utterly confused. He had no idea what had transpired between Sierra and the chieftain, and if someone didn't tell him soon he'd either explode or go insane.

He stared fixedly at the tipi into which Sierra had disappeared, wondering what to expect next. He didn't have long to wait. The woman who had given him water earlier, the same woman who accompanied Sierra just now, approached him. She knelt before him and drew a knife from one of her knee-length moccasins. Ram flinched, then relaxed visibly when she cut through his bonds.

"Come." She motioned him to follow and waited impatiently as he rubbed circulation back into his raw wrists. When he tried to rise, pain exploded in his head. Clucking her tongue, Prairie Flower was beside him instantly, helping him to his feet. To his utter embarrassment, he was forced to lean on her for support.

"Where are you taking me?" he asked, gazing with mute longing toward Sierra's tipi.

"I am Prairie Flower, sister to Strong Hand. You belong to me now."

"The hell I do!" Ram roared. He reached deeply into a reservoir of strength to add substance to his protest. "What have you done with my woman?" He shook free of Prairie Flower, took two steps and staggered, negating the effect of his heated protest. He was weaker than he thought. The head wound he'd sustained, the countless bruises, and the beating from the women and children all combined to render him as weak as a newborn kitten.

"Come, Yellow Hair," Prairie Flower said, urging him forward. "Talks Brave will come to no harm. Prairie Flower will tend to your injuries."

Ram could not help smiling at the name Sierra had been given. Talks Brave. It suited her perfectly. Through some miracle, she had talked her way out of a desperate situation. He only hoped she hadn't taken them from the frying pan into the fire. When Prairie Flower tugged his arm impatiently, Ram had no option but to follow. As long as he knew Sierra was safe, he'd bide his time until his strength returned.

Sierra peeked through the tent flap, watching intently as Prairie Flower slit through Ram's bonds and led him away. She held her breath when he stumbled, and rage consumed her when the Indian maiden reached out to steady him. Was Ram so naive that he didn't know what the woman wanted from him? He'd probably be more than willing, she thought, disgruntled. Prairie Flower was a beautiful woman and he was a virile man. He'd probably fulfill his duty with gusto. Surrendering to exhaustion, Sierra sank down onto the sleeping mat and closed her eyes.

She was tired, so tired. And worried about Ram. He had suffered serious injuries, and despite her fear that he would succumb to Prairie Flower's charms, she prayed the woman would treat his wounds. Sighing wearily, she slid into a restless sleep.

Some distance away in another tipi, Ram eyed Prairie Flower warily as she stripped the tattered shirt down his arms and tossed it aside. From somewhere in the depths of the dimly lit lodge, she found water and a strip of soft deerskin, which she used to bathe his head wound and numerous cuts and scratches. Once they had been cleansed, she spread them with a soothing salve and bound his head with a clean deerskin strip. When she tried to remove his trousers, he resisted violently. But in the end, Prairie Flower had her way. He was too weak to sustain prolonged resistance, and the determined woman soon rid him of his trousers, boots, and small clothes. When he was completely naked, she eyed him appreciatively.

"Dammit, look all you want," he ground out defiantly. "But if you're looking for something more, you'd do well to look elsewhere. I'm too damn tired to do justice to any woman." Sending Prairie Flower a look that dared her to object, he stretched out on the sleeping mat, pulled the blanket up to his chin, and closed his eyes. Sleep came almost instantly.

Prairie Flower let out an angry puff of breath, but Ram's soft snoring made her realize he was indeed too exhausted to serve the purpose for which she intended him. Heaving a sigh of regret, she stripped off her tunic and slid beneath the blanket. The warm body pressed intimately against his back made little impression upon Ram. He had already succumbed to sleep, unaware that Prairie Flower slept beside him.

* * *

Sierra awoke to the certain knowledge that she wasn't alone. Rolling to her side, she saw a pair of naked legs braced inches from her face. Alarm shuddered through her as her gaze followed the legs upward, past a tautly stretched breechclout, bronze chest, and scarred shoulders. She gasped in dismay when the unsmiling face of Firewalker came into view. His dark, smoldering eyes reminded her of an animal of prey.

"W-what do you want?"

The silence in the tipi grew oppressive as his hot gaze devoured her. She was so stunned to see him that she failed to notice her saddlebags slung over one of his broad shoulders until he shrugged and they dropped to the ground beside her with a dull thud. Then he turned abruptly and ducked through the tent flap.

Sierra collapsed in relief. For a time she feared that Firewalker intended to go against Strong Hand's wishes and harm her. Sunlight slanted through the smokehole, allowing the welcome light of day into the dim interior of the lodge. Realizing that it was morning, Sierra rose from the sleeping mat, her thoughts on Ram. She wondered if he'd spent a peaceful night. If his sleeping arrangements were left up to Prairie Flower, she supposed Ram must be smiling this morning.

"I hope he enjoyed himself," she muttered. All men were the same. One woman was as good as another in bed.

Then her thoughts turned to more pressing

matters, aware that she looked a mess and was desperate for a bath. And she had a pressing need to find a private place to attend to personal matters. Rummaging in her saddlebags, she removed a clean blouse, drawers, shift, towel, soap, comb, and brush. Logic told her that the Indians would have made camp close to water, and she intended to find it.

Rolling her clean clothing in a towel, Sierra left the tipi. The village was just beginning to stir; she could smell food odors wafting to her on a lazy breeze and her stomach rumbled. She fervently hoped that Strong Hand had made provisions to feed her and Ram while they waited for Wind Rider.

Sierra paused outside the tipi to look around and get her bearings. When she saw several women drift toward a path leading through the woods, she decided to follow. She walked slowly but surely, ignoring the curious glances aimed in her direction. She was rewarded for her diligence when the path led to a clear mountain stream. It was narrow but fairly leapt and danced over its rocky bed, forming rapids that looked treacherous. When the women followed the stream around a curve, Sierra was close on their heels. Rounding a bend, she halted abruptly, staring with pleasure at a small pool formed where the stream bed made a lazy loop. Several women were already bathing and splashing each other in obvious enjoyment.

Sierra watched for a few minutes before deciding to join them. No men were in evidence, and she suspected that they bathed in a place separate from the women. She stripped off her blouse and skirt and waded in. Turning to watch, the women began to giggle, pointing at her shift and drawers, which she'd left on for propriety's sake. The Indian women, Sierra noticed, had stripped bare. She had to admit it would be much easier to wash without the encumbrance of clothing, and after a short debate with her conscience, she pulled off her underwear and cast it aside.

Sierra felt like a new woman when she returned to camp an hour later. After bathing, she'd washed her dirty clothes and spread them out on bushes to dry. Her next priorities involved appeasing her hunger and talking to Ram, not necessarily in that order. One of her problems was solved when she saw Prairie Flower leave her lodge and walk briskly toward the river. She carried a water jug in one hand and a blanket over her arm. The moment she was out of sight, Sierra ducked into the Indian woman's tipi, praying that Ram hadn't left yet for his own bath. She was surprised to find that not only hadn't Ram left, but he was still sleeping soundly.

His bare legs and torso poked out of either end of the blanket, which was bunched around his middle. Sierra saw no evidence of a second mat and could only assume that Prairie Flower had shared Ram's sleeping mat. She could still see the impression of the woman's body. She made a choking sound deep in her throat, which sounded curiously like a sob.

Ram awakened with a start, confused and disoriented. For a moment he couldn't recall where he was or why. His head throbbed and his body ached. Gingerly he sat up, unaware that he was naked and his private parts were barely concealed by the blanket.

He saw Sierra and frowned, trying to recall events of the previous day. "Sierra. What—what happened? Where are we? God, I feel like hell."

"We're in an Indian village," Sierra explained, her expression softening when she noted his pain and confusion. "Don't you remember?"

Ram frowned. "Oh God, I remember now. Are you all right? None of those savages hurt you, did they?"

"I'm fine, Ram." She dropped to her knees beside him. "What about you? You don't look so good."

"Prairie Flower treated my injuries. My head is pretty damn hard, so I reckon it will heal."

"Did Prairie Flower please you last night?" Sierra couldn't help asking. Jealousy was like a ravening beast inside her.

"Prairie Flower? What in the hell are you talking about? I went to sleep almost immediately."

Sierra's relief was instant and complete. "You mean you didn't . . . You and Prairie Flower didn't . . . She wants to make a baby with you."

"What! Hell no, we didn't. Nor do I intend to. What do you take me for, some damn stud? Where is she, by the way?"

211

"Gone to the river to bathe. I saw her leave."

"Then tell me what in the hell happened last night. I nearly went insane worrying about you. What did you say to Strong Hand to make him change his mind about killing us?"

"I told him I was Wind Rider's sister. I was grasping at straws, but I knew Firewalker meant to . . ." Her words fell off. "I had no idea it would work so well. Firewalker's reaction truly stunned me. At least we're safe until Wind Rider arrives and tells Strong Hand I'm his sister."

"They've sent for Wind Rider? Oh, God, Sierra, what if he isn't your brother? Even if he is, you have no guarantee that his years of living with savages hasn't changed him. What if he isn't the loving brother you remember from your childhood?"

"I was only three when I saw him last, but I know he'd not turn against me. According to rumor, my brother has returned to white society. He is employed by the government in some capacity."

"If that is true, then why does Wind Rider's name strike terror in the hearts of these savages? I fear you've come all this way for nothing. It's highly improbable that Wind Rider is your brother."

"No, Ram, I'm sure you're mistaken. I have to believe that Wind Rider is my brother. I've come so far and we've so much to lose if he isn't."

"Yeah, our lives," Ram mumbled resentfully.

"We've got to get out of here. Where in the hell are my clothes?"

He spied his saddlebags lying nearby and rummaged through them until he found what he was looking for. When he'd removed a clean change of clothing, he threw aside the blanket and lunged to his feet. A surge of liquid heat melted Sierra's bones as she watched him dress. She flushed and looked away, needing no reminders of the paradise she had found in his arms. Once Ram was fully dressed, he grasped her hand and said, "Let's get out of here."

"Where are we going?"

"To find Strong Hand. If he thinks he can give me to his sister and expect me to perform stud service, he's badly mistaken. I'm not letting you out of my sight. I saw the way Firewalker looks at you, and I don't trust him. We're safe as long as they think you're Wind Rider's sister. I think we should make a few demands of our own."

Ducking through the tent flap, they walked hand in hand through the village. Sierra felt the menace of dark eyes following them and was relieved when no one tried to stop them. They found Strong Hand sitting before his lodge. He was eating and licking food from his fingers with slow relish. He burped loudly and spared them an inscrutable glance.

"We wish to talk to you, Strong Hand," Ram said in a voice that brooked no argument.

Strong Hand raised a dark eyebrow, his eyes unreadable as he searched their faces. After a suspenseful pause, he motioned them to a place beside him. His woman placed a bowl of steaming food in Ram's hand, and since he was hungry, he began eating. Whatever it was tasted delicious, and when he turned to offer some to Sierra, he saw that she had also been given food and was digging in.

Strong Hand waited until they had finished eating before relaxing against his backrest and directing his dark, impenetrable gaze at Ram. "Speak, Yellow Hair."

Ram cleared his throat and considered carefully everything he wanted to say. "Prairie Flower is beautiful and desirable, but I already have a woman. You cannot give me to another. I will share Sierra's tipi until her brother arrives."

The corners of Strong Hand's lips stretched upward into a grimace. Though his expression could not be described as friendly, neither could it be considered threatening. "You speak like a man with a choice, Yellow Hair, when in truth you have none. Why should I consider your words when you have no position in my village? You and your woman are captives. I could still order your death if it pleased me. My dealings with white eyes have taught me that they are a treacherous people. They wish to drive us to reservations and kill our buffalo."

"Have you forgotten Wind Rider?" Sierra dared to ask. "I am his sister. I am not your enemy."

Strong Hand sent her a guarded look. "Wind Rider is friend to the Indian. If you are truly his sister, you will come to no harm and your man will live. When you see Wind Rider, you must thank him for your lives."

"He's coming, then?" Ram asked.

Strong Hand nodded. "He will come."

"What about Prairie Flower? No one, man or woman, can order me to perform as a man if I do not desire to do so." He sent Sierra a speaking look, one that warmed her heart.

"I would have thought less of you had you meekly mated with Prairie Flower," Strong Hand admitted, gaining new respect for the powerful man who would have made a good warrior. "Prairie Flower will be angry, but you have my permission to move freely within the limits of the village. If Wind Rider does not claim kinship with Talks Brave, Prairie Flower can do as she pleases with you—I will not interfere—and Firewalker can claim Talks Brave. Go now, while I think of a way to appease my sister. She can be fierce when she does not get her way."

Ram could barely contain his glee. He knew little about Indians, but he had heard that they respected courage. It wasn't courage that made him reject Prairie Flower. He had no desire to bed the woman and that was all there was to it, even though he knew he could face severe punishment, or even death, for his refusal.

"Thank you," Ram told the chieftain as he grasped Sierra's hand and led her away. They hadn't taken two steps when Prairie Flower appeared, directing her vicious temper at her brother.

Fortunately, Strong Hand was prepared to deal with his sister's abusive tirade. His harsh words had a quelling effect, and her fiery outburst came to an abrupt halt. Hands on hips, she glared at Strong Hand, then turned her malevolent scowl on Sierra. Strong Hand put an end to it with a single word and a chopping motion of his hand. Abruptly Prairie Flower turned and stalked away.

"Let's get the hell out of here," Ram said, pulling Sierra toward the tipi she had occupied the previous night.

Once inside the lodge, Ram jerked Sierra into his arms and kissed her hungrily. She moaned low in her throat, arching against him as she returned the kiss.

"I was so worried," Ram said, pulling her down onto the sleeping mat. "I had no idea what was going on. Thank God you were able to handle the situation. I don't think I've ever felt so helpless or frustrated in my life. Until Wind Rider arrives, we can enjoy a short reprieve."

Sierra frowned. "What do you mean?"

"Have you considered what will happen to us if Wind Rider claims he isn't your brother?"

"I know Wind Rider is my brother. He *has* to be."

"Be realistic, Sierra. By your own admission, eighteen years have passed since you last saw your brother and sister. If they weren't killed outright, do you really think they could have survived the harsh life they were forced to live? Don't get your hopes up, sweetheart. I think we should plan to escape before Wind Rider arrives."

Sierra drew back in alarm. "No! Go if you want, Ram, but I'm staying. I've come too far. I deserve to know the truth."

"You don't deserve to die," Ram said with aching tenderness.

"If Wind Rider isn't my brother, I prefer to believe he'll not allow Strong Hand to harm us."

Ram shook his head in disbelief. "I wish I had your faith."

"I have to believe in Wind Rider, Ram, I just have to. If you want to leave I'll help you, but I won't go with you."

"Little fool. Do you think I'd leave without you?"

"You made me no promises," she reminded him.

A bleak smile stretched Ram's lips. "I can't. If circumstances were different . . ."

"But they aren't, are they?" She glanced down at her hands, refusing to show him the depth of her feelings.

"No, dammit, they're not!" He looked as if he wanted to explain, then his eyes went murky and he clamped his mouth tightly shut. Explaining now would accomplish nothing. The story of his life was far from pretty, and it was bound to get uglier.

Rising abruptly to his feet, he ducked through the tent flap.

"Ram, where are you going?"

"I need air."

He couldn't bear to see Sierra hurt, and continuing this conversation was sure to cause her pain. Guilt plagued him. He had taken her virginity and he still wanted her with a desperate, compelling need that tore him apart every time he looked at her. She deserved better than what he could offer her, which was too damn little.

Ram wandered down the trodden path to the stream, finding the bathing place without difficulty. He stripped quickly and immersed himself in the cold water, needing to douse the fever in his blood. He briefly considered escape again, but knew he could not leave Sierra behind. Come what might, they would face the danger together.

When he returned to the village, Sierra was standing beside a group of women, watching them perform various chores. Some were scraping stretched-out deer and buffalo hides, others were preparing a variety of food, and still others were sewing beads in intricate patterns on tunics and shirts.

"I had no idea Indian women worked so hard," she said as he walked up to join her.

"I suspect there's much we don't know about Indians," Ram remarked with grudging respect.

Twice that day food was brought to them by an old woman, who shyly placed bowls before them and scooted away. Later she returned for the empty bowls, taking them away as silently as she'd brought them.

When night claimed the peaceful camp, Ram spread out their sleeping mats. He gazed at Sierra across the dim interior of the lodge and felt the restless prowl of sexual yearning deep inside him. Intuitively he knew he'd have the devil's own time finding sleep this night.

Chapter Eleven

Sleep eluded Sierra. She recalled Ram's warning about Wind Rider and feared he might be right. She didn't know what she'd do if Wind Rider wasn't her brother. What if the rumors she'd heard were untrue? She tried not to think about the unpleasant consequences should Wind Rider prove to be a fierce savage like Strong Hand and his warriors.

She moaned and thrashed restlessly on her pallet, unaware that Ram was also having difficulty finding sleep. A strangled sob slipped past her lips, and she turned her face into the mat to stifle any further outburst. She was no coward, she told herself. She'd come a long way to find Ryder, and she had to have faith; she had to believe that Wind Rider was her long-lost brother.

Ram heard Sierra's soft sounds of distress and wanted to leap across the short distance separating them and comfort her. But he knew exactly where that would lead and forced himself not to react. Unfortunately, his body chose to ignore his mind's dictates.

"Sierra? Are you all right?"

"Ram . . ." His name left her lips on a sigh. There was no mistaking the plea in her voice and the raw need to comfort her drove Ram. Throwing aside his blanket, he was beside her instantly.

"What is it, little love? Don't be afraid—I won't let anyone hurt you."

"Oh, Ram, I am so frightened. I've come so far and dreamed about finding my family for so many years—what if it's all been a fantasy? I've been thinking about what you said earlier and decided it's ridiculous to base my belief that Wind Rider is my brother on rumor.

"Worse yet, I've involved you in my problems. If I hadn't insinuated myself into your life, you wouldn't be in danger now. I'm sorry, Ram."

Ram brushed the tears from her pale cheek with the pad of his thumb and she came willingly into his arms, her slender body molding into the curve of his. "I don't regret a damn thing, little love."

His mouth settled over hers with the same hard hunger that tortured his body, sinking deeply into the hot center of her mouth, teasing her with deep, thirsty thrusts of his tongue. Sierra returned the kiss, her body arching up to meet his, stroking his back, his shoulders, as if she couldn't get enough of touching him. She rubbed against him and heard his frenzied groan, answering it with a soft gasp. When Ram broke off the kiss, he was panting as if he'd just run a race.

"We have to stop now, little love, before it's too late."

Her hands slid down his hips and played over his thighs, refusing to let him go. She needed him, wanted him. She didn't care if he had another woman waiting for him in Denver. Tonight was all that mattered. Tonight and all the nights that followed until fate and circumstances parted them. If she could never be with Ram like this again, at least she'd have this night.

"Make love to me, Ram." Her eyes glowed brightly with the promise of paradise.

Holding her tightly, Ram struggled for control. "You don't know what you're saying, little love." His voice was gruff with need. The need to sheath himself inside her seared him from the inside out.

"I've never been more serious in my life," Sierra said, sending him a scorching look as she rotated her hips against his loins.

"Sierra, Sierra," he whispered, dragging his mouth across her aching lips. "If things were different, I'd give you the world."

"I don't want the world, Ram. I want you. Now." She needed to fill herself with the hardness and taste of him, to know that he was hers for this brief moment in time, to hold him and be held.

Pleasure exploded inside Ram as he took her mouth, savoring it, tasting her, caressing her, lured and ripped apart by her passion. Holding her hips, he rubbed her against the hard length of his arousal. They were both shuddering, making no pretense of hiding their hunger from one another.

"My God," he whispered. "You truly are a witch, Sierra Alden. Don't ever change—you're perfect just the way you are. But . . . are you sure, little love?"

Her answer was to nuzzle his neck, nipping at the tender flesh behind his ear and instantly soothing it with her tongue. Ram's fingers tightened on her pliant flesh, sending delicious little shivers along her spine.

Sitting back on his haunches, Ram began removing Sierra's clothing, exposing her lush body in all its naked splendor. Moonlight filtered through the smokehole above, turning her flesh to molten gold. "You're so damn beautiful, it hurts my eyes to look at you. I want to give you so much pleasure that you'll never forget this night, little love."

"I won't forget it, Ram, not ever."

His eyes never left hers as he slowly stripped away his own clothing. When he was naked she stared at him, at the strength of his arousal, at the hard promise of his masculinity. He groaned in response to her perusal and lowered himself atop her, straining against her, his body

GET YOUR 4 FREE BOOKS NOW—A $21.96 Value!

Mail the Free Book Certificate Today!

Get Four Books Totally FREE – A $21.96 Value!

PLEASE RUSH
MY FOUR FREE
BOOKS TO ME
RIGHT AWAY!

Leisure Romance Book Club
65 Commerce Road
Stamford CT 06902-4563

AFFIX
STAMP
HERE

throbbing with sweet, aching need. Sierra felt her flesh melt and run like thick honey against him and she spread her legs eagerly.

Ram grinned down into her glittering eyes. "Oh, no, little love, not yet. We've got all night."

Sierra felt every incredible inch of him, rock-hard and smelling of sweet mountain sage, against her body. She relished the heat and hardness of him. A soft gasp slipped past her lips when she felt the slide of his hair-roughened chest down her body. He paused briefly at her breasts, his mouth teasing as he kissed and suckled the pouting tips. She writhed and moaned his name as her world slowly disintegrated. Blazing a searing path down her body, he stopped briefly to kiss and lick her navel before placing a teasing kiss at the soft curls between her legs. Shock shuddered through her. Did people do such things? She stiffened and tried to push him away.

"I won't hurt you, little love," Ram whispered raggedly. "You'll like it, I promise."

Unable to speak, Sierra shook her head in vigorous denial.

"Let me, please let me . . ." He lowered his head and found the petals of her sex with his tongue, parting her, finding her slick and swollen with desire.

"Oh, Ram, I don't . . . I can't . . ." Her vision dimmed; her mouth worked wordlessly. Ignoring her silent plea, he continued his hot pursuit, rendering her helpless, lost to everything but the liquid heat of his mouth. He was creating such a frenzy of need within her that her protests soon turned to small cries of pleasure.

"You like this, don't you, little love?" Ram asked, looking up briefly. "Don't fight it. Let yourself go. I'll not leave you."

His pleasuring added a new dimension when he slid a finger inside her, pushing it in and out in rhythm with his plunging tongue, which had settled on a spot so sensitive that Sierra nearly screamed aloud when he discovered it. She felt the pressure build to nearly unbearable heights, felt tiny little eruptions along her nerve endings, and grasped Ram's shoulders to keep from tumbling over the edge of the bottomless pit opening beneath her. Her climax came abruptly, violently, as her body exploded into a thousand jagged pieces. She thought she had given everything she had to give but learned her mistake when Ram slid up her body and thrust into her. He filled her so completely, so gloriously, that her tremors began anew.

Panting to pace himself, sweat rolled off his body as he buried himself deep inside her. He could feel her contractions luring his swollen flesh and gritted his teeth to keep from ending it too soon. He remained motionless until he felt Sierra's breathing ease and her body relax, then he renewed the slow seduction of her senses. He kissed and licked and nipped, all the while thrusting and retrieving, driving her inexorably upward, past the threshold of pleasure to ecstasy.

"I can't wait, little love," Ram gasped, having

stroked himself past the limit of human endurance. "Oh, God, I've never felt . . . This is incredibly . . . Sierra!"

His body jerked violently as he spilled his seed, the taste of her on his lips acting as an aphrodisiac that lured him beyond mere pleasure into the realm of raw rapture. He feared he had left Sierra behind until he heard her small cries of completion and felt the contracting of her sheath against his swollen flesh, intensifying his bliss. Incredibly, she had reached a second climax.

Tottering on the fringes of awareness, Sierra felt Ram pull out of her and collapse beside her, breathing hard. He reached out and dragged her into his arms. She snuggled close, sighing contentedly. She couldn't recall experiencing anything that even remotely compared with what she'd just shared with Ram. If this was all she would ever have of him she could die happily, knowing she'd experienced something so earth-shattering that it defied description.

"What are you thinking?" Ram asked curiously. In the short time they had left together, he wanted to be privy to her every thought, know what was in her heart, fulfill her every desire. His greatest fear was that once she learned what he'd been keeping from her she'd despise him, and he wanted to store away this blissful time to retrieve from his memory and enjoy at his leisure.

"I was thinking about what you said to me when we were tied to that stake outside and thought we were going to die."

"I said a lot of things."

"You said you'd have married me if it were possible. What did you mean? What's stopping you? Is it Dora? Do you love her so much?"

Ram went still. Love Dora? At one time Dora was his life, but she had betrayed him. She had taught him that women couldn't be trusted. Since then he had used them for one purpose only. Until he met Sierra. He had no reason to trust her; their first meeting had been anything but memorable. Undaunted, she had insinuated herself into his life and no amount of discouragement had turned her away. Then something totally unexpected had happened to him. Sierra had burrowed her way into the deepest chambers of his heart and made him want her with a fierce need that had utterly defeated him.

For the first time in many years, the icy barriers guarding his heart began to melt and he felt the shackles of resistance dropping away as if by magic. Against his will, a tenuous trust slowly grew between him and the stubborn young woman who rested so confidently in his arms.

Trust. The word sounded hollow, without meaning. He'd thought he'd lost the ability to trust until Sierra had shown him the way. And how did he repay her? By taking her virginity and offering nothing in return. She deserved an answer to her entirely too reasonable question.

"My feelings for Dora are confusing," he said guardedly.

For years he'd fed on his hatred for Dora, yet he honestly couldn't define exactly how he felt. It lay somewhere between hate and pity. He wanted her to pay for disrupting his life, for thrusting him into hell, and he could say with assurance that he no longer loved her.

"Dora and I go way back. She has nothing to do with us . . . about how I feel about you."

"She has everything to do with us," Sierra said softly. "Are you still determined to see her when we reach Denver?"

"I have to. I've waited a long time for this meeting. The thought of seeing her again has kept me sane these past ten years."

Pain. Deep, gut-wrenching pain lanced through Sierra. Why couldn't Ram love her as much as he loved Dora? "Will you tell me about it?"

"God, Sierra, don't ask that of me."

How could he admit how naive he'd been, how stupid to trust a woman so completely and love so blindly? No, he decided firmly, Sierra would be better off not knowing what he intended to do to Dora and Jason once he found them. He was seriously thinking about taking the law into his own hands. And if he went back to prison, at least he'd go with the sweet taste of revenge on his lips. His obsessive need for revenge made it impossible to make promises to Sierra, especially promises he was unlikely to keep.

Sierra felt Ram's anguish keenly and was stunned by it. "I won't press you, Ram, nor will

I give you up without a fight. For a few days you are mine and mine alone. Forget Dora, forget everyone. There is only us. And there are still hours left till dawn. I want to pretend you're mine for as long as I can."

"I feel like a damn heel," Ram spewed bitterly. "You deserve better, little love. I've forgotten how to trust. My heart is an empty shell. I've taken so much from you and given so little in return."

Sierra sighed, hurt by Ram's inability to confide in her. She didn't understand his obsession with Dora. What had she done to him? And who was Jason? "What you've given me is enough to last a lifetime. If you won't tell me what this is about, at least you can love me again."

Their second joining was slow and leisurely, with none of the urgency that had driven them earlier. The edge had been blunted on their appetites, and their loving was sweet and achingly tender. Afterward Sierra cried, knowing that she could never take Dora's place in Ram's life. He could deny it all he liked, but she knew in her heart that Dora was the only woman Ram would ever love.

Outwardly, the days they spent in Strong Hand's camp remained relatively calm and without mishap. Inwardly, Sierra's distress increased. She did not know when Wind Rider would arrive and looked for him daily. For the most part, Strong Hand's people ignored her and Ram. It was obvious that they were biding their time until Wind Rider arrived and either accepted or denied kinship with her. If he refused her, she would be given to Firewalker and Ram would belong to Prairie Flower.

After a week in Strong Hand's village, Sierra's nerves were frayed beyond repair. Only during those hours she spent in Ram's arms each night, after they closed the flap on their lodge and retreated into a world of their own making, did Sierra feel safe.

During those private moments Sierra sensed an almost desperate urgency to Ram's loving and assumed it was due to their precarious situation. Yet try as she might, she couldn't dispel the chilling sensation that there was more to Ram's desperation than their present danger warranted. He had hinted at things that confused and frightened her. If they lived through these dangerous days, she feared Ram would face an even greater challenge—one which involved a woman named Dora. But questioning him seemed to send him into a moody silence. He had made it perfectly clear that the part of his life concerning Dora was to remain private.

"What are you thinking, little love?" Ram asked when they were sealed in the private world of their lodge that night. They had just made love during a fierce thunderstorm, and their passion had surpassed the violence of the elements.

"This is all going to end soon, isn't it, Ram?"

Ram sighed. The warmth of his breath sent a shattering wash of sensation over her.

"It should never have happened in the beginning. Lord knows, I fought it as long as I could."

Sierra grinned impishly. "You never had a chance. If only—"

"No, don't even think it. I don't know what is likely to happen when we reach Denver, or even if we *will* reach Denver. There is one promise I can make, though. If I'm still able once I finish my—business, I'll find you."

It wasn't enough, not nearly enough, but Sierra reckoned it was all she was going to get. It sounded as if his business might be serious, or even life-threatening.

"I need a promise from you, Sierra," Ram continued seriously. "If our loving results in . . ." he paused and cleared his throat . . . "a child, come to me immediately. I'll be staying at the Denver Hotel. No matter what happens to me, I'll make sure you and our child are taken care of for life."

Sierra only heard part of his words. The part about something happening to him. She blinked rapidly. "What could happen to you?"

"Various things," he said vaguely. "Promise me, little love. Promise you'll come to me if you suspect our loving has produced a baby."

Sierra's chin angled for battle. If he didn't want her now, why would a child change his mind? "I will repeat your own words, Ram—I can make you no promises."

Ram raked his fingers through his hair, cursing fate, cursing Dora, cursing his inability to control his passion where Sierra was concerned. "Dammit, Sierra, I'm serious."

"So am I. I don't think you have anything to worry about, but if I'm wrong, I'll make the decision when the time arrives. That's the best I can do."

Ryder Larson sat in council with Many Coup, chief of a renegade band of Sioux. When the ceremonial pipe was passed to Ryder, he solemnly sucked in a lungful of smoke, slowly blew it out, and passed the pipe to the next man, who repeated the process. Ryder, in his capacity as Indian agent, had been trying for months to get Many Coup to settle his people on the reservation for the winter. If he wasn't successful, many tribes, this one among them, would not survive. A hard winter, lack of game, a severe shortage of food and blankets, and debilitating illnesses would decimate many of the militant tribes entrenched in their mountain camps.

Ryder was the last person in the world who wanted to cage plains Indians on reservations, but he was a realist. If the once proud race was to survive, their lives must be preserved by those in a position to do so. He was devoting his life to that cause. Hannah, his beloved wife, understood his need to better the way of life of his adopted people, but he still regretted leaving her for long periods of time while he visited various tribes scattered throughout the area, distributing food and medicines provided by the government.

There were too many dishonest agents for Ryder's liking. Some agents lined their own pockets by selling goods supplied by the government and replacing them with shoddy merchandise, or more often, none at all, leaving the Indians vulnerable to starvation and illness. He and several other honest government-appointed agents were attempting to change all that, but it was a thankless, time-consuming job that kept him away from his family longer than he would like. His reward came in knowing that he'd helped the People survive.

Ryder had an advantage that other agents lacked. He had been raised by Cheyenne and understood the culture and people better than he did his own white race. He was universally respected and admired by Sioux, Cheyenne, and Arapaho alike. The People called him Wind Rider, a name he bore with pride. He and his sister Abby, known to the People as Tears Like Rain, had returned to white society against their wills. With the help and love of their respective spouses, they were learning to cope with a world they didn't understand.

Hannah had stood by him and loved him in spite of his warlike activities against whites. And Abby's husband Zach had helped her adjust to the white world by showing her that all whites weren't cruel. They were lucky, he and Abby, to have had each other during their growing years, luckier perhaps than their little sister Sierra, who was still lost to them despite their best efforts to find her.

Ryder returned his attention to Many Coup,

waiting for the old chief to speak. He'd been in the village for two days, trying to convince Many Coup to take his people to the reservation for the winter, and he was anxious to go home to Hannah and Lacy, their two-year-old daughter.

"Because we trust and respect you, Wind Rider, I will take my people to the reservation," Many Coup said as he laid down the pipe. "I am old, and my people are tired of war. Our children's lives are at stake. We will leave when the sun has risen in the sky two times."

"I know it isn't a solution to your problems, Many Coup, and that some of the young braves will refuse to go, but I can promise your people food and blankets to see them through the winter until game is available in the spring."

Ryder relaxed as they spoke of the problems they might encounter during their travels east to the reservation, elated that he had succeeded in saving another tribe from extinction. Regrettably, there were still many chiefs he'd failed to convince. Strong Hand, an Arapaho chieftain, continued to plague travelers and attack army patrols. Ryder feared it would be only a matter of time before the army found them and wiped them out to the last man, woman, and child. He'd give anything if he could save them from that fate.

Lost in his own thoughts, Ryder did not notice a lone horseman riding hell-for-leather toward them until a warning was given by a sentry. Ryder saw at a glance that the Indian was Arapaho. His horse was lathered as if he'd ridden long and hard. He skidded to a halt beside the council, leaped from his pony, and addressed Ryder directly.

"I am Standing Bear. I have traveled far to find you, Wind Rider. I bear a message from the great Arapaho chieftain, Strong Hand."

Curious, Ryder rose gracefully to his feet. "You have a message for me? Speak, Standing Bear."

"I am to take you to our village. You come now."

Ryder's handsome features wore a look of stunned disbelief. For months he'd been looking for Strong Hand's camp, and now the reclusive chieftain was summoning him with no explanation. "Can you tell me what this is all about?"

Standing Bear shook his head. He'd been instructed not to divulge the reason for the summons. The wily chieftain wanted to judge Wind Rider's reaction to the woman who claimed to be his sister without giving him the advantage of a warning or explanation.

"You will learn soon enough. If you call yourself friend to the People, you will answer Strong Hand's summons without question."

"I will come, Standing Bear."

What Ryder truly wanted was to return home to Hannah and little Lacy. What he did was to bid Many Coup good-bye, promise to visit him on the reservation, and ask that his mount be brought to him. An hour later, having been given pemmican, parched corn, and fried Indian bread to sustain him during his journey, Ryder left the village with Standing Bear. He had no idea what Strong Hand wanted, but he welcomed the opportunity to persuade the chieftain to take his people to the reservation.

Sierra and Ram made love that night with a poignancy that was both sweet and disturbing. Sierra moved through the following day beneath a dark cloud of anticipation. Some sixth sense told her that the moment of truth was nearly at hand, and she felt both fear and exhilaration. She could be seeing her brother very soon and that excited her. But beneath the joy, fear of losing Ram brought a disturbing sadness.

She had never expected to meet a man like Ram Hunter. She had never thought she'd fall in love so completely or care so deeply. Yet she knew that once she and Ryder were reunited, the part of her life that included Ram would come to an end. Circumstances she could only guess at, since Ram had not confided in her, would force them apart.

The afternoon was sunny and warm as Sierra and Ram walked hand-in-hand to the river. With mutual consent they found a secluded spot beneath a canopy of trees and made love. It had happened spontaneously. They hadn't planned on loving, but neither could they have prevented it. They had ducked beneath the trees, dropped to the ground in a frenzy of need, and made love without removing their clothing. They were still lying in each other's arms, aglow in the aftermath of wild passion, when Firewalker burst through the trees.

"Talks Brave, where are you? You must return to the village at once."

Sierra expelled her breath on a long shuddering sigh and sent Ram a look so filled with fear and anticipation that it made him want to take her away where no one could harm her. If it had been at all possible, he would have taken her away long ago. But Sierra had been so convinced that Wind Rider was her long-lost brother that she'd adamantly refused to leave.

"He's here," Sierra whispered shakily. Ram took her hand and squeezed. She sent him a misty smile. "I'm ready."

They stepped out of the woods together. Firewalker saw them and frowned, aware of what they had been doing. With more force than necessary, he prodded them toward the village. "Wind Rider has arrived."

Ryder was in a nasty mood as he rode into the village. Standing Bear had driven him relentlessly, insisting that they sleep and eat in the saddle instead of stopping to make a proper camp at night. If he had an inkling of what to expect, he wouldn't be so grumpy, but Standing Bear had remained uncommunicative. They rode into the village shortly after midday. Tension seemed high as they approached Strong Hand's lodge, and Ryder was quick to note that nearly the entire population had gathered, whispering among themselves and gazing expectantly at him. Strong Hand stepped outside his lodge to greet him.

"Welcome, Wind Rider, we have been expecting you."

"Why have you summoned me?" Wind Rider asked with asperity.

Sierra and Ram paused at the edge of the clearing. Sierra's feet felt wooden, her legs heavy as she slowly walked toward the stranger who had just ridden into camp. He was dressed in buckskins, which accentuated the leashed strength of his lean, muscular form. He moved with the long, confident strides of a man comfortable with his surroundings and his identity. He wore his longish black hair clubbed at the back of his neck with a rawhide thong, and his exposed skin was tanned a deep bronze. From where she stood, Sierra couldn't make out the color of his eyes, but knew instinctively that they would be gray.

Strong Hand's gaze focused on something just past Ryder's left shoulder, and Ryder felt the hairs rise on the back of his neck. He turned slowly, feeling his own tension accelerate, his heart pounding. He was more than a little stunned when he saw a white woman and man walking toward him. He was aware from Strong Hand's intense perusal that something was expected of him, but he didn't know what. True, he hadn't expected to see white captives, especially captives who were still alive and apparently unharmed. He spun around to face Strong

Hand, one dark eyebrow raised in honest surprise. The chieftain's face remained inscrutable, offering nothing.

Sierra walked toward Wind Rider on quaking legs. She was so shaken that she had to concentrate in order to remember to breathe. Wind Rider had seen her now and waited for her to approach. She could tell by his expression that Strong Hand had told him nothing about her. She felt her courage fleeing and wished she could flee too, until Ram bent down and whispered into her ear. "Don't falter. Take courage. I'm right beside you."

Ryder had enough wits about him to notice that the young woman was a real beauty. She was close enough now for him to see the sun reflecting off her thick black hair. A timid smile stretched the lush fullness of her lips, and her gray eyes glittered like . . . Ryder went still, shock shuddering through him. He shook his head, trying to bring his imagination under control before it conjured up images from the past that had existed only in his memory.

Sierra was standing so close to Wind Rider now that she could reach out and touch him. Their eyes met, gray on gray, bonding with complete understanding and familial recognition.

"Dear God, who are you?" Ryder's words were strangled, his throat so tight he had to force them past his lips.

"Ryder? It is you, isn't it? I—I'm Sierra. I've traveled a long way to find you."

Ryder felt his world tilt crazily. "Sierra? Little Sierra?"

Sierra laughed happily. "Not so little anymore."

They stared at one another for the space of a heartbeat, then Ryder opened his arms.

Chapter Twelve

Strong Hand's inscrutable expression gave nothing of his thoughts away as Sierra flung herself into Ryder's open arms. If the chieftain had any doubt about Sierra's identity, Wind Rider's exuberant welcome dispelled them instantly.

"I am convinced," he said bluntly. "Talks Brave did not lie; she is your sister."

"Talks Brave?" Ryder grinned down at Sierra, amused by the name she had been given. "Talks Brave is indeed my sister. We were separated many winters ago. Thank you for not harming her, Strong Hand. She is very dear to me."

"Talks Brave and Yellow Hair came very close to losing their lives. They were spared when Firewalker expressed his desire for Talks Brave and Prairie Flower spoke on behalf of Yellow

Hair. Had Talks Brave not claimed kinship to you, she would have become Firewalker's woman."

"Yellow Hair?" Ryder looked past Sierra to where Ram stood, his body tense and watchful. Ryder took careful note of Ram's protective manner toward Sierra, of his powerful build and good looks. He set Sierra slightly away from him and asked, "Who is Yellow Hair, Sierra?"

Sierra swallowed visibly. "His name is Ramsey Hunter. I—we were traveling on the same stagecoach."

"Alone? My God, Sierra, what ever possessed you to set out alone through dangerous territory?" He spared Ram an ominous glance. "What is Hunter to you?"

"Just a friend," Sierra lied. "And you mustn't blame him. I sort of—tagged along with Ram. It wasn't his fault that—"

"I'm capable of defending myself, Sierra," Ram said, stepping forward. He should have known how damning their behavior would appear to Ryder when he realized that Ram and Sierra had been unchaperoned traveling companions. Did Sierra's brother suspect they were more than companions? Ram wondered. No matter, he was fully prepared to accept the entire blame for what happened between them.

"Perhaps this conversation should take place in private," Ryder said, sending Ram a quelling look. The relationship between Ramsey Hunter and his sister, if indeed there was one, needed to be clarified. He turned to Strong Hand. "My sister and I have need of privacy."

"Take your sister and her man to their lodge. We will prepare a feast tonight to celebrate your reunion."

Ryder's mouth tightened. Strong Hand's words implied that Hunter and Sierra had shared the same lodge during their period of captivity. He also referred to Hunter as Sierra's "man."

"What were you and Strong Hand talking about?" Sierra asked. Since the conversation with Strong Hand hadn't been conducted in English, she had no idea what was being said.

"I told Strong Hand we needed privacy. There is so much we need to catch up on. Come, we'll go to your lodge." He slanted Ram a chilling glance. "You too, Hunter."

Ryder and Sierra sat side by side inside the tipi; Ram sat across from them, his expression wary. It was obvious that Ryder Larson didn't like him very much, and Ram couldn't blame the man. He had taken Sierra's innocence knowing he could not offer marriage.

"Start from the beginning, Sierra," Ryder said gently as he gazed tenderly into gray eyes so like his and Abby's that it was uncanny. "How did you know where to find me? And whatever possessed you to leave your home with a man like Hunter?"

Ryder didn't know Ram, but he was a good judge of character and he'd seen plenty of men like Hunter since his entry into white society.

They were takers and users. The hard gleam in Hunter's eyes told Ryder all he needed to know about the man.

Sierra looked from Ryder to Ram, sensing a hostility she could neither explain nor prevent. The tension flowing between them was nearly tangible. "I was taken to San Francisco by my adoptive parents after they found me wandering on the prairie," she explained, hoping to diffuse the volatile atmosphere. "I knew my first name and little else. But I never forgot you and Abby, never. As I grew older, the Aldens tried to discourage my interest in finding you and Abby. They told me you were both dead and sent me East to school in hopes I'd forget my real family. But I never did."

Ryder's expression softened. "Abby and I never forgot you, little sister. We even hired detectives to find you. Was your childhood painful? Were the Aldens strict and unloving?"

"Oh, no, just the opposite," Sierra said. "They loved and indulged me outrageously. Father's business acumen made him rich and I was denied nothing."

Ryder nodded gravely. "I am glad. But what prompted you to leave your home to search for me and Abby? Didn't you know how dangerous it was? And," he said, slanting Ram a withering look, "where does Hunter fit into the picture? Is he your husband?"

"No," Sierra said without thinking. "I didn't meet Ram until I returned from school just recently. I left San Francisco after I heard an

246

amazing story about white Indians. The story concerned a brother and sister who had been raised by savages and recently returned to civilization after years of captivity."

Ryder's eyes darkened with anger. "My people are not savages. Abby and I were not captives. We were loved by our foster parents. I have found many whites to be more savage than the People. I loved and respected my adoptive father and mother."

"I'm sorry, I didn't mean . . ." Sierra was at a loss for words. Evidently Ryder had been affected deeply by his years with the Indians.

Ryder relaxed visibly and his dark expression lifted. "No, Sierra, I'm sorry. It's difficult sometimes to forget how badly I was treated in the past by white men, despite being one myself. Learning to trust my own kind has not been easy, but with Hannah's help, I am slowly overcoming my distrust of white society."

"Hannah? Who is she?"

Ryder's smile lit up his face. "Hannah is my wife. Without her I could not exist in the white world. We have a daughter. Lacy is two years old."

"I have a niece!" Sierra squealed delightedly.

"And a nephew. Abby has a son. His name is Trey, and he is nearly three. But enough of me, little sister. You still have not told me why you were traveling with Ramsey Hunter. By your own admission, you hardly know the man."

"That's not entirely true," Sierra began, only to be interrupted by Ram.

"Perhaps you should ask me that question," Ram said. "I am a friend of Lester Alden. Sierra needed an escort, and since we were both traveling to Denver, I offered my protection. We left San Francisco on the Wells Fargo stagecoach."

Stunned, Sierra stared at Ram. He was deliberately lying to save her embarrassment. It hadn't happened at all as he'd described. He had told her repeatedly that he didn't want to become involved in her harebrained scheme.

"Were you the only two people on the coach?" Ryder asked curiously. "Why were no other captives taken by Strong Hand's warriors?"

"The stage on which we were traveling became involved in an unfortunate accident before reaching Salt Lake City. Since the next stage wasn't due for a week, we decided to travel to Denver by horseback."

"Are you saying you've been alone with my sister since Salt Lake City?" Ryder asked quietly—almost too quietly. "Strong Hand said you were sharing a tipi."

Ram flushed. "Strictly for Sierra's protection. I felt it necessary to remain close. Firewalker wanted her. He still does."

"Your efforts on my sister's behalf are commendable," Ryder said with a hint of sarcasm. The harsh reality of his next words brought a gasp from Sierra. "Will we be holding a wedding in Denver?" He might as well have come right out and asked if Ram had bedded Sierra.

The bluntness of Ryder's question stunned Ram. Before he could form an answer, Sierra rushed to his defense. "Ryder! Please. This is neither the time nor the place for this discussion. I'm safe—that's all that matters. We've been reunited at last, and I want to enjoy our reunion. How soon can we leave?"

"Sierra, I'm perfectly capable of answering your brother's question," Ram said tersely. He faced Ryder squarely. "Your sister is of age, and whatever happened between us, if anything actually did happen," he stressed, "is our business. I feel obligated to say, however, that there will definitely be no wedding in the near future."

Ryder lunged at Ram, rage shattering his tenuous control. Leaping to her feet, Sierra insinuated herself between them, begging for restraint despite the pain of Ram's harsh words. "Please, can't you see how much this is hurting me? Ram is right. We owe explanations to no one. All I want now is to visit my family and put all this behind me."

Ryder's temper cooled instantly. If Hannah was here, she'd berate him soundly for flying off the handle the way he'd just done. His ways were still Cheyenne despite his efforts to fit into white society. If he had his way, he'd apply Cheyenne justice to bring Ramsey Hunter to heel.

"Forgive me, Sierra, I have no right to question or accuse. My protective instincts are working overtime. I can't wait to take you home. Abby will be ecstatic. And I know you will like my wife Hannah and Abby's husband Zach."

"I'm looking forward to it." Hannah sighed happily. If she couldn't have Ram, her recently discovered family would help ease the pain of their parting.

"I must speak with Strong Hand," Ryder said as he rose to his feet. "I'm hoping to convince him to take his people to the reservation for the winter, where they will be provided with food, medicines, and blankets. He will be difficult to convince, but I must try. I will ask him to provide another lodge for Hunter tonight."

Ram glared at Ryder but said nothing. When Sierra looked as if she wanted to object, Ram sent her a warning glance. She swallowed her protest and said, "I heard you were employed by the government in some capacity."

"The governor once saved my life, and I'm repaying my debt by working with the Agency of Indian Affairs. One day I'll tell you about it. I am still working with the agency because I feel strongly about helping the People. I do not want to see the plains Indians wiped out. Their heritage must be preserved at all costs, and I will continue to help them as long as I can make a difference in their quality of life."

Ram stared at Ryder, giving grudging respect where it was due. He couldn't ever recall meeting such a selfless or giving individual. It seemed inconceivable that this man had been raised by savages yet still remained true to his moral beliefs and the pride he carried within him.

*   *   *

Sierra stretched out on the sleeping mat, missing Ram's comforting presence beside her. True to his word, Ryder had arranged for Ram to be given a lodge separate from hers. In fact, she and Ram had spent precious little time together since Ryder's arrival. The feast had lasted for hours, with dancing and drinking and general merriment. Seated between Ryder and Strong Hand, Sierra had sent covert glances longingly at Ram during the long feast. Prairie Flower had claimed a place beside Ram, and Sierra fumed with impotent rage as she watched the Indian woman's crude attempts at seduction.

A surprising development during the evening came when Firewalker approached Ryder, engaging him in a heated discussion. Later, when Sierra asked what it was all about, Ryder laughingly told her that Firewalker had offered ten horses for her. He went on to say that the offer was quite generous by Indian standards and she should be flattered that the fierce brave wanted her enough to part with ten horses. When she expressed outrage, Ryder had placed an arm around her shoulders and assured her that he wouldn't sell her at any price.

The camp was quiet now, but sleep eluded Sierra. She missed Ram's arms around her and feared she'd never again know the magic of his kisses or feel the strength of him moving inside her, taking her to paradise. With grim determination, Sierra decided that she couldn't let him go without a proper good-bye.

Tossing aside the blanket, she crawled to the opening of the tipi and peered outside. The flat white disc of the moon rode high above the mountain peaks, casting an eerie glow on the sleeping camp. She stared with longing at the tipi where Ram slept. Throwing caution to the wind, she crept out into the cool mountain air, moving cautiously toward the man she loved.

Ram shifted restlessly on the sleeping mat, feeling empty and lonely without Sierra. In his mind's eye he pictured his life stretching endlessly before him, plagued by sleepless nights of wanting, needing . . . Was he destined to spend what remained of his life unfulfilled and empty? A sudden movement at the tent opening captured his attention, and he peered through the darkness. A beam of moonlight filtered through the smokehole, revealing the slim figure of a woman.

"Sierra." He whispered her name on a breathless sigh.

He noted a slight stiffening of her narrow shoulders before the woman spoke. "It is Prairie Flower."

Ram sat up abruptly, pulling the blanket around his naked hips. "What in the hell do you want?"

She came down on her haunches beside him and jerked off her tunic. She was naked beneath it. "Yellow Hair is alone tonight. I will ease your loneliness." Her dark eyes slid greedily over the broad expanse of his bare chest.

"Thank you, Prairie Flower," Ram said, trying to ignore the sleek smoothness of her golden body and blatant invitation in her dark eyes, "but I am not lonely and have no need of your company."

Prairie Flower's eyes narrowed spitefully. "What kind of a man are you? Are your loins too weak to pleasure more than one woman? Is your blood cold? Am I not beautiful enough to please you, or my skin not white enough?"

"You are lovely, Prairie Flower," Ram said truthfully, "but I do not want you. You would be better served to find a man who appreciates you."

A low hiss whistled through Prairie Flower's teeth as she shot to her feet. "If you weren't under Wind Rider's protection, I would order my brother to put you to death. Perhaps," she hinted slyly, "I will think of something better." Whirling on her heel, she plunged through the tent flap into the moon-drenched night in all her naked glory.

"What in the hell is that supposed to mean?" Ram muttered beneath his breath.

Moving silent as a wraith toward Ram's tipi, Sierra was stunned when she saw Prairie Flower bursting from the lodge. Pain exploded in her brain. The randy bastard, she thought, feeling keenly the agony of betrayal. He couldn't even wait until he left the Indian camp to take another woman. Determined to let Ram know exactly what she thought of his tomcat antics, she burst into the lodge like a vengeful banshee.

Still reeling from Prairie Flower's late-night visit, Ram wasn't expecting another nocturnal intruder and assumed that Prairie Flower had returned for another attempt at seduction.

"It won't work, Prairie Flower," Ram said sternly. "I said I didn't want you and I meant it. There is only one woman I want right now, and she is as unattainable as the moon and stars."

Sierra expelled a shaky breath. His words sang through her blood. Ram hadn't bedded Prairie Flower. "Perhaps if you reach high enough, you'll find the moon and stars within your grasp."

"Sierra! My God, what are you doing here? Your brother will have my hide if he finds you here."

Sierra dropped to her knees beside him. "This may be the only time we'll have to say good-bye. My brother hasn't known me long enough to judge my feelings for you. I love him dearly, but he can't possibly know what is right for me."

"He wants what is best for you, little love, and he doesn't think I'm what you need. Can't say as I blame him," Ram observed dryly. "Your brother has good sense."

Sierra sighed heavily. "I don't want to talk about Ryder right now. I don't want to talk at all." She searched his face, conveying with a searing look exactly what she wanted from him. "Give me something to remember all the lonely nights to come without your arms to comfort me."

"Aw, God, Sierra, don't you think I hate the thought of parting as much as you do?"

"I don't know, do you?"

Ram closed his eyes, grappling with his conscience. He lost the battle and pulled Sierra down beside him, dragging her against him with a hunger that nearly tore him apart. She sighed softly as his mouth came down hard on hers. Instant warmth flared in the pit of her stomach, making her shiver with delicious anticipation. With delicate strokes he touched his tongue to hers, exploring the silken texture of her mouth, tasting her heat, her need, mingling it with his own.

For a magic moment, Sierra forgot that they were parting, perhaps forever. Forgot that there was another woman in Ram's life. She simply savored the kiss in a hushed atmosphere of awe and want. The slow rasp of Ram's tongue over hers sent slivers of fire to the hidden places of her body, preparing them for a deeper joining, bathing her in liquid heat.

"I could kiss you forever," Ram groaned against her lips. "You taste of sweet mountain air and sunshine." He shifted his hips, trying to ease the agony between his legs. He wanted her so badly that he was already hard and throbbing. His fingers shook as he struggled with the fastenings on her blouse and skirt.

"Let me help you," Sierra said as she pushed his hands aside. When she lay before him in all her naked glory, he tossed aside the blanket covering his loins, shoved her legs apart with his knees, and knelt between them.

His gaze traveled the length of her body with hot possessiveness, thinking her the most glorious creature God had ever created. When she arched upward, inviting his caress, he happily obliged. Cupping her mound, he slid a finger inside her, nearly exploding when he found her hot and wet for him. He closed his eyes and groaned helplessly against the tide of emotions rolling over him. No longer could he describe what he felt for Sierra as lust. There was more to it than that—much, much more. If he could live his life over, there would be no Dora, no Jason, no emotion called revenge. Unfortunately, he didn't believe in miracles. Life could not be repeated no matter how badly one wanted it; therefore, Ram had only this night to demonstrate the depths of his feelings to Sierra.

Sierra felt the heat of his hand against her, the steady thrust of his finger, and released a shuddering sob. Suddenly she wanted to give him the same kind of pleasure. Gazing at him in unabashed delight, she reached down between his thighs, closing her hand around his thick length. Ram nearly shouted when she squeezed and pulled, forcing him to grow harder, thicker. The breath hissed harshly from his tight throat. Gritting his teeth against the exquisite, painful pleasure, he allowed her to continue for a breathless moment before stilling her hand.

"Stop!" he gasped harshly. "I don't want it to end like this."

Balancing himself on his outstretched arms, he watched her face, feeling himself dissolving as he rubbed the smooth round tip of his sex against the wet, slick lips between her legs. He loved looking at her when he made love to her, adored the way she gasped and arched against him, giving him unlimited access to her straining breasts. Almost reverently he accepted her offering, nibbling and licking the hardened nubs, then drawing them each in turn into the heat of his mouth.

When he'd nursed his fill, he gripped and lifted her buttocks and eased into her, stretching her, filling her with his throbbing length. Wanting even more of him, she wrapped her long legs around his hips, taking him deep, rejoicing when he cried out in keening ecstasy. Abruptly he rolled over, taking her with him. Sierra squealed in delight when she found herself on top, firmly impaled, riding Ram as she would a wild stallion.

"Ride me, little love. Take the reins and do as you please."

Her expression grew rapturous as she moved experimentally, relishing the feel of his swollen length stroking her clenching tightness, going deeper than he'd ever gone before. She rode him wildly, thrusting herself up, then down, again and again, hips bucking, head thrown back, teeth clenched. Grasping her buttocks, Ram deliberately slowed her movements into a more leisurely pace, fearing it would end too soon.

"Not so fast, little wildcat," he moaned as if in pain. "It's too soon. Not yet . . . Not yet . . ."

He rolled over again, pressing her down into the sleeping mat, breathing hard, trying desperately to bring their unrestrained passion under control. But it was burning too hot to be contained. A powerful explosion was building inside him, and he couldn't hold it back. He speared her deeply, pulled nearly all the way out and plunged again, until his hips were pounding against hers in unrestrained abandon.

"Ram! I can't . . . Oh, God . . ."

Sierra's climax burst upon her in wave after wave of grinding, gut-wrenching pleasure. Ram gave a shout and galloped after her.

"Thank you, Ram," Sierra whispered when her breathing returned to normal.

"For what? You gave me as much pleasure as I gave you."

"For giving me something I'll never forget, no matter what happens to our lives."

Her words nearly ripped Ram apart. Never had he felt so helpless, never had life seemed so unfair. Since no reply could do justice to what he felt in his heart, he simply held her close. When the first muted streaks of dawn appeared on the distant horizon, Sierra stirred fretfully, knowing they must part soon.

"I know, little love," Ram said, kissing the top of her head. "You must leave. We'll be together until we part in Denver."

"But we won't be like this again. Why, Ram? Why won't you tell me what you're hiding? I believe you care for me. Why won't you trust me with your problems? They can't be so terrible, can they?"

The pain in Sierra's voice convinced Ram that he'd been wrong to keep her in the dark about his past. He opened his mouth to confide his deepest secrets when an angry voice shattered their euphoria.

"If you're in there with Hunter, Sierra, I'm going to kill the bastard. If my sister is good enough to bed, she's good enough to wed."

"Oh, God, it's Ryder."

"Get dressed," Ram said, scrambling into his pants. "I'll try to placate him until you're ready."

Sierra could hear them exchange angry words outside the tipi, but they had moved just far enough away to prevent her from deciphering what was being said. With shaking hands she pulled on her clothes.

Ryder faced Ramsey Hunter with murder in his heart. He trusted few white men, and Hunter had done nothing to earn his trust. He had gone to Sierra's tipi to make sure she'd be ready in time to leave and found it empty, and he knew without being told where he'd find her. When Ram stepped out of the tipi alone, Ryder wanted to tear his heart out.

"Either face my gun or marry my sister," Ryder said without preamble. "What kind of man are you? Have you no conscience? I'd be willing to bet my sister was an innocent until she met you."

"No matter what you think of me, I care deeply for your sister."

"Deeply enough to marry her?"

Ram struggled for breath. "I can't. And I won't draw against you. Sierra would hate me. If you want to kill me, go ahead."

"Don't you dare hurt him, Ryder!" Sierra had come out of the tipi in time to hear Ram's words. "He didn't come to me, I went to him. If you harm him, I swear I'll turn around and return to San Francisco."

Ryder went still. Didn't Sierra realize that the bounder had quite possibly ruined her life? How could she fancy herself in love with a man without morals? Had her adoptive parents taught her nothing about life?

"I'm older than you, honey, and having just found you, I'm naturally protective of you." He sent Ram a contemptuous glance. "A decent man would offer to marry the woman he ruined. Hunter deserves to be shot."

Sierra's chin rose belligerently. "I don't want to leave, Ryder, so don't force me to. Promise me you won't hurt Ram."

"I can fight my own battles, Sierra," Ram said harshly. In truth, he couldn't blame Ryder for flying to his sister's defense. He'd probably do the same if the tables were turned.

"Promise me, Ryder," Sierra said stubbornly.

Ryder's love for his sister defeated him. "Very well, Sierra, I'll respect your wishes. But I'll be damned if Hunter is going to get his hands on you again."

* * *

Sierra wasn't unhappy to leave Strong Hand's village. When Ryder had returned with her to her tipi, he stayed to help gather her meager belongings and was horrified when he discovered a rattler in her sleeping mat. Sierra had been too shaken up to think coherently, but Ryder had calmly shot the snake, fiercely grateful that Sierra hadn't slept in her own sleeping mat last night. If she had, she might not be alive today. He hated to admit it, but her desire for Ramsey Hunter had most probably saved her life.

Up until the moment of their departure, Firewalker had persistently badgered Ryder to accept the ten horses he had offered for Sierra. Of course Ryder had refused. Even more upsetting was the way in which Prairie Flower stared at her, as if she were a ghost. Sierra had a strong suspicion that the snake in her sleeping mat was the work of the vindictive Indian woman.

Ram had been horrified when he heard about her close call, and the furious look he gave Prairie Flower told Sierra that his thoughts coincided with hers.

"I probably will never see Strong Hand again," Ryder said as they rode from the village. "He decided not to move his people to the reservation. I fear they will all perish. Even if they manage somehow to survive the winter, the army will find their hiding place and few of them will live to tell the tale."

He sounded so sad that Sierra couldn't find it

in her heart to speak harshly of Strong Hand, his sister, or their people.

"That's the Great Divide ahead," Ryder said, pointing toward the towering peaks in the distance.

Even in late August, the peaks and deep crevices were sprinkled with glittering snow. Sierra could see creeks and small waterfalls rushing down steep inclines to gather in valleys stretching below. Aspens, spruce, fir, and pines presented breathtaking contrasts in varying shades of yellow and gold-tinged green. Wild animals abounded in the clearings of lush grasses and shrubs, adding yet another infusion of color to the muted greens and golds of the higher elevations.

"It's beautiful," Sierra said reverently.

"Don't be surprised to see whole herds of elk or deer at the edges of clearings. Or wild mustangs."

To Sierra's chagrin, Ryder allowed Ram and Sierra scant opportunity for privacy on the trail. Ryder felt little sympathy for Ramsey Hunter. White men, he thought derisively, were still very much a mystery to him despite his best efforts to understand them.

Ryder seemed familiar with the mountain trails, leading them across narrow bridges, through well-trodden passes, and down into valleys lush with vegetation. At night when they made camp, either Ryder or Ram hunted game for their evening meal, and since water was abundant, their canteens were always as full as their bellies. Three days later, the Great Divide was behind them. The high country fell away in varying degrees until the horizon came down to meet the mile-high ground upon which Denver had been built.

Sierra gained a wealth of information from Ryder during their days on the trail, catching her up on the years during which they had been separated. She had heard so much about Abby, Zach, Hannah, and the little ones that she was eager to meet them at long last.

"Will you take me to your home or to Abby's?" Sierra asked.

"I thought I'd take you to meet Abby first," Ryder replied. "She and Zach bought a large house in town just recently. They loved the farm, but Zach's freighting company has grown so prosperous in the past two years that he felt it necessary to move closer to his business. They rent the farm out to sharecroppers.

"Hannah loves our place on the river and wouldn't move to town for any reason, but she does like to visit Denver occasionally. Abby has been begging us to come to town for a long visit, and this might be a good time. After I drop you off at Abby's house, I'll continue on home and return in a few days with Hannah and Lacy."

"Sounds wonderful," Sierra sighed. She was happy, but not as happy as she would have been if she and Ram weren't parting.

She had gained so much during this journey. She had found a family she had only dared dream about, discovered passion, and fallen in love with an exceptional man.

The passion had been returned in abundance. The love had not.

Chapter Thirteen

Descending from the lofty granite heights of the Rockies, Sierra stared in fascination at the ever-changing scenery. Snowcapped peaks gave way to foothills and dense groves of firs. Graceful aspens, already turning yellow for fall's colorful display, were replaced by cottonwoods, pines, piñon, and juniper. The descent was breathtaking—almost distracting enough to turn Sierra's mind from Ram and what promised to be a painful parting. Perhaps not painful for him, but definitely for her.

The silence was deafening. Sierra heard nothing but the creak of leather and muffled thud of hooves on the pine-needle-strewn path as they descended the high trail. The keening cry of a soaring eagle startled her, and she shielded her eyes to gaze upward into a sun-drenched sky.

"Did you ever wonder why you were named Sierra?" Ryder asked, his voice shattering the peace and tranquility of the forest.

Sierra looked at her brother with renewed interest. "Upon occasion. But since no one really knew the answer, I gave up wondering."

"Our parents dreamed of settling on the Western frontier even before you were born," Ryder said, digging deep into his memory. "Had you been a boy, you would have been named Rocky, but since you were a girl, and the only mountain range that lent itself to a girl's name was the Sierras, you were called Sierra. If I recall correctly—it's been so long—both Abby and I were thrilled with the choice."

Sierra smiled wistfully, happy to have even that small piece of information about her past.

Gradually they descended to the foothills, and Ryder reined to a stop, pointing to a collection of buildings rising in the distance. "There's Denver. And that's Cherry Creek. It separates the city from Aurora."

"It's bigger than I remembered," Ram said, reining in beside them.

"You've been here before?" Sierra asked, recalling how little she knew about Ram.

Ram nodded. "About eight years ago. Did a little prospecting along the creek. Even built a cabin but didn't stay long."

"Let's ride," Ryder said. "I can't wait to see Abby's face when I introduce you. Perhaps I'll have a little fun before I tell her who you are."

He kneed his mount and trotted off. When Sierra prepared to follow, Ram grasped her reins.

"This might be our last chance to speak privately," he said in a stilted voice. Sierra searched his face, fragile hope dying when she saw the bleak look in his eyes. She should have known better than to think he'd had a change of heart about marrying her.

"I never wanted to hurt you," he said earnestly. "What happened between us was—"

"—wonderful," Sierra said firmly. "And inevitable. Please don't make it sound demeaning. It was as much my fault as yours. I care for you, Ram. My mistake was not realizing how much you cared for Dora. I had no chance with you right from the start, did I?"

"No," he said slowly, "but it's not because—"

"Please, Ram, don't lie to me, I don't think I could bear it."

It nearly broke Ram's heart to let Sierra believe he loved Dora, but circumstances made it necessary. She needed to forget him and get on with her life. He was thankful that she had a new family to help her recover. But there was a matter of vital importance that needed settling before they parted.

"Before we reach Denver, I want your promise to let me know if—if you're increasing."

"Why?"

"My God, Sierra, how can you ask? I'd never deny a child I've created, especially one whose mother I care about."

Sierra stared at him.

"Your promise, Sierra," Ram said from between clenched teeth. "If I don't get it, I swear I'll tell Ryder that you might be carrying my child."

"Don't you think he already suspects as much?"

"Maybe he does and maybe he doesn't, but when I get through with him, he'll have no reason to doubt."

"He might insist that we marry."

"I think not," Ram said with such conviction that Sierra flinched inwardly. Ram knew that once he told Ryder the truth, there would be no forced wedding. He might find himself facing the business end of Ryder's gun, or that deadly knife he carried, but there definitely wouldn't be a wedding.

"Very well, Ram, I promise. But I don't think you have anything to worry about."

With a heavy heart, Sierra spurred her mount and shot off after Ryder before Ram could stop her. Tears blurred her vision, and she dashed them away. Despite Ram's rejection, she did not regret the hours she'd spent in his arms—blissful hours when the world around them receded, hours when he belonged solely to her. Not even the mysterious Dora had intruded upon the love they shared so briefly. But beneath their moments of shared happiness, she sensed a sadness in Ram. No, she amended, not so much a sadness as a silent anguish, a need for something she could not give him. She prayed Dora could give him what he needed.

Experiencing Ram's passion and discovering her own had been the high point in her life, but she wanted more than fleeting passion from him. She wanted to share his hopes, his dreams, his silences, his laughter. She wanted to bear his children, to earn his trust and respect. She wanted to feel his joy, his sorrow, everything that a woman could share with the man she loved.

She wanted to be loved in return.

The feeling that she had somehow failed Ram persisted as they rode through the misty twilight into the city of Denver. If Ram had trusted her enough to confide in her, she might have been able to help, but obviously Ram could not overcome his distrust of women long enough to take her into his confidence. What had Dora done to hurt him so badly and why did he still love her?

"Here's where we part company, Hunter," Ryder said, turning to Ram. "Follow this road to the livery and turn left at Dowling Street. The Denver Hotel is located halfway down the street. You can't miss it. I'm taking Sierra to our sister's home. If you care about Sierra, you'll not try to contact her during your stay in town."

Sierra wanted to tell Ram that Ryder's wishes weren't hers, that she'd be happy to see him, but Ryder slapped her horse's rump, and the mare took off down the street at a brisk canter.

"Don't forget what I said, Sierra," Ram called after her. "You gave your promise."

Ram's hands were shaking when he reined his mount toward the hotel. There was only one other time in his life when he'd felt so bereft, so utterly alone, and he'd spent the last ten years feeding on his hatred for the woman who had caused those emotions. He strongly suspected that he'd spend what was left of his life empty of all emotion, and for reasons that had nothing to do with Dora.

Ryder knocked on the door of the large, stately house and flashed Sierra a grin. "Remember now, not a word until I introduce you. Abby will think all kinds of things when she sees you with me, none of them kind, but I can't resist teasing her a little before I introduce you."

"That's a dirty trick to play on our sister," Sierra said with a hint of rebuke.

"Don't worry, she won't be angry when she learns who you are. Keep your head down so she won't see your eyes too soon and spoil the surprise."

Suddenly the door opened, revealing a lovely, obviously pregnant young woman with honey-blond hair and intelligent gray eyes. Sierra was struck immediately by the family resemblance.

"Ryder! What a grand surprise. It's not often that my favorite and oh-so-handsome brother drops in for a visit. Have you been out to the farm yet?" Ryder shook his head. "How fortunate that you came here first."

She gave him a hug and pulled him into the room. Sierra followed in his wake. "What do you mean by that remark?" Ryder asked curiously. "Is there some reason I shouldn't go out to the farm?"

"You wouldn't have found Hannah and Lacy home had you gone first to the farm. Zach went out to check on them yesterday, and Hannah seemed so lonely that he brought her and Lacy to town for a visit. Now we can have a real family reunion."

"Yes, indeed, a real family reunion," Ryder repeated innocently as he dragged Sierra from behind him into full view. Placing a strong arm around her waist, he gave her an affectionate squeeze. Horrified, Abby took one look at the lovely young woman who had accompanied Ryder and blanched. She sent Ryder a fulminating scowl. The tender way Ryder looked at the woman, his gray eyes shining with love, brought Abby to a premature conclusion. She didn't want to believe it of Ryder. He was the last person in the world she would expect to take up with another woman. Until now, his whole world had revolved around Hannah and Lacy.

"My God, Ryder, what have you done? Who is this woman? How could you? I never thought you'd stoop to this. How dare you bring a lightskirt into my home?"

Suddenly Zach burst into the room. "What is

it, Abby? I heard you shouting clear upstairs." Then he spied Ryder, grinning from ear to ear, his arm around a woman Zach had never seen before. He gave his brother-in-law an uncertain smile while his sharp blue eyes assessed Sierra carefully. "Good to have you back, Ryder." Zach's sweeping glance missed nothing, noting Sierra's beauty and graceful figure. He cocked a blond eyebrow at Ryder, as if to question his sanity.

"Calm down, sis," Ryder said, laughing softly. "I've brought someone for you to meet. Someone who is very dear to me."

A loud gasp from the doorway captured Sierra's attention. A petite, auburn-haired woman with vivid green eyes was looking at Ryder as if he'd just broken her heart.

"Ryder?"

"Hannah!" Dropping his arm from Sierra's waist, Ryder gave a whoop and bounded toward his wife, lifting her from her feet and swinging her around in joyful welcome.

"Now wait a damn minute," Abby said, hands on hips as she watched Ryder's bizarre behavior. Someone owed her an explanation, and it had better be good. She trusted her brother and knew he loved Hannah too much to discard her for another woman. "What is this all about, Ryder?"

"Put me down!" Hannah cried, struggling to escape Ryder's strong embrace. She couldn't think straight with his arms around her. "Are you trying to tell me something, Ryder? Who is that woman and what is she to you? If she thinks she can take you away from me, she'll have a fight on her hands. And if I win, I may kill you before I'll forgive you."

Ryder laughed uproariously. He couldn't recall when he'd had such a good time. Did his family actually think he'd bring home a mistress? It was time to put an end to speculation. Setting Hannah down on her feet, he went to Sierra, placed a protective arm around her shoulder, and brought her into the family circle.

"I did indeed bring home another woman." Hannah's cry of distress and the murderous expression in Zach's eyes convinced him that his little joke must be brought to a speedy conclusion. Placing a finger beneath Sierra's chin, he lifted her face. "Open your eyes, honey, and meet your family. That feisty blonde is your sister Abby, and that ugly fellow next to her is her husband Zach. And that little copper-haired hellion with blazing green eyes is my wife Hannah. This lovely young woman," he said, thrusting Sierra forward, "is Sierra. Sierra Larson Alden."

Clearly upset with Ryder for the trick he had played on his family, Sierra's gray eyes darkened to the color of storm clouds, but they were still unmistakably Larson eyes. But if she had expected an exuberant welcome, she was disappointed. Absolute silence prevailed. It grew so still in the room that Sierra wanted to turn and run away, back to Ram, all the way back to San Francisco. Why did no one speak? Wasn't anyone besides Ryder glad to see her?

Several excruciating minutes passed before profound shock wore off, replaced by shouts of happiness. Abby sobbed and clung to Zach for support, so great was her shock. Hannah burst into tears, knowing what finding Sierra meant to the family. Everyone began jabbering at once.

Abby was the first to regain her composure, rushing forward to hug Sierra with fierce joy. "I didn't think I'd live to see this day," she said brokenly. "Ryder and I have hoped and prayed but never truly expected to find you. The detective we hired took our money but gave us very little hope. Welcome home, Sierra."

"Oh, Abby," Sierra sobbed as the two sisters embraced, "I've dreamed of this moment. I may have been young when we were separated, but I never forgot you or Ryder, never gave up hope, never!" She said it so fiercely that Abby recognized a determination as strong as hers and Ryder's.

"You're a Larson, all right," Abby said laughingly. "And it's not just the eyes that give you away. Come in and sit down. You must tell us everything about your life. I want to know about the people who adopted you, and about your husband, if you have one."

Ryder frowned, still fuming over Ram Hunter's refusal to marry Sierra. "Sierra is not married. She can fill you in on the rest."

Abby sensed Ryder's anger and wondered about it as she directed Sierra to a comfortable chair. The family closed ranks around her.

"Where are the children?" Sierra asked, anxious to see the younger members of her family.

"Sleeping," Hannah said. "I've just put Lacy and Trey to bed. They're as wild a pair as you'd ever want to see when they're together. We usually put them to bed as soon after supper as we can." Suddenly she recalled her manners. "Oh, you and Ryder must be starved. Come out to the kitchen. You can eat while you tell us all about your life. I'm dying to know how Ryder found you."

The food was delicious. Between mouthfuls Sierra related the rather boring facts of her dull life as the pampered daughter of Holly and Lester Alden. Her years at school had been as uneventful as her years of growing up in San Francisco with servants to see to her every whim. When Abby clamored to know how she had gotten to Denver, she repeated Ram's lie, divulging little except that a friend of her father's had escorted her. She tried to keep the excitement from her voice when speaking about Ram but fooled neither Abby nor Hannah, who had experienced countless problems of their own before finding love with their mates not to recognize the depth of Sierra's feelings for Ramsey Hunter.

When Sierra launched into the tale of how she met Ryder at Strong Hand's camp, Abby's eyes widened. "You were Strong Hand's captive? I remember meeting him once. He was quite fierce, even by Indian standards. Thank God you remembered Ryder's Indian name. Ryder has been trying to convince Strong Hand to take his people to the reservation for the winter."

"If I hadn't mentioned Wind Rider, I would have been given to Firewalker," Sierra related. "And Ram . . ." She reddened and stared at her hands. "Prairie Flower wanted Ram."

"Just like Tears Like Rain wanted me," Zach said, smiling fondly at Abby. "I must admit, becoming a fierce Indian maiden's slave didn't appeal to me at the time, but it did have its rewards." His smile turned into a wicked grin, and now it was Abby's turn to blush.

"Tell me all about your life with the Cheyenne," Sierra said eagerly. She had talked enough about herself and needed to take her mind off Ram. Had he gone to Dora immediately or would he wait until tomorrow? she wondered dimly.

They talked late into the night, each relating a brief summary of his or her life. When it was Ryder's turn, he spoke slowly, his eyes never leaving those of his beautiful wife. With amazing insight, Sierra sensed that Ryder wasn't reconciled to living as a white man and that he was still confused about his identity. But no one could doubt his deep love for his wife and his commitment to the Indian people.

Ryder and Hannah drifted off to bed first. They hadn't seen one another in over two weeks, and Sierra could tell they were hungry for each other. If she hadn't experienced love firsthand with Ram she would never have known that. Zach left next, sensing Abby's need to be alone with Sierra. He kissed Abby's forehead and told her to take her time.

"I should go to bed myself," Sierra said, sighing tiredly. "So much has happened to me since leaving San Francisco, it's almost like living a dream. Whoever would have thought I'd attempt a cross-country trip by myself, or be captured by Indians, or meet my brother under circumstances that could hardly be called normal? You and Ryder are everything I ever dreamed you'd be. I can hardly wait to meet the children."

Something Sierra said stuck in Abby's mind. "I thought you said Ramsey Hunter accompanied you. If that is true, you didn't exactly travel alone." She searched Sierra's face, as if trying to read her sister's mind.

Sierra flushed and looked away. "Well, yes, there was Ram. I didn't mean . . . that is . . ."

Abby reached out and patted Sierra's hand. "Do you want to tell me about it, honey? I am older than you and somewhat more experienced. Is there something I should know about Ramsey Hunter? Is he really an old family friend? Is he old at all?"

Sierra shook her head. Lord, no! Ram wasn't old, he was . . . "Ramsey Hunter and father are

277

friends, but Ram isn't old. Around thirty, I would imagine."

"And much more experienced than you, little sister. I sense something is bothering you. Did . . ." She hated to ask but felt the need to protect her sister. "Did he take advantage of you?"

Sierra shook her head in vigorous denial. "The answer is no to both questions, Abby, and I really don't want to talk about Ram. I'll always be grateful to him for saving my life when the stage went into the ravine, but in all likelihood I'll never see him again. Besides, I'm engaged to Gordon Lynch. Gordie works for Father at the bank and I expect we'll be married when I return to San Francisco." The lie nearly stuck in her throat.

Abby grew alarmed. "Don't even think about returning! You just got here. Let us enjoy our visit, and I promise not to ask questions you don't wish to answer. I'll show you to your room, honey, and tomorrow you'll meet the children."

Grateful for Abby's understanding, Sierra gave her sister's arm a squeeze before they ascended the stairs together.

Ram paused before Room 214 and rapped softly.

"It's late. Who is it?" The man's voice was gruff and impatient.

"Ramsey Hunter." Ram had already arranged for his own room at the Denver Hotel and couldn't wait till morning to settle this pressing piece of business.

The door opened immediately. "Mr. Hunter. I'd almost given up on you. Where have you been? You should have arrived in Denver weeks ago."

"You wouldn't believe me if I told you," Ram said, rolling his eyes heavenward. "Suffice it to say, I was unavoidably detained, Crookshank. Thank God you waited."

Crookshank gave Ram a hard look. Everything about the man had a hard edge to it— from his lean, sinewy body to his angular, square-jawed face. "There is the matter of my fee, Mr. Hunter."

"You'll get your money," Ram said tersely, "but first tell me, have the birds flown?"

Crookshank grinned without mirth. "Still here, Mr. Hunter. I don't think they have any idea you're hot on their trail. It took a good deal of digging to find them, but I finally tracked them down. You'll find the man at the Silver Nugget almost any night of the week. He's a regular at the poker table. Sometimes the woman accompanies him. She's a damn good-looking piece. I've been watching them for over two weeks. He uses her to distract the other players while he deals from the bottom. Sometimes he uses her in other ways," he hinted, sending Ram a meaningful glance.

"You've done a damn fine job, Crookshank," Ram said. "You'll get your money and a bonus just as soon as the bank opens in the morning.

Where I can find them?"

"They rent a ramshackle house on Broadway, Number 742."

Ram left soon afterward. After supper and a hot bath, he went to bed, but sleep eluded him. A vivid picture of Dora floated before his eyes. He imagined her the way she'd looked when he kissed her good-bye before leaving to visit his parents that day ten years ago. He heard her sweet lying lips telling him how much she loved him, recalled how her lush body pressed against his with seductive promise. God, he had loved her!

Abruptly his thoughts turned to Sierra. There was no comparison between a deceitful jade like Dora and a woman as fiercely honest and brave as Sierra. Sierra was sunshine and freshness and sweet light after years of living in darkness, nurturing his bitterness and hatred. When he left San Francisco, he had every intention of killing Jason and devising a just punishment for Dora. After meeting Sierra and learning to care about someone again, he was having second thoughts—not that the pair didn't deserve harsh punishment. He'd dreamed too long of revenge. He'd never killed in cold blood and wasn't certain he could do so now. Yet if he turned them over to the law, they might not get what was coming to them.

Damn Dora!

So beautiful . . . So passionate . . .

So deadly.

He remembered . . .

God, he didn't want to remember. It hurt too much.

Chapter Fourteen

The nightly crowd at the Silver Nugget was behaving in their usual rowdy manner as Ram and Crookshank shared a bottle at a table tucked away in a dark corner. Jamming his hat lower over his forehead, Ram slouched forward, his blue eyes cold and intense as he watched the play at one of the poker tables. He'd sat at this same table every night for a week, watching Jason and waiting for Dora to appear. His patience had been rewarded when Dora walked through the door earlier, clinging to Jason's arm.

Ram's eyes narrowed as he watched Dora distract the players seated around the poker table. He hadn't expected to find her still as lovely as the day he met her. With cool appraisal, his gaze slid over the smooth creaminess of her alabaster skin, the full lushness of her red lips, the silken texture of her pale blond hair. She had changed little in ten years, he reflected, his eyes settling on the ripe thrust of her breasts against the low-cut gown she wore. The provocative way she leaned forward provided every man who cared to look with an unrestricted glimpse of extravagant curves spilling from the neckline of her bodice.

"See what I mean," Crookshank said as he strained to get a better view of the generously endowed Dora. "Now watch Jordan. Even an inexperienced gambler could see him dealing from the bottom if he wasn't blinded by the woman's charms."

Ram nodded grimly. It was just as Crookshank had described. A man would be a fool not to stare at Dora. Her blond beauty hadn't diminished in all these years, and her body had matured with spectacular results.

"My work here is finished," Crookshank said, rising to his feet. "I'm off on a new job tomorrow. It's been nice working for you, Mr. Hunter."

They shook hands and Ram wished him well. In a matter of seconds, Crookshank was forgotten as Ram returned his attention to Dora and Jason. Long-repressed memories crowded together inside his head. Images of Dora, her passion exploding as she writhed beneath him, her hot mouth and seeking hands driving him wild with love for her. He remembered Jason, coming to live with them as a young lad when no one else wanted him, eagerly accepting a job at the Cow Palace, not once indicating how much he resented Ram.

Shaking his head to clear it of painful memories, Ram sucked morosely on his drink, waiting, watching. . . . It was long past midnight when the game finally broke up. One by one the players drifted away, except for one man, who engaged Jason in earnest conversation. A snort of disgust slipped past Ram's lips when he saw money changing hands. A few minutes later, Jason spoke with Dora and she left with the gambler. Though she didn't look particularly happy with the arrangement, she had made no vocal complaint, giving Ram the impression that she had done this kind of thing before.

Jason left a short time later, and so did Ram. He had much to think about, plans to make. Having seen Dora and Jason again after all these years had served only to intensify his hatred and brought a renewed vow to seek revenge. Somehow, some way, Dora and Jason would be punished for the two years they had carved out of his life. And for all the years that followed. They'd find him not so easily gulled this time around.

It was Dora's fault that he'd been unable to offer Sierra the kind of life she deserved. Had he known where to find Dora, he could have resolved things long ago and been free to return Sierra's love.

*   *   *

Sierra took comfort in and gained joy from her family, but not happiness. Only Ram could give her the kind of happiness she craved, but regrettably Ram didn't want her. With each passing day, Sierra learned more and more about her extraordinary family. She had been astounded when Abby told her how she and Zach had saved White Feather's life just moments before the Sand Creek Massacre. She learned that Summer Moon, White Feather's widow, was still happily married to Coyote and lived on the reservation. They had a son together, in addition to the son Summer Moon had borne White Feather.

If she had Ram's love, her life would be complete, but Ram didn't love her. Though Sierra tried to conceal her sadness over the loss of Ram in her life, Abby had not been fooled. She learned just how much Abby was attuned to her feelings about a week into her visit. Hannah had already gone back to the farm with Ryder and Lacy when Abby suggested a trip to town. Sierra agreed with alacrity, and they left Trey behind with his nurse.

"Is there anything I can do to help?" Abby asked as they traveled down a pleasant, tree-lined street.

Sierra stared at her. "Help me? I don't know what you mean."

"I think you do, honey," Abby said gently. "I know something is bothering you. Is it Ramsey Hunter? I can't help feeling there's something you're not telling me about your friendship."

Sierra flushed. Abby had come too close to the truth for comfort. "Whatever is or was between us is over."

"How do you know if you refuse to discuss the problem?"

"Do you see Ram knocking down the door to see me?" Sierra asked resentfully.

"I know Ryder doesn't think much of Mr. Hunter, but I usually form my own opinions."

"I chased after him once and I won't do it again, that's all I'm going to say. Please, Abby, don't spoil this outing. Let's just enjoy our reunion."

Abby's heart went out to Sierra. She wanted to help, but unless Sierra confided in her there was nothing she could do. "Shall we stop at Bradley's Tea Room for refreshments?"

Sierra's face lit up. "Oh, yes, let's do. I'm really partial to those little cakes they make at Bradley's."

After enjoying a relaxing hour in the tea room, Sierra and Abby left arm in arm. They had just reached their buggy when Sierra saw Ram walking in their direction. Ram saw Sierra and was nearly overcome by the sight of her. He thought her more beautiful even than he remembered. He hadn't counted on bumping into Sierra like this, seeing her again, feeling all those emotions he remembered so well, and he wondered if fate had a hand in throwing them together when he least expected it. There were so many things he wanted to tell her before his confrontation with Dora and Jason today, things he should have told her long ago.

"Hello, Ram," Sierra said, gazing intently into his face. She thought he looked haggard.

A light in Ram's eyes kindled at the sight of Sierra. "Hello, Sierra, how are you?"

"Well enough, and you?" It nearly killed Sierra to exchange small talk with Ram when what she really wanted was to throw herself into his arms, kiss him until she grew dizzy, and feel him returning the love and passion she felt toward him. "This is my sister, Abby Mercer. Abby, you've heard me speak of Ramsey Hunter, I'm sure."

Abby sent Sierra an amused glance. So this was the man Sierra had been pining for since her arrival in Denver. She offered Ram a slim hand, liking what she saw. Ram was much like Zach, she decided as she studied him with avid curiosity. She wished she knew what had happened between Ramsey Hunter and her sister, and why Ryder disliked the man.

"How do you do, Mr. Hunter. Sierra has indeed spoken of you. I've wanted to thank you for taking such good care of her."

Ram looked startled. "Not good enough care, Mrs. Mercer, since I couldn't save her from captivity. Her own ingenuity did what I couldn't."

"Nevertheless," Abby said warmly, "you saved her from possible death when the stagecoach went down the ravine. Sierra told us all about the accident."

"It was nice seeing you, Ram," Sierra said, reluctant to part. "Have you . . . taken care of your business yet?"

Ram gave her a searching look. "No, not yet, but I intend to very soon."

Abby looked from Sierra to Ram, sensing the significance of all that was left unsaid between them and wondering if Ram's business concerned Sierra. Perhaps Ryder was right, she thought worriedly. Perhaps it was in her sister's best interest to keep Sierra and Ramsey Hunter apart. The very air seemed to vibrate between them. "I'm suddenly feeling very tired, Sierra. Let's return home and continue our outing another time."

Sierra sent Abby a concerned look. "Are you unwell? Is it the baby?"

Abby shook her head. "I'm merely tired."

"I've been hoping for a word alone with Sierra, Mrs. Mercer. I've been wanting to call on her, but your brother made it abundantly clear that I wouldn't be welcomed in your home. If you wish to leave, perhaps you'll allow me to see Sierra home later. There is a matter of some importance I need to discuss with her."

Abby's warmth cooled immediately. If Ryder had forbidden Ramsey Hunter to call on Sierra, then something indeed must be wrong with the man. Something Ryder and Sierra had failed to mention. She glanced at Sierra and was shocked at the expression of naked hunger on her sister's face. She'd never forgive herself if Ramsey Hunter hurt her little sister. If he did, he'd find himself at the receiving end of Cheyenne justice, for like Ryder, she hadn't entirely discarded everything she'd learned at White Feather's knee.

"The livery is just around the corner," Ram said, searching Sierra's face. "I'll rent a buggy and take you for a ride into the foothills. I'll have her home early, Mrs. Mercer."

Abby sent Ram a wary glance. Lord, Ryder would be fit to be tied if she allowed Ram to spirit Sierra off without a chaperon. "That really wouldn't be proper. Perhaps it would be more circumspect if you bought Sierra lunch at the hotel and brought her home immediately afterward."

Sierra sighed in exasperation. "Abby, really, I am twenty-one, after all, and I've been alone with Ram before."

"That's what I'm afraid of," Abby muttered beneath her breath as Ram assisted her into the buggy. Lord, what have I done? she asked herself as she watched them walk away. She'd never forgive herself if Ramsey Hunter turned out to be a first-class scoundrel. But there was no denying she'd liked him, and she was usually a good judge of character. She had no choice now but to pray Sierra knew what she was doing.

"Are you happy with your new family?" Ram asked as they walked toward the livery.

"Deliriously happy," Sierra grinned. "They're everything I've ever wanted and more."

"Abby seems nice."

"She is, and so is Ryder, despite your animosity toward one another. You can't blame Ryder for being protective of me."

Ram said nothing. Ryder had good reason to dislike him. He had taken his sister's innocence and refused to marry her. Silence prevailed until they reached the livery, where Ram arranged to rent a buggy for the day.

Sierra didn't ask where Ram was taking her as they left Denver behind. She was too happy just being with him again to ask questions.

"Have you seen Dora?" Sierra asked when she could no longer bear the silence.

Ram gave her a sharp look. He didn't want to talk about Dora. He regretted having blurted her name out in his sleep, giving Sierra the impression that he cared for the woman. "Not yet."

"She is in Denver, isn't she?"

"She's in Denver," Ram said tightly, "and I intend to see her very soon, but not for the reason you think."

Sierra stored that bit of information away for later consideration. "Did you mean what you told Abby? Did you really want to see me?"

"You know damn well I did. But I was—"

"—afraid of Ryder?" Somehow Sierra couldn't believe Ram feared Ryder.

"No, not Ryder. I didn't trust myself. I can't control myself when I'm with you, Sierra, and I didn't want to hurt you again."

"Why haven't you seen Dora? What are you waiting for?"

"The right time. Have you sent a telegram to your father in San Francisco?" Ram asked, adroitly changing the subject.

"Of course—did you think I wouldn't? I love Holly and Lester Alden. I didn't want them worrying unnecessarily."

Ram fell silent, simply enjoying Sierra's company.

"Why did you suggest this ride, Ram?"

Ram halted the buggy in a peaceful glade between two mountains. A bubbling creek meandered through the grassy glen. He turned to look at Sierra, his face harsh with anguish. "There's something I need to tell you, Sierra. At first it didn't seem necessary for you to know, but after we . . . became close, it was wrong of me to keep the truth from you."

"The truth? I'm not sure I want to know."

"Let's walk a little way," Ram said, helping her down from the buggy. His hands lingered on her waist so long that she could feel the searing heat of his palms through her clothing.

"It's beautiful here," Sierra sighed. "So peaceful."

"I'm quite familiar with this area," Ram said. "I once prospected along this creek."

Taking her arm, Ram guided her along a narrow path that took them through trees and rocks that looked as if they had been placed there by God in the beginning of time. The quiet was shattered only by their uneven breathing as they climbed upward along the slight incline. If Ram was looking for a private place for their talk, he had found the perfect spot, Sierra thought. They could have been the only two people left on earth.

"Let's rest here," Ram suggested, pointing to a misshapen fir tree growing beneath the shadow of a huge rock. He took off his coat and laid it at the foot of the tree, waited for her to sit down, then settled beside her. When his arms went around her, she didn't complain, melting against him in hungry yearning.

The smoldering heat of Ram's eyes kindled into liquid flames, consuming her in raw fire. An exquisite sensation shot through her when her breasts met the muscular heat of his chest. The moment he touched her, she realized just how desperately she had ached to feel him hold her again.

"Oh God, Sierra, you feel so damn good in my arms. The last few days have been pure hell without you." He touched her cheek with fingers that were less than steady. Then he bent his head to taste the trembling corners of her mouth.

Sierra sighed blissfully when he probed the sultry heat of her mouth with deep thrusting movements of his tongue, stroking her, wanting her with a hunger that was slowly destroying him. When Ram finally ended the kiss, he was wholly, totally aroused. Sierra felt the hardened ridge through the layers of her clothing, rubbing herself against him in sensual abandon. This was what she wanted, what she had yearned for to make her complete.

"Ram . . ."

The huskiness of Sierra's voice caressed his senses, dragging a groan from him.

"I didn't bring you here for this, little love, but I hope you want me as much as I want you. If you want to stop this now, just say the word and we'll leave."

Sierra took hold of his hand and placed it over her breast, where her heart raced out of control. "Can you feel my heart pounding? Until you touched me, it was just a whisper inside my chest. Now I can hardly contain its wild thumping. It beats for you, Ram, only for you. Your touch is like magic."

Ram's breath broke when he felt her nipple harden at his touch. He bent his head, dragging his teeth against it through her clothing, then wetting it with his tongue. Sierra made a throaty sound as she arched against him, wanting more.

"I want you, little love. I want to sheath myself inside you and feel you tighten around me. I want you so damn much, it's embarrassing."

Ram felt the tremor that went though Sierra as clearly as she did.

Sierra's throat was so dry that speech was impossible. But her luminous gray eyes provided Ram with the answer he sought. Passionately, he took her mouth as his fingers released the fastenings on her dress, pulling the edges of her shift apart, baring her breasts to his sight and touch. When his mouth moved down to cover a cresting peak, Sierra's provocative cry frayed the cords of his restraint. With shaking hands, he skimmed her leg, raising her skirts until he'd bared the treasure lying hidden beneath the layers of her clothing. He found the slit in her pantalettes and cupped her, testing her warmth with probing fingers.

Sierra arched and thrust her loins against his hand, bathing him in liquid heat. "Oh, Ram, please."

"I know, little love, I want the same thing," Ram gasped raggedly. "I want you naked beneath me, but this is neither the time nor the place. I never meant to take you in haste like this, but I can't help myself. Open for me, sweetheart. I've never needed you as much as I do now."

He shifted slightly, fumbled with his trouser opening, and pressed between her legs. Sierra felt the smooth, wet tip of him probing her heat and the solid thrust of him into her throbbing center. Then he was stroking, retreating, stroking again, consuming her with sensual fire. It flared all around her as she writhed beneath him, convulsing her inside and out. Within seconds he felt the pulses of his own climax surging powerfully into her clenching heat.

Ram waited until his breathing returned to normal before he lifted himself from Sierra and began repairing the mess he'd made of her clothes. When she was decent, his gaze probed deeply into the silver depths of her eyes. "Forgive me, Sierra. I'm a total bastard."

Sierra sat up abruptly, staring at him. "I don't understand."

"I didn't bring you here for this. There's something I need to tell you. Something I should have told you before we reached Denver but never got the chance."

"Are you finally going to tell me about Dora?" The catch in Sierra's voice told Ram just how deeply his reticence had hurt her. She might hate him afterward, but it was better than letting her think he loved another woman.

"It's time you knew about Dora and our . . . relationiship."

She searched his face. "Do you still love her so much?"

"My God! Is that what you think? I feel nothing but contempt for Dora. It's you I care about."

Stunned, Sierra said shakily, "I thought you loved Dora."

Ram sighed. "At one time I loved her, but that love died years ago. She put me through hell and ran off with my best friend."

"Don't lie to me, Ram. You wouldn't be chasing after her all these years if you didn't still love her. Ten years is a long time to hold a grudge."

"Not if the woman was your wife and she betrayed you in the worst way possible. Not if her lies made your life a living hell, and she and your best friend had planned it all."

"Wife?" Her voice was so low that Ram could barely make out her words. "Dora is your wife?"

His wife. Dora was Ram's wife. My God, what a fool she'd been not to realize it.

"I'm sorry, sweetheart, but yes, Dora is my

wife. We were married over eleven years ago. I was a naive youth of twenty-one, so damn in love I could see none of the flaws my family pointed out to me. She had the face of an angel and the body of a temptress. She told me I was the only man she would ever love."

"I . . . I don't want to hear this, Ram." It hurt too much to hear Ram speak of how much he had loved another woman.

"Hear me out, Sierra," Ram pleaded. "I spent one year in blissful ignorance before my world collapsed. I had no idea that Dora and Jason were lovers."

"Lovers! You've mentioned Jason before. Your wife must have been either crazy or stupid to take a lover when she had you."

Ram sent her a grateful smile. "I was young, gullible, and inexperienced then. Jason was older, wiser in the ways of women, and as I discovered too late, greedy. I was only seven years old when my parents took Jason into their home to raise. He was fifteen. His parents had been killed by Indians, and he had no relatives. Jason and I, along with my brother, became inseparable. When Jeff joined the Texas Rangers, Jason and I became closer than ever.

"Then I met Dora. We were both eighteen. She had moved to town to live with her grandmother. I fell in love with her instantly. I should have inquired why she'd been sent by her parents to live with her grandmother, but I was too much in love."

Sierra gave a sad little smile, imagining how

wonderful it would be to have Ram's love.

"My parents sent me to Houston to school, but I couldn't endure being away from Dora. I returned for good two years later and asked Dora to become my wife. I had no idea she and Jason had grown close during my absence."

"Why didn't Dora marry Jason?" Sierra asked curiously.

"Jason was an orphan. He had no money, nothing except his job on my parents' ranch. On the other hand, my parents were well off. When I married, they offered me half interest in the ranch, if I wanted it, and if I didn't, they would set me up in business. I chose to become a businessman, since ranching didn't appeal to me.

"My family wasn't happy with my choice of wife, but being loving parents, they accepted Dora. About that time I learned that Hiram Walker was looking for a partner. He owned a saloon called the Cow Palace and was getting on in years. He wanted a younger man willing to take an active part in the business. The Cow Palace was a thriving business and I jumped at the chance to become part owner. Shortly after my marriage, I became partners with Hiram."

"What did Dora think about the arrangement?"

"She wasn't too happy about the long nights I put in at the Cow Palace but eventually came to accept it. Especially when the money started rolling in. I banked my profits in a joint account and when Dora suggested that I put my share of the Cow Palace in her name, I agreed. I'd have done anything for her. I figured the business would give her security should anything unforeseen happen to me.

"Hiram and I got on exceptionally well. I hired Jason to work for us because he expressed a desire to leave the ranch. Six months later, Hiram shocked me by naming me sole beneficiary of his estate. He had no relatives and considered me the son he never had. Upon his death, the Cow Palace would be all mine—or Dora's, as it turned out."

Ram's voice grew harsh, and Sierra sensed the rage building inside him. "Go on. Something happened to Hiram, didn't it?"

"Hiram was killed during a robbery. In a way I blame myself. Counting the day's take was usually my job. He was in the office shortly after closing time when he was shot in the back. He bled to death before help arrived. The back window was open, and the money and gold he had been counting was missing. I've always felt guilty for not being there that night."

"Where were you?"

"I went out to the ranch to visit my parents. Mother hadn't been feeling well, and it was a quiet night at the Cow Palace, so I decided to ride out to see her and Pop. On the way home, I was caught in a fierce storm. Lightning struck a tree as I was passing by, and that's the last I remembered for several hours. When I came to, my horse had bolted and I had to walk back to town."

Sierra got the distinct impression that Ram

had reached the crux of his story.

"The sheriff was waiting for me when I got home. I was arrested for Hiram's murder. According to Jason, he was just leaving the saloon for the night when he heard the shot and ran to investigate. He said he saw the murderer escaping out the window. With great reluctance, he admitted that I was the man he saw going out the window.

"Then Dora, my beautiful wife, said that I had been acting strange for days." His voice was harsh with bitterness. "The sheriff searched the house and found the money from the Cow Palace hidden at the bottom of a chest.

"Since I couldn't account for the lapse between the time I left the ranch and arrived back home, I was charged with murder and brought to trial a month later. The evidence was more than enough to convict me. Jason's testimony and Dora's tearful confession that I was jealous of Hiram turned the jury against me. Dora deliberately lied during the trial. She testified that after Hiram named me beneficiary of his estate, I had often expressed my desire for his death. I was convicted of murder and sentenced to life in prison."

Sierra gasped in shock. "Life! How horrible. How did you get out? Did Dora change her story? Or"—she gulped—"did you escape?"

Ram smiled grimly. "I must admit I thought of escape many times during the two years I was incarcerated. Neither Dora nor Jason had anything to do with my release. In fact, my brother told me they had conveniently disappeared after cleaning out my bank account and selling the Cow Palace.

"I had been in prison a little over a year when I befriended a man who bragged about one of his friends who had cheated the law. His name was Pell Carson. Carson spoke glowingly about a friend who had committed a murder and let another man take the rap for him. When I'd gotten all the details, the story was too much of a coincidence to be ignored. When I finally wheedled a name out of the man, I alerted my brother, who recruited the Texas Rangers to find the real killer.

"Another year was to pass before he was apprehended and confessed that he'd been paid to murder Hiram Walker by a man named Jason Jordan. After two years, I was free and a warrant was issued for Jason. He and Dora have eluded the authorities for eight years."

"It must have been horrible for you," Sierra said, dashing the tears from her eyes.

Ram's face hardened. "I was a changed man when I left that prison. I was harder, meaner, conditioned to survive in a hostile environment. I trusted no one. The ability to trust and feel love had been beaten from me by sadistic guards. Life was cruel and harsh, but I adjusted and survived. The hardest part was the gut-wrenching loneliness. I had abundant time to fan the flames of revenge. My experience with Dora taught me that women were not to be trusted for any purpose other than to satisfy lust."

"Have you been searching for Dora and Jason all this time?"

Ram nodded. "I'd no sooner run across their trail than they would disappear again, sometimes days or hours before I arrived. The thought of Dora and Jason as lovers, laughing at me behind my back, enraged me. I wanted to kill Jason."

"Do you want to kill Dora, too?"

Ram paused and glanced down at his hands, surprised to see them shaking. "I don't know. You won't believe how often I've thought about strangling her with my bare hands. I thought I had found them in Silver City but learned they left town abruptly just days before I arrived. I was feeling defeated when I met Pete Wills, a down-and-out prospector. He needed a grubstake and persuaded me to throw my lot in with him. Since returning to Waco didn't appeal to me, I used the last of my money to become partners with old Pete. He swore he was within days of striking a rich vein. It actually took two years of backbreaking work before we hit a vein as wide and deep as Pete predicted."

"I'd heard you'd made your money from mining," Sierra mused thoughtfully.

"At least I can thank Dora for that," Ram said with bitter emphasis. "Once I had money again, I hired a detective to trace Dora and Jason. When I received word that they were in San Francisco, I sold my interest in the mine and left a rich man. But once again, Dora and Jason had slipped from my grasp. I paid the detective to continue his search and remained in San Francisco, buying property and investing my money. Then, little wildcat, I met you."

"Are you sorry?" Sierra asked.

Ram grinned. "You sure as hell made life interesting for me. But I never meant for things to get out of hand between us. Unfortunately, I can't seem to control myself where you're concerned."

"So what happens now?" Sierra asked. "Does this change anything between us?"

Ram chose his words carefully. "If anything unforeseen happens to me, I wanted you to know the truth. I've already visited a lawyer and made provisions for you. Jason is nearly as good with a gun as I am. Though I think it unlikely, he could kill me if I call him out."

Sierra gasped in alarm. "You can't mean to challenge him! It's against the law. If you kill him, you could end up in prison again. Is that what you want?"

"At least I'll know I'm in prison for a reason," Ram said bitterly.

"Don't do it, Ram! If you care for me at all, don't do it."

Ram sent her a look so filled with anguish that it nearly broke her heart. "Don't ask that of me. I've spent ten years planning my revenge."

"I love you, Ram. Doesn't that make a difference in your plans?"

Ram groaned as if in pain, hating what he had to do. "No," he said finally, "no difference at all."

Chapter Fifteen

Sierra rose stiffly to her feet, hurt, angry and feeling incredibly stupid. Ram's words made his position perfectly clear. It made no difference that she loved him, no difference at all. Vengeance ruled his head; hatred occupied his heart. He planned on taking the law into his own hands.

"Take me home, Ram. I should have listened to Ryder. I was a fool to think you cared for me." She turned and started back down the path.

Ram leaped to his feet, grasping her arm and turning her to face him. "I do care for you."

"Forgive me if I don't believe you." She flung the words at him like stones. "I should never have forced myself on you when you were so adamantly opposed to taking me to Denver. I made a pest of myself and I'm sorry. Don't

305

worry, I'll not trouble you again. Kill Jason if you must, do whatever you want to Dora, I no longer give a damn."

Ram would never know just how costly those words were to her.

"You don't understand, Sierra," Ram said, dragging his fingers through his hair. "This has been going on for ten years, until it's become a festering sore inside me, too painful to forget or ignore. My parents went through their savings and had to sell the ranch to finance the search for the real murderer. Thank God they were able to buy it back when I struck it rich. I want revenge, Sierra. I *need* revenge for my own peace of mind. When this is over, if I'm still alive, there will be time for us."

Sierra laughed harshly. "There is no us, Ram. There never was. It was foolish of me to think otherwise. I don't regret making love with you, though obviously it meant very little to you."

"That's not true!"

"Then prove it!" Sierra shot back. "Forget this damn vendetta against Dora and Jason. They aren't worth your time or trouble."

Ram's face hardened. "I can't."

Wresting her arm from his grasp, Sierra took flight down the rocky path, stumbling and sliding, yet somehow remaining on her feet until she reached the buggy. When she tried to fling herself into the conveyance, Ram was beside her, lifting her onto the seat.

"Please, Sierra, listen to reason," Ram begged

as he climbed into the driver's seat and took up the reins.

"Don't talk reason to me, Ram Hunter! You're as stubborn as a mule. And arrogant, and self-centered, and totally without the sense God gave you. As for me, when I return to San Francisco, I'll be planning a wedding. I've made Gordon wait long enough."

"Gordon!" Ram spat the name out on a curse. "You don't belong with that milksop."

Of course I don't belong with Gordon, Sierra's heart cried out in silent rage. *Only you're too pigheaded to listen to reason.*

"My life is no longer your concern," Sierra said. "You have your problems and I have mine."

"Dammit, Sierra, why do you think I tried to stay away from you? Even before I left San Francisco, I sensed you'd be too great a distraction to me. No," he amended, "more like a fatal fascination. I was obsessed with you. No woman since Dora has affected me the way you do. I know I have no right to stop your marriage to Gordon but—"

"You're right, Ram, you have no right, no right at all."

Sierra was numb. It hurt to think how little influence she had on Ram. She'd been dead wrong to think she meant anything to him. Obviously he'd used her to sate his enormous lust while her imagination had worked overtime, dreaming of a life with Ram, loving him, wanting him.

"I'm sorry," Ram whispered, wishing things could be different.

His heart had been empty for so long that until now he had failed to recognize the depth of his feelings for Sierra. He realized now that he loved her and feared he had destroyed the only pure emotion he'd had in ten years. But in order to be true to himself, he had to see this business with Dora and Jason through to the bitter end.

"I'm sorry, too, Ram."

Ram stared at the small, rundown house that Dora and Jason had rented. After a tense ride back to town, he'd taken Sierra home. Before they parted, he had reminded Sierra about her promise to tell him if a child resulted from their loving. Sierra had merely stared at him before jumping to the ground and racing inside the house. Infused with an overwhelming sadness, Ram drove away and did not look back.

With difficulty, Ram banished Sierra from his mind and concentrated on sweet revenge. He checked his gun riding low on his hip, tested the smooth glide and weight of it in his hand, then slid it back in its holster.

His resolve firmly in place, Ram approached the door, wondering how he would react to seeing Dora again after all these years. At one time she'd been his love, his life, then she had betrayed him. Steeling himself for an explosive confrontation, Ram rapped on the door.

Mentally prepared for a volatile confrontation, Ram tensed as the door opened. Dismay settled over his features when he saw a young lad who looked to be seven or eight years old standing in the opening. Staring at Ram with eyes the color of a clear blue sky, the towheaded boy's friendly smile was so familiar that Ram felt a gut-wrenching jolt deep inside him.

"Who in the hell are you?"

The boy blinked, intimidated by Ram's size and fierce scowl. "I'm Tommy. Who are you?"

Ram's eyes narrowed. "Tommy? What is your mother's name?"

Tommy looked puzzled but answered politely. "Dora."

Ram felt as if he'd been gut-shot. "Who is your father?" Ram had no idea Dora and Jason had a child, and his mind whirled with what that meant in terms of the revenge he'd planned so carefully.

Tommy's expression grew wary, his fright visible in the innocent depths of his eyes. He was spared a reply when Dora appeared in the hallway.

"Who is it, Tommy? How many times have I told you not to open the door to strangers?" For years she and Jason had survived one step ahead of the law, and every time someone knocked on the door she feared the worst. Tommy stepped behind her skirts as she approached the door.

"Hello, Dora."

Dora reeled back in shock, stumbling over Tommy, who scooted out of the way in the nick of time. "Dear God, it's you!"

"You're wise to implore God, Dora." Ram's voice was cold, implacable, utterly lacking in mercy.

"What do you want, Ram? Why can't you leave us alone? I'm tired of moving from place to place, fearing to look over my shoulder lest I find either you or the law hot on my heels."

"You should have thought of that before you and Jason murdered Hiram, stole my money, and ran away. Do you have any idea the kind of hell you put me through? Each day in prison was like a year off my life. Just thinking about you and Jason in bed together drove me to the brink of madness."

Dora's face drained of all color. "It wasn't my idea, Ram, honestly," she said, dragging her tongue over lips so dry that she could hardly speak. Ram stared at the tip of her pink tongue, recalling with stunning clarity the countless times she'd dragged her hot little tongue over his body. "It was all Jason's idea. He hated you, did you know that?"

"Were you lovers before we were married?" She shook her head. "Tell me the truth, dammit!" Ram said, stalking her.

"Mama, I'm frightened. Why does the man want to hurt us?" Tommy's question brought Ram up short as he stared at the small boy, who was trying his utmost to shrink into the woodwork.

Ram frowned. Frightening a child wasn't his style. The presence of the child had thrown him into a state of confusion. "I don't want to hurt you, son." Lord, he needed to think. He hadn't counted on a child. A child changed everything.

"No, Tommy, Ramsey Hunter doesn't want to hurt you, just me and your mother." Ram's gaze shifted to the doorway behind Dora. Jason stood in the opening, leaning against the doorjamb. Though his body looked relaxed, Ram knew Jason was as tightly coiled as a rattlesnake. "I knew you'd show up sooner or later, Ram. Now that you've found us, what do you intend to do?"

Ram slanted an uncertain glance at Tommy. "Send your son away so we can speak freely."

Jason turned to Tommy and snarled, "You heard, kid, get the hell out of here."

Tommy lingered a moment longer than Jason thought necessary. Before Ram realized Jason's intention, Jason had backhanded Tommy across the face, sending him flying into the wall. "Get the brat out of here, Dora, before I give him the licking he deserves. You spoil him."

Appearing frightened by Jason's brutality, Dora hustled Tommy to his feet. Whispering words of comfort into his ear, she sent him to his room. "Must you be so cruel, Jason?"

Ram was stunned into silence. Since he'd entered the house, nothing had gone right. Did Jason always abuse his son? The boy seemed a good enough sort. "You weren't always a bully, Jason, what happened?"

"I'll tell you what happened," Jason snarled. "You and Jeff had everything while I was merely tolerated by a family who really didn't want me.

No one wanted me. I envied you. Your family had money. You and Jeff had the best of everything while I had nothing. But what really rankled was the fact that Dora accepted your proposal instead of mine. After you were married, I schemed and planned to get even with you. Did you think I enjoyed working for you, doing your bidding? But I had the last laugh, Ram—I slept with your wife before you did and continued to do so even after you were married. You were so enraptured with Dora, you never even guessed she wasn't a virgin."

"So you paid to have Hiram killed and accused me of murdering my partner," Ram said bitterly. "You and Dora railroaded me into prison. But I foiled your plan, didn't I? You forgot Jeff was a Texas Ranger and determined to prove me innocent. The man you hired was found and confessed, Jason, and I was finally free. Now you're the wanted man."

"I'd heard you were free," Jason sneered, "and knew you'd come looking for us. I figured the law might not catch up with us, but you would. We've moved so many times in ten years, I can't even remember all the places we've been. Which will it be, Ram? Are you going to kill us? Or will you turn us over to the law?"

"I haven't made up my mind," Ram admitted.

"Please, Ram, let us go!" Dora pleaded. Her eyes were wild with fear. "Think about Tommy. What will happen to him if you kill us or send us to prison?"

"You should have thought of that before you

slept with Jason and conspired against me."

Despite his harsh words, learning about Tommy had changed everything. He could not find it in his heart to harm the parents of an innocent child.

"You don't understand," Dora cried on a rising note of panic.

Ram searched her face, unimpressed by her startling beauty and the ripe body he'd once found so fascinating. A pale halo of blond hair framed a pair of almond-shaped eyes as dark as midnight, and her sensuous lips had lost none of the lush fullness he remembered so vividly. Her lashes fluttered helplessly and her breasts heaved distractingly as she begged Ram to spare her life.

"Would you harm the mother of your son?"

Ram went still. He couldn't have heard right. "What did you say?"

"She said it's entirely possible that Tommy is your son," Jason repeated harshly. "Then again, he could be mine. My personal opinion is that he's yours. I can't stand the brat. I tolerate him because he's Dora's son, but every time I look at him I see you, a man who had everything I wanted, all I've ever desired."

Confusion, dismay, and disbelief warred within Ram. If Jason was trying to bewilder and disarm him, he had succeeded admirably. Not for one minute did he believe Tommy was his son. This was just another ploy to hurt him. He knew it as well as he knew his own name, yet . . .

"You're lying. Only a bastard would use his own son in such a despicable manner. How old is Tommy? Seven? Eight? He couldn't possibly be mine."

"Tommy is nine, nearly ten," Dora said smugly. "Believe what you want, Ram, but the possibility exists that Tommy is your son. At times he's so much like you, it's uncanny."

Recoiling in horror, Ram refused to believe that the poor, abused boy was his son. He preferred to think that Dora and Jason had devised a cruel method of tormenting him. They had counted on his reluctance to harm the parents of an innocent child. Tommy was their protection. He had to believe that, needed to believe it, else he couldn't live with the knowledge that his own child was being so abused.

Everything was different, yet nothing had changed, Ram thought dismally. Revenge still burned hotly within him, but Tommy and the question of the boy's paternity had shot Ram's plans for revenge all to hell.

"I can see you still have doubts," Jason said. "I know you want to kill me. Go ahead, but keep in mind you'll be killing an unarmed man." He pulled aside the tails of his coat, revealing his lack of weapons. "If you need proof, ask Tommy how old he is. The boy won't lie."

"Call him," Ram said. He had no idea why he fell in with Jason's suggestion so readily. Perhaps it was his burning need to have another look at the boy.

Jason nodded to Dora. She left the room and

returned minutes later with Tommy in tow. The left side of the boy's face was swollen and discolored, and his frightened expression and wild eyes tore at Ram's heart.

"How old are you, Tommy?" Jason asked harshly.

Tommy shot him a puzzled look. "You know how old I am, Papa."

"Don't sass me, boy," Jason said, raising his hand as if to strike the child again.

"Touch the boy again and you're a dead man," Ram said with lethal intent. Never had he felt such a compelling urge to do bodily harm to another man. A man who picked on helpless children deserved less than contempt.

Tommy looked at Ram with renewed interest. No one had ever come to his defense before, not even his mother. He'd suffered Jason's cruelty for as long as he could remember, and it felt good to have a protector.

"I'm nine, nearly ten," Tommy said.

The directness of the boy's blue eyes startled Ram as he searched Tommy's face for a hint of the truth, seeing nothing but a pleasant, towheaded boy with blue eyes that could have been inherited from either him or Jason. True, the boy's hair was blond, unlike Jason's, which was dark brown. But he could have gotten his hair color from his mother. Both he and Jason had blue eyes, while Dora's were a darker shade of midnight blue. Unfortunately, nothing in the boy's features gave Ram the answers he sought.

"Satisfied, Ram?" Jason smirked.

Ram was far from satisfied. Did he or did he not have a son? Not even Dora knew for sure. The one thing he did know was that he had to get away where he could think clearly. Whatever he did would affect the life of an innocent child. And from what little he'd seen, the child had already suffered enough.

"You can thank the boy for a temporary reprieve," Ram said tersely. "But you haven't heard the last from me. I'd advise you not to skip town again. If I don't find you, the law will."

"What are you going to do?" Dora asked warily. "I'm tired of running, Ram. Can't you forget and forgive and let us go? Look at you. Apparently you've prospered over the years, while our lives have been a living hell, never knowing when you or the law would show up on our doorstep."

"Forgive?" Ram made a harsh sound deep in his throat. "It's far too late for forgiveness. I've lived with bitterness too long. You were my whole world. Now look at you, whoring for a man who treats you and your son like dirt."

Without conscious thought, Ram's gaze settled on Tommy, his expression darkening when he noted the boy's bruised face and wide, frightened eyes. A jolt of something deep and moving shuddered through Ram—a recognition, a bonding he was totally unprepared for and did not welcome. Dragging his gaze from the small boy, Ram turned his attention back to Dora and Jason.

"I'm giving you a short reprieve, but you can

count on my returning once I've sorted things through in my mind. Maybe I'll let the law handle this after all."

Whirling on his heel, Ram stormed through the door, leaving a thoroughly shaken Dora in his wake.

"Oh God, Jason, I knew he'd find us one day. Do you really think he'll set the law on us?"

"I don't put anything past Ramsey Hunter," Jason said bitterly. He glared down at Tommy, who stood beside his mother with a bewildered look on his face. "I knew the brat would come in handy one day. Learning about Tommy has confused Ram. I think we can forget Ramsey Hunter for good."

"You've forgotten something, Jason," Dora bit out, "Tommy could be *your* son."

"Not damn likely," Jason muttered, giving Tommy a vicious shove as he stormed out the door.

Sierra spent the next several days in a state of anxiety. She prayed that Ram hadn't done anything foolish, like taking the law into his own hands. She hadn't heard from him in over a week and hoped he had taken her advice to forget his long-standing grudge. Instinct told her Ram wasn't the type to carry a grudge for ten years without demanding retribution. She tried to tell herself she didn't care, but convincing her heart was difficult.

Ram had made his choice whether she liked it or not. She had foolishly allowed him to make love to her again, but it had made no difference in his plans. Nothing she'd said or done had changed his mind. Ram had used her for the last time, she vowed. Even if she didn't marry Gordie, she'd not succumb to his passion again. She had learned a valuable lesson. Love didn't conquer all. Pitted against revenge, it came in a distant second.

Then something happened that turned Sierra's world upside down. She had not had a monthly since the first time she'd made love with Ram. She had expected it daily for the past two weeks, and when it did not arrive she assumed it was because her system was reacting to the upheaval of leaving San Francisco and everything that had followed. When she'd vomited upon arising two days in a row, she even had an explanation for that. She blamed it on something she'd eaten the night before.

Sierra touched her breasts, recalling how she'd noticed the unaccustomed tenderness a few days ago, shortly after being with Ram. She'd rationalized that by telling herself he'd been unnecessarily rough with her. But Ram was never rough. His hands were always gentle, no matter how aroused he became.

Pregnant. She'd only just begun to think of herself in those terms. Certainly she'd been with Ram often enough in the past for him to make her pregnant. She recalled her promise, the one he'd forced her to make. Even if she told him about her problem, there was little he could do about it. The fact remained that Ram was married to Dora. The feeling persisted that Ram *wanted* to be married to Dora, else he would have found a way to divorce her long ago. He loved Dora. He would always love her.

So where did that leave her? Sierra asked herself. Without a husband or father for her unborn child. What would her family think? Would the brother and sister she'd just found despise her? Would they send her back to San Francisco to bear her child in shame? Her fall from grace would probably kill her adoptive parents; she couldn't possibly go back to San Francisco to bear her fatherless child. Lord, what a mess she'd gotten herself into.

Sierra wandered downstairs. She had just lost her meager breakfast and hoped Abby hadn't noticed her green face when she had excused herself from the table so abruptly. Her foot had just touched the bottom stair when she heard a pounding on the front door. When Abby didn't appear immediately, Sierra called out that she'd answer the door. The color drained from her face when she opened the door and saw Gordon Lynch standing on the doorstep.

"Gordie! What are you doing here?"

"I'd prefer not to let the neighbors know how foolish you've been," Gordie said succinctly as he stepped inside and closed the door behind him.

Wearing a suit and hat in the height of fashion and carrying a walking cane, Gordie looked every bit the successful businessman that he was.

319

"Well, Sierra, I must say you certainly have led me a merry chase. Do you have any idea what you've put me and your parents through? Running off with Ramsey Hunter was foolish and reckless behavior. Fortunately, Lester has been able to squelch gossip by telling everyone you'd gone to Sacramento to visit relatives. There's been a wealth of speculation on your sudden disappearance, but thank God no one has questioned your father's explanation.

"Whatever possessed you to run off with a man like Hunter, Sierra? We were to be married—did that mean nothing to you? Your poor distraught father implored me to fetch you home, and of course I agreed. I've been in Denver two weeks trying to find you. I didn't even know your sister's last name, or have the slightest notion where to find you.

"I finally wired your father and he supplied me with your sister's name and address. After I left San Francisco, he received a telegram from you, giving details of your family. You can't imagine my relief when I learned you and Hunter had parted ways in Denver and you were staying with your sister. Lester felt strongly that Hunter wouldn't take advantage of you, but I don't trust the man."

Sierra had just about all she could take of Gordie's verbal abuse. "You have no right to chastise me, Gordon. I'm not married to you yet. I did what I felt was necessary. My parents never took my desire to find my siblings seriously. Now that I've found them, I'm not leaving until I've ended my visit. My sister is expecting a child soon, and I intend to be with her when she gives birth."

"Perhaps I can extend my stay, dear," Gordon cajoled, aware that Sierra was growing belligerent. "I can't remain away from the bank forever, but I'm willing to compromise. We can be married in Denver before we leave. You can't afford any more speculation or gossip."

"Did I just hear someone mention marriage?" Abby walked into the room, wiping her hands on her apron.

"Abby, this is Gordon Lynch. He just arrived from San Francisco. Gordon, this is my sister, Abby Mercer."

Gordon turned on the charm. "How do you do, Mrs. Mercer. I'm so pleased Sierra has finally found her siblings. I'm Sierra's fiance."

Abby sent Sierra a shuttered look. "Sierra's fiance? How—how nice. Please come in and sit down. I'm sure you and Sierra have much to discuss. Did I hear you right? You did mention a wedding, didn't you?"

"I did indeed, Mrs. Mercer," Gordon beamed. "Sierra and I plan to marry right here in Denver. This trip will serve as our honeymoon. Sierra's father is all for the match."

Sierra scowled at Gordon, trying to think of a polite way to tell him that she had no intention of marrying him.

"How soon do you intend to marry?" Abby asked, surprised by the unexpected appearance of Sierra's fiance.

"Very soon. Say, two weeks? Will that give you enough time?"

Abby stared at Gordon Lynch thoughtfully. He was handsome in a dapper way, but not muscular or virile like Zach or Ryder—or Ram Hunter. His manner was brusque and impatient and decidedly patronizing where Sierra was concerned. But if he was what her sister wanted, she'd offer no objections.

"Two weeks isn't sufficient time to plan a wedding," Abby replied, waiting for Sierra to either confirm or protest.

"I'm not sure I want to get married," Sierra said, finally finding her voice. "I've just found my family and want to enjoy being with my brother and sister a while longer."

"Don't be ridiculous, dear," Gordon said with a hint of annoyance. "Your family wants what's best for you. If you recall, you agreed to our marriage. I was deeply hurt when I learned you had left town without anyone's knowledge. You're not going to disappoint me again, are you?"

"This is an important decision, Sierra," Abby said. "Think carefully before you commit yourself."

Gordon didn't seem like the kind of man her sister needed. Abby suspected there was more between Ram and Sierra than either had admitted, but since meeting him on the street that day, Sierra had acted strangely and refused to talk about their relationship. In fact, she'd insisted that she never wanted to hear Ramsey Hunter's name again.

Sierra recalled the day she had told Gordon to go ahead with their wedding plans. She hadn't been enthusiastic then and she certainly wasn't enthusiastic now, even though it meant giving her child a father. Before she agreed to marry Gordon, she felt an obligation to tell Ram he was going to be a father. She had given her promise, after all. What she wouldn't admit, even to herself, was that she desperately wanted Ram to find a way for them to be together. For their child's sake, if not for love.

"Of course Sierra is going to marry me," Gordon said in a businesslike tone. "She knows our marriage is advantageous to both of us."

When Sierra did not protest, Abby assumed her sister's silence lent agreement to Gordon's proposal. "Well, then, if it's settled between you, I suppose we'll have a wedding."

"I'll leave the details to you and Sierra," Gordon said, pleased that everything had worked out to his satisfaction. "If you don't mind, Mrs. Mercer, I'd like a private word with my fiancée."

"Of course," Abby said uncertainly, "there are things I must attend to anyway." She sent Sierra a concerned look, disturbed by her sister's apathy. Sierra's silence left Abby with an uneasy feeling about this whole affair with Gordon.

"I'm glad your sister is being reasonable about this," Gordon said once they were alone. "Why can't you be more like her? I can't begin to tell you how distressed I was when I learned you had left town with Ramsey Hunter. You acted irresponsibly and recklessly. Hunter isn't the type to act without ulterior motives. I regret my bluntness, dear, but I must know. Did Hunter take advantage of you? You were alone with him long enough. I won't hold it against you, you understand, but I must know if the bastard seduced you."

No matter Sierra's answer, Gordon wasn't about to break off their engagement. Oh, no, there was too much at stake. Once he married Sierra, the bank would fall into his hands like a ripe plum. Upon the death of the elderly Aldens, Sierra's inheritance would belong to him. He was counting too much on Sierra's wealth to let the lack of a maidenhead change his mind.

Gordon's question was met with stony silence.

"Did you hear me, dear? Please answer my question."

"Your question does not deserve an answer," Sierra said with cold fury. "As for marriage between us, I seriously doubt it will happen."

Gordon knew immediately that he had pushed Sierra too far. He supposed he'd find out on their wedding night whether or not Hunter had seduced her. The important thing now was getting her to the altar and securing the Alden fortune for himself and his heirs. He was truly fond of Sierra, but where money was involved, he was too astute to allow feelings to interfere with important issues.

"Forgive me, dear. I didn't mean to distress

you. Forget I mentioned it. We can discuss our plans more fully when I return tomorrow."

Giving her no time to protest, Gordon pulled Sierra into his arms and kissed her soundly. When she felt the wet slide of his tongue into her mouth, she trembled in revulsion. How could she marry a man whose kisses repulsed her?

Ramsey Hunter had ruined her for any other man.

Chapter Sixteen

Sierra spent the next three days listening to Gordon expound on his plans for their wedding. She blanked out most of what he said, taking little interest in the conversation. Upset over Sierra's lack of interest in her wedding, Abby made a special effort to find the cause of her sister's indifference. She knocked on the door to Sierra's room one morning shortly after Zach left for his office and grew alarmed when she received no reply. Furthermore, the strange noises coming from inside the room were anything but reassuring.

The door was unlocked and Abby let herself inside. "Sierra, are you all right? I heard a strange—" She stopped dead in her tracks when she saw Sierra clutching her stomach and retching into a basin. "My God, are you ill? Why didn't you tell me?"

Rushing to Sierra's side, Abby placed a supportive arm around her waist and steadied her while Sierra emptied the contents of her stomach. When she finally stopped heaving, Abby took the basin from her hands, set it on the floor, and settled her in bed. "Lie down, honey. I'll get a cloth for your head and some water to rinse out your mouth."

Sierra felt so miserable that she merely nodded, grateful for her sister's help. It no longer mattered who knew she was pregnant, for they'd find out soon enough whether she told them or not. She might as well face the unpleasantness now and get it over with.

"How long has this been going on?" Abby asked anxiously. "I'll send for the doctor."

"No, no doctor, Abby, please. I—I know what is wrong with me."

Abby frowned in consternation. "You know what is wrong and haven't told me?"

Sierra nodded and lowered her gaze, too ashamed to look Abby in the eye. "I—I'm going to have a baby."

The air whooshed from Abby's lungs in a loud hiss. "You're pregnant? Who is the bastard who did this to you?" Suddenly comprehension dawned. "No, don't tell me. It's Ram Hunter." Her voice had a bitter edge to it.

Abby sat on the edge of the bed, pulling Sierra into her arms. "Don't worry, honey, I'll take care of you. There will be a wedding, all right, but it won't be between you and Gordon. Zach and Ryder will convince Ramsey Hunter that a marriage proposal is expected."

"Oh, Abby," Sierra wailed, "you don't understand. Ram is already married. He and his wife have been separated for ten years, but he's still married nonetheless. A detective just recently located his wife in Denver."

"Oh, Sierra, I'm so sorry. But perhaps all isn't lost. Now that Ram knows where his wife is, he can obtain a divorce before your baby is due. You love him, don't you?"

"I want to hate him, but I can't," Sierra whispered, dashing tears from her eyes. "But it doesn't matter whether I love him or not. Ram still loves Dora. He's never stopped loving her."

"Are you sure?"

"As sure as I can be," Sierra said shakily. She looked at Abby with stricken eyes. "What am I going to do?"

"Right now you're going to rest," Abby said. "When you feel better, we'll talk more about it."

Sierra grasped Abby's hand. "No, I want you to know everything about Ram. He's not as bad as you think. He doesn't even realize he loves Dora, but it's obvious to me. What she did to Ram is beyond understanding. She's a monster, Abby. How could he still want her? He says he only wants revenge, but I'm afraid he's going to do something terrible and regret it."

Her curiosity piqued, Abby said, "Very well, if it will make you feel better, perhaps you should tell me."

Sierra took a deep breath and expelled it. She told Abby everything, beginning with the day she and Ram met and ending with their most recent encounter several days ago. She didn't mince words when she explained Dora's role in Ram's life. When she finished, Abby appeared deep in thought.

"That explains a lot," Abby finally said. "But it doesn't excuse what Ramsey Hunter did to you. He took your innocence knowing he couldn't offer marriage."

Though Abby and Zach had made love before their marriage, their situation differed from Sierra's. Zach had been quite eager to marry her and did all in his power to get her to the altar. But this was her little sister, and Hunter had no intention of marrying her.

"I told you, Abby, I literally threw myself at Ram. He couldn't help himself."

"He could have told you he was married; it might have made a world of difference had you known. Do you really think Ram means to harm Jason and his wife?"

Sierra's silver eyes glowed hotly. "I hope not." Her voice held a note of indecision. "Ram isn't the type to kill in cold blood. Besides, I believe he still loves Dora despite the fact that when Ram and I are together, something seems to explode between us. I've never experienced anything like it before or expect to again."

"You've got to tell Ram about the baby, honey. He has a right to know he's going to be a father. He has a responsibility to you whether or not he's married. And you've got to think long and hard before you commit yourself to marriage to Gordon."

Sierra acknowledged Abby's sound advice with a nod. "You're right. I'm not a sniveling coward. I don't need Ram to help me to raise his child, but I did promise I'd tell him if . . . if . . ." Her words fell off; she was aware that there was little Ram could do about her pregnancy. "I know now I couldn't possibly marry Gordie. It wouldn't be fair to him. If you don't mind, I'd like to stay in Denver, or at the farm with Ryder and Hannah, until my child is born. I'll understand if neither you nor Ryder wants me. But if I return to San Francisco, it would be difficult to explain to my parents."

"You can stay wherever you like for as long as you like, Sierra. Speaking for both myself and Ryder, I can truthfully say it will make little difference to us. You're our sister, and we love you. Why don't you take a short nap? You'll feel much better after a good rest."

After Abby left, Sierra felt as if a suffocating weight had been lifted from her. Telling Ryder was going to be much more difficult, she decided. As hot-headed as he was, he'd likely go gunning for Ram, and that was something she didn't want.

Vividly she recalled everything she loved about Ram. She remembered every single detail of his handsome face and hard-muscled body. Closing her eyes, she imagined his thick chest pressing her down into the fragrant bed of pine needles when they last made love, the heat of his mouth as he kissed her, the magic of his touch on her breasts, between her legs. Tongues of fire licked at her, and she touched her breasts, imagining it was Ram's hands she felt. Groaning in despair, Sierra flopped over onto her stomach and surrendered to sleep.

She awoke two hours later feeling much better, but not good enough to face Ram. Another day slipped by before she felt well enough to make the trip to Ram's hotel. A rather nasty confrontation with Gordon provided the impetus she needed to act.

Gordon arrived early that afternoon to tell her that he'd engaged a church and minister to perform their marriage and asked about her plans for a modest reception afterward.

Sierra sighed heavily. "Make all the plans you want, Gordie, I'm not ready yet to get married. I would appreciate it if you'd return to San Francisco and wait for me. We'll talk about marriage when I get home."

An angry flush spread upward from Gordon's neck. "Now see here, Sierra, I'm not returning to San Francisco without you. The Aldens expect us to come back as husband and wife, and come hell or high water we're going to be married a week from Saturday."

Sierra stared at her hands. "I can't marry you, Gordie."

Gordon's eyes narrowed suspiciously. "Why? Is there something you're not telling me? I won't stand for any more of your foolishness, Sierra. If you have a valid reason for postponing our marriage, you'd better tell me now."

Sierra would rather die than tell Gordie she was expecting Ram's child. "I don't love you."

Gordon snorted derisively. "Love? What has love got to do with us? We've always gotten along well together. We're fond of one another. I can think of no other woman I'd want to marry. All I ask is that you behave properly and bear my children without complaint. You always were a fanciful creature. Life is not fantasy, dear, it's reality. I'll have the bank, and you'll have everything your heart desires."

Everything except love, Sierra thought dismally. "Fondness isn't the right kind of foundation upon which to base a marriage, Gordie. It won't bring happiness."

"Love grows from fondness. Few people are in love when they marry. I won't take no for an answer, Sierra. I don't care if you've planned a reception or not, the wedding will take place on schedule."

Sierra nearly laughed aloud. Once Gordie met Ryder, he'd know better than to force her into something she didn't want, but she'd let Gordie find that out for himself. In many ways Ryder was still a fierce Cheyenne warrior.

"I'll come back tomorrow," Gordon said sourly. "Perhaps you'll be in a better mood by then. Are you feeling well? You're looking pale today."

"I'm fine, but I doubt my mood will have improved by tomorrow."

He patted her hand condescendingly. "Nevertheless, expect me tomorrow afternoon."

"Ryder and Hannah will be in town day after tomorrow," Abby said once Gordon was gone. She'd been in the next room when Gordon arrived and she'd heard everything. "I can assure you, he will set Gordon Lynch straight. If that's what you want," she added sharply.

"I can't marry Gordon and let him believe Ram's child is his," Sierra said, sending Abby a tremulous smile. "I'm going to see Ram this afternoon."

"I'll go with you," Abby said with firm resolve.

"No, Abby, thank you, but this is something I have to do alone. Besides, you're too close to your time to be traipsing around town. I'll be fine, truly."

Ram sat in his room nursing a bottle of the best brandy the hotel had to offer. The turmoil and indecision churning inside him haunted his every waking hour and tormented his sleep. He hadn't had a good night's sleep since learning he might or might not have a son. He had seen how badly Jason treated the boy and it nearly tore him apart just thinking about the abuse Tommy had suffered through the years. Sweet Jesus! It was as likely that Tommy was his son as Jason's. Jason was aware of the odds and had stubbornly refused to claim the boy. He preferred to punish the boy for an accident of birth.

Ram's dilemma was daunting. Sierra had been right all along. She had begged him to forget and forgive, but he couldn't find it in his heart to do so. His stubbornness had caused him to lose the one woman who meant anything to him. How could he have been so stupid?

He'd lost the desire to kill Jason the moment he'd laid eyes on Tommy. Maybe even before that, if he wanted to be truthful. As for Dora, punishment was no longer feasible. She was the mother of the child who could be his son. He still hated Dora; that hadn't changed. But he also pitied her. Perhaps even more than he hated her.

Ram sighed and rested his head in his hands. What in God's name was he going to do about Tommy? He felt an obligation to the boy whether or not he was Tommy's father. Jason hated the boy, and Dora was either unwilling or too weak to defend her son against Jason's abuse. Perhaps she feared Jason as much as Tommy did. Or more likely, she just didn't give a damn.

His life had become hopelessly mired, and he didn't know how to dig himself out. He wanted Sierra with a desperate, consuming hunger, and he grieved over losing her. He admired Sierra and he'd never admired another woman. His heart had been dead and buried until he met her. She had fire in her, and courage. How many women would journey across untamed country to locate lost siblings? Damn few, he reckoned.

Vividly he recalled the taut firmness of her breasts, the cherry nipples that rose so temptingly to his caress, the tightness, the slickness of her as she took him inside her. Her kisses tasted of sweet sunshine. There was no pretense in her response to him. She had given him everything—her heart, her soul, her body. He had taken her innocence and given her nothing in return except pleasure. He didn't even have the right to tell her he loved her until he rid himself of a wife he should have discarded years before.

Ram was half-way through the bottle of brandy when he heard a racket in the hallway outside the door. His senses dulled by alcohol, Ram responded slowly. Too slowly.

"Ram, open the door! It's Dora. Please open up—I need to speak to you."

The chair flew back with a clatter as Ram jumped to his feet. "Dora, what in the hell do you want?"

"Please, Ram, I'm desperate. Tommy is with me."

The boy's name did what Dora's pleas could not. Ram flung open the door. Dora rushed inside, dragging Tommy with her. Ram shut the door and turned to face Dora, his brows raised.

"I had to come, Ram," Dora began breathlessly. "I couldn't take it anymore. Jason has been drinking steadily since you came to town. He's afraid of what you're going to do. He beat me and then started on Tommy." She raised her face to the light, revealing a bruised cheek and a black eye.

Ram spat out a vile oath. "I should have killed the bastard when I had the chance." He placed a finger under Tommy's chin, lifting it to the light. "Did he hurt you, son?"

Tommy's face was grotesquely swollen, but he gave Ram a weak smile despite his injuries. "It's all right, sir, I'm used to it. But I don't like him hitting Mama."

"Stay here," Ram said tightly as he started toward the door.

"Where are you going?" Dora cried.

"To arrange for a room for you and Tommy. I don't care what you and Jason do, but I won't stand for his abuse of Tommy.

Ram left, returning a few minutes later with a key to the adjoining room. "Put Tommy to bed. He looks exhausted."

Dora rose obediently, sending Ram a grateful look. "Thank you, Ram. I was a fool to leave you. You'd never hurt me or Tommy."

Ram sent her an oblique look that spoke eloquently of his contempt.

When Dora had disappeared into the next room, he poured himself another drink and pondered this newest development. In a matter of minutes, his life had gone from bad to worse. He laughed harshly. Years ago he'd sworn vengeance against Dora. How ironic that he now found himself offering protection to a woman he'd sworn to punish.

Only an inch remained in the bottle when Dora returned through the adjoining door. "Tommy is asleep. I thought we could talk."

"Talk," Ram repeated sourly. "I wish it were that simple."

"I want to be your wife again," Dora said, sidling up beside Ram. "I was a foolish young girl when I left you all those years ago. Jason was older and more experienced. He—he beguiled me. I didn't know what I was doing when I agreed to help him convict you for Hiram's murder. He spun such glorious tales of how wonderful it would be if we could be together all the time, living on your money. I was just a wide-eyed girl, for God's sake!"

Ram laughed harshly. He had no sympathy for Dora. "You were never a wide-eyed girl."

Ignoring him, Dora continued. "In the beginning, I had no idea Jason planned Hiram's murder. Afterward I was forced to go along with Jason's plans. He thought we were in the clear when you were convicted and jailed. For two years, we lived like kings and had great fun together. Believe it or not, Jason was thrilled when Tommy was born. But when I confided that the child could be yours, he changed.

"He hated Tommy from the beginning. The first few years weren't too bad. We had the money from the Cow Palace and your bank account. Then we heard that you'd been cleared of murder charges and released from jail and that Jason had been charged with the murder of Hiram Walker. The pressure of trying to stay one step ahead of you and the law changed Jason. He lost heavily at the tables and became cruel and abusive. And when he couldn't make enough money at the card table, he—he sold me to other men for a few hours' pleasure."

"Do you want to hear about my years in prison, Dora?" Ram sneered. "I could match you horror for horror."

Dora flushed and looked away. "Will it help to say I'm sorry? Take me back, Ram. We have a son together. I'll be a good wife, I swear it. We're still married. There's nothing to stop us from taking up where we left off."

"You forget one thing, Dora. I'm no longer a gullible boy. I don't want you."

Her hips swaying seductively, Dora walked slowly toward Ram. "You could love me again, I know you could. Look at me, Ram. Am I not still beautiful?" Boldly her fingers opened the front of her dress, baring her breasts to him. "At one time you loved my breasts. They're still as firm and white as they ever were. And my legs, Ram." She hoisted her skirts up to her thighs. "They're still slim and shapely. Remember how good we were in bed? It can be that way again if you take me back."

To prove her point, Dora perched on Ram's lap, cupped his cheeks with her hands, and kissed him. Her mouth was wet and hot, her tongue a flaming sword thrusting past his teeth. When she felt the stirring of his shaft beneath her bottom, she smiled and rubbed her breasts against his chest in a most provocative manner. With catlike grace, she slid off his lap and knelt between his legs, smiling up at him through hooded lids as she released his swollen shaft from his trousers. Licking her lips with greedy anticipation, she bent her head to take him between her lips.

Spitting out a curse, Ram leaped to his feet. "Damn you! It won't work, Dora. Once a whore, always a whore. Save your whore's tricks for men who appreciate them. Did you find out I'm wealthy? Is that why you're here?"

Dora's eyes narrowed into catlike slits. "I want us to be a family," she lied. It hadn't taken her long to discover that Ram had grown filthy rich during the past ten years. "Don't worry about Jason. I already told him I was leaving him. What's wrong with you? You used to adore everything I did to you. You used to love me."

"You made a mockery of that love. It's too late for us, Dora. For Tommy's sake, I'll give you money for a new start without Jason, but that's all I'm willing to do."

Dora came to her feet in a rush. "What about Tommy? Is that what you want for your son? I know you don't believe me, Ram, but Tommy *is* your son. I—I want to be with you again. Seeing you has made me realize how much I still love you."

Ram went still. Tommy. God, could he walk away from the boy, knowing he might be his son? "I truthfully don't know what to believe, but I'll see that Tommy is taken care of."

"I don't want your money—I want you. Taking me back is the only way to free us from Jason. You've seen how he treats us. Tommy deserves better than that. Tommy deserves a father who will love him."

Ram glanced at the adjoining room where Tommy slept, wondering what it would be like to be a father. He decided he'd like it just fine if the mother of his child was Sierra. Yet he couldn't deny that Tommy touched his heart in a way he'd never expected. He'd do what he could to see that the boy was kept safe, but no amount of persuasion could make him take Dora back.

"You can stay here until you decide what you want to do with your life and where you want to go. That's the best I can do right now."

"I know once you get to know Tommy you'll love him," Dora said, confident of her ability to seduce Ram. It hadn't failed her in the past. Ram had always been such a fool over her. After she had learned how prosperous he was, she'd quickly decided to leave Jason. She was tired of being Jason's punching bag and sick of the kind of life they led. Once Jason had been an exciting lover, but no longer.

She and Jason had gone through the money from the Cow Palace and Ram's bank account within a short time. Jason's bad luck at the tables and lack of skill with cards had quickly depleted their small nestegg. It wasn't until he started using Dora's charms to distract the players that he managed to recoup their losses and live comfortably again. On those rare times when Dora's spectacular body and face failed to influence the outcome of the game, Jason made up his losses by selling her for the night to the highest bidder.

"Tommy isn't the issue, Dora," Ram said, rounding on her. "The lad is an innocent pawn. You should have married Jason instead of me and saved us all a lot of grief."

"I made a mistake. I let Jason blind me to everything that was decent and good. I was as much a victim as you, Ram—why can't you accept that?"

Ram's spine remained stiff and his resolve unyielding. Intuitively, Dora realized that desperate measures were necessary if she wanted to win Ram. She had not bothered to repair the damage she'd done to the front of her dress earlier and she sidled up to Ram, pressing her naked breasts against his chest, tearing open his shirt and merging their flesh. Ram sucked in a scalding breath. He didn't want Dora, didn't even like her, but he was a virile male and his loins reacted without conscious effort on his part. He spat out a curse and pushed her away, but Dora clung tenaciously to his neck.

Sierra paused outside the door of Ram's hotel room. It had taken all her courage to come this far, but she knew it had to be done. Abby had convinced her that Ram should know he was to become a father, and reluctantly she agreed. Her face flamed when she recalled the hotel clerk's raised eyebrows and knowing smile when she'd asked if Ram was in his room. She should have brought Abby along, she supposed, but her sister was so heavily pregnant now that she knew it would be uncomfortable for her to travel about town in a buggy.

Wishing she could disappear into the wood-work, Sierra rapped lightly on the door. When she received no answer, she knocked again. The clerk had assured her that Ram hadn't left his room all day.

Ram heard the knock on the door and con-sidered the possibility that it could be Jason. Dora heard it too and wondered the same thing. While Ram was debating the best way to handle the situation, or even whether to open the door at all, Dora decided it would serve her purpose to have Jason see her and Ram together like this. She'd already told Jason she intended to leave him, but he had laughed at her, saying it would be a cold day in hell when Ram took her back. If he caught them in one another's arms with their clothes all awry, he would assume Ram had relented.

"Someone is at the door, Ram," she said, winding her arms even more tightly around his neck.

"Dammit, Dora, let go of me!"

"If that's Jason at the door, it wouldn't hurt for him to see us like this. Then he'd know just where he stands with me."

"He might have a gun. Did you think about that possibility?" Ram bit out, trying to push her away from him.

Sensing that she was losing control of the sit-uation, Dora took matters into her own hands. "Come in," she called loudly. "The door is open." She knew it was open, for she hadn't seen Ram

343

lock it after he had returned to the room earlier.

Had she misunderstood the hotel clerk? Sierra wondered when she heard a feminine voice invite her inside. She glanced up to check the room number and saw she hadn't made a mistake. Intuition told her to turn and run as fast as her legs could carry her, but curiosity demanded that she open the door. With shaking hands, she turned the knob and stepped inside.

Never had Sierra come so close to fainting. Bitter bile rose up in her throat, and the room seemed to spin around her. The gorgeous blonde in Ram's arms had to be Dora. Sierra viewed the scene with distaste. Dora's shapely arms clung to Ram's neck. The front of her dress gaped open, revealing the rounded perfection of a pair of coral-tipped breasts. Ram's shirt hung open; his trousers were unbuttoned and the edges gaped, revealing a hint of crisp, tawny hair.

"Oh God, oh God . . ." Sierra's complexion took on a green tinge and she clutched her stomach, fearing she'd spew forth its meager contents. Sheer guts kept her upright, and iron will, reinforced with several deep breaths, brought her nausea under control.

Shock waves shuddered through Ram. Having Sierra find him like this plunged him into the deepest pit of hell. "Sweet lord, Sierra, I'm sorry. It's not what you think." He gave Dora a vicious shove, breaking her hold on his neck. Once free of her, Ram whirled around, hastily fastened his trousers, and jammed his shirt into his belt. When he turned back to Sierra, his face was contorted with agony.

Dora made no effort to cover herself. "Who is this woman, Ram, honey?"

Ram groaned as if in pain. "This is Sierra Larson Alden, a—friend of mine. Sierra, this is—"

"—Dora," Sierra said in a strangled voice. "I need no introductions, Ram."

A pleased look curved Dora's lush lips. "Ram told you about me? Then you know I'm his wife."

Still reeling from shock, Sierra nodded. She'd always suspected that Ram still loved Dora, and finding them together like this reinforced that belief. She wasn't stupid. Obviously she had interrupted something extremely intimate and private.

"Did you know that Ram and I have reconciled and are back together again?" Dora asked. Astutely, she sensed that Sierra was a threat to her, and she wanted to put an end to it.

"For God's sake, Dora, shut up!" Ram snarled. "You have no right to say something that's not true."

Dora's red lips pursed into a sensuous pout. "She's bound to find out sooner or later, Ram."

Ram took a step in Sierra's direction, reaching out to her, his face stark with emotion. Sierra retreated out of reach, fearing she'd shatter if Ram touched her. "Forgive me for intruding. Had I known you and Ram were—were together again, I wouldn't have come today."

Dora's eyes narrowed thoughtfully. The tension, the hungry yearning flowing between Ram and Sierra was as powerful as a lightning bolt, and she didn't like it one damn bit. Was this young woman the reason she hadn't been able to tempt Ram? Dora gave Sierra a thorough inspection that was almost insulting. The girl certainly was lovely, she admitted with grudging admiration. And years younger than her own thirty-two. But she had something Sierra didn't, Dora thought smugly. She had a son who could claim Ram as his father.

"Sierra, please don't think—"

"Ram, have you told Sierra about our son?" Dora asked sweetly before Ram could finish his sentence.

"Damn you, Dora!" The harshness of Ram's voice startled Sierra. And it must have awakened Tommy, who had been sleeping in the adjoining room. He appeared in the doorway, his eyes swollen from sleep.

"What's wrong, Mama? Has Pa—Jason come for us?" Just this morning, his mother had told him it was no longer necessary to call Jason Papa, which suited him just fine. "Is he going to hurt us again?"

Tommy looked so frightened that Ram couldn't help replying, "No, son, no one is going to hurt you again."

Through the roaring din of her emotions, Sierra stared at Tommy. The boy, so like Ram that he took her breath away, ripped away Sierra's last shred of composure, leaving her exposed to more hurt than she could bear. Why hadn't

Ram told her he had a son? She felt as if she had never really known him. The swelling in her throat became unbearable. She stared at Ram as if seeing him for the first time.

Ram felt Sierra's anguish as deeply as he did his own. Pain lanced through him. His eyes turned dark and murky. With dawning horror, he knew he had lost Sierra forever. Any hope he'd harbored of reclaiming Sierra's love once he divorced Dora had been swept away by a woman who wasn't good enough to walk in Sierra's shadow.

Her heart hammering, her breathing ragged, Sierra clawed her way through the shadowy mists surrounding her and spun on her heel.

"Sierra, wait!" Ram reached out to stop her, but she slipped through his grasp. "You came here for a reason—what is it?"

What, indeed? Sierra thought wretchedly. Telling him about the baby seemed ludicrous after what she'd just seen. Obviously she had to tell him something, but what?

Without pausing in her flight, she glanced back over her shoulder and said, "Gordon Lynch is in Denver. We're to be married a week from Saturday. I wanted you to be the first to know."

Sierra's words had the desired effect. Ram's thunderstruck expression was awesome to behold.

Chapter Seventeen

Sierra fled from Ram's room as if the devil were nipping at her heels. She didn't slow down until she reached the lobby, and then only for decorum's sake. Haunted by disturbing thoughts of Ram and Dora together, she rushed blindly out the door into the street. A startled cry left her lips when someone grabbed her from behind, abruptly halting her wild flight.

"Sierra, what are you doing here? Were you looking for me?"

Sierra nearly collapsed in relief when she saw it was merely Gordon, not Ram as she'd expected. She stared at Gordie through a shimmering mist of tears, which she dashed away before he could see them and ask embarrassing questions.

"Sierra? Are you all right? I asked you a question. Have you come to see me?"

Suddenly Sierra knew what she must do. Since Ram was lost to her, she had only one option left.

"Yes, I came to see you. I needed to talk to you, Gordie. Do you still want to marry me?"

Gordon gave an exasperated look. "What is wrong with you, Sierra? Of course I want to marry you. Our wedding is a week from tomorrow, remember?"

"Walk me home, Gordie. There is something I need to tell you. Afterward, if you still want to marry me, we can talk about the wedding."

"You're acting very strangely, dear. What is this all about? You know how I abhor surprises."

Sierra took Gordon's arm, and they proceeded down the street. When they came to a quiet street with little traffic, Sierra stopped and turned to face Gordon, her expression grim. Gordon frowned, baffled by her strange behavior. Once they were married, he intended to put a stop once and for all to Sierra's melodramatic behavior. He supposed he was going to hear another of her fanciful notions. Sierra's doting parents shouldn't have spoiled her so outrageously, he thought.

"I don't really think we should hold a discussion here on the street," Gordon said impatiently. "Can't this wait until we get to the house?"

Sierra released a shaky sigh. "No, it can't wait. After I've explained, I'll understand if you want nothing more to do with me."

Gordon sent Sierra a sharp glance, beginning to understand. "Does this have anything to do with Ramsey Hunter?"

"It has everything to do with Ram. He and I . . . I'm . . ."

"You need go no further, Sierra. I think I know what you're trying to say. I suspected all along that you and Hunter had an intimate affair, and I prefer to think he seduced you. You're an inexperienced child compared to Hunter. I've already forgiven you your indiscretion."

Gordon was angrier than he let on. If not for the bank and Sierra's inheritance, he'd take her for his mistress. But Gordon was not stupid. Marrying Sierra despite her lapse had much to commend it, including Sierra's gratitude for overlooking her slightly soiled condition. Her gratitude would give him license to do as he pleased for the duration of their marriage. If she complained, all he had to do was bring up her little affair with Hunter.

Sierra chewed on her bottom lip, knowing that Gordon was in for an even bigger shock.

"You're partly right, Gordie, but there is more to it than that."

Gordon blinked. "More? I don't understand."

Sierra's eyes closed on a wave of despair. At that moment she truly hated Ram Hunter. "I'm carrying Ram's baby."

Sierra might as well have said she had two heads. Gordon stared at her in absolute horror.

"I beg your pardon. I don't think I heard you right, Sierra."

Squaring her narrow shoulders, Sierra looked unflinchingly at Gordon. Nothing or no one was going to make her ashamed of what she had done. She had loved Ram. His child was growing inside her, and she loved it already. Life would be easier for her and her child if she was married, but it wasn't necessary. If Gordon still wanted to marry her, so be it, but if he balked, she'd walk away from him and never look back. She was astute enough to know that Gordie wanted the bank and her inheritance badly; it seemed she had no choice but to offer herself and her child in return for a respectable marriage and a name for her child.

"You heard me right the first time, Gordie. I'm carrying Ram's child. Do you still want to marry me?"

"Isn't that something you should be asking Hunter?" Gordon said stiffly.

"For reasons I won't go into at this time, Ram can't marry me."

"You mean he won't marry you," Gordon sneered derisively. "At least you had the decency to tell me before the wedding."

"I'd never do that to you, Gordie. Believe what you want, but I am fond of you. What is your answer? If it's no, there will be no hard feelings. But if you say yes, it has to be unconditional. I won't stand for you mistreating me or my child. I know how badly you want the bank, and if you do not treat me with the respect I deserve, I'll see that you never get it. In return for your name, I'll be a good wife to you. The kind of wife you've always desired."

Gordon looked at Sierra with renewed interest. Instead of being devastated at bearing a child out of wedlock, she was tackling the problem with dignity. It was true that his main concern was gaining control of the bank, but he'd always been fond of Sierra; they'd known one another for years. And no matter how much he might despise Ramsey Hunter, he could never be deliberately cruel to an innocent babe.

Besides, old man Alden would be so grateful to be getting a grandchild so soon, he'd be appropriately generous to his son-in-law. And in Sierra he'd have the kind of wife he'd always dreamed of. Having her grateful and beholden to him did have merit. And of course there would be children of his own, many of them. So many that Sierra would have no time to look at another man.

"I'll expect you to bear my children," Gordon said.

"Of course."

"And I don't want Ramsey Hunter's name ever mentioned in my hearing."

"I agree wholeheartedly." Nothing would be more painful than hearing or talking about Ram. She'd have his child to remember him by and that was enough.

"If you give me any reason not to trust you in the future, all the promises I've made will be terminated. I can be as cruel and vindictive as the next man if my good will is compromised."

Sierra nodded grimly, aware that her life as Gordon's wife would never be the kind of life she'd always wanted for herself. He'd be forever watching her, wondering if she'd been with another man because of her history. He wouldn't be able to help himself. And although he insisted that he'd not be cruel to Ram's child, her knowledge of human nature told her it wasn't going to be easy for him to keep his word.

"You'll have no reason to distrust me, Gordie. I intend to keep my part of our bargain."

"Very well, Sierra, we have a deal. Let's hope neither of us lives to regret it. You've hurt me deeply, but I'm going through with the wedding nevertheless. Your parents need never know about your shame."

"So be it," Sierra said tersely. She started to proceed down the street, but Gordon stopped her.

"I think you owe me more than that, dear. In the past you've demonstrated little of the warmth I know you're capable of. I think I deserve a small token of affection. In a few days we'll be man and wife, and I'm looking forward to all the benefits due me as your husband."

After casting a covert glance down the street to make sure it was still deserted, Sierra closed her eyes and offered her mouth for Gordon's kiss.

Gordie had different ideas. "I want you to kiss me, Sierra. As if you really mean it."

Sierra's eyes flew open, and she sent Gordon

a startled look. His implacable expression indicated that he intended to hold her to the bargain she had just made. Moving closer, her lips touched his briefly, tentatively. Still not satisfied, Gordon grasped her shoulders, pulling her hard against him as he took her mouth in a bruising kiss that left her gasping for breath. He took advantage of her open mouth, thrusting his tongue past her teeth to sample her sweetness. But his passionate assault did not end there. Fired beyond control, Gordon forgot they were in public view as his hands slid from her shoulders to her breasts, kneading and molding the firm mounds to fit his palms.

Sierra froze but did not pull away. In a few short days, Gordie would have a legal right to her body. She suppressed a shudder of revulsion and forced herself to relax and accept the caress, knowing that never again would Ram touch her like this. Gordon would be her husband, and only Gordon would have the right to do all those wonderful things she'd done with Ram. Unfortunately, they wouldn't be so wonderful with Gordon.

A sob caught in Sierra's throat. Dear God, what had she done?

How could she allow Gordon into her bed?

How could she expect Gordon to uphold his part of their bargain when she couldn't respond to him as a wife should?

How could she forget Ram?

* * *

355

The moment Sierra rushed out of his hotel room, an anguished cry left Ram's throat. His first inclination was to run after her and force her to listen to his explanation. There had to be some way to convince her that appearances were often deceiving. He was halfway out the door before he realized that he couldn't rush out into public view with his shirt gaping open and his trousers unevenly buttoned. Spitting out a curse, he hastily set his clothing to rights, grabbed his coat, and headed out the door.

"Where are you going?"

Ram turned and stared at Dora, having already forgotten her. "Stay with your son, Dora—he needs you." Without waiting for a reply, he left the room, his angry strides betraying his mood.

He pushed through the front door of the hotel just as Sierra and Gordon rounded a corner. Seeing them together nearly tore him apart. Imagining them as husband and wife, engaging in all those activities allowed to married people, renewed his determination to do all in his power to prevent Sierra from marrying Gordon. She didn't love Gordon, for God's sake! Reason left him as he followed the couple down the street.

When they stopped abruptly on a deserted street, Ram stepped behind a lamppost to watch. Concealed from their view, he saw them speaking earnestly together and wondered what Sierra and Lynch found so interesting. He wanted to tear Gordon limb from limb when he saw them kissing a short time later. But when he saw Gordon's hands covering the breasts of *his* woman, he wanted to commit murder.

Not trusting the violence building within him, he turned and fled.

"That's much better, dear," Gordon said smugly. "I'm well satisfied that we'll deal well with one another."

"I promised I'd make you happy, Gordie," Sierra said, sadly aware that she was sacrificing her own happiness for a marriage she could barely tolerate. "I'd best be getting home now. I don't want to worry Abby."

"That's another thing, Sierra," Gordon said with a hint of censure. "There will be no more reckless behavior or walking the streets alone after we're married." He offered his arm. "Come along, I'll see you home. It wouldn't do to have your family worry about you."

"You can't do this, Sierra," Abby cautioned. Her brow furrowed in obvious concern. "You don't have to marry Gordon Lynch if you don't love him. Maybe it would help if you told me what happened between you and Ram Hunter."

"There is no hope for me and Ram, Abby. I don't ever want to hear that man's name again. Gordon knows about the baby and has agreed to all my terms. I believe that marrying Gordie is best for me and my child, and that's all that matters." She sent her sister a teary smile that did little to ease Abby's fears. "So, my dear sister, we're having a wedding. Will you help me pick out a dress to wear? There isn't time to have something made to order."

"Of course, if that's what you want."

"Will you be my matron of honor? I'd like Ryder to give me away."

"I'd be honored," Abby said, still not convinced that Sierra was completely rational. She gave every indication of having suffered some kind of shock. "I'm sure Ryder will be delighted to give you away. You can ask him yourself tomorrow."

When Ryder arrived the next day, he reacted with surprise to Sierra's announcement of her marriage to Gordon Lynch. He hadn't forgotten her infatuation with Ramsey Hunter and couldn't believe she had gotten over him so soon. He'd only known Sierra a short time, but she didn't strike him as a fickle miss who'd forget a man she fancied herself in love with so easily.

After Ryder met Gordon Lynch, he was more puzzled than ever over Sierra's choice of husband. He certainly wasn't a man Ryder would pick for his sister, though truth to tell he was far more suitable than Hunter, who had earned his contempt when he refused to marry Sierra.

As the day progressed, Ryder became more and more concerned over Sierra's decision to marry Gordon. When he questioned Abby, she was deliberately vague about everything concerning their sister, which did little to ease Ryder's mind. He had a nagging suspicion that there was more to Sierra's decision to marry Lynch than she was telling him. Ryder sensed that Ramsey Hunter was the cause of Sierra's haste to marry. After talking over the matter with Hannah in the privacy of their bedroom that night, Ryder decided that a call on Ram was definitely in order.

Ram awoke the next morning with a purpose that sent him out into the crisp September morning bright and early. Even if it took all day, he intended to rent a house for Dora and Tommy. The hotel was no proper place for a child, and he wanted to get the boy safely out of Jason's reach. He intended to pay a year's rent on a house in a quiet neighborhood where the boy could live a normal life. Then he planned to hire a lawyer and start divorce proceedings. He hadn't decided yet whether to ask for custody of Tommy. He still found it hard to swallow Dora's claim that he was Tommy's father, even though he had already decided to support the boy.

Regret rode Ram relentlessly. He regretted not telling Sierra he was married when he first met her. He regretted not pursuing a divorce more vigorously in those early years after Dora left him, and he regretted driving Sierra into Gordon Lynch's arms.

Too late, he lamented sadly. Too late for everything.

Or was it?

*   *   *

Ryder stormed into the Denver Hotel, his face dark and inscrutable, his silver eyes as turbulent as storm clouds. He frightened the poor hotel clerk so badly that the man was barely able to repeat Ram's room number. Ryder paid little heed to the heads poking out of rooms up and down the hall as he pounded loudly on Ram's door. One look at Ryder's scowling features convinced them that retreat was the better part of valor.

Ryder's face registered his shock when the door was opened by a towheaded lad. Ryder's expression was so fierce that Tommy took a shaky step backward. He had been in the adjoining room, heard the pounding on Ram's door, and decided to answer the summons.

"I thought this was Ramsey Hunter's room," Ryder said, his expression softening when he noted the boy's fear.

"This is Mr. Hunter's room, but he isn't in right now. Can I help you, Mr . . . ?"

Ryder's head swiveled at the sound of a female voice. He saw a woman standing in the doorway of an adjoining room and his mind went blank. "Larson. Ryder Larson. Who are you?"

Dora's mind worked furiously. Where had she heard that name before? In a moment it came to her. Ram had introduced Sierra as Sierra Larson Alden. Her eyes narrowed, and a sly smile curved her lips. "I'm Ram's wife and this is Tommy, our son."

Suddenly everything became clear to Ryder. Hunter couldn't marry his sister because he already had a wife. Rage exploded inside him. The bastard! Never would he understand the society that spawned such men. The Cheyenne had laws to deal with adulterers like Ramsey Hunter.

"Where is your husband, Mrs. Hunter?" Ryder asked, noting without interest the woman's seductive beauty.

"He left early without telling me where he was going. Are you a friend of Ram's?"

"Hardly," Ryder snorted.

Dora wet her lips, smiling with sultry invitation. "Call me Dora." She thought Ryder every bit as handsome as Ram. "Would you like to come in and wait? Tommy can go into the adjoining room while we . . . talk." She sent him a dazzling smile.

Ryder easily saw through Dora. He recognized her for what she was and thought justice well served. Ramsey Hunter deserved a whore for a wife. "I don't have time, Mrs. Hunter. I think I've learned everything I need to know."

When Ryder left the hotel, he was clear in his mind about a lot of things. It occurred to him that Sierra was marrying Lynch because she couldn't have Hunter. He wondered how long she had known about Ram's wife. Unfortunately, there was nothing Ryder could do about it except hope that Sierra's marriage would be a happy one. Lynch was a respectable businessman, and he did have the Aldens' blessing. If

361

both Sierra and Lynch were satisfied with the arrangement, he'd not interfere.

Ram found the perfect house for Dora and Tommy and planned on moving them in on Friday, the day before Sierra's wedding. Jason turned up at the hotel on Thursday. It wasn't as if Ram hadn't been expecting him. He had, in fact, looked for him long before now.

"Where is Dora?" Jason asked curtly as he searched the empty room. "I've come to take her home."

"You can have Dora if she'll go with you, but you can't have Tommy no matter what Dora does."

"You can have the brat," Jason sneered. "I never did believe he was mine. He's been a thorn in my side these past ten years. It's Dora I want. Where is she?"

Suddenly Jason looked past Ram through the open door of the adjoining room, where Dora stood poised on the threshold. "I'm here, Jason, and I'm not leaving. I'm tired of being slapped around. I want to be Ram's wife. He knows how to treat a woman."

Ram sent Dora a fierce scowl. "Leave me out of this, Dora. I washed my hands of you long ago. I thought I made that clear."

"I can change your mind, Ram. I know you very well, and I don't believe you'd abandon the mother of your son."

"I have only your word as proof that Tommy is my son," Ram said with waning patience.

"Don't leave me, Dora," Jason pleaded desperately. Without Dora he was nothing. He had been obsessed with Dora from the moment he first saw her. He had never wanted to hurt her, but sometimes she made him so angry that he couldn't control his temper. Moving from place to place, hiding from the law and Ram, had made their relationship tense and volatile. Lack of money caused dissension, followed by fierce arguments resulting in violence. Their problems were complicated by Tommy, who reminded him daily of Ram.

"I'm still Ram's wife," Dora insisted stubbornly, "I'm going to return to my husband."

"Like hell," Ram muttered darkly.

Jason sent Ram a look so filled with malice that it sent icy shivers down Ram's spine. "I'm desperate, Dora. I'll kill Hunter before I let him have you."

"Take your threats and get the hell out of here, Jason." Ram took a menacing step forward, and Jason quickly retreated. "I suggest you leave town as quickly as possible. Tomorrow I'm going to the sheriff. I imagine there's an old wanted poster on you around somewhere. Meanwhile, I'm going to wire Jeff that I've found you. I suspect the state of Texas will be glad to hear you've finally been located."

"Bastard!" Jason spat viciously. "You haven't heard the last of me yet."

"Write me from prison," Ram sneered. "When the shackles rub your wrists and ankles raw, and your back aches from forced labor and beatings by sadistic guards, you'll feel something of what I suffered those two years I was jailed unjustly."

Anger made Jason more determined than ever to keep the woman he'd considered his all these years. He glared at Dora, his eyes burning brightly with jealous rage.

"You won't have him, Dora, mark my words. You're mine. You'll always be mine. Can't you see Ram doesn't want you? Once he's gone, you'll come crawling back to me on your knees."

Whirling on his heel, he stormed away.

"I've never seen Jason so angry," Dora said, stepping close to Ram. "I think he means to do you bodily harm."

"He can try," Ram said tightly. "You're welcome to go with him, you know, but Tommy stays. You gave birth while still married to me, and for all intents and purposes he's my son. I'll take care of him whether or not he's my flesh and blood. The boy has suffered Jason's abuse for the last time."

"Ram . . ."

Ram frowned. "What is it now, Dora?"

"I really do love you. I've just begun to realize how much. We can start over again, you and I. We have a son; he deserves both his parents."

Ram snorted derisively. "I'm too wise to let you make a fool of me again, Dora. I've learned my lesson well. I've visited a lawyer and started divorce proceedings. I'll bring the papers around for you to sign in a day or two."

Dora's eyes widened. "I'll not sign them."

"You will if you know what's good for you. The law hasn't forgotten that you're an accessory to a foul crime."

"That was ten years ago," Dora scoffed. "It seems unlikely that the law is still interested in me."

"We'll see. Go back to your room and tell Tommy he'll be moving to a new house tomorrow."

"It's that girl, isn't it? What is Sierra to you? Her brother—at least I think he was her brother—came here to see you."

Ram went still. "What did he want? What did you tell him?"

"I told him I was your wife and Tommy was our son. He seemed quite interested. He left without leaving a message."

Ram stared at her for the space of a heartbeat, then grabbed his hat and coat and stormed from the room. In two days, Sierra was going to marry Gordon Lynch, unless he found a way to stop the wedding.

Minutes later, he found himself standing on Sierra's doorstep. He didn't bother analyzing his purpose for being there as he rapped loudly on the door.

Hannah answered his knock. Her eyes widened when she saw Ram. Ryder had told her all about his visit to Ram's room and what he'd learned. "What do you want?"

"I want to speak to Sierra."

"She's not here." She started to close the door in his face but Ram held it open with his palm.

"It's important."

"I told you, she's—"

"It's all right, Hannah, I'll see Ram." Sierra appeared at the door, looking so beautiful that she stole Ram's breath away.

"Are you sure, Sierra?" Hannah asked, reluctant to leave. Both Zach and Ryder were out, and she knew that neither she, Abby nor Sierra was strong enough to evict Ram if he didn't want to leave.

"I'm sure," Sierra said, though in truth seeing Ram again was painful in the extreme.

Hannah hesitated briefly, then turned and walked into an adjoining room.

"Why did you come here, Ram?" Sierra whispered shakily. God, he was handsome. Did he know what he did to her?

"To talk some sense into you, little love. Dora means nothing to me. What you saw in my room wasn't what it appeared."

Sierra blinked back scalding tears. How easily he lied to her. Her expression was sober and touched with anguish. "It was difficult to mistake what you two were doing. But don't get me wrong. It's none of my business what you do with your wife. I can't blame you for wanting her—she's lovely. Why didn't you tell me you had a son?"

Ram grit his teeth in frustration. "I don't want Dora, and I didn't know I had a son until a few days ago. I'm not even sure Tommy *is* my son. Dora can't even say for sure, since she was sleeping with both me and Jason at the time."

Sierra wanted to scream at Ram. She knew who had fathered *her* unborn child. It was Ram, pure and simple. She searched her heart and found a smidgen of pity for Ram. It must be frustrating not knowing if he was really the boy's father. "I'm sorry, Ram, but that's no concern of mine. I think you'd better leave now. With my wedding taking place day after tomorrow, there is much to be done."

"You can't marry Lynch, Sierra. I won't let him touch you. You belong to me."

"You can't stop me."

"Dammit, Sierra, I'm getting a divorce. In six months to a year, I'll be free and we can be married. I . . I need you. You burst unexpectedly into my life and performed a miracle. Your caring healed wounds I believed too deep to cure."

Sierra searched Ram's face, the liquid silver of her eyes dull with regret. Six months to a year. Too late, much too late. She didn't want to bear a child out of wedlock. Besides, she knew what she'd seen in his room.

"I'm sorry."

She turned abruptly and walked away. When Ram made as if to follow, Hannah blocked his path. "Let her be, Mr. Hunter. Go home to your wife and child and leave Sierra alone."

"I'll leave," Ram said with quiet determination, "but you can tell Sierra I haven't given up. And tell her . . . tell her . . . Never mind, I'll tell her myself."

Chapter Eighteen

The day of Sierra's wedding began on an ominous note, with Sierra emptying the contents of her stomach into a basin. Pale, weak, and listless, she barely made it down to breakfast, surprised to see Abby looking even more wan than she was. Dismissing her appearance with a shrug, Abby insisted that she was fine. And since her baby wasn't due for another three weeks, the table talk gradually got around to the wedding and Sierra. By that time Sierra was beginning to recover from her queasy stomach and was able to act, albeit not very convincingly, like an eager bride.

The weather outside was as dismal as Sierra felt. An ominous gray sky hinted at an impending storm, and an occasional roll of thunder made the weather appear even more threatening. Glancing out the window of the breakfast room, Sierra grimaced at the misty fog that had settled over the city. Her dark mood seemed to match the gloomy day.

The wedding was scheduled for eleven o'clock, and after breakfast Sierra returned to her room while Hannah and Abby fussed over her hair and clothing like mother hens. Sierra had no idea that her family suspected her heart wasn't in this wedding. For the child's sake, she had decided to go through with this marriage and be a good wife to Gordon. She knew of few men who would be willing to marry a woman carrying another man's child, and she was grateful to him for his sacrifice.

"You look lovely," Hannah said wistfully as she stepped back to admire the elaborate hairdo she'd created for Sierra. "I hope Gordon realizes how lucky he is."

"Are you all right, honey? You look pale." This from Abby, who was looking rather pale herself.

"I'm fine, Abby. Have Ryder and Zach left for the church yet? They were to join Gordon to await our arrival."

"I heard them leave a few minutes ago. Zach said he'd bring the buggy around to the front door before he left."

"I'll drive," Hannah offered.

"I'll check the children and their nurse before we leave," Abby said as she walked from the room. Her steps were slow and dragging, but she was determined to conceal her discomfort so as not to spoil her sister's wedding day.

"I'll get our wraps," Hannah said as she hurried after Abby. "Come down when you're ready, Sierra—it's growing late."

Alone at last, Sierra dropped the facade she'd tried to maintain during the morning. Tonight she'd be lying in Gordon's arms—tonight and every night for the rest of her life. How could she bear it? How could she respond to a man she didn't love? How could she forget the splendor of Ram's loving? She had to if she wanted her marriage to succeed.

Her body trembled with the memory of Ram's hands on her. She closed her eyes and recalled the magic of his kisses, the strength of his arms, the way his body adored every inch of hers. He had taught her passion, and she had been humbled by the earth-shattering experience.

There was a power about Ram that she couldn't resist—a raw sensual masculinity that made other men pale in comparison. There was something dangerous about him, too. A quality men feared and women adored, it emanated from every sinew and muscle of his big, hard body.

But Ram was married. Married with a child. He hadn't cared enough about her to tell her he had a family, and she'd been blinded by her love for him. She had truly intended to tell him about the baby, but when she saw him and Dora together, their clothing awry, their bodies entwined, she'd been too devastated to function properly. She'd long suspected that Ram loved

Dora, no matter how often he had denied it or how badly Dora had hurt him, so she shouldn't have been surprised to see them together like that. But it hurt—oh God, it hurt.

She had hoped . . . But her hopes had been dashed, and not even a baby could mend what was wrong between her and Ram. She was better off with Gordon, she tried to tell herself. She owed him so much. He truly was a good friend.

"Are you ready, Sierra?"

Hannah's voice drifted to her from the bottom of the stairs. "Coming, Hannah." Dragging in a steadying breath, Sierra squared her shoulders and opened the door to her room.

Ram leaned against a tree across the street from the Mercer home, his clothing wet from the cold drizzle that had begun falling at daybreak. He had arrived early, even before the first lamp was lit inside the house. Shivering in the cool, wet predawn, he had remained rooted to the spot regardless of his discomfort. He had noted movement in the house as the occupants rose to meet the day and he continued his silent vigil, waiting for something—anything. His breathing quickened when he saw Zach and Ryder, dressed in their Sunday best, leave the house.

After Zach brought the buggy around to the front door, both men had ridden off on horseback. To the church, Ram supposed. After an interminable length of time, the front door opened and three women stepped outside.

Ram had eyes for no one but Sierra. Dazzling in a blue velvet cloak that billowed out in shimmering folds around her slim body, her beauty was breathtaking. The vivid blue color provided a perfect setting for the lustrous black curls peeking from beneath her hood, framing the pale oval of her face. Ram stared at her, noting her unnatural paleness. He wondered if she was regretting her decision to marry Gordon Lynch. Lord, he hoped so.

Desperation rode Ram. Despite his resolve to stop the wedding, he'd devised no workable plan. If he barged into the church, he'd have to contend with Ryder and Zach, and they would quickly put an end to his interference. Yet Ram could not make himself leave, eagerly devouring Sierra's beauty. If there was a God, He'd find a way to stop a marriage that would only bring Sierra unhappiness.

Pulling her hood closer about her head to protect her hairdo against the cold drizzle, Sierra settled her skirts around her in the buggy, waiting for Hannah to give Abby a hand up. She slid over to make room for her ungainly sister. Abby had one foot on the riser when she bent over and clutched her stomach. Her cry of distress brought Hannah instantly to her side.

"Abby, what is it? Is it the baby?"

"I don't know," Abby said, panting.

"Let me help," Sierra said as she started to climb down to aid her sister.

"No," Abby said weakly, "you'll be late for

your wedding. Go on without me. Tell Zach I didn't feel up to attending. It's still too early for the baby, but I don't want to take unnecessary chances. Perhaps it's the excitement," she added hopefully.

"I'll stay with Abby," Hannah offered. "Can you drive yourself, Sierra?"

"Yes, but I don't think I should leave. What if—"

"Nonsense," Abby scoffed. "I've already had one child, remember? It's probably nothing. You go on, and Hannah and I will follow later. If by chance we don't make it in time, the preacher's wife can act as witness. I don't want to spoil your wedding, honey."

Leaning heavily on Hannah, Abby hobbled slowly back to the house. Sierra waited until they had disappeared inside before scooting over to the driver's side and reaching for the reins. She nearly jumped out of her skin when someone leaped up beside her, snatched the reins from her hands, and slapped them smartly against the horse's rump. The startled animal clattered off down the street at a brisk clip. The sudden motion flung Sierra backward, and she grasped the side rail to keep from being tossed out.

"Ram!" Her brain whirled in confusion. "What do you think you're doing?"

Ram didn't bother to answer, concentrating instead on guiding the buggy through the crowded streets.

"Dammit, Ram, answer me! You're going in

the wrong direction. I'll be late for my wedding."

Ram slanted her a dark look that spoke eloquently of his thoughts on that subject. "You can't marry Lynch. You don't love him."

Sierra stared at him. "I thought you didn't believe in love."

Ram fell silent. Careening through town at breakneck speed was hardly the proper time to discuss love.

"Where are you taking me?"

Silence.

"This is kidnaping."

More silence.

It wasn't until they left town that Sierra realized where Ram was taking her. They were traveling in the direction of that secluded, magical place in the foothills where they had made love beneath a twisted pine tree. So much had happened since then that it seemed like an eon ago. A fragmented picture flashed before her eyes of Ram bending over her, exciting her with his hands and mouth, thrusting, stroking, adoring her with every part of his body. He had made her feel loved then. But that was before she had learned about Ram's son, and found Dora and Ram together in a way that left little doubt in her mind as to what they had been doing.

They had left the bustling city far behind when Ram turned the buggy onto a rutted trail winding upward into the foothills. The rain was falling faster now, and Sierra pressed against the back cushion, shivering beneath her cloak. When they reached the creek, Sierra expected Ram to stop, but he continued on, following the meandering stream a few hundred yards west. If the day hadn't been so dismal, Sierra would have been enthralled with the vivid yellow, red, rusts and greens of the aspens.

The skies opened up, releasing a drenching downpour just as Sierra spotted a cabin sitting on the bank of the stream. She was grateful to see shelter of any kind as a clap of thunder rattled the nearby trees and lightning streaked across the heavens.

Ram halted the buggy at the sagging front door, jumped to the ground, and lifted Sierra from the conveyance. He sprinted with her in his arms into the cabin, nearly ripping the door from the rusted hinges in his haste to get her out of the rain. Ram went immediately to the crude hearth and started a fire, using dry wood piled beside it, while Sierra surveyed the dilapidated room in open curiosity.

Why had Ram brought her here? What did he expect to gain by making her miss her own wedding? He couldn't marry her himself, so why did he torment her? By now Gordie would be seething with anger over being left standing at the altar, and she suffered a pang of guilt. She wondered if Ryder and Zach were searching for her. She shuddered, fearing what they would do to Ram when they found him.

Ram rose with exaggerated nonchalance, dusted off his knees, and turned to face Sierra, finding her every bit as upset as he expected her to be. "It should be warm in here in a few minutes."

"What is this place? Who owns it?"

"It's an old prospector's cabin," Ram explained. "Believe it or not, I'm the owner. I built it several years ago when I came to Denver looking for Dora and Jason. They had already left, and for a time I lost track of them. Having nothing else to occupy me, I decided to try my hand at prospecting. I lived here and prospected only six months before I learned that Dora and Jason were in Silver City and left in haste. I was surprised to find that the cabin hadn't changed much since I left. I came back several days ago, stocked it with dry wood, and cleaned it up somewhat."

Sierra wasn't impressed. "Did you plan to bring me here all along?"

"Perhaps I did have it in the back of my mind, but I didn't know how I would arrange it. It's private here, and no one will disturb us. I knew that if I took you to my hotel room, your brother would come gunning for me. He doesn't much like me."

Silver eyes assessed him keenly. "Can you blame him?"

"I reckon not, but he doesn't understand. I never meant to hurt you. For years revenge ruled my life. It made me insensitive to all but my own needs. Lord knows, I fought the attraction between us as long as I could. I refused to acknowledge the depth of my emotions where

377

you were concerned. Even after I took your innocence, I couldn't admit how much you'd come to mean to me.

"All I could think of was punishing Jason. I might have been tempted to kill him if not for Tommy." His voice dropped to a husky whisper. "I tried to deny my emotional attachment to you, but each time we loved made a mockery of my denial. I love you, Sierra. You can't marry Lynch. I want you to marry me when my divorce is final."

Sierra sank down into the nearest chair. Heat crawled up her neck, and her breath came in jerky gasps. Hearing those words from Ram left her shaken and confused.

Noting her flushed cheeks and misty eyes, Ram dropped to his knees beside her. "It's warm in here. Take off your wet cloak, and I'll spread it out to dry. I don't want you getting sick." When Sierra made no effort to comply, he lifted it from her shoulders and spread it across a chair before the fire.

"You love me?" Sierra repeated, finally finding her tongue. "What about Dora? What about revenge? I find it difficult to believe you'd forget and forgive what happened all those years ago. It's been a part of your life for too long."

"So it has," Ram agreed. "But when I learned you were going to marry Gordon, revenge no longer mattered to me. I realized our future together was more important than the past. Dora and Jason have suffered their own kind of hell. For ten years, they have been hiding from me and running from the law."

"Did you decide this before or after you bedded Dora?" Sierra asked with asperity.

Ram stood up, pulling Sierra with him and dragging her into his arms. "I never bedded Dora, little love. You're the only woman I want, the only one I love. I realize that what you saw in my room looked damning, but Dora's attempt at seduction didn't work. I don't want Dora. My love for her died a long time ago."

Still not convinced, Sierra said, "She's the mother of your son."

"Tommy is a fine lad any man would be proud to claim. But the fact remains that no one knows for certain if he's my son or Jason's."

"Will you let Jason have him?" For some reason, Ram's answer was important to Sierra.

"No!" Ram declared forcefully. "I've made provisions for Tommy. But I don't want to discuss Tommy right now. I'd rather talk about us—and our future."

Sierra moistened her dry lips with the tip of her tongue. "I'm going to marry Gordie. He—he's been good to me."

"The hell with Gordie," Ram spat, pulling her hard against him. "Can you deny what you feel in my arms? Can you truthfully say you experience the same things with Lynch? Does he make your flesh burn, your heart pound? Does he give you the same kind of pleasure I do? Think, little love, think of the splendor we shared, the paradise that awaits us still. I want you, Sierra, and I think you want me."

He kissed her, and her senses reeled out of control. Ram groaned, feeling it, tasting it, matching her passion with an even greater passion. She kissed him back, her arms rising to clasp his neck, pressing against him with hungry yearning.

"God, Sierra, I want you so damn much I'm humbled by it," he whispered against her ear. He kissed her neck and felt her muscles go taut under his soft touch. She returned the caress, timidly sliding the tip of her tongue along the side of his neck up to his ear.

It was too much. Ram's control broke. With a growl, he lifted her in his arms and strode toward the cot in the far corner of the room. Then, in a flurry of lace and silk, he removed every stitch of her clothing, his eyes pools of blue flame, awed by the visual feast spread out before him. She reached for the blanket.

"Don't," he said, staying her hand. His eyes locked with hers as he began removing his own clothing.

Sierra watched him in unabashed pleasure, wondering how she could ever have considered marrying Gordon and sharing this kind of intimacy with him. With almost painful longing, she watched Ram reveal each tantalizing muscle and sinew. She wanted to look away but hadn't the will. She desperately wanted to believe he loved her, and she did what her heart demanded—accepted his gift of love for the fleeting pleasure it brought her. Only the good Lord knew what tomorrow would bring.

Ram knelt on the cot, adoring every inch of her with his eyes. She was sleek, feline, her body graceful and firm. Her skin had the sheen of pearls, and he reached out almost reverently, his hand skimming lightly down the pulsing hollow of her throat to the ripe fullness of her breasts. He paused to test one nipple with the tip of his finger, smiling when it rose impudently to meet his touch.

He moved on, down her flat belly to her hips and the pale ivory of her thighs. His palm stroked her smooth flesh from hips to knees, sliding up the insides of her thighs slowly, turning them to quivering jelly.

Everywhere Ram touched she tingled, and he touched her everywhere. She cried out when his hand moved higher between her thighs. Separating her moist folds, he thrust one finger into her honeyed warmth.

"Ram . . . Ram . . ." Her eyes flew up to meet his, filled with a desperate hunger that nearly unmanned him.

"I've never wanted a woman the way I want you," he said softly, lowering his mouth to take her lips.

Sierra recognized his urgency and was awed by the leashed strength of his desire. There was so much power in the taut muscles and sinews of his body that she was amazed at his ability to contain it. Her thoughts skidded to a halt when Ram's tongue swept into her mouth. His taste inflamed her.

Lingering over her lips but briefly, Ram's

mouth moved down her body, kissing and nibbling, making her writhe beneath him. When he palmed a breast and sucked the nipple into his mouth, Sierra moaned, the sweet torture painfully arousing.

"I want you inside me now," Sierra pleaded on a raspy sigh.

"Soon, little love." His mouth trailed a burning path from her breast to her naval, his tongue darting inside the sensitive indentation to tease and plunder.

It can't be soon enough, Sierra thought. Did he enjoy tormenting her?

As if in answer to her silent plea, Ram pressed her legs apart and settled between her thighs. His hands sifted through the soft dark hair protecting her sex, separating the moist petals and lowering his mouth to the swollen bud at the entrance. Clutching at the bedding, Sierra arched against the heat of his mouth and gave a startled cry.

Waves of throbbing pleasure rushed over her, and the roar of passion blotted out the sound of rain pounding against the tin roof. Grasping her hips to hold her in place, Ram's mouth and tongue made relentless forays into her heated center, lapping, sucking, flinging her higher and higher, until she reached the pinnacle of ecstasy.

With a burst of white-hot flame, profound ecstasy sent her over the edge, spinning, spinning . . . Her body went rigid, spasming beneath the wet lash of his tongue.

Still vibrating from her violent climax, she felt his thick, pulsing shaft probing the throbbing entrance to her core. With fierce possession, he thrust himself inside her, the heat of his passion consuming her. He gave a hoarse shout as waves of sheer, stunning pleasure swept through him and he slid deeper, deeper still, until he felt his tip nudge her womb.

He moved very slowly at first, wanting to prolong that magical time within her, and incredibly, Sierra felt passion stir again inside her. When he felt her response, his slow strokes became a raging tempest, like a crashing of waves and the din of a storm, a storm building within him. She shivered against him, loving the taut, slick feel of his bronzed muscles, the tempered strength of his arms and legs. When ecstasy claimed her, she exulted in the knowledge that she was giving Ram the same kind of ecstasy he gave her. She felt the constriction of his body, heard the hoarse pleasure of his cry, and then the easing of his body as he fell beside her, spent.

"Do you still want to marry Lynch?" Ram asked when his heart had slowed to a steady thunder.

Never had Sierra been aware of so many things at once. She was aware that it had stopped raining and the sun was shining through the dingy window. She was aware of the intense feelings whirling inside her. And she was aware that Ram loved her and wanted her. Their child would be born with a mother and father who loved it. This would be a perfect time to tell him about the baby, she thought dreamily. One day they would be together, no matter how long it took for Ram to obtain his divorce.

Ram searched Sierra's face, sensing that she was about to tell him something important. He didn't think he could bear it if she told him she still intended to marry Lynch.

"Sierra . . ."

"Ram, I . . ." Her words were interrupted by violent pounding on the door.

"Hunter! I know you and my sister are in there. Either you come out, or I'm coming in."

"Oh my God, it's Ryder!" Sierra cried, pulling the blanket up to her chin.

"How in the hell did he find us?" Ram asked, diving into his pants.

"Ryder was raised by Indians. He learned his tracking skills from the Cheyenne. Abby told me he's wonderfully adept at all Indian skills."

"Just my luck," Ram muttered sourly.

"Hunter! I'm coming in."

Ram took one look at Sierra and felt her embarrassment as keenly as he did his own. It rankled to think that her brother was always bursting in on them at inappropriate moments.

"I'm coming out!" Ram shouted as he pulled on his boots and buttoned his shirt. "Get dressed," he hissed as he stepped out the door. Sierra scrambled for her clothing.

"You bastard!" Ryder spat viciously. "I told you to keep away from my sister. You have a wife and child, Hunter—why won't you leave Sierra alone? She left Gordon Lynch standing at the altar."

"I couldn't allow her to marry Lynch," Ram said evenly. "She doesn't love him."

"So you decided to make Sierra your mistress," Ryder said from between clenched teeth.

"No! I love Sierra. I've filed for divorce and plan to marry her, if she'll have me."

"She damn well won't have you. She's lucky Lynch still wants her."

"Let me answer for myself," Sierra said as she stepped out the door.

"Not now," Ryder said, grasping Sierra around the waist and hoisting her onto the back of his horse. "Abby needs you."

Dear God, she'd forgotten all about Abby. "How is she? Is it the baby?"

"We don't know yet. The doctor hadn't arrived yet when I left."

"How did you find us so soon?"

"Several people saw the buggy careening down the street and recalled the direction it was heading. The rest was simple tracking."

"I need to go to Abby," Sierra said, sending Ram a look that spoke eloquently of her anguish.

"Of course you do," Ram agreed. "We'll talk later."

"Leave the buggy at the livery," Ryder said tersely as he turned his mount toward town.

Ram watched Sierra and Ryder until they were out of sight. Then, with a heavy heart, he turned and reentered the cabin. He had no idea if Sierra meant to go through with her marriage to Lynch, for Ryder had interrupted at a crucial moment. For all he knew, Sierra was on the verge of telling him she didn't love him, that she wanted Lynch. He knew he had reached her on one level, for their passion had been too hot to contain. But whether he had reached her heart was debatable. Before he left the cabin, he glanced back at the rumpled bed, recalling those dazzling moments of ecstasy he had found in Sierra's arms.

Was that all he was ever going to have of her?

Chapter Nineteen

"I had every intention of marrying Gordie until I saw Ram," Sierra explained to Ryder as they neared the city. "Is he at the house?"

"He wanted to go to the sheriff and charge Hunter with kidnaping," Ryder replied shortly, "but I convinced him to go back to the hotel and do nothing until he heard from me. I wasn't sure whether you went with Hunter willingly or he kidnaped you. Hannah caught just a fleeting glimpse of you driving off with him. Lynch left, but he wasn't too happy about the whole mess. Can't say I blame him."

"I'm sorry. It's not what I intended. I had no idea Ram would show up when he did. He—he wanted to talk me out of marrying Gordie. That's why he brought me to the cabin."

"He doesn't deserve you, honey. Besides, he already has a wife."

"That's something else you don't understand. Abby is the only one who knows what Ram has been through. He's not what you think."

"What is he? The bastard used you—how can you defend him?"

"He didn't use me, Ryder, he loves me. He wants to marry me."

Ryder snorted in disbelief. "He isn't the only man who's used that excuse to get a woman into his bed."

"Ram's not like that."

"If there is something I don't know, Sierra, maybe it's time you told me."

"Yes, I want you to know. It's a long story that began ten years ago. After you've heard it, I know you'll feel differently about Ram."

"Perhaps," Ryder said doubtfully.

Sierra took a deep breath and told Ryder everything she knew about Ram and his marriage to Dora. She left out nothing, including the murder of his partner, Jason's involvement, Dora's betrayal, and Ram's shock when he learned about Tommy.

"Whew," Ryder whistled, setting his hat back on his head. "You sure have a knack for getting yourself into complicated situations, little sister."

"You do understand now, don't you?"

"I agree I might have judged Hunter harshly, but that doesn't absolve him of guilt where you're concerned."

"I love you for wanting to protect me," Sierra said, giving him a shaky smile.

"You were young and inexperienced, and Hunter took unfair advantage of you."

"If anything, I took advantage of him," Sierra admitted. "There is something else you should know. I'm carrying Ram's child."

"Good God!" He reined his horse to an abrupt halt. "I'll kill the bastard!"

"You'll do no such thing, Ryder Larson. He's the father of my child."

"No wonder you agreed to marry Lynch—you were desperate for a father for your child. None of us felt your heart was in it, but we were willing to abide by your wishes. After all, Lynch was your fiance and he did have the Aldens' blessing. We want your happiness, honey. What are you going to do? Does Lynch know about the baby? Obviously, Hunter can't marry you since he still has a wife. A divorce takes time."

"I told Gordie about the baby, and he still wanted to marry me. But I can't marry Gordie now—not after learning that Ram loves me. I'd like to stay in Denver until my child is born, if that's all right with you and Abby. I don't know how long it will take for Ram's divorce to become final. Our conversation ended rather hastily after you arrived."

Ryder gave her a piercing look. "You had more than enough time if conversation was all you were engaged in."

Sierra flushed and looked away. How easily her brother saw through her. "Nevertheless, as soon as I make certain Abby is all right, I'm going to Ram's hotel. I really do need to talk to him. There was too much left unsaid. He doesn't know . . . Never mind, he'll know soon enough."

Ryder looked stunned. "You mean Hunter doesn't know about his child?"

"He'll know before the day is out."

Sierra returned home to an exuberant welcome, although no one had doubted Ryder's ability to find her. She was more than grateful when few questions were asked about the hours she'd spent with Ram. Though curious, her family didn't pry, and she appreciated their restraint.

Sierra's first concern was Abby, who was not with the others in the parlor when she arrived home.

"Abby is fine, Sierra," Zach assured her when she asked about her sister. "It was a false alarm. The doctor ordered her to bed until she delivers. I'm going to take very good care of her."

"Thank God," Sierra breathed shakily.

"Thank God you're all right," Zach replied sincerely. "Go on upstairs—Abby will be relieved to see you."

Sierra hurried upstairs and found her sister sleeping peacefully. She tiptoed out and went back downstairs to join the others.

"She's sleeping," she told them when they looked at her questioningly. "I'll look in on her later. If you don't need me, I have an errand to run."

"Sierra," Hannah cried, "you can't leave

again—it's almost dinner time. Can't it wait until tomorrow?"

"This can't wait," Sierra said stubbornly.

"I'll take you," Ryder offered. "And bring you home when you've finished your—errand." The harsh planes of his face told her there was no way she was leaving the house unaccompanied.

"Very well. Shall we leave?"

"This really isn't necessary," Sierra said as Ryder lifted her onto his horse's back and mounted behind her.

"Let me be the judge of that, little sister. I'll take you to Hunter's hotel and wait for you in the lobby. I'll give you an hour, no more. That should be plenty of time to tell him about the baby."

Ram climbed slowly up the stairs to his room, his mind in turmoil. Damn Ryder Larson, he thought with a hint of malice. If not for Larson, he and Sierra would have everything settled between them by now. God, he loved her. Until Sierra had fallen into his life and taught him to feel again, his heart had been an empty shell. Impudent beyond belief, spoiled certainly, and incredibly persistent, Sierra filled his life with sunshine and light. She was sweet, and kind, and passionate, and beautiful; he was damn lucky he had found her. Luckier still that she loved him.

Or did she? He broke out in a cold sweat when he thought of how close she had come to marrying a man she didn't love. She had been about to tell him something when Ryder interrupted them, and he wondered if she was going to say she no longer loved him. Lord knew, he didn't deserve her. He had lied to her and taken her innocence knowing he couldn't marry her. He had hurt her in more ways than he cared to count.

With a heavy heart, Ram inserted the key in the lock. The door swung open before he turned the key, and he stepped inside. Preoccupied with thoughts of Sierra, his mind didn't register the fact that the door hadn't been locked.

"Ram, where have you been? You've been gone nearly the entire day."

Ram started violently. "How did you get into my room, Dora? You nearly frightened the daylights out of me. Is Tommy all right?"

"Tommy is fine. I left him with the housekeeper you hired. I had to see you, Ram, and asked the maid to let me inside. You haven't been to see us since you moved us, so I came to you."

"I'm tired, Dora. Can't this wait until tomorrow?"

Dora stared at him narrowly. "Something happened, Ram. What is it?"

"Nothing that concerns you. Go home to Tommy. My lawyer will call on you soon with arrangements for our divorce. You'll note that I've made generous provisions for both you and Tommy."

"I don't want a divorce. I'm afraid of Jason. What if he doesn't leave town? What if he—"

"If he doesn't leave town, he'll be arrested to-morrow and charged with murder. He may not have done the deed himself, but he paid to have it done."

"I swear I didn't know what Jason intended, Ram. Jason told me he stumbled onto the murder after it had been committed, and I believed him. I didn't know he was responsible until later. I admit I lied in court, but I never expected you to be convicted."

"Like hell!" Ram snorted. "You couldn't wait to get your hot little hands on my money and run off with Jason."

"You'll never know how much I regret it."

"It's too late, Dora. I love someone who will never betray me. After our divorce, I'm going to marry Sierra. If she'll have me."

Dora's eyes widened. "If you're referring to Sierra Alden, I heard she was going to marry her fiance from San Francisco today."

"It never happened. She doesn't love him. Go home, Dora."

Ryder delivered Sierra to the hotel as he'd promised and waited in the lobby, albeit reluctantly, while Sierra ascended the stairs to Ram's room. The door was ajar, and the sound of voices wafted to her through the opening. She recognized Ram's voice, raised in anger, and when a female voice responded, she knew Dora was in the room with him. Like a coward, she almost turned and fled, until she recalled Ram's emphatic denial of any kind of involvement

393

with Dora. Squaring her shoulders, she pushed the door open and stepped inside.

Dora saw her first. "Come in," she said with biting sarcasm, "you might as well join in the discussion."

Ram's expression revealed his shock. Sierra was the last person he expected to see here tonight. He was surprised Ryder had allowed it.

Sierra anticipated his question. "Ryder is waiting downstairs for me. I had to see you, Ram."

"Where is your fiancé, Miss Alden? Ram told me your wedding was called off. Too bad."

Ram sent Dora a quelling look.

"Should I leave and come back another time?" Sierra asked uncertainly.

"No! God, no. Dora was just leaving."

Dora bristled at Ram's curt dismissal. "Come with me, Ram," she pleaded, "come home with me and Tommy. We need you."

Ryder stared impatiently at the stairs, his expression watchful. After checking his timepiece, he saw that only fifteen minutes had elapsed since Sierra had ascended the stairs, and he settled back into the chair, fighting the urge to tear up the stairs and make certain she was all right. There was no explainable reason for his tension, just a gnawing feeling in the pit of his stomach.

A few minutes ago, he had seen a man enter the lobby and climb the stairs. He wouldn't have thought a thing about it if the man hadn't paused at the foot of the stairs and glanced furtively over his shoulder before continuing. Ryder could tell by his staggering gait that he was liquored up. The hair rose on the back of his neck, but since he had no reason to suspect the man of anything sinister, he forced himself to relax.

Weaving from side to side, Jason paused outside the partially opened door to Ram's room. He'd learned the room number when he'd inquired the day before. His expression hardened when he heard Dora beg Ram not to abandon her and the boy. He couldn't lose Dora—not now, not ever. He had spent long days and sleepless night thinking about what he was going to do, and it finally came to him. He had to kill Ramsey Hunter. He'd thought about killing Ram ever since he learned that Ram had been released from prison and was looking for him and Dora.

Nothing had worked out as he'd planned. Ram was supposed to be blamed for Hiram's murder and put away for life. Then he'd have Dora all to himself. He had hated sharing her with her husband and thought he'd found a way to be rid of Ram forever without actually killing him.

Pushing the door open, Jason stepped inside the room. The tension was so thick that no one noticed him until he slammed the door shut with a bang. Once he had their attention, he drew a gun from his belt and aimed it at Ram's chest. The six-shooter was cocked and aimed before anyone could react.

"Ram isn't going anywhere with you, Dora." His voice was calm—too calm. "You belong to me. This time I'm going to make damn sure Ramsey Hunter is out of our lives."

"Don't be a fool, Jason," Ram said. "You'll never get away with killing me."

"I'm willing to take the chance. I'm tired of running from you. The law I could outsmart, but not you. This time I'm gonna get rid of you permanently."

Sierra finally found her voice. "Ram, he's going to kill you!"

Jason eyed Sierra narrowly. "Who in the hell is she?"

"No one you need concern yourself with, Jason. Let her leave. She has no part in this."

"So she can bring the law? No, the woman stays. Don't interfere, lady, if you know what's good for you."

"Dora!" Sierra cried, visually measuring the distance to the door. "Do something! Talk to him."

"I can't do a thing when he's like this," Dora said. Her voice quivered from fear. "He's been drinking. I've learned to stay away from him when he's drunk."

Ram saw Sierra's furtive glance toward the door and knew she'd never make it, given Jason's vicious mood. "Don't try it, Sierra," he cautioned. "When Jason comes to his senses, he'll realize just how foolish he's acting and leave."

"I'm not leaving until I finish what I came for," Jason said, weaving dangerously. "I should have known better than to hire someone to do a job I could have done better myself. Better yet, I should have had *you* killed instead of Hiram. It might have been you if you hadn't taken it into your head to visit your parents that night."

Sierra held her breath, fearing Jason would lose control and fire the gun without realizing what he'd done.

"I'm not armed, Jason. You'd be killing an unarmed man."

Jason sneered. "Good. I wouldn't have a chance if you were armed. This is the way it has to be."

Down in the lobby, Ryder grew more anxious as the minutes ticked by. Something nagged at him, something he could not explain. The need to climb those stairs was like a gnawing beast inside him. He knew he had promised Sierra an hour, but he could no longer ignore the inner voices telling him to walk up those stairs. His expression hardened as he sprang to his feet. Despite his promise to Sierra, he was going to follow his intuition. It hadn't failed him yet.

What happened next took place so quickly that Sierra was hard put to explain it later. In fact, she could barely recall the events leading to the tragedy. Ram started forward at the same time that Jason squeezed the trigger. Dora screamed and threw herself in front of Ram. The bullet hit her squarely, and she fell to the ground. Ram was so stunned that he dropped to his knees beside Dora, immediately searching for a heartbeat. Finding no sign of life, he rounded on Jason, his face contorted with rage.

"You bastard! You've killed her." Ram had harbored thoughts of punishing Dora for years, but he would never have resorted to cold-blooded murder.

"No! Not Dora. I never meant to hurt Dora. It's your fault. You've always stood between us."

Jason aimed again, and Ram knew he could never rise fast enough to stop him. At this close range he was as good as dead. He sent a quick glance at Sierra, putting his feelings into one searing look.

At that precise moment, Ryder burst into the room, took in the situation in one sweeping glance, and fired off a shot at Jason. Jason's finger, already on the trigger, jerked reflexively as his arm shot up. The bullet went wild, finding its mark in Sierra. A soft cry hissed past her lips as she crumpled to the floor.

Ram saw Sierra fall and felt his world spin dizzily. Abandoning Dora's lifeless form, he crawled to Sierra, tears coursing down his cheeks.

"Sierra—oh my God, Sierra." His anguished cry was that of a wounded animal. He lifted her head, cradling it against his chest as he rocked her back and forth in his arms. "It's all my fault, little love. I brought you to this."

By now people were gathering outside the door. When the manager poked his head inside the room, Ryder barked out a few sharp commands. One was for a doctor and the other to summon the sheriff.

"Move aside, Hunter," Ryder said, shoving Ram out of the way so he could get to his sister. Relief shuddered through Ryder when he saw the steady rise and fall of her chest.

Ram was in a daze. If anything happened to Sierra, he couldn't live with himself. She looked so white and still that he feared for her life. Then the doctor arrived, and Ram hovered over them while the medical man made a hasty examination.

"Can she be moved?" Ryder asked anxiously. "She can't stay here."

"Take her to my office. It's not far. The bullet has to be removed as soon as possible."

"I'm going with you," Ram said, finally finding his tongue.

"She doesn't need you, Hunter, she has her family." Ryder's implacable tone implied that he held Ram responsible for everything that had happened to his sister. "I reckon the sheriff will want an explanation, and you're the only one who can give it."

Ram watched helplessly as Ryder gathered Sierra gently in his arms and carried her from the room. He knew Ryder wouldn't let anything happen to her, but he desperately wanted to be with her. When he heard her moan, he started to follow despite Ryder's warning. Then the sheriff arrived, making it impossible for Ram to leave.

Long, agonizing hours passed before the sheriff was satisfied with Ram's explanation of the double killings and allowed him to leave.

"I'll wire Texas first thing in the morning," Sheriff Dooley said as he finished writing out his report. "If Jason Jordan is wanted in that state, there's no reason to hold you for further questioning. I'll get a statement from Mr. Larson and his sister later. I'm still confused about Miss Larson's reason for being in your hotel room, but after hearing your statements I don't think I need delve too deeply into that aspect of the case. I'm sorry about your wife, Mr. Hunter."

"Thank you," Ram said, aware that Dora had saved his life. It was probably the only purely unselfish thing she'd ever done.

Ram was nearly out of his mind with worry over Sierra. He knew he should tell Tommy about his mother before someone else did, but all he could think about was Sierra. He held himself fully responsible for her injury and wouldn't blame her if she wanted nothing more to do with him.

"Am I free to leave?"

"Certainly. I suppose there are arrangements you need to make."

Arrangements. His face went blank. Then it dawned on him. The sheriff was referring to the disposal of Dora's body. He owed her a decent burial and intended to make certain she received one. As for Jason, he owed the man nothing, but he supposed he'd see that Jason was decently buried and a marker provided for his grave.

"Yes," Ram replied, rising. "I'll take care of all the arrangements."

It was very late when Ram left the sheriff's office a short time later. He was torn between going immediately to Tommy and his need to see Sierra. Since Tommy was likely to be in bed now, seeing Sierra was his primary concern. Unfortunately, he had no idea where the doctor's office was located. There were several practicing physicians within the sprawling city. Logic told him the office had to be close to his hotel, considering the haste with which the doctor arrived once he'd been summoned, but he didn't want to waste precious time looking for it. So he went instead to the Mercer home.

Every lamp was lit in the large house despite the late hour when Ram rapped on the door. He was seething with impatience when Hannah finally answered the summons.

"Mr. Hunter. What do you want?"

"I want to see Sierra."

"That's impossible."

"Where is she?"

"She's sleeping. The doctor gave her something for pain." Ram was trembling so badly and appeared so shaken that Hannah's soft heart went out to him. He seemed so genuinely concerned that she feared Ryder might have misjudged the man.

"I won't bother her. I just need to look in on her, for my own peace of mind. I've been beside myself with worry."

"Worry won't change what you've done to my sister." Ryder materialized from one of the rooms off the foyer, moving to block Ram's entrance.

"Do you think I wanted this to happen?" Ram rasped harshly. "My God, I love Sierra. I'd rather it had been me."

"Because of you, one woman is dead and another lies wounded. I strongly urge you to leave and not return. You've caused Sierra enough trouble to last a lifetime."

"Just tell me, is she all right?"

Ryder and Hannah exchanged guarded looks. "The doctor says she will recover. No permanent damage has been done," Hannah said, her voice softening.

Ram nearly collapsed in relief. "I'll leave for now and return tomorrow."

"Come back as often as you wish," Ryder returned, "but it will do you no good. You are not to see Sierra under any circumstances. You've done her enough harm."

"I couldn't agree more, Hunter." Gordon Lynch appeared from the interior of the house to lend his support. "If not for you, Sierra and I would be married by now and on our honeymoon. We're still going to be married, just as soon as she's well enough to walk down the aisle."

Rather than make an ugly scene, Ram capitulated. Not that he was giving up on Sierra. Oh, no, he'd be back. Every day, if need be. Until he heard from Sierra's own lips that she didn't want him.

Once Ram was gone, Hannah had serious doubts about turning him away. "I think you were too hard on him, Ryder. The poor man appears devastated. I think he truly loves Sierra. Furthermore, I think she loves him."

"Sierra doesn't know what she wants," Gordon grumbled, forestalling Ryder's reply. "Marrying me is the best thing for her right now. She'll forget that rogue once she's reconciled to becoming my wife. Now, if you'll excuse me, I'll get on back to my hotel. If Sierra regains consciousness, tell her I'll be back tomorrow."

"I don't like it, Ryder," Hannah said the moment the door closed behind Gordon. "We're not considering Sierra's feelings. It should be her decision whether or not to see Mr. Hunter."

"Sierra is in no condition to make decisions right now," Ryder said. "I can't forgive Hunter for what he's done to her. If she decides she wants to see him once she is able to make decisions, I'll be the first to apologize."

Ram and Tommy were the only mourners at Dora's graveside. After the brief service, Ram led Tommy away. He'd explained Dora's death as best he could, and the boy took it as well as could be expected. Once Ram explained that he'd not abandon the boy, Tommy appeared resigned to the loss of his mother. In fact, he shyly expressed his eagerness to live with Ram in San Francisco. Dora had already told Tommy that Ram was his father, and he seemed to accept the fact quite readily. The fragile bond forged between Tommy and Ram strengthened with each passing day.

Ram returned to the Mercer home every day, twice a day, for the next four days, and each time was told Sierra was too ill to see him. On the fourth day, he noticed the doctor's buggy parked at the curb and decided to linger long enough to question the man about Sierra's condition. If she was still desperately ill after four days, then her wound was more serious than he'd been led to believe. His patience was rewarded when Doctor Lister emerged from the house twenty minutes later. Ram intercepted him before he reached the curb.

"I'm Ramsey Hunter, Doctor. Can you tell me anything about Miss Larson's condition?"

The doctor adjusted the spectacles more comfortably on his nose and gave Ram a thorough appraisal, "You look familiar, Mr. Hunter. Are you a friend of the family?"

Ram did not flinch from the doctor's probing gaze. "I'm a friend of Miss Larson's. A very *good* friend."

"I think I'm beginning to understand," Doctor Lister said, seeing more than Ram intended.

"About Miss Larson—can you tell me anything at all to put my mind at ease? She was in my hotel room the night of the shooting. I hold myself responsible for her injury."

The doctor stared at Ram over the rim of his spectacles, relying on intuition and his astute judgment of character before speaking his mind. After several tense moments, during which Ram nearly exploded with impatience, the doctor seemed to reach a decision.

"I don't know what you are to the young lady, Mr. Hunter, but I can guess. You'll be pleased to know that she will recover from her injury with no ill effects. Right now she needs quiet and tender care, which her family seems to be providing. The length of her recuperation will depend on many things. Her frame of mind for one."

"Frame of mind? I don't understand."

He searched Ram's face. "I'm assuming you're the man responsible, otherwise I'd not tell you this. I tried to save the baby, but it was out of my hands. The loss came as quite a blow to her. Sorry to be the bearer of bad news, Mr. Hunter, but the young lady will recover, and she will be able to have other children one day. *After* she's married," he stressed. "Now if you'll excuse me, I have other patients to visit."

Ram stared at the doctor in profound horror. A baby! Sierra had been pregnant with his child! My God, no wonder she didn't want to see him. She had good reason to hate him. In a few short months, he'd brought her more grief than most people experienced in an entire life-time. No wonder her family despised him. The best thing he could do for Sierra now was to take himself out of her life and let her recover in peace.

With heavy step and heavier heart, Ram forced himself to walk away from his last chance at happiness. For Tommy's sake, he'd survive, but without Sierra, his life held little meaning.

As he walked against the wind, the moistness on his face was due less to the damp air than from the watery mist gathering in the corners of his eyes.

Chapter Twenty

Sierra awoke to crushing pain. She had drifted in and out of consciousness so often that she had no conception of the passage of time. Had it been yesterday that she'd been shot by Jason Jordan? Her brain was still muddled when it came to details. She recalled seeing Dora throw herself in front of Ram, then everything happened so quickly that she had difficulty sorting through those confusing events. Vaguely she recalled Ryder bursting into the room, then everything went blank until she woke up in her own bed with her family hovering over her. Through the pain came the knowledge that Dora had saved Ram's life. She'd always be grateful to Dora for that.

Her brow furrowed as she concentrated on what little she recalled of the events. Intuition told her there was something she should remember—something vitally important to her, something that was almost too painful to recollect.

Her hands flew to the thick bandages padding her chest, aware that it covered the wound where the bullet had entered her body, but her pain went deeper than that. An aching emptiness inside her drew her hands to her flat stomach. An agonized groan passed her lips when the terrible truth burst upon her.

She had lost Ram's child!

Her cry brought Hannah rushing to her side. "Sierra, are you all right?"

Startled to hear another voice so close at hand, Sierra asked, "How long have you been sitting there?"

"You haven't been left alone since you were hurt. Either Ryder, myself, or Zach sits with you night and day. Is there something I can get you? The doctor said you're going to be fine."

"What about Abby?" Sierra asked, concerned when Hannah failed to mention her sister.

"She's still confined to bed," Hannah explained. "The doctor said the baby could come at any time. Zach is having the devil's own time keeping her down."

Sierra tried to sit up, and raw pain exploded in nearly every part of her body.

"Oh, Sierra," Hannah cried, feeling her sister-in-law's pain as if it were her own. "You're not strong enough to move around yet. The doctor said your wound is healing well, but excessive movement can tear open the stitches."

"I feel so helpless," Sierra complained. "You have enough to do with Abby down in bed."

"You're going to be just fine, honey. You're not to worry about anything."

Tears welled in Sierra's eyes. "Nothing will be the same again. I lost my baby."

"I know. I'm sorry. You don't have to talk about this now, Sierra."

"I want to. I never even got to tell Ram about the baby." Her brow furrowed, as if her memory were somehow deficient. "Where is Ram? I don't recall seeing him."

"There was his wife's funeral to arrange and his son to care for," Hannah said, dissembling. "His mother's death must have been difficult for the boy to accept. But Gordon is here. He's barely left your side through all this."

"Did I hear someone mention my name?" Gordon Lynch strode into the room, looking pleased to see Sierra awake and speaking lucidly. "You're looking exceptionally well today, dear. I'm more than pleased with your speedy recovery."

Sierra attempted a weak smile. "You're a good liar, Gordie, but I do thank you. I must look a fright. Hannah said you've hardly left my side. I'm touched by your concern."

"I'm your fiance, dear. Why wouldn't I be concerned?"

"If you'll excuse me," Hannah said, sensing Sierra's need to be alone with Gordon, "I'll see to the children."

"How are you feeling?" Gordon asked, taking the chair Hannah had just vacated.

"Like I've been run over by one of Zach's freight wagons."

"You'll feel better. The doctor says you're lucky to be alive. You've lost a lot of blood, not just from the bullet wound but from . . ." He flushed and looked away.

Sierra swallowed convulsively. "You can say it, Gordie. I lost Ram's baby." Tears gathered at the corners of her eyes and trickled down her cheeks. She turned her face away in an effort to hide her heartbreak. It didn't work.

"It's for the best, dear. As soon as you're better, we'll be married. I've wired your father that we'll be wintering in Denver. I told him you wanted to be on hand for the birth of your sister's child and that we'd return after the mountain passes open in the spring. I said nothing about our wedding being delayed, or about your . . . accident. It's kinder to let him think we're taking an extended honeymoon."

"I can't marry you," Sierra said softly. "I don't love you. I was only going to marry you because of the baby, but that's no longer necessary."

"You're ill, dear, and you're not thinking clearly."

"Don't you see, Gordie? Ram no longer has a wife. There is nothing to stop us now from marrying."

"He still has a son."

"I'll be his mother," Sierra said with fierce determination. "Ram needs me now as much as I need him."

"If that's true, why isn't he here with you? Why hasn't he been to see you? Why," he challenged, "has Hunter taken his son and returned to San Francisco?"

Of course he'd never tell Sierra that Hunter had come to the house repeatedly up until the day he left for San Francisco. He hoped her family would follow his example and lie about Hunter coming to see her. It wouldn't help Sierra's recovery to know that Hunter had been turned away.

The pain Sierra felt before was nothing compared to the gut-wrenching agony Gordon's words brought her. The previous pain was merely of the flesh, but this affliction cut knife-deep into her heart, into her very soul. The color drained from her face, and the sound that began deep in her throat startled Gordon from his complacency.

"Are you all right, Sierra? Should I call Hannah or Ryder?"

"No," Sierra whispered on a shuddering sob. "Please leave now, Gordie. I'm . . . tired."

Gordie rose with alacrity. "Of course. How thoughtless of me not to realize it. I'll pop in later this evening. The doctor said you need lots of rest. You have all winter to recuperate. But I'm far more impatient. We'll marry as soon as you're able to walk down the aisle."

Alone at last, Sierra closed her eyes, recalling every word Gordie had said about Ram. Could it be true? Had he really left Denver? It was late in the year; if he hadn't left now, she knew he'd be forced to winter in Denver. How could he leave without telling her? Ram loved her, didn't he? Why would he leave at a time when nothing stood in the way of their being together? Had Dora's violent death in some way altered his feelings for her? Her mind utterly rejected that possibility. Ram loved her. He did!

Then a frightening thought came to her. Had Ram somehow learned about the baby? Was he angry because she hadn't told him? Was he upset because she was going to marry Gordie while carrying Ram's child? Her brain whirled with unanswered questions and terrifying answers, until she could no longer think coherently. The pain remained, until Hannah returned a short time later and administered a dose of laudanum.

Chapter Twenty-one

Ram surveyed the evening crowd gathering inside the Lucky Lady with a bored expression. Since returning to San Francisco, he'd gained little pleasure from the kind of life he'd once enjoyed. If not for Tommy, he'd probably become more of a lush than he already was. Thank God for the experienced and caring housekeeper he had been lucky enough to find. Some nights he consumed so much devil's brew that he never even made it to the new home he'd purchased after his return. Lord knew he tried to be a good father to Tommy. For his son's sake, he had bought a grand house on the hill and hired servants to staff the place.

"I don't know what in the hell happened to you in Denver, but you sure ain't the same man who left San Francisco last summer." Lola

413

paused beside Ram, rolling her eyes in disgust when she saw the condition he was in. "What's gotten into you, Ram? You've been home for four months, and you're as much fun as a man who just lost his grubstake at the wheel."

Ram eyed Lola narrowly, wishing she'd just go away and let him drink in peace.

"And you're drinking too much. What kind of example are you setting for your son?"

"Since when did you get so sanctimonious?" Ram grumbled. "If I drink too much, that's my business. Your job is to keep the saloon running and see that I'm not being cheated."

"You're my business, Ram," Lola said earnestly. "We're friends. I can't stand to see you ruining yourself with drink. Is it because of the boy's mother? Why didn't you tell me you were married? What happened in Denver?"

Ram glared at Lola and calmly tossed down the contents of his glass. It hurt too much to think about Sierra, let alone talk about her. He told himself that giving up Sierra had been the selfless thing to do, but his heart utterly denied it. Every time he recalled the agony he'd put her through, he wished it were possible to rewrite the past. If he could, there would only be Sierra, and a love that would endure forever. And they would have the child she had lost because of him.

"Don't pry, Lola. Tommy's mother is dead. That's all you need to know."

"I could make you forget her, honey. You've been celibate as a monk since you came home.

I can help you, Ram. I know what you like, what you need." She caressed his cheek, her eyes sultry with invitation.

"I'll let you know when I want you," Ram muttered in a voice slurred from drink. He poured himself another generous helping of whiskey, raised his glass in salute, and tossed it down his throat.

"I'll be here when you want me, Ram," Lola said, shaking her head in disgust as she walked away.

Ram watched the seductive sway of her hips, thinking that he should accept her offer and bed her. The last time he'd had a woman was when he'd made love to Sierra in the cabin. When he closed his eyes, he could still picture her face as he brought her to pleasure, her ebony hair surrounding her like a dark cloud and her eyes glowing brighter than newly minted silver dollars. He remembered the firm fit of her breasts against his hands and the delicate warmth and heady scent of her aroused body. His memory needed no jogging to recall how perfectly their bodies fit together, how tightly she clasped him within the welcoming warmth of her sheath. Just thinking about loving her made him hard, and he adjusted the fit of his trousers while his mind continued the journey down dangerous paths.

"Ramsey Hunter, where have you been keeping yourself? Do you mind if I join you?"

Startled from his reverie, Ram was more than a little surprised to see Lester Alden lowering himself into the chair Lola had just vacated.

"Sierra and Gordon will be arriving home soon," Lester said, watching closely for Ram's reaction.

Ram said nothing.

"I never did thank you properly for looking after Sierra. She left San Francisco without my knowledge, but knowing she was with you relieved my mind considerably. She's always been headstrong, but what she did was downright foolish. I know you were more or less forced into the role of chaperon, and I appreciate what you did for her. I know I've already thanked you, but one more time won't hurt."

"No thanks are necessary, Lester. I'm glad it all worked out for Sierra."

Lester shook his shaggy head. "I never would have believed her siblings were alive after all this time. The last telegram I received announced the birth of a daughter to Sierra's sister. Gordon said he and Sierra were remaining in Denver for an extended honeymoon. The passes will soon be open, and I expect word to arrive any day now about their arrival."

"I know you'll be happy to see her again," Ram offered dispiritedly.

"You'll never know how glad," Lester said fervently. "I have hopes of seeing a grandchild or two before I leave this earth. Who knows," he added cryptically, "one may already be started."

"You're that certain they're married?" Ram asked harshly.

Lester gave Ram a startled look. "As certain as I could be. I haven't received confirmation, but I assumed they were married some time ago. But enough of my daughter. How is that son of yours? Holly asked me to invite you both to dinner—just name the day. You're a surprising man, Ram. No one suspected you had a family."

"No family, just a son. Tell Mrs. Alden I'll let her know about dinner."

"Of course. Take your time. Well, I'd best get on home, Holly is waiting supper." He sent Ram a searching look. "Take care of yourself, Ram. You don't look well. Come by the office when you can spare the time—I have a business proposition to discuss with you."

"I'll do that, Lester," Ram said, not really interested. Truth to tell, nothing much interested him these days.

A month later, after giving Lester Alden's words careful consideration, Ram found himself seated in Alden's office. The knowledge that Sierra and Gordon were returning to San Francisco had spurred him into action. He needed something to keep his mind occupied and his energies focused, something other than the Lucky Lady, which he planned to get rid of soon. Buying the saloon had been a passing fancy anyway.

"I'm glad you stopped by, Ram," Alden said, shaking Ram's hand warmly. "I think you'll be interested in what I have to say."

"That's why I'm here," Ram said. "What kind of business proposition did you have in mind?"

"Three other investors and myself are pooling our money and financing a railroad spur north into Oregon, perhaps as far north as Seattle. We need young blood in our group, and I immediately thought of you. The initial investment won't overburden you, since there are five of us putting up capital. We've already secured the government contract for our venture and have begun purchasing rights-of-way along the route. What do you say, Ram? Are you with us?"

Ram gave the matter several minutes of serious thought. "Before I make a decision, Lester, you should know that I intend to take Tommy to Texas to visit my parents as soon as school is out in late spring. If you still want me after that, I'll throw my lot in with you."

"You won't be sorry, Ram. There's little risk to the venture, and you're sure to double or triple your investment."

"I'm selling the Lucky Lady, so I'll have plenty of time to devote to the railroad and whatever it takes to get it going."

"Do you have a buyer yet?"

"I'm selling to Lola."

"I didn't know your—er, Lola had that kind

of money." From the tone of Lester's voice it was obvious that he thought Lola was Ram's mistress.

"She doesn't. I haven't spoken to her yet, but I've already visited my lawyer and had papers drawn up. If she agrees, I'll sell the Lucky Lady to her for ten percent of the profits."

"Are you sure you know what you're doing? You might be able to find a cash buyer if you look around."

"I don't need the cash, and I know Lola will do a damn fine job of managing the saloon. She proved her business acumen while I was in Denver. I found no fault with the way she ran things in my absence."

"What you do with the Lucky Lady is your concern, Ram," Lester said. "I'm looking forward to working with you on our new venture." He reached out to shake Ram's hand, sealing their bargain.

Just then one of the bank clerks stuck his head in the office. "Mr. Alden, the stagecoach has just arrived. The station manager sent word that your daughter is on it."

Lester's face lit up. "I received a telegram from Sierra shortly after I spoke with you that day at the Lucky Lady. Please excuse me, Ram. It's been many months since Sierra left and I'm anxious to see her."

Ram stood. "I understand, Lester. I'd feel the same were I you. We'll talk more about our venture later."

Lester was out the door before Ram finished

his sentence. Ram followed slowly, his heart thumping so erratically that he expected it to jump out of his chest. Sierra was back. Sierra and her husband. The thought was painful in the extreme. How could he bear it? How could he remain in the same city knowing she was close by, sleeping every night in her husband's arms?

Perhaps he should move to Texas with Tommy, he thought dully, then in the same breath decided against it. Tommy loved San Francisco. He'd made many new friends, something he never had before. It would be cruel to uproot him again. Ram no longer cared or even wondered if he was Tommy's father, for it didn't matter anymore. Tommy had become an integral part of his life. He had lost Sierra but thanked God he still had Tommy.

Without conscious knowledge of having walked there, Ram found himself standing across the street from the Wells Fargo depot. The stage was already discharging passengers when he arrived. He saw Lester, his face anxious as he waited for Sierra to alight.

When Gordon Lynch stepped down and turned to offer a hand to someone behind him, Ram held his breath. Then he saw her. She was even lovelier than he remembered. He could hardly breathe as he drank in the sight of her. He saw at a glance that she appeared fully recovered from her ordeal. He smiled in fond recollection when he saw the ridiculous bit of feather and fluff perched atop her dark hair.

She'd never been very practical when it came to hats, favoring outrageously inappropriate headgear that ill suited the occasion. When she saw Lester, she rushed into his open arms. Lynch hovered nearby, looking somewhat grim.

Jealousy raged through Ram at the thought of Sierra and Gordon together. Damn! He needed a drink and he needed a woman, and not necessarily in that order. Turning abruptly on his heel, he left the tender scene behind as he strode briskly back to the Lucky Lady.

As happy as Sierra was to see her father, something was missing to make her homecoming complete, and she knew exactly what it was. Ram. Then, from the corner of her eye, she saw him. She wanted desperately to go to him, to tell him what was in her heart, but it would have to wait. She needed to explain to her father first.

"Is that Ram standing across the street, Papa?" she asked her father while Gordon was seeing to their luggage.

Lester turned his head just in time to see Ram disappearing around the corner. "Why, yes, I believe it is. I'm worried about that man. He hasn't been the same since he returned home. But enough about Ramsey Hunter. Your mother is waiting anxiously for you at the house. We want to hear all about you and Gordon and your winter in Denver. And of course we'll want to know every detail about your brother and sister and their families."

* * *

Ram slammed into the Lucky Lady like a man possessed. He stormed up to the bar and barked, "Whiskey, Slim, the whole damn bottle."

"Aw, Ram, I don't think—"

One look at Ram's steely glare, and the bartender quickly complied. "Find Lola and send her up to my suite." Grasping the bottle by its neck, he took the stairs two at a time.

Nearly one-fourth of the bottle had been consumed before Lola rapped on the door and breezed inside without waiting for an invitation. "You wanted to see me, Ram, honey?" Her hair was tousled in delicious disarray and her wrapper was hastily tied at her waist, as if she'd just arisen from bed. Since her nights rarely ended before dawn, she usually slept until mid-afternoon.

Sprawled in a chair, Ram stared at her, his eyes haunted, his expression bleak. "I'm tired of living like a monk, Lola. Come here and show me what I've been missing all these months."

Lola's eyes lit up. "You mean it, honey? Hot damn, I've waited a long time for you to come to your senses." Hips swaying provocatively, she sidled up to Ram, took the glass from his hand, and set it carefully on a nearby stand. "You don't want that, I'm all the stimulant you need." Taking his hands, she pulled him to his feet.

Curling a hand around her neck, he pulled her roughly against him, and kissed her hard. Her mouth opened beneath his ruthless probing and he thrust his tongue inside, hoping to recapture the same kind of magic he'd experienced with Sierra. When it didn't happen, he squeezed her breasts and pumped his loins against her, desperate to stir a response from his reluctant body.

"Not so fast, honey," Lola panted breathlessly. "We've got hours before the evening crowd arrives."

It might take hours, Ram thought sourly as he cursed his flaccid flesh. Damn Sierra for spoiling him for any other woman! He wanted Lola, but his manhood wasn't cooperating. Had he turned into such a lush that it affected his ability to perform? Then and there he made a vow never to touch another drop of alcohol.

"Let's take this nice and easy, honey," Lola purred as she unknotted his cravat and tossed it aside.

His coat came next. She pulled it down his arms and threw it over a chair. His vest followed. Then, one by one, she slipped the buttons from his shirt, pulled it off, and added it to the growing pile of clothing. When he was bare from the waist up, she stepped back into his arms, running her hands through the soft golden fur growing over rippling muscles and corded tendons.

"I'd forgotten just how wonderful you felt," Lola whispered against his lips as her hands roamed freely over his firm flesh.

"Take your clothes off," Ram growled, hoping

the sight of her naked body would arouse his recalcitrant flesh.

Thus far, nothing she'd done had stirred or aroused him. With Sierra, all he had to do was look at her and he grew instantly hard. Was he destined to go through life without ever again responding to a woman's touch?

"What's the hurry, honey?" Brazenly she cupped him between the legs. Her eyebrows flew up in honest surprise.

"I'm sorry," Ram muttered, looking away.

"It's the liquor, honey. It's nothing to be ashamed of. I just need to work a little harder, that's all."

She released the belt of her wrapper and pulled it open, her large breasts and shadowy triangle clearly outlined beneath the sheer material of her nightgown. Her nipples were long and distended, and Ram stared at them, visually comparing them with the firm pink buds cresting Sierra's breasts.

Ram turned away, clearly unmoved by the sight of Lola's voluptuous body. He resented the fact that she wasn't Sierra. He'd never forget his little love. Maybe one day his memory would dim, but not now, not while love for Sierra burned hotly within him.

"It's no use, Lola. I—I'm not in the mood."

"I can put you in the mood, honey." She reached for him.

Ram backed away. "You're wasting your time. But all is not lost, Lola. I've been wanting to talk to you, anyway. How would you like to buy the Lucky Lady?"

"Buy the Lucky Lady?" Excitement animated her features. The prospect of owning the saloon clearly appealed to her. Then, abruptly, her face fell. "You're teasing me. You know I can't afford it."

"I'm not teasing. I've grown bored with the place, and I know you will make a success of it."

"Sure I can, but I don't think the bank will give me a loan."

"I'm willing to sell for ten percent of the profits. The papers are already drawn up and ready for your signature. My lawyer is expecting you to call on him at your leisure."

Real tears shimmered in Lola's eyes. "This is the nicest thing anybody has ever done for me." Her voice trembled with emotion. "You'll not regret it, Ram. If I can't have you as a lover, I'll settle for a friend."

Ram smiled and offered his hand. "Friends it is, then."

She stared at his hand, shoved it aside, and wound her arms around his neck. "This calls for more than a handshake." Lifting her head, she offered her lips to seal the bargain.

Neither Ram nor Lola heard the soft metallic sound as the door opened and closed.

"Take your hands off of him."

Clasping the gaping edges of her wrapper, Lola whirled on her heel, surprise turning to understanding when she saw Sierra standing in the open doorway.

Ram was shocked enough for both of them. His mouth dropped open in genuine dismay. His emotions were raw and exposed; his throat worked convulsively. Overwhelmed by the sight of Sierra, he shuddered and exhaled sharply.

"Are you slumming, Mrs. Lynch? What in the hell are you doing here?" He wanted to call back his words but couldn't. Jealousy was a sickness inside him. Did she enjoy taunting him? Didn't he hurt enough?

Sierra's heart went out to Ram. His expression was guarded, his eyes desolate. His words were barbed and resentful, but she knew that down deep he hadn't meant them. Unless . . . Did he no longer love her? Had Lola taken her place in his heart?

A suffocating sensation thickened Sierra's throat. "I hoped we could speak in private." She sent Lola a speaking glance.

Lola was too astute not to grasp the drift of things. She realized now why Ram had been drinking heavily and avoiding her bed. It was as plain as the nose on her face that Sierra and Ram had become close during his absence. The tension between them was as volatile as a smoldering volcano.

"Sure, honey, I was just leaving anyway. You're welcome to the big lug. Maybe you can get a rise out of him. I sure as hell couldn't." Laughing heartily, hips swaying provocatively, she sashayed out the door, leaving the heady scent of perfume in her wake.

"Does your husband know you're here?" Ram's voice shook despite his best effort to control his desperate yearning for a woman he couldn't have.

Sierra reached out to him, her voice choked with emotion. "Ram." She longed to throw herself into his arms and stay there forever. "I didn't marry Gordie."

Chapter Twenty-two

Ram felt the color drain from his face. "Why are you tormenting me? If this is your idea of a joke, I don't think it's very funny."

Sierra's heart constricted as fear raced through her. What if Ram no longer cared for her? She realized that she was risking her pride by coming to him like this, but pride was a cold substitute for the heat of his touch, the fire of his kiss. "It's true, Ram. I wouldn't joke about something like that. I didn't marry Gordie because I don't love him."

Ram was afraid to let himself hope. "If I recall correctly, your mind was set upon marrying Lynch not too long ago."

Sierra flushed and looked away. She wanted to tell him about the child she'd lost, but the hurt was still too raw. "I made a mistake. I know

now I couldn't have gone through with it. Besides, you weren't free to marry me at the time."

"Your father told me you and Lynch were married in Denver."

"I didn't realize Gordie let Papa think we had married. I think he still hoped to convince me to marry him once I'd recovered. We never told Papa about my . . . injury."

Ram searched her face. "You *are* recovered, aren't you? You look . . . wonderful." She looked more than wonderful, she looked so damn good that it was all Ram could do to keep from dragging her against him and kissing her until she wanted him as desperately as he wanted her.

Sierra gave him a dazzling smile, nearly stopping his heart. "I'm fine, Ram. As good as new." Her smile suddenly faltered and her eyes grew misty. "Well . . . almost."

Ram took Sierra's hands in his and searched the silver depths of her eyes. He wanted her to know that he shared her grief about their child. "I know about our baby, Sierra. It nearly broke my heart. I hold myself responsible for putting you through such terrible agony."

Sierra's eyes misted, and she dashed away the tears forming there. "How did you find out?"

"I spoke with the doctor. I was beside myself with worry, and Ryder refused to let me see you. One day I waited outside your door for the doctor to leave."

"I . . . I'd hoped you wouldn't find out. But perhaps it's best that we talk about it. I wanted our child, Ram. I'm sorry about the way Ryder and my family treated you. It was their way of protecting me. Once I was well enough to assure them I wanted only you, they expressed regret for treating you so shabbily. Believe it or not, Ryder went looking for you on my behalf. He wanted to apologize. I couldn't believe you had left Denver."

Still holding her hands, he brought one of them up to his lips and placed a tender kiss on the palm. When his mouth traced a path down the fragile flesh inside her wrist, Sierra felt something inside her shatter.

"Leaving you was the hardest thing I've ever done. When you lost our baby, I realized I was no good for you. I took your innocence knowing I could never marry you. You deserved better, sweetheart. I've brought you nothing but grief and pain. I felt you'd be better off without me and decided to leave and let you marry Lynch. Can you ever forgive me?"

He dropped her hands, and Sierra reached up and brushed his cheek. She felt the prickle of whiskers against her palm, a sensation that was startlingly erotic in its simplicity.

"There is nothing to forgive you for. You didn't take my innocence, I gave it to you. It wasn't your fault I lost our babe. Bad luck, rotten timing—call it whatever you want. I was in the wrong place at the wrong time. No one could have predicted what happened. I was lucky; I recovered. Dora wasn't so lucky."

"Have you any idea how much I love you?"

Ram asked in a voice made hoarse with emotion. "I don't deserve you, Sierra."

Sierra gave him a teasing smile. "I thought I was spoiled, and obstinate, and reckless, and infuriating, and—"

Ram halted her litany with a breath-stopping kiss, raw with hunger and need. He kissed her until her lips parted and the sweetness of her mouth welcomed his tongue. He kissed her until she was panting and breathless. He kissed her until his need to taste her had been filled.

"You're everything you just described, but so much more," he said when he finally released her mouth. "You're sweetness and sunshine and—and—I can't breathe, let alone think, with you in my arms. I can't remember when I've ever wanted you more."

"More than you want Lola?"

A confused look crossed his features. "Lola? If you think I want Lola, you're dead wrong. I've lived like a damn monk since returning from Denver. I wanted no other woman. No one but you would do for me."

Sierra sent him a skeptical look. "That's not what it looked like to me when I walked in here a few minutes ago."

Ram had the grace to flush. "I was at the Wells Fargo depot when you arrived."

"I know, I saw you."

Ram looked somewhat startled but reserved comment. "I saw you with Lynch and something snapped inside me," he continued. "I imagined you lying in his arms each night, responding to him as you did to me, and decided it was time to let you go from my life. I planned to use Lola to help me forget you. I tried, but my flesh refused to obey. I never thought I'd see the day when I'd be unable to respond to a woman." He sent her an amused look. "I might have been forced to live the rest of my life as a monk." A shudder rippled over his bare torso at so horrendous a thought. "Is there a chance for me, Sierra? Can you forget the pain I've caused you and love me again?"

"I'm afraid not, Ram."

Ram's heart plummeted to his feet, and the expression on his face made Sierra almost sorry she had teased him.

"How can I love you *again* when I never *stopped* loving you?"

"God, Sierra, don't do that to me. How soon can we marry?"

"I want the Aldens to give me the wedding they've always dreamed of. They've given me so much, I don't want to disappoint them. Is a month too long?"

Ram groaned. "A month. I don't think I can keep my hands off you that long."

"What about Tommy? Will he accept me as his mother?"

"He'll love you just as I do," Ram assured her. He searched her face, struggling for the right words to explain his feelings for the boy. "I don't really know if Tommy is my son, Sierra, but it no longer matters. I'm all Tommy has. He depends on me, and I've come to love him dearly."

433

"I understand and can't wait to become his mother. There will be children of our own, of course, but Tommy will always be special."

"I don't know how in the hell I'm going to wait a whole month."

He pulled her into his arms, needing to touch her, to feel her warmth. He kissed her passionately, his hunger for her a physical ache inside him. His tongue found hers, drew upon it, thrusting more and more deeply into her mouth, imagining he was delving into the moist heat of her body instead. She felt his hand cover her breast, the fingers pulling at her nipple. The heat and hardness of his loins surprised her as he cupped her buttocks and brought her against the white-hot center of his arousal.

"I said we'd marry in a month, not that we had to wait a month to love each other," Sierra whispered against his lips. "I've dreamed of being in your arms like this all winter. I was so afraid that dreams were all I was ever going to have of you."

His hands were shaking as he swept her from her feet and carried her into the bedroom, following her body down onto the soft surface. Passion exploded as he tore her clothes from her body, flinging them to the floor. His eyes never left hers as he ripped off his boots and trousers and lowered himself against her body. Closing his mouth over her nipple, he teased it with the swirling tip of his tongue, bathed it in the liquid heat of his mouth, then sucked on it until the pink bud swelled and hardened.

A small sound left Sierra's throat and she arched up against him. It had been so long that she'd nearly forgotten the magic of Ram's loving. His hands moved and stroked ceaselessly, her belly, her breasts, her thighs, touching her everywhere but that sweet, aching triangle where she longed for his touch. Just when she thought she would die with wanting, he began to stroke it with the tips of his fingers. Her eyes closed, and a rapturous sigh left her lips.

"Open your eyes, little love, I want to watch your expression when I give you pleasure."

Sierra's lids flew open, her eyes dilated as he wet his fingers in his mouth and dipped them into the sweet, swollen petals of her sex. She cried out and arched against him as his fingers sought the most sensitive places, then plunged deeply within her, rotating his palm against her mound.

The rush of her breath was sweet against his lips as his mouth devoured hers. After a soul-destroying kiss, his lips began a slow decent down her body, tasting her breasts, the cunning indent of her waist, her hips, her thighs, finally reaching that place where his fingers worked incredible magic upon her. She arched violently upward, hands clutching the bed clothes as he slid his tongue against the tender flesh his fingers had just abandoned. Again and again, with maddening slowness, his tongue dragged over her, relishing the wild arching of her body, the trembling sighs.

Sierra feared she would disintegrate when his

tongue grew bolder, stroking, delving, tasting, plunging. Her fingers tore into his flesh, his hair, the rumpled bedding beneath her. Ruthlessly his torment continued, savoring her fragrant moistness, ignoring the pounding inside his head as tension and need gripped him.

His tenuous grip on restraint almost snapped when a cry burst from her. He felt her arch against him, then go taut. Pulsating waves of incredible pleasure swept over him as he felt the hot spurt of her body's sweet release. He stayed with her until the last tremor left her, her wetness and warmth stirring him to white-hot desire. Her eyes turned smoky as he rose above her and thrust inside her. He held her close, groaning as her body closed around him, pushing himself into the deepest part of her.

Slick, hot, yielding, their bodies joined and melded. Again and again he filled her, retreated, his hands clutching her buttocks, molding her to him, forcing her to arch against his driving loins. His climax came in a volatile burst of seed that exploded from him in a burning rush. It caught him, pierced him, shattered him. When he fell atop her, he was surprised to feel her trembling beneath him, providing him with ample proof that he had touched her soul.

Easing himself to her side, Ram pulled her into the curve of his body. How could he have been foolish enough to think he could ease himself with Lola when no one but Sierra would ever do for him?

"Are you sure you want to wait a month before we marry?" he asked when his breathing returned to normal.

Warm and contented in the cradle of his arms, Sierra murmured something unintelligible. Making no sense of her words, Ram repeated his question.

"After remaining celibate for months, one more month will seem like child's play," she murmured drowsily. "We'll still see each other often."

Ram groaned. "That's what I'm afraid of."

Bodies entwined, they lay in perfect contentment, neither willing to break the magic spell. Finally, Sierra sighed and said, "I suppose I should leave."

"Not yet. Stay a while longer. I'll take you home and inform your parents that we intend to marry. Was Lynch bitter over your decision not to marry him?"

"Gordie certainly was persistent, but I finally got through to him. I've always known he was more interested in the bank and my money than me. He was pleased when I told him I'd talk to Papa about appointing him president of the bank. I also suggested that he court the daughter of J.D. Carrington. He's far richer than Papa, and Barbara Carrington is much more suited to him than I am. And don't worry about Papa. I've already explained about us. He seemed quite pleased."

"You have a solution for everything, don't you, sweetheart? I'll bet your brother and sister hated to see you leave."

"Ryder, Hannah, and Lacy are in Washington. Ryder was asked to serve on the Commission of Indian Affairs. He really hated to leave but felt he'd be in a better position to help the Indians in Washington. By the way, Hannah is expecting another child."

"And Abby? Your father told me she had a healthy baby."

"A girl this time." Sierra's voice broke when she recalled the bittersweet agony of holding her tiny new niece. It should have been her own babe she held in her arms. "It was an easy birth after her earlier scare. They plan on visiting Boston soon to show off the baby to Zach's brother and sister."

"Do you think they'll ever visit San Francisco?"

"They promised they would. As soon as train travel is available. Another year and we'll be able to travel coast to coast."

"I have a trip in mind for us, little love. I'd like to take you and Tommy to Texas to meet my parents and brother."

Sierra could see that Ram was excited about visiting his family. "You plan on returning to San Francisco, don't you?"

"Of course. Your father and I are going to be business partners in a railroad venture."

"What about the Lucky Lady?" She couldn't deny the twinge of jealousy she felt at the thought of Ram associating on a daily basis with Lola.

"I'm bored with the saloon and decided to sell

it. If I'm going to be a family man and upstanding citizen, devoting my evenings to the Lucky Lady isn't appropriate behavior for a future pillar of society."

"You're selling the saloon? Oh, Ram, you don't know how much that pleases me. I'm sure Tommy will appreciate seeing more of you."

"We're wasting precious time talking," Ram reminded her as his hands made a slow, sensual journey over her naked flesh.

His expression was dangerously provocative. Sierra's tongue flicked out to moisten her lips, leaving a slick silken sheen. Ram stared at it, then lowered his mouth to taste her. A little puff of air left her throat and he breathed in her scent, returning it as he deepened the kiss. His mouth was hot and liquid, and suddenly Sierra felt the need to give him as much pleasure as he gave her.

A low groan escaped his lips and a shudder shook him as her fingers closed around the rigid length of his staff.

"Dear God!"

Anticipation seized him when she rose to her knees and knelt beside him. Long silken hair tickled his thighs as she bent her head and tasted him. Pleasure turned to pain, then to unbearable torment when he felt the liquid warmth of her mouth bathe him. A hoarse cry ripped from his throat. With a swift, violent motion, he lifted her bodily and brought her down atop him.

"Ride me, little love. I'll be your wild stallion."

*　　*　　*

Later, after the wildness of their mating had subsided, Sierra stirred sleepily, sent Ram a wistful smile, and asked, "Will it always be magical between us, Ram?"

"If you mean our loving, nothing will ever change that, sweetheart. Love is what makes the magic, and I will always love you. I'm sorry I put you through hell."

"It no longer matters, Ram. I love you too much to relive the past. We'll have other children. Perhaps we've already started one."

Ram sent her an amused grin. "If not, it won't be for lack of trying." He sighed with exaggerated impatience. "It's going to be a damn long month."

Author's Note

Dear Readers,

I hope you enjoyed my Trails West trilogy. It was fun writing about the three Larson siblings and their adventures on the Western frontier. If you haven't read *Tears Like Rain* and *Wind Rider*, the first two books of the trilogy, they can be ordered from Leisure Books.

In December 1995 watch for *The Lion's Bride*, a medieval romance set in the year 1067, during the reign of William the Conqueror. The story is an exciting battle of wills and clash of passions that involves the heroine's ability to foresee certain things in the future.

I enjoy hearing from readers and personally answer all letters if a self-addressed stamped envelope is enclosed. Write to me in care of Leisure Books at the address in the front pages of this book.

TEARS LIKE RAIN — Connie Mason

WIND RIDER
Connie Mason

Romantic Times Storyteller Of The Year

A white man by birth, Wind Rider has given his heart to the Indians who raised him. Grown to a mighty warrior, he lives to protect his people from the invasion of settlers who will take their land. But who will defend him from the exasperating Irish beauty whose soft, sensuous touch sears his very soul?

An indentured servant desperate to escape her cruel master, Hannah McLin will do anything to be free—even trust a Cheyenne brave. Amid the splendor of the untamed wilderness, she won't allow herself to admit her attraction to his hard-muscled body. She can't yield to the bold, passionate longing in his silver eyes. But the closer they come to the safety of civilization, the hotter Hannah burns to succumb to the fiery caresses of the man called Wind Rider.

___3692-4 $4.99 US/$5.99 CAN

Beyond the Horizon

Connie Mason

"Connie Mason writes the stuff that fantasies are made of!"
—*Romantic Times*

As the sheltered daughter of the once prosperous Branigan family, beautiful Shannon is ill-prepared for the rigors of the Oregon Trail, but she is still less prepared for the half-breed scout Swift Blade. His dark eyes seem to pierce her very soul, stripping away layers of civilization and bearing her hidden longing to his savage gaze. His bronzed arms are forbidden to her, his searing kisses just a tantalizing fantasy. But as the countless miles pass beneath the wagon wheels, taking them to the heart of Indian territory, Shannon senses that this untamed land will give her new strength and the freedom to love the one man who can fulfill her wild desire.

_3798-X $5.99 US/$6.99 CAN

Dorchester Publishing Co., Inc.
65 Commerce Road
Stamford, CT 06902

Please add $1.75 for shipping and handling for the first book and $.50 for each book thereafter. NY, NYC, PA and CT residents, please add appropriate sales tax. No cash, stamps, or C.O.D.s. All orders shipped within 6 weeks via postal service book rate. Canadian orders require $2.00 extra postage and must be paid in U.S. dollars through a U.S. banking facility.

Name _____

Address _____

City _____ State _____ Zip _____

I have enclosed $_____ in payment for the checked book(s).
Payment <u>must</u> accompany all orders. ☐ Please send a free catalog.

DANCE of the FLAME

ELAINE BARBIERI

**Elaine Barbieri's romances are
"powerful...fascinating...storytelling at its best!"
—*Romantic Times***

Exiled to a barren wasteland, Sera will do anything to regain the kingdom that is her birthright. But the hard-eyed warrior she saves from death is the last companion she wants for the long journey to her homeland.

To the world he is known as Death's Shadow—as much a beast of battle as the mighty warhorse he rides. But to the flame-haired healer, his forceful arms offer a warm haven, and he swears his throbbing strength will bring her nothing but pleasure.

Sera and Tolin hold in their hands the fate of two feuding houses with an ancient history of bloodshed and betrayal. But no matter what the age-old prophecy foretells, the sparks between them will not be denied, even if their fiery union consumes them both.

_3793-9 $5.99 US/$6.99 CAN

**Dorchester Publishing Co., Inc.
65 Commerce Road
Stamford, CT 06902**

An Angel's Touch

Time Heals
SUSAN COLLIER

Tired of her nagging relatives, Maeve Fredrickson asks for the impossible: to be a thousand miles and a hundred years away from them. Then a heavenly being grants her wish, and she awakes in frontier Montana.

Saved from the wilderness by a handsome widower, Maeve loses her heart to her rescuer—and her temper over the antics of his three less-than-angelic children. As her angel prods her to fight for Seth, Maeve can only pray for the strength to claim a love made in paradise.

_52030-3 $4.99 US/$5.99 CAN